Crack in the World

By

Maribeth Shanley

Perseverance Books
Published by Indigo Sea Press
Winston-Salem

Perseverance Books
Indigo Sea Press
302 Ricks Drive
Winston-Salem, NC 27103

This book is a work of fiction. Names, characters, locations and events are either a product of the author's imagination, fictitious or used fictitiously. Any resemblance to any event, locale or person, living or dead, is purely coincidental.

First Perseverance Books edition published
January, 2016
Perseverance Books, Moon Sailor and all production design are trademarks of Indigo Sea Press, used under license.

For information regarding bulk purchases of this book, digital purchase and special discounts, please contact the publisher at
indigoseapress.com

Cover design by Stacy Castanedo

Manufactured in the United States of America
ISBN 978-1-63066-347-6

For my best friend and husband, Bob Bibb, who has always encouraged and supported me.

My sister, Colleen, who has never been afraid to go against the norm as she reflected on our childhood and family life.

My friend, Brenda Bernard, who saw my talent and encouraged me to write this novel.

My publisher, Mike Simpson, who saw a novel worth publishing, gave me constructive advice and invited me to resubmit.

I am very fortunate to have such a wonderful support group!

Chapter One

Emily woke early that first Sunday in the new bedroom she shared with her two younger sisters, Lily and Katie in East Providence, RI. She thought she heard voices downstairs, so she got up, went to the top of the stairs and listened. She heard her mother, Sarah, saying good-bye to her father, Joe. She then heard a door close, so she walked over to the window which faced the front of the house. She could see the driveway from the window as she watched Sarah help her maternal grandmother, Bertie into the front seat of their car. Emily recalled that the previous evening she overheard her mom tell her dad she and Bertie were going to the 8 a.m. Mass the following morning. That meant her father was downstairs, alone. A feeling of fear told Emily to be very quiet. She didn't want her dad to know she was up. *God, don't let him hear me. I don't want him to bother me this morning,* she thought.

As she watched their car disappear over the crest of the hill, something caught Emily's eye. She squinted as she looked across the street to a meadow that sat in back of the brown house directly across the street. At the edge of the meadow she saw what appeared to be a strange tree. From her window the tree looked as if it was growing sideways. She had never seen a tree so intriguing or inviting, so she slipped out of her pajamas into her jeans, and sweatshirt. She then held her tennis shoes close to her chest and tip-toed back over to the door of the bedroom, stepped out into the hall and listened. Hearing nothing, she tip-toed half-way down the stairs, cocked her head and listened harder. She was sure she could hear the bathroom shower. Believing her dad was in the shower, she quietly walked down the remaining stairs making sure she avoided the creak in the second stair from the bottom, said another prayer and slipped out of the house.

It was beautiful outside! The sky was blue, the air was crisp and the smell of spring filled her nostrils. She took a huge breath as she thanked the heavens for not giving her away, sat down on

1

the front stoop and slipped on her tennis shoes. She then stood up and took in another deep breath as she walked across the street and through the yard of the brown house to the tree. She was right. It was a very unusual tree which was indeed growing sideways.

Wow, what a cool tree; better be careful though. That's all I need, to go back home all scraped up, she thought. So she put her right foot on the tree trunk, hoisted herself up and stood for just a few seconds making sure the tree could support her. Once she felt confident that she wouldn't fall off, she walked up the tree trunk to the first large branch that jutted upward toward the sky, grabbed the branch and sat down. *Dad would never think to look for me here. I'm safe up here. I'm going to wait till Mom and Grandma come home before going back in.*

With her legs dangling as she happily swung them back and forth, she looked out over the meadow and thought, *it's so pretty up here. I love this tree. This can become my secret hiding place.* She then crossed her arms, hugged herself and thought, *it's cozy and I feel extra safe* as her eyes darted over the green field. She spotted a rabbit and two little babies. She hugged herself again and took in yet another big breath of air.

****

The boy in the brown house had just gotten up. He was in the upstairs bathroom when he parted the window curtains, looked out the back window of the house and saw Emily. Captivated by her image, he was curious to know who she was. *Could she be from the family that moved in across the street?* He wondered.

He couldn't take his eyes off her. She was tiny yet, with the sun now framing her body, she seemed larger than life. Her long hair, flame red, caught the early morning sun and a light breeze tossed it to and fro. He blushed to himself as he watched her. But, he didn't want to miss this opportunity; so, he tore himself from the window, threw on his jeans, shirt, and tennis shoes and grabbed a light jacket. It was April in Rhode Island so he knew he'd be chilled without the jacket.

He ran down the stairs as Martha, his grandmother called out to him, "Where are you going, Sean?"

"To say hi to the new girl who just moved in. I'll be at the slant tree. I won't be long."

"Don't forget your mom will pick you up at 8:30. I don't want to send you home without breakfast; your mom will think I'm neglectful."

"Ok Grandma. Call me when breakfast is ready. Bye. Gotta go before she's gone."

He stood at the base of the tree when the little girl turned to see him staring.

"Oh, I'm sorry. Am I trespassing?"

"No. The tree isn't ours. I saw you from the upstairs window and was curious. Are you my grandma's new neighbor?"

"Yes, we moved in Friday. It's so pretty here. I saw the tree from my bedroom window and couldn't help myself. I had to come see it. I've never seen a tree like this!"

"Do you mind if I come up?"

"Come on up! My name's Emily. What's yours?"

"Sean Mahoney. Pleased to meet you Emily. What's your last name?"

She brushed her hair back with her hand. "Callaway."

He smiled as he sat down. "Emily Callaway. I like that."

"Thanks, Sean." Emily said as she turned beet red.

Sean couldn't help blushing as well. He couldn't take his eyes off her. He'd never seen such a pretty girl as he noticed her milk white skin with tiny brownish freckles, full cherry red lips and flame red, curly hair.

She pointed to the brown house, "Is that your house?"

"No. It's my grandma's house. I'm here for the weekend. I live just outside Boston with my mom. It's far, but not too far. I'm going home today. Grandma will probably call me for breakfast soon,"

"I've never seen a tree like this," repeated Emily as she moved over giving him more room to sit. "How did it get like this?"

Sean scratched his head and squinted from the sun. "I'm not totally sure; but when my gramps was alive he used to tell me about a hurricane that came through and knocked the tree over. Bay View convent owns this land but no one ever removed the tree so it just grew sideways like this. The kids call it the slant tree."

She stretched her body looking for the convent. "Slant tree. I like that. Where's the convent?"

He raised his arm and pointed. "Oh, it's up there. You can't see it from here. There's a grapevine grove up there too. Sometimes you can see the sisters picking grapes. I think they make wine with them."

He then smiled and asked, "Are you an only child?"

"God, no. I have an older brother and two younger sisters. My grandmother lives with us too. She's not well though. She has a hard time walking and can't remember much of anything; but I love her. I remember when she was well. She used to be a lot of fun. Now she's just sad."

"What happened to her?"

"She had something called a stroke. I don't understand it but it made her act like a child. It makes me sad. I love my grandma with all my heart. She used to be my best friend; but, now she hardly ever remembers my name." Her tone was sad as it trailed off.

Looking puzzled he asked, "What about your parents?"

"Well, my mom doesn't work and my dad's in the Navy. That's why we're here. He was transferred to a base here."

Emily then asked Sean, "What about your parents?"

Sean answered. "My mom works for a lawyer's office." Then his voice sounded crestfallen. "I don't have a dad. He died several years ago."

"I'm sorry, Sean. What…."

Her question was cut short when they heard someone calling Sean's name.

"Sean!" yelled Martha. "Breakfast is ready and you only have 20 minutes to eat it. Hurry up boy!"

Sean looked over his shoulder to see his grandmother standing on the stoop holding the screen door open. He waved at his grandma then extended his hand to Emily.

She extended hers and they shook which made Emily again blush.

"When will you be back?" she asked.

"I'll be back the weekend after next. Can I visit with you again?"

"I'd love that. I need to go in too. Mom just pulled into the driveway. She went to early Mass this morning with Grandma. I'm sure she'll be wondering where I am."

They both jumped down off the tree, smiled and waved good bye.

Standing at the door, Sean waited a little while as he watched Emily run across the yard, then street. She turned as she reached her door and smiled.

She was surprised he was still watching; so she waved again and went in.

Sean ran in through the screen door slamming it shut as Martha called out, "What's the matter with you, boy. You're going to break that door one of these days. Now hurry up and eat. I left a plate on the table for you."

Soon, Martha walked back into the kitchen. She was putting the last pin in her hair as she rounded the corner. Sean had already finished eating and was cleaning his plate and utensils as she entered.

"That's a good boy. You'll make someone a wonderful husband one day. You're so considerate."

"Grandma, what's a stroke? Emily's grandma had one. Emily said her grandma is sad now."

"Well, Sean, a stroke is when someone has a blood clot that travels to the brain and either bursts or blocks off the blood supply which causes the brain to suffer from lack of oxygen. It's what killed your grandpa. He had what's called a massive stroke."

"Oh."

Sean stared off into space wondering about his grandpa and Emily's grandma's sadness. He remembered how alive and full of energy his grandpa was just months before he died. It made Sean sad to think about his grandpa and now Emily's grandma.

"So, Sean, what's Emily like? You did say her name is Emily, right?"

"Yea, Emily. Well, she's really sweet and seems very smart. Oh (he blushed), she's also cute. I think I'm going to enjoy my visits more now. Uh, uh…I mean I already enjoy my visits. I just…." Sean turned even redder.

Martha laughed in a girlish manner, "I get it, Sean. I wasn't this old forever you know. I remember the first time I met your grandpa. Now he was a looker. Are you all packed and ready to go? I think I just heard your mom's car drive up."

"I just have to throw a few things into my bag. I'll go do that now. Love you, Grandma!"

"I love you too, Sean."

As Sean flew up the stairs, his mom, Beth walked in the door looking worn out.

Beth's voice reflected how tired she was. "Hi, Martha. Has Sean been good for you?"

"Sean is always good, Beth; he reminds me so much of Davie when he was Sean's age. Plus, I think he has a crush on the little girl who just moved in across the street. Her family moved in a few days ago. Looks like a brood of kids. I counted four," laughed Martha.

"You look tired, Beth. Have you been having a hard time sleeping again?"

Beth dropped to one of the wooden kitchen chairs, "I've been working a lot. I worked till about nine last night and then a little when I got home. I take the bar next week and I've been studying like a dog. I just hope I pass it. My boss told me he'd ask the partners to give me a shot at practicing with them. That would mean a pretty sizeable raise which we sure could use."

Martha patted Beth's hand. "I'm proud of you, Beth. I know your dad would've been proud of you as well. So would Davie. I know he's looking down and smiling at everything you've accomplished these past five years. He'd be proud of how you're raising his son. I sure am. Sean's such a good, sweet boy."

Martha changed the subject. "How's your mom doing?"

"She's doing ok. My youngest sister finally got her degree in medicine and has moved back in with Mom. Sal's going to do her internship at the hospital a few miles from Mom's house. That should work out well for both of them. I worry about Mom sometimes though. She never knows when to slow down."

Martha chuckled. "Your mom's a go getter, that's for sure. Is she still selling real estate?"

Beth nodded her head. "Yes. That's what I mean about never slowing down. She just pushes herself."

Martha tilted her head slightly and grinned. "Well, I guess that's where you get your drive."

Beth chuckled. "Well, I guess I can't argue with that one now, can I."

They both laughed as Sean popped back into the room.

"Ready, Mom!"

Beth got up from the kitchen table and patted him on the head. "Thanks for being ready on time, Sean. Now, kiss your grandma and go load up the car, we need to get going. We don't want to be the ones late for my boss' party."

He pecked Martha on the cheek. "Ok. Love you, Grandma. I'll see you two Fridays from now. Say hi to Emily if you see her, ok?"

"I will, Sean," Martha smiled. "Now be a good boy for your mom. I love you too."

Chapter Two

Full of smiles, Emily practically danced into her house.

Joe, sat in his Lazy Boy chair watching TV when he looked up, scowled and almost whispered, "Where have you been? I was looking for you this morning."

Emily's cheery smile immediately dissolved as she answered with a slight stutter, "Uh, uh…I went across the street. There's a tree I wanted to see. "

"Well, next time, ask me if you can go out. Now, go find your mom. She was looking for you to help her unpack some of the kitchen boxes."

"Yes, Daddy."

Emily slowly walked into the kitchen, then down the hall to her mother's bedroom. She knocked, then opened the door when Sarah responded, "Come in."

"Emily, where have you been? Your dad didn't know where you went. Are you ok?"

Now more animated Emily exclaimed, "Oh, yes. I looked out my window this morning and saw this very unusual tree across the street and in the back of the house, so I decided to go check it out. It's really a cool tree, Mom. The kids call it the slant tree. It was knocked down during a hurricane and just began growing sideways. You can just walk straight up the tree just like a ramp. On the other side of the tree is a meadow with tall grass. It's really beautiful!"

"How did you get so much information about the tree, Emily?"

Emily sat on her mom's bed. "Oh, the boy across the street visits his grandmother. He came out to see who I was. He's really very sweet and polite."

Sarah nodded. "That's nice, Emily. Now, I really could use your help today. There are lots of boxes in the kitchen to unpack and you're the only one I trust to help me. Your brother and sisters just aren't as responsible as you."

Emily was disappointed that her mom changed the subject so quickly. She wanted to talk more about the tree and Sean. However, Sarah seemed her usual distracted self and only appeared focused on Emily's assistance in unpacking.

Then Emily asked about her siblings. "What will Paul, Lily and Katie be doing while we're unpacking boxes, Mom?"

Not noticing Emily's mood change, Sarah said matter of factly, "Well, Paul is going to go explore the neighborhood and your two sisters are coloring in the bedroom."

Emily frowned, then mumbled an injured "Ok."

As she left her mom's bedroom and scuffled down the hall toward the stairs she pondered, *I don't know why I have to do all the chores. Paul never has to do anything. He gets away with murder.*

Although she accepted that her younger sisters weren't expected to help around the house, she just couldn't understand why her older brother *always* got off the hook. Yet, as usual, Emily didn't complain. She simply disappeared into herself feeling wounded and unimportant.

She thought about complaining that Paul wasn't helping, but she stopped herself. The last time she expressed her feelings about Paul she got into trouble. So she kept her mouth shut, and headed toward the stairs. She told Sarah she'd be back down shortly.

As she climbed the stairs she purposely changed her mood and thought about Sean. *He made me feel special. I think he thinks I'm pretty. Maybe that's why he blushed. I sure hope I didn't blush. I hate blushing. It's so immature.*

By the time she climbed the last stair, she managed to completely change her mood and skipped to her room. She opened the door only to see her two sisters on the floor with their crayons spread out all over the wooden floor.

She got perturbed. "Hey Katie and Lily don't spread out your crayons like that. This is my room too; and, I don't want to live in a wreck of a bedroom before we even have a chance to get used to it."

The youngest, Katie immediately started picking up the

crayons but Lily lipped back, "We'll do whatever we want to do, Miss Prissy Pants. This is our room too! Besides, you're not Mom. You can't tell us what to do!"

Emily looked totally disgusted then walked over to the closet as she accidently stepped on a couple of crayons causing them to break and crumble.

"Hey," yelled Lily, "What'd you do that for?" "I'm going to tell Mom you broke our crayons!"

Emily looked back at Lily and shrugged her shoulders. "Go ahead. That's what happens when you spread them all over the floor like that. Besides it was an accident. I didn't know I was stepping on them."

"Fine," yelled Lily as she reluctantly began helping Katie pick up the crayons.

Just as quick as she had become distracted, Emily refocused on her encounter with Sean and wondered if he would call his grandmother and ask about her.

I hope he does. I think I like Sean. I can't wait to see him again.

She brushed her hair, changed her shirt, and then went back downstairs. She so wanted to go see what other kids lived in the neighborhood, but she resigned that would have to wait.

As she arrived in the kitchen, Joe's younger brother Pat was sitting at the kitchen table talking to Sarah. "Hi Uncle Pat," she mumbled unenthusiastically...then she asked..."Where's Dad, Mom?"

Taking a sip of coffee, Sarah replied and pointed to one of the boxes across the room. "He went up to the drugstore to get a Sunday paper. Start with that box, Emily; and be careful not to break anything."

Emily dutifully walked over to the box, opened it up and began unpacking plates and glasses. Sarah then pointed to the cabinet they should be placed in. Emily nodded and began placing them in the cabinet.

About an hour into unpacking, Emily jumped up, told Sarah she needed to run upstairs for a minute and left.

About fifteen minutes later she came back down the stairs only to hear Pat talking to Sarah.

"Emily is lazy, Sarah. She reminds me of my sister Phyllis. Phyllis was lazy too."

Emily was crushed. Although she had no idea why, Emily knew no one in her dad's family really liked their sister, Phyllis. It hurt to be compared to Phyllis especially since Emily knew she was anything but lazy. She felt even more wounded when Sarah didn't defend her to Pat. She just agreed and said nothing more.

Emily walked back into the kitchen just as Joe came in from the garage. Pat looked over at Emily with a huge smirk on his face. Emily quickly assessed the situation. Neither of her parents were looking so she glared the most hateful stare she could muster at Pat. He looked stunned but said nothing. He just got up and followed his brother into the TV room.

Emily felt triumphant that she was able to communicate her anger at this stupid man. *What does he know about lazy anyway. He's just a jerk.* She then brushed it off and buried herself in thought as she continued unpacking.

Three hours later, Pat got ready to leave. He spent most of his time at the house watching golf with Joe. As he left, he patted Emily on the head and told her to be good. She knew her parents weren't looking so she yanked her head away and threw him another disdainful glare.

He made a few stupid jokes and left as Emily thought, *I hope I don't see that jerk again for a long time. I've never liked him anyway.*

Chapter Three

About an hour later Sarah told Emily they'd unpacked enough boxes for one day and gave her permission to go out and explore the neighborhood. Emily was ecstatic.

As she stepped out the door she breathed deeply and remarked to herself that spring's perfume was especially wonderful in Rhode Island. She so loved spring as she recalled her morning adventure. Spring was her favorite season. *Everything looks so new and perfect,* she thought as she looked around noticing how fresh and green the grass was. Then she looked up and down the street as far as she could see and marveled at all the colorful tulips. She bent over to pick a red one from the front of her house when she saw Martha across the street. She immediately thought of Sean and decided to take the tulip over to her.

Martha was weeding around the front bushes as Emily walked up. Startled, Martha looked up, covered her eyes from the glaring sun and greeted Emily.

"Hi, Emily; Sean told me all about you this morning. He was quite impressed with you. I'm Martha and I'm pleased to have you as my neighbor."

Emily smiled, squatted down next to Martha and said, "Hi, Martha. I'm glad to meet you too. I liked Sean as well."

She handed Martha the tulip, "Here, Martha. I picked this for you. I hope you like red. Your tulips are beautiful! You must like yellow. There are *so* many of them!"

"I do like yellow. It's my favorite color. I guess because it's so bright and cheerful; but I also like red. It's bold and makes a big statement, don't you think?"

Emily giggled. "Oh, yes. Red is my very favorite color. I think it screams look at me, don't you think?"

Martha cocked her head. "Well, Emily, I think you're right

about that. Hmm…Sean said you were a very bright young girl. He was quite smitten with you I must say."

Emily blushed to which Martha smiled approvingly, "I think I'm going to enjoy having you as my neighbor, Emily. You're welcomed to come over any time you wish. In fact, I'd love you to visit me as often as you'd like; that is as long as it's ok with your parents."

"They won't mind. Now, I think I'm going to walk down the street. I think I saw some kids my age down there."

"Yes, there are several kids your age down there. You're about eleven or twelve; am I right?"

Emily answered proudly. "Yes, I'm eleven; but I'll be twelve this December. I'm in sixth grade."

Martha pondered with, "Hmm…Sean is going to turn twelve in three weeks. His mom is having a small birthday party for him. I'll see if I can get you an invitation. You could ride up to Quincy with me. That's where Sean and his mom live. Would you like to do that?"

"Oh, yes. Thank you for inviting me. Of course I'll have to ask my mom; but I would love to go to Sean's birthday party."

"Great! Now, run along. I know you have lots more to do with your time than hang around an old lady like me."

Emily giggled and called back as she skipped away, "You're not at all an old lady. You're a very pretty grandmother. See you later, Martha."

Feeling very flattered and young, Martha literally leapt to her feet, picked up her garden tools and walked to the garage side of her house.

She smiled as she thought, *what a lovely girl. I'm so glad Sean made friends with her.*

As Martha rounded the corner, she heard her phone ringing. She dropped the garden utensils on the stairs and ran in to answer it.

"Hello."

"Hi, Grandma; it's Sean."

Martha laughed, "Well, Sean who else would it be? You are my only grandson now aren't you?"

Sean giggled, "Yea. I guess so. Have you met Emily yet, Grandma?"

"Well, as a matter of fact, she just left. She came over to give me one of her mom's red tulips. She's a very sweet and charming young girl. She was quite impressed with you. How was the party you and your mom went to today? Did you meet any nice kids?"

"Yea, it was pretty fun. I met a couple of kids. They're going to my school next year. They live in Worcester, but are moving here when school gets out. Their dad just passed the lawyer test and is going to work for Mom's boss. Their dad's not married. I think he likes Mom."

"How do you feel about that, Sean? Does your mom seem to like him as well?"

Sean paused. "I'd be ok with it. He seems like a really nice man and treats Mom nice. I'm not sure if Mom likes him though. You know she still cries about missing Dad; but I wish she could start being happy again."

"Sean, you're such a thoughtful young man. Why don't you tell her that you're ok if she starts dating again? It might take a huge weight of worry off her shoulders. It also might give her permission to lighten up a little. What do you think?"

Sean took several seconds to respond. "You might be right, Grandma. I think Mom is worried about me. Maybe if I can let her know that she doesn't need to worry she'll lighten up. Thanks, for the hint, Grandma."

Martha felt very proud of her young grandson. "Anytime, Sean; anytime."

"Well, gotta go, Grandma," exclaimed Sean. "Mom's calling me. We're going to run some errands and then go out for dinner. Love you lots, Grandma."

Martha said lovingly, "And I love you too, Seanie. Call me later this week ok?"

"I will Grandma…promise!"

****

Emily walked down the street. Half way down she stopped. She could hear a trickling sound. She tilted her head to listen carefully realizing a creek was close by. She walked to her left and saw the creek.

Sitting on a log was a turtle. She walked down to the edge of the stream and petted the turtle as it immediately ducked inside its shell. "Hi Mr. Turtle. I'm sorry I scared you. I won't hurt you, promise! I love turtles and frogs." Some of the girls from her old neighborhood made fun of her for liking such "nasty creatures," the girls called them.

"Emily, don't you know that turtles and frogs are for boys and not girls," Mandy McBride once stated in a very snotty manner.

But Emily just blew her off by saying, "Well, girl or no girl, I like them. I think they're beautiful. When I grow up I'm going to study them," to which Mandy snapped, "Emily you are so stupid sometimes."

As Emily thought about Mandy she pondered how some people could be just plain cruel. She *tried hard* to never be mean. *People should like what they want to like whether they're a boy or a girl*, Emily resolved.

Then, she waved goodbye to the turtle and walked back up to the street and began walking down to the bottom cul-de-sac. As she passed the white house on the right she heard some girls giggling. She looked over and saw a couple of girls about her age jumping rope. Usually Emily was shy about meeting new people for the first time, but she knew if she didn't make the first move, she may not get to meet anyone. So she mustered her courage, walked up the driveway and called to the girls.

"Hi, I'm Emily. I just moved into the green house up the street. Can I jump rope with you?"

The three girls stopped and all three looked her way.

"My name's Jeannie," called the one in the middle; the one actually jumping the rope. "This is Lisa and her baby sister, Karen. Come on up."

Emily walked up to them just as Lisa stopped swinging her end of the rope. Jeannie nearly tripped over the rope as it dropped to the ground, but Emily was close enough to grab Jeannie's arm braking her fall.

"Phew, thanks. My mom would have killed me if I got skinned up today. I fell off my bike yesterday and had to go to the hospital for stitches," Jeannie exclaimed as she rolled down her right sock to show Emily the three stitches on her ankle bone.

15

"Ewe, I hate needles," exclaimed Emily. "Does it still hurt?"

"No, but it sure did yesterday after I realized I cut it," responded Jeannie.

"Yea," piped in Lisa. "You didn't even know you were bleeding till I told you so. Say, Emily, why don't you swing the rope with Karen so I can jump."

"Sure," replied Emily.

After about ten jumps Lisa got tired and jumped out of the range of the rope. "Wanna see some of the cool stuff around here, Emily?"

Looking approvingly, Jeannie exclaimed, "Yea. We were about to have a tea party on the rocks. Hey Karen, go get the cool aid and cups and meet us up on the rocks?"

Karen grumbled, "Why do I always have to be the one to go get everything?"

"Because you're the baby of us," answered Lisa, "So, hurry up. We're thirsty. And bring the bag of chips with you too."

Karen grumbled again under her breathe, threw her end of the rope down and stomped into the house. The other three girls ran around the right side of Lisa's garage. There on the right side and in back of the house next door was the biggest pile of not rocks but boulders Emily had ever seen.

Her eyes got big as she called out to the two girls who were now climbing, "Wow. Is this the rocks? Where'd they come from?"

Jeannie looked back over her shoulder. "No one knows. They've been here ever since we all moved in and that was eleven years ago for me. I was born on this street. They're pretty cool aren't they? We have tea parties up here. It feels like we're in our own castle."

They all began giggling and jabbering as they finished climbing to the top. They were seated on individual boulders as Karen came out of the house loaded down with a plastic bottle filled with red cool aid, four plastic cups and she was carrying the bag of chips with her teeth. As she arrived at the bottom of the pile, she dropped the chips and yelled, "Hey, someone come down and help me. I can't carry everything up by myself."

Emily obliged, climbed back down and helped Karen carry the cups and chips up to the top. They all sat around a flat topped boulder which served as a table.

Emily was so pleased she made the first move to meet these three girls, especially Jeannie she thought; because she immediately felt a special connection to her. "This is one of the coolest places I've ever lived. This morning I sat on the slant tree and met this really cute boy."

Lisa scowled then poked Jeannie and said, "Did you meet Sean? You better watch out cuz Jeannie has a big crush on him."

Emily immediately became embarrassed then bashfully remarked, "Uh, yea. I think he said his name is Sean. He seems pretty nice, but I'm not interested in him at all."

She didn't want to jeopardize not being welcomed so she immediately changed the subject by pointing to the tree stand on the back side of the rocks, "How far back do those trees go?"

Jeannie was a carefree spirit so she wasn't as disturbed by Emily's comment about Sean being cute as Lisa seemed to be. Instead, she brushed it off. Besides, she immediately liked Emily so she was the one who answered.

"Not too far. We call them the woods. It can get pretty dark back in there and there's a covered well half way into the woods. We could walk back there in a few minutes if you'd like but we better do it soon because in about an hour it's going to be dark and none of us want to be in the woods after dark."

"Ok. I'd like to see the well. What's down in the well?" asked Emily.

Karen finally spoke, "Nothin much, but a kid fell into the well and got killed. After dark his ghost walks around in the woods. That's why we don't go in there when it's dark."

"Oh, really? Have any of you seen his ghost?" asked Emily.

"No," answered Karen, "But my brother and his friends have."

"Oh, they're just making that up," laughed Jeannie, rolling her eyes.

"I don't know," Lisa retorted, "Billy was scared to death when he came home that night. Maybe he really did see that kid's ghost."

"Well, if we're going to go see the well, we better go now. I have to be home in fifteen minutes," commanded Jeannie.

They all climbed down from the rocks, stored their trash under a loose rock on the ground and walked into the woods.

Later Emily recounted to her mom how dark and scary the woods seemed to be; and, told her that the well was even scarier. When they came out of the woods they walked out a side path.

"Mom, there's even an old broken down milk truck in the field next to the woods. It's all pretty mysterious down there!"

"Well, Emily, you just be careful."

Chapter Four

The next few weeks went by in a blink. That first Thursday in their new house, Emily and her siblings started their new classes at St. Joseph's school. Before she knew it, two Thursdays had gone by and she remembered the next afternoon Sean would be back visiting Martha.

As Emily fell asleep that Thursday night, she thought about the cute boy she met several days ago, and hoped he remembered her. She also hoped she would be able get to know him better without offending Jeannie. She took a shine to Jeannie and hoped they could become friends.

That following morning Emily woke up to find herself wedged between her bed and the wall.

From the bottom of the staircase, her mother called her and her siblings. "Paul, girls, time to get up and ready for school. Hurry up. Your dad is going to drop you off this morning and he needs to leave in 20 minutes."

As her two sisters got up she tried to free herself from her snare. *How did I get here?* Emily wondered.

Then she remembered. She felt sick to her stomach all over again as she recalled what happened the night prior; but she didn't have time to dwell too long because Lily and Katie were bickering.

It's just as well, thought Emily feeling emotionally trapped and alone.

Then she remembered what day it was. *It's Friday! All I have to do is get through this day and Sean will be back.*

Her mood transformed instantly as she thought, *I don't have time to be sad. Besides, what good would it do? I can't tell anyone anyway. I'm just going to be happy today. I can't wait to see Sean! I can't wait to get to know him. Maybe he'll help me feel happy.*

So Emily spent the next several minutes shaking off her sadness and feelings of being out of control of what happens to her in her house. She thought, *I'm just going to concentrate on later. I want to be happy and not sad. Feeling happy makes me happy.* She was determined as she went about her business of getting dressed. Then she grabbed her brush and ran down the stairs calling to her mom.

"Mom, Mom, can you braid my hair today?" I want to wear these new barrettes. They match my new shirt."

"Ok, hurry up. We only have a few minutes. Your father is getting very concerned about being late for his meeting with Admiral James," yelled Sarah.

Soon, she was ready to go. She threw on her jean jacket, picked up her books and her lunch box and ran out the door. Paul and the two girls were already out at the car arguing who would sit up front as Joe walked out.

Joe got in the driver's side and said, "Emily, why don't you get in the front. You can sit in the middle next to me."

"That's ok, Dad. Lily can sit there if she wants. I don't mind sitting in the back seat."

"*No!* Lily, you sit in the back. Emily let's go. You don't want to make me late do you?" growled Joe.

Without a word, Lily stuck her tongue out at Emily and climbed in the back seat as Emily reluctantly climbed in the front and moved to the middle, close to her dad. Paul then climbed in and sat between Emily and the window.

Joe patted Emily on her knee. "That's a good girl, Emily."

Cringing from his touch, Emily adjusted her seating as she moved closer to Paul. Joe didn't seem to notice as he concentrated on backing out the driveway.

For Emily the drive to school seemed painfully long. All she could smell was Joe's strong after shave and his sickening sweet breathe from the alcohol he drank the night before. She could feel the heat from his body and that made her want to throw up, but instead, she shook off the feeling and slipped inside her own mind again and thought about Sean and how happy she would be when she finally got to see him later in the day.

As they arrived at the school her three siblings jumped out of the car and ran up to the school yard. She slid across the seat to get out as well, but was stopped dead in her tracks.

Joe grabbed her shoulder and squeezed. "Emily, wait!"

"Yes Dad?" she recoiled from his grip as she turned to look at him.

"I'm sorry I scared you last night."

Emily didn't want to talk to her dad; *especially* about the night prior. She just wanted to get away from him; so, she muttered, "It's ok, Dad."

"Well, I just want to make sure you continue to remember your promise to me about not telling anyone." He squeezed her shoulder even tighter.

Now visibly shrinking from his painful grip, Emily spoke in a very tiny voice which quivered, "Yes, Daddy; I remember. I won't tell anyone."

Joe let up on his grip and said, "Good girl. Now go on. I don't want you to be late for the school bell."

As Joe drove away, Emily dropped her book on the sidewalk.

Sister Liam bent down and picked it up. "Hi, Emily; are you ok today?"

"Yes Sister Mary Liam," Emily responded through a few sniffles.

She looked up and the sister asked, "Emily are you crying? What's wrong dear?"

"No, sister; I just got some dust in my eye. That's all. I'm ok."

"Ok. Now hurry along. We're ready to go inside," said the sister as she patted Emily on the head.

All day Emily had difficulty concentrating. She was terribly embarrassed when Sister Liam called her during math class. She wasn't paying attention when Sister Liam finally smacked the wooden pointer on the blackboard and said very loudly, "Emily, it's time to come back down to earth," to which the class laughed.

Emily shrunk in her chair then decided she had more to worry about than her teacher scolding her in front of the class.

She had been thinking about her dad and last night then about what he said to her as she tried to get out of the car. *I so hoped he was finished with bothering me.* But after last night and now the conversation, Emily realized things may never be different for her.

She did her very best to get through the rest of the day when finally the bell rang and it was time to go home. Emily collected her belongings and started out the class door as Sister Liam called.

She pointed to the chair next to her desk. "Have a seat right here, Emily."

Emily sat down.

Sister Liam put her pen down and looked up. "Emily, what's going on with you today? You were miles away all day long. You've been a very good student since you arrived two weeks ago, but today...well, I don't know. Is everything ok at home?"

"Yes, sister. I'm sorry but I just haven't felt very well today. My head has been hurting all day; but I'll be better next week. I promise."

"Well, ok then. I just don't want to see you fall behind. You're a very good girl and a wonderful student. If I can do anything at all, I hope you will let me. Now, run along. Perhaps when you get home your mom will let you lie down for the rest of the day."

"Maybe so. Thank you very much, Sister Mary Liam."

That afternoon, Emily and her siblings rode the bus home. When the bus stopped at the top of their street and the driver opened the doors they all got off. Lily and Katie took off running while Paul got off with a few other boys he'd made friends with.

Emily was the last one off the bus. She began her 1/8 mile trek down the street to her house which was half way down the long hill. As she reached the crest of the hill she saw Sean's mom's car and her heart beat faster. She quickened her step when, from behind, she heard a voice calling her name. She stopped and turned around to see Jeannie running down the street to catch up to her. She waited, hoping she could get in her house before Sean came out.

Jeannie was out of breath when she caught up to Emily. "Hey, where are the other kids?"

"Oh, they all took off running. I didn't feel like hurrying. Jeannie, I wish you and I could go to the same school. That would be cool, don't you think?"

Jeannie giggled at her new friend. "Yea it would. But, unfortunately I'm not Catholic and my parents refuse to pay for a

Catholic school. They think you Catholics get brainwashed. Besides, I really like going to the public school."

As the two girls approached Emily's house, Jeannie remarked, "Oh, isn't that Sean's car? He must be staying with his grandma this weekend."

"Oh, I didn't notice. Maybe he is. Well, I better go inside. I probably have chores to do. Maybe I'll see you tomorrow."

Jeannie continued walking down the hill as she called back, "Well, not in the morning. I think we're going to see my aunt and uncle. Maybe tomorrow afternoon or Sunday, how about that?"

"Sounds good, Jeannie. See you later, ok?"

Emily walked over to the side door of her house and hesitated as she watched Jeannie disappear past the two houses to the left of hers.

She turned and was about to open the door when she heard a familiar and welcoming voice calling.

"Hi Emily!"

She turned around to see Sean walking across the street.

"Oh, hi, Sean." She tried to contain her excitement. *I don't want him to think I'm a stupid, giddy girl*, she thought.

He came close and they both sat on the step and began talking about their week when Sarah opened the door.

Startled, Emily looked up and said, "Oh, Mom. This is Sean. He visits his grandma, Martha across the street."

"Nice to meet you, Sean. Unfortunately, Emily can't play right now. She has chores to do; but you're welcomed to come back tomorrow morning if you'd like."

"Nice to meet you too, ma'am. Ok, Emily…I guess I'll see you tomorrow." Sean extended his hand to Emily. She smiled then shook his hand. When he turned to walk away, she chuckled to herself. She thought his behavior was strange but polite in a curious way.

As Emily and her mom closed the door, Sarah said, "He seems like a nice boy, Emily."

Emily giggled, "He's very polite, but peculiar too. He shook my hand."

Sarah was visibly distracted and even agitated, so without thinking she coldly said, "Emily, I need you to set the table for dinner." Then, Emily detected a sadness in her mom's tone, "But don't put a plate on the table for Grandma."

"What's wrong with Grandma, Mom? Is she sick?"

Sounding mechanical, "She's not feeling well." Then Sarah again with that tone of sadness replied, "*Plus* your father requested that we have an evening meal without her at the table."

Emily complied thinking how mean her dad could be toward her grandma. After she finished setting the table, Emily went to Bertie's room which was just off the family TV room.

"Hi, Grandma."

Bertie was sitting in a chair staring out the window as she turned toward Emily and smiled. Emily sat on the side of Bertie's bed next to her chair. As she stroked Bertie's hands she began telling her about school, the neighborhood, Jeannie and especially Sean. She knew nothing she was talking about would register with Bertie; yet, as she remembered how interested Bertie used to be in her, she continued to talk. She needed someone to tell about what's been going on in her life outside the family and house. Emily was bursting with optimism; and she desperately needed to share her hopefulness.

A few hours later as she continued to stroke Bertie's hands she asked, "Don't you feel good, Grandma?"

Bertie looked at Emily with sad, empty eyes and shook her head no.

"That's ok, Grandma. I love you, you know that don't you?"

Bertie looked up and for a split second she resembled the person Emily used to know as she responded, "I love you too, Emily. You're such a sweet, kind girl."

Emily was taken completely by surprise. She couldn't remember the last time Bertie remembered her name. She often called her Sarah, so Emily became overwhelmed with joy as she stood up, bent down and hugged Bertie as tight as she possibly could. But the moment didn't last very long as Emily turned to see Sarah standing in the doorway telling her to come out for dinner.

"Can I eat here with Grandma, Mom…please?"

"If your dad agrees, then yes you can. I think Grandma would appreciate the company. Now come on out and at least you can bring back Grandma's plate."

Emily turned back to Bertie and whispered, "I'll be right back, Grandma."

Emily stood up, stroked Bertie's head only to realize that the moment of recognition was completely gone. She felt sad yet determined to encourage her dad to let her come back and eat with Bertie. Emily's love for Bertie was evident; and, for the first time in years Emily felt the warmth of Bertie's love for her. It was still there, only obscured by her stroke.

As Emily walked to the kitchen she felt a tear escape the corner of her eye. She was overwhelmed by that special moment as she recalled how, prior to her stroke Bertie seemed interested in Emily the person.

Bertie doted over her. She often took Emily on the city bus to the downtown area when they lived in Florida. Her grandma's attention made up for how unimportant the rest of her family made her feel.

When Emily arrived in the kitchen everyone except Sarah was seated at the kitchen table. There was a lot of chattering as Lily and Katie played with their Barbie dolls.

Joe looked at Emily. "I understand you want to eat with your grandma."

"A...Yes, Daddy, please? She just seems sadder tonight than usual. I'm hoping I can cheer her up just a little."

"Well, I guess you can. Okay, girls," Joe barked at Lily and Katie, "Put down the dolls and let's have a little quiet now. I want to be finished by 8:00 so I can watch TV. Paul, pass me those rolls."

Emily felt relieved as she took Bertie's and her plates from the shelf.

As Emily picked up the plates Sarah said, "Go ahead, Emily. I'll bring your glass of milk and Grandma's tea."

After dinner, everyone except Emily retired to the TV room to watch TV. Bertie fell asleep in her chair but Emily woke her and helped her get ready for bed. As she covered Bertie, she kissed her and told her she would always love her, turned off the light and walked through the TV room to the kitchen where she knew the dishes were waiting for her to clean. An hour later she finished cleaning up the kitchen, then slipped off through the house, climbed the stairs and went to her room where she put a

CD in the CD player she got last Christmas, put her earphones on and began listening to Neil Young's CRAZY HORSE.

She turned off the light, went over to the window and knelt on the bench that sat just under the window. She saw a soft glow of light in the top left window of the house across the street. Emily watched as a small figure walked in front of the window. The figure stopped and she could see Sean was also looking out his window. She wondered if he was thinking about her. Just then the song "We Never Danced" played. She loved this song because it tugged at her heart.

She recalled the first time she heard it. It was the theme song from one of her favorite movies, "Made in Heaven." *I wonder if Sean and I will ever get to dance together. I hope so.* As the song ended she felt for the replay button and played the same song over. As it began, a tear trickled from the corner of her eye. She was again thinking of what Bertie said to her just a few hours earlier and trying even harder to imagine a day when life would be better for her.

Chapter Five

The next morning Emily woke to find that she was all alone in her bedroom. She got up, threw on her robe and slippers and headed down to the kitchen. Sarah was busy making pancakes as she turned to see Emily.

"Emily, where'd you go last night?" She then said, "Here," as she handed Emily a plate consisting of two pancakes and a strip of bacon.

"I didn't feel like watching TV so I went up and listened to one of my CDs. Where's Dad?"

"He left about two hours ago to play golf. Listen, the girls and Paul are already outside. Why don't you finish there, get dressed and go on out as well."

"Don't you want me to clean up the kitchen, Mom?"

"No, I'm giving you the morning off. I want you to have a good time today. You deserve it, Emily. I also want you to know that I very much appreciate that you sat with Grandma last night. I think it really made her feel good. She seems to be in better spirits today than she has been in a while. Then Sarah gently said, "You know, Emily, your grandma still loves you even though she doesn't show it. She's very sick and can't help herself."

"I know she still loves me, Mom. She called me by my own name last night. I'm glad I made her feel better. She deserves to be happy, Mom." Emily drank the last of her milk, then carried her plate and glass to the sink. "I hate that Grandma is so sad."

"I know, dear. I do too. Now run along and have a nice day, ok?" Sarah said gently as she kissed Emily's cheek.

Once Emily got dressed and brushed her hair, she looked out the front window and saw Martha and Sean in their front yard. She hurriedly put on her jacket, tied her tennis shoes and ran down the stairs so fast she slipped on the last step and almost fell

27

but caught herself by grabbing onto the stair rail. She flew out the door! As she shut the door behind her she looked up to see Sean waving for her to come over.

"Hey, Emily!"

"Hey, Sean; hi Martha!" Emily shouted equally enthusiastically.

Sean was standing next to Martha as she was bent over cutting a few of her tulips.

"I usually have to do chores every Saturday, but Mom's giving me the day off."

Now standing Martha asked, "That's wonderful, Emily. Where's your brother? Is he doing chores?"

Emily looked down at the ground. Her mood and facial expression immediately changed to reflect pain as she kicked a small rock back into Martha's front garden.

"No," she mumbled. "He rarely gets stuck doing chores. I guess because I'm the oldest girl, I do all the chores."

Martha watched Emily's gesture. Her intuitiveness detected an extreme sadness in Emily.

Then Sean exclaimed, "Hey Emily, wanna go see the grape vine grove I was telling you about?"

"Sure, that would be fun. Let's go." Emily immediately bounced back and responded now with much enthusiasm.

The two children ran around the back of the house as Martha heard her phone ringing. She smiled to herself as she rounded the corner of the house and saw the two children running hand in hand. She answered the phone, "Hello."

"Oh hi, Martha." It was Beth. "Martha, I hope you don't mind; but I'd like to pick Sean up tomorrow evening around 9 rather than in the morning."

"That'd be fine, dear. What's going on? Not that it's any of my business."

"Of course it's your business, Martha. I'm actually going on a date."

With a bit of excitement in her voice, Martha asked, "Well, Beth…who's the lucky man?"

"His name is Bill Haskell. He starts with the firm next Monday. We met him at the office party last weekend. I think

Sean may have mentioned him to you…which, by the way, thanks for talking to Sean. I've been concerned about how Sean would take me seeing anyone new. He's the one who encouraged me to say yes to Bill."

There was a smile in Martha's voice when she responded. "Well, I was just encouraging Sean to continue with the line of thinking he was already doing. He's very concerned about your happiness. He misses Davie tremendously; but he's more concerned about the here and now and that has a lot to do with you being happy. When you're happy, he allows himself to be happy. Talk about happy. He and Emily just ran off to the grape vines."

Then, Martha became serious. "You know, Beth, there's something about Emily. I can't put my finger on it; but I get this feeling deep in my gut that she's not very happy."

"Really? What do you think is going on?"

"I just don't know, but it was something in her voice and the way she got a faraway look when I asked about her family. It might be nothing more than a run-away imagination; but…well…I don't know."

"Well, maybe she'll talk to Sean. He seems to really care about her."

"You're right, Beth. Well, listen, you have a wonderful day tomorrow with Bill and don't give Sean a second thought. Ok dear?"

"I will, Martha; and, thanks for being so supportive. You know, I don't say this very often, but I love you like a second mom," Beth said choking on her words just a little.

"I love you too, Beth. Bye, bye."

Martha hung up the phone and sat at the table for a few minutes wondering if it was her imagination. She then decided not to dwell on anything but instead stay vigilant and probe as much as she could without seeming invasive. She didn't want to scare Emily off.

She just seemed so sad, burdened and distant, Martha thought.

****

29

Sean and Emily ran through the meadow. Suddenly Emily tripped and fell. Her knee barely missed a rock but the corner of the rock ripped a tear in her jeans.

"Ouch," Emily squealed.

Sean, who had been running a few steps ahead, stopped and turned then walked back and crouched down next to Emily. "Are you ok?"

"Yes. But I almost wasn't. I just missed landing on this rock which tore my jeans. Mom's going to kill me."

"Awe, don't worry! When we get back I'll ask Grandma to sew the tear. She's a great sewer. See!" He pointed to several tears in his jeans.

"Do you think she will?" asked Emily with a slight quiver in her voice.

"Sure. Grandma really likes you. Now come on," he said as he stood, extended his hand and helped Emily to her feet. She began walking with a slight limp.

"Are you sure you're ok?"

"Yea, I'll be ok in a minute." They walked a little further; then she started running.

"See, I'm all better," she yelled as Sean ran to catch up.

Then they saw something moving above several tall bushes.

Sean grabbed Emily's jacket and whispered, "Shhh. Someone's there."

He pointed as they both crouched down.

They heard two female voices and Sean whispered as he stood and peeked. "It's the sisters. We're almost to the vines."

"Should we go back?" asked Emily.

"No, most of them are usually very nice. Let's see if they're the nice sisters."

He took her hand and they walked slowly as if they were just out for a stroll. As they arrived at a slight clearing just before the vines, the two sisters turned and looked startled.

"Oh, we're sorry sisters; this is my new neighbor, Emily. I wanted to show her the grape vines," said a polite Sean.

The sister standing closest smiled and spoke. "Hi Emily! My name is Sister Mary Joseph, and this is Sister Mary Theresa."

Both sisters had white aprons on and the aprons were loaded with grapes.

"We'd shake your hands but we don't want to drop the grapes, come on with us!" Sister Mary Joseph smiled broadly.

The two nuns walked a short distance to where they had a huge metal pail. They dumped the grapes in the tub and turned back toward the children.

"There," said Sister Mary Joseph as she wiped her hands on her badly stained apron.

"And, what's your name, young man?" asked Sister Mary Theresa.

"I'm Sean Mahoney and this is Emily Callaway. Pleased to meet you," Sean extended his hand.

The two sisters looked at their hands which were also stained, and laughed.

"Well, Sean Mahoney and Emily Callaway, I hope you'll forgive us but we don't want to get any purple on your hands. But, we have some lovely lemonade just behind that tree. Would you two like a glass of lemonade?" Asked Sister Mary Joseph.

"Oh, yes, please," exclaimed Emily. "I love lemonade!"

"Me too!" said Sean.

They all walked over toward the tree. Behind the tree sat a small table with two chairs. On the chair was a small blanket.

Sister Theresa removed the blanket and spread it on the ground. "You two children can sit on the blanket if you'd like. I'm afraid if I try to sit there we'd have to call the fire department to get me up again."

Both children giggled as they sat. Sister Joseph poured lemonade into two paper cups and handed them to Emily and Sean. Then Sister Theresa handed them each a napkin and a few chocolate chip cookies.

"These were made this morning," said Sister Theresa.

"Umm," said Emily. "Thanks, chocolate chips are my favorite!"

Sean also thanked the sisters and exclaimed, "This is the best lemonade I've ever had!"

They all sat and chatted for a while as Sean asked what they did with the grapes. The nuns told them they did indeed make wine.

"In fact," explained Sister Mary Theresa, "Our convent bottles and sells the wine. The money from the sales goes to the

Sisters of Mercy fund which helps provide clothing for the poor children in Providence."

Both Sean and Emily were very impressed with that explanation.

About a half hour passed and Sean said, "Well, sisters, we really need to get going, but thanks so much for giving us lemonade and cookies."

They all got up and shook hands since now the sisters' hands although still stained were dry. Emily made a mental note as to how soft both sisters' hands were.

Then she asked Sister Theresa, "Are you named after Sister Theresa, the Little Flower of Jesus?"

"Why yes, I am. I'm also a huge admirer of the present Sister Teresa of Calcutta. Why Emily, how do you know about the Little Flower of Jesus?" asked Sister Theresa.

"Oh, I read about her in my catechism book last year. She's my favorite girl saint."

"That's wonderful dear. She was French and her actual name was Sister Theresa Lisieux, which is the small town in Normandy, France where she was born," explained Sister Theresa.

"Yes, I remember," smiled Emily.

The four parted company as Sean and Emily turned around and began walking as the two nuns watched smiling from ear to ear.

"I so love when the children come to visit us," said Sister Theresa.

"Wow, Emily," exclaimed Sean, "I'm impressed. I didn't know any of that stuff."

"Oh, it's no big deal, Sean. I just love the story about this 15 year old girl who just seemed to be so sweet."

Sean watched Emily's mouth move as she talked. He wasn't yet aware, but he felt something really special for this little red head.

"Let's go see if Grandma can fix your jeans, then we can make some sandwiches and go eat them on the tree," said Sean hoping she would say yes.

"I hope she can fix them. These aren't that old. I don't want my mom getting mad at me for playing too rough."

Sean began running as Emily called out, "Do you mind if we walk back, Sean? I don't want to take a chance and fall again."

"Sure, Em," cutting her name short. "Do you mind me calling you Em?"

She smiled sweetly. "No. I kind of like it. That's what Grandma used to call me. She was the only one. Now you're the only one."

They walked back and as they did, Sean bent down to pick a few buttercup flowers. He handed them to Emily and said, "These are for you, Em. I'm so happy you moved in across the street."

Emily blushed. "Thanks, Sean. No one's ever given me flowers before."

They arrived back at the house and went inside. Sean called to his grandma who was sitting in her living room.

Martha walked out and saw Emily standing next to the kitchen table and exclaimed, "Why Emily, those are very pretty buttercups. Let's put them in some water shall we?"

Emily felt so welcomed in Martha's house and that made her smile. "That would be nice, Martha. Sean picked them for me. If it's ok though, I think I'll keep them over here for safe keeping. My sisters will ruin them if I take them home. They're so immature! Is that ok, Sean?"

"Yes, Em. That way, when I see them they'll remind me of you." He smiled back to which Emily blushed.

Watching these two, sweet children interact filled Martha with such joy. She smiled as she took the buttercups from Emily's hand. She reached up into one of her cabinets and pulled out a small vase and put the flowers in it. "This is a perfect size vase for your perfect buttercups, Emily."

Then Martha pulled a small round lace doily from a drawer and laid it in the middle of the kitchen table and placed the vase on the doily.

Pleased as punch at this moment Martha asked, "There, now would you kids like something to eat?"

Sean said, "Yes, please, Grandma. We wanted to eat sandwiches on the tree. Is that ok?"

"Yes, Sean, let's fix three sandwiches."

Then Sean blurted, "Oh, I almost forgot. Can you sew Emily's jeans? She fell and tore them."

Martha bent down to inspect the tear as Emily pointed to it.

"I sure would appreciate it, Martha. I don't want my mom to find out. They're not that old and I'm afraid she'll get mad at me for playing so rough."

"Of course I will, dear. Sean, run upstairs and get a pair of your jeans so Emily can see if they fit while I patch hers."

Sean darted up the stairs as Martha and Emily prepared three egg salad sandwiches. When he came back down he was carrying a pair of jeans, smiled and handed them to Emily and then jumped in to help his grandma finish preparing lunch. Emily came back out from the bathroom. The jeans were too big causing the legs to drag on the floor. She kept tripping as she walked back into the kitchen.

"Sean, can we eat in here and then after my jeans are fixed go sit on the tree? Is that ok?" asked Emily as she tripped again.

"Sure," said Sean. He laughed as Emily tripped once more. They both laughed as Martha put two plates with an egg sandwich each on the table.

"You two sit and eat while I patch these jeans," smiled Martha.

Sean waited for Emily to sit first, then he sat down as Martha poured two big glasses of milk and put them on the table.

She picked up Emily's jeans from the counter. "Take your time. I'll be back soon."

Sean and Emily were laughing when Martha came back.

"There." She held up the jeans. "You can barely see they've been torn."

Emily took the jeans, examined them and exclaimed, "Wow, I can't even find where you fixed them. Thanks so much, Martha."

She hugged Martha around the waist.

Martha patted Emily on the head and lovingly said, "Why don't you go change and then the two of you can get out of here."

As Emily stumbled over Sean's long jeans into the bathroom, Sean cleared the table and started washing off the plates and glasses.

Shortly Emily reemerged with her right sized jeans on and she and Sean went out to the slant tree.

"This has been one of the nicest days of my entire life, Sean. I really enjoyed visiting with the sisters and I just love your grandma. She reminds me of my grandma when she wasn't sick. Thank you for making me feel so welcomed in my new home." She was smiling from ear to ear.

"Em, it was really boring here before you moved in. Yea, I played with some of the other kids in the neighborhood but you're different. I feel…well, good when I'm with you. It's kind of the way I felt before my dad died. He and I were best buddies. I miss him a lot; but now, with you I don't feel so lonely."

He moved a little closer to Emily so their shoulders touched. They spent the rest of two hours sitting in the tree talking and laughing.

After a while Emily asked, "Sean, do you mind if I ask about your dad?"

He was brimming with pride at the request. "No, Em, I love talking about my dad!"

"How did he die?" she asked.

With grief in his voice, "About five years ago he was coming home from a trip and it was raining really hard. He was driving down one of the mountains in Vermont and was in back of a semi-truck. The truck lost its brakes and jack knifed. My dad didn't have time to stop and ran right into the truck. He was in a coma and died a week later."

Emily frowned as she put her hand on his and said, "I'm so sorry, Sean. Tell me more about him. I would love to hear more!"

Sean immediately became animated again. No one had ever asked him about his dad and he just loved talking about him.

Emily smiled and felt warmth all over as she watched Sean gesture with his hands and arms as he spoke, "Dad was a children's doctor. He went to Vermont to look at a hospital he was thinking about working at. He loved to hike and Vermont is a great place for hiking. He and I used to go hiking all the time. Just the boys he would say. We had so much fun. He taught me all sorts of things, like what plants are good to eat and which ones are poisonous. He taught me how to fish and he could even catch a fish with his bare hands! He didn't even need a fishing pole! It was *so* amazing to watch. Lots of time, when we'd hike, we'd bring sleeping bags and a tent and cooked on an open fire. I remember sitting out in fields with him at night. The sky would be clear and you could see all the stars. He'd look up at the stars, put his arm around me and would tell me what all the constellations were as he pointed to each one. I know where Leo, Andromeda, Hercules and all of them are. My favorite is the Little Bear constellation where the North Star is. Its real name is Ursa Minor and the North Star is the brightest in the constellation. Dad would say, Sean, if you ever get lost at night, just look up at the sky and you'll know exactly where you are." Then Sean's eyes welled up with tears. "I just miss my dad so much."

Overwhelmed with emotion for this sweet boy, Emily put her arm around Sean and said, "Oh, Sean, I'm so, so sorry. I wish I could have met him. He sounds wonderful."

"He was." Then he turned to her. "Thanks, Em for letting me talk about him. You're the first person that's ever asked. I think we're going to be good friends."

"I think so too, Sean. I think so too."

****

Later that evening as Emily lay in her bed she thought about her conversation with Sean. She felt happy for him that he had that type of relationship with his dad, even if it was for just a short while. It made her want to get to know Sean better.

He makes me feel special and happy.

On the other hand, she felt extreme sadness that she wasn't able to discuss her father with so much pride and love in her heart. *I wish with all my heart I could talk about Dad like Sean talks about his dad. His dad sounds like he loved Sean a lot. If only Dad loved me a lot too,* she thought. *But I can't talk about Dad because I know he doesn't love me. He only wants to bother me. I'm pretty sure Dad hates me.* As she began to drift off to sleep, she wondered if her dad had ever loved her like she longed to be loved by him. Her thoughts saddened her so much that she turned onto her side, curled up into a ball and cried herself to sleep.

Chapter Six

April and May flew by for the children. There was only one week left until summer vacation began.

By this time, there were three friends playing in the meadow, woods, grape vines and having long conversations on the slant tree.

Jeannie had become *the* intricate third member; yet, Emily continued to hide her special feelings for Sean out of respect for Jeannie. Sean, on the other hand was pretty obvious which of the two girls he was smitten with; yet, at the request of Emily, he tried hard to hide his preference. The three of them were sitting on the slant tree one Saturday afternoon when Sean went in for some snacks.

"Hey, Jeannie, have you asked your parents if you can go to Sean's cookout party next weekend?"

"Yes, and yes, I can go. It should be fun. How about you? Do you also have permission to go?"

"Yes. I wasn't sure at first but Mom likes Martha so she talked Dad into letting me go. It should be tons of fun! I love cookouts!"

Then Jeannie turned sideways so she could address Emily directly.

"Listen, Emily. I know how much you like Sean; and, it's pretty obvious how much he likes you. I just want you to know its ok with me. Besides, I've met the new boy who just moved into the house at the very bottom of the street. I really like him and I think he likes me. I also want you to know that I really appreciate what you've been doing."

Emily looked up and acted surprised. "What do you mean what I've been doing?"

Jeannie giggled a little then said, "You know. You've been trying really hard to not let on how much you like Sean. I know too you've been trying to hide it because you didn't want to hurt my feelings. I just want you to know that; but I also want you to know that I can tell there's something special between you and Sean."

Emily scratched her head as Jeannie continued, "Awe come on, Emily. Don't tell me you can't feel it. Sometimes I swear I can almost see beams of light going from Sean to you and then from you to him. I can't explain it but I think it's kinda cool."

Emily blushed. "You're right. I've had a special *feeling for* him from almost the first time I met him. It's kind of weird; but nice."

Their conversation was cut short when Sean yelled as he pushed open the screen door with his left foot, "Hey, guys. Can one of you help me carry some of this?"

Both Jeannie and Emily whipped around to see Sean trying to balance three cans of soda and a bag of cookies.

Jeannie looked at Emily and with a snicker said, "You go help him. He's your boyfriend anyway."

The girls giggled. Then rather than running down the tree, Emily jumped to the ground and ran over to help Sean.

That was how the entire summer went for the three which soon became four once Jeannie introduced Phillip from down the street to Sean and Emily. With Sean's mom, who was now working at the law firm as a lawyer vs. a paralegal and also seeing Bill Haskell on a regular basis, Sean spent most of the summer at his grandma's house.

Emily's summer had been so much fun, in her mind she managed to minimize all the bad stuff that had happened to her. Besides, her dad, a helicopter pilot, had spent the better part of the summer on board the US Naval aircraft carrier, the USS Constellation. He wasn't due back until October, long after the beginning of the new school year.

Two weeks prior to the startup of school, Sarah announced to her children that she intended to take them and her mom to the shore for a long weekend. Emily, who usually loved going to the shore, looked very sad when Sarah made the announcement.

"What's wrong, Emily? I thought you'd be happy," asked Sarah.

Emily tried to look happy. "I am, Mom. It's just that we only have two more weeks before Sean has to go back to living at home and visiting only once a month."

"Well, what if I told you that I've already invited him to come with us. Would you be able to get excited then?"

"Are you kidding? Uh, uh…you aren't kidding are you Mom?" begged Emily.

"No, I'm not kidding. I asked Martha yesterday. I'm surprised he hasn't already mentioned it. Then, maybe Martha hasn't told him yet. I've rented three cabins so I figure Grandma and I will take one of the cabins, Paul and Sean the other and you girls the third."

"Holy cow, Mom! I can't believe you'd do that. Thanks so much. I really, really am excited now!"

That long weekend at the beach was one of the best family weekends Emily could remember having in a very long time.

Paul and Sean got to know each other better and seemed to like each other quite a bit. In fact, they both teased Emily endlessly the entire weekend which she thoroughly enjoyed. Sean continued the teasing nearly the entire trip home as he poked Emily in the side making her giggle. Paul even threw a wet towel over Emily's head making her giggle even more.

As the three finally tired of their antics, Emily smiled and thought, *even Grandma seemed to have fun.*

Then, a sleepy Emily leaned her head against the window on the passenger side of the back seat and stared at her mom. Emily watched her mom the rest of the trip home recognizing how different she acts when her dad wasn't around.

"She just seems so much more alive and in charge; almost like she becomes a totally different person," Emily said as she repeated her thought to Martha that evening after helping Sean carry one of his bags over to his house.

Martha asked, "How does your mom act when your dad is at home, Emily?"

"Well," she said thoughtfully, "She lets him tell her what to do; and she acts like she's not very smart. Sometimes she talks in a baby voice to him. I don't know how to explain it. I just really like my mom so much more when dad's not at home. It almost makes me wish he'd be gone more; but I know that's not a nice thing to say. He is my dad after all."

"That's ok, Emily. Everything you tell me remains here with me. If you ever want to express your thoughts or feelings, please…I want you to feel comfortable that everything is confidential. Ok?" Martha assured Emily.

"Ok, Martha. Thanks for not thinking I'm a bad person for saying those things. I love my dad; but sometimes…well…," Emily's voice trailed off. Then she changed the subject. "I better go say goodnight to Sean and get back home. I need to help Mom unpack."

"Ok, dear," said Martha as they hugged.

As Martha watched Emily round the corner to the living room she pondered Emily's comments. She was becoming very friendly with Sarah who she liked quite a bit; but Emily's comments made her think about Sarah.

Typically when she and Sarah were together, Joe wasn't around; yet, she could detect a sense from Sarah that she felt inferior to her husband and even feared him a little. On a few occasions Sarah complained at how intolerant of Bertie Joe was; yet, at the same time, Sarah was hesitant of criticizing Joe because, "After all, he took my mother in and doesn't push me to put her in a home."

Martha also felt that something else wasn't quite right in the household. It bothered her tremendously, yet she couldn't get a handle on what made her feel so uncomfortable.

****

Emily climbed the stairs to Sean's room and knocked. He opened it and thanked her for helping him carry the bag she handed him.

"I had a great time, Emily! It was fun too, getting to know Paul better. He's pretty cool," laughed Sean.

"I did too, Sean! I had a ton of fun. I'm glad you got to come with us. It made the weekend extra special. I could also tell that Paul really likes you too. You know, I think Grandma even had a good time, don't you think, Sean?"

"Yea, I think she did. She loved when you buried her feet in the sand. She giggled like a little girl. Say, Em did you like the clam cakes your Mom got this morning for us to eat? That was a special treat. Don't you think?"

"I love, love, loved them! I've never had anything like that. I can't believe they had clams in them. I usually hate slimy things like oysters, but the clam cakes were absolutely yummy!" exclaimed Emily using her hands and arms to describe how much she loved them.

At that very moment, Sean reached out, grabbed Emily's arms and pulled her close. He kissed her on the cheek and then on the lips. Then he stepped back and said, "I'm sorry. I should have asked you. You just made my heart skip ten beats just then. I really like you, Emily."

"I like you too, Sean. I need to run home now." She turned and as she walked out of the room she stopped, looked back over her shoulder and said, "You don't have to apologize, Sean. I liked your kiss. In fact, I don't think I'll wash my face for several days now."

They both laughed and waved good-bye.

When Sean heard the front door shut, he went to the window and watched Emily cross the street. *I shouldn't have kissed her; but I like her a lot. I'm glad I kissed her.* Then he smiled to himself when he thought about Emily not washing her face for several days. He was so happy to know Emily because she filled a void in his heart left when his father died. She made him feel alive again.

Chapter Seven

Soon summer ended and everyone was back in school. Emily began attending a new school.

Instead of riding the bus, she now walked up the hill and down Pawtucket Avenue about two blocks to Bay View Academy. She liked it there. Her teacher was nice and she was even taking art classes after school from Sister Mary Karen, who was older than sin, but very talented as she encouraged Emily's creativity.

One late October afternoon as Emily walked home carrying an oil painting she painted for her mom, she realized her dad would be home in a few days.

She felt a glut of mixed emotions; happy, sad, apprehensive, guilty and scared all at once.

Her feelings for her dad were a jumble of junk she just didn't know what to do with. When he was nice, he was a lot of fun; like those Sundays he would gather all the children in the kitchen and make fudge.

She thought how she much preferred having those thoughts about her dad; but, she wasn't always able to keep the other thoughts and dreads from entering her world. She doesn't recall all the details, but she remembers the first time it happened.

Emily stopped walking, stared down at the sidewalk and got totally lost in thought as she recalled the evening her dad was headed to the liquor store.

She was just six years old. Although she had forgotten, prior to that night, Emily was a happy little girl. She felt special and very much loved by her father. In fact, Joe's step-mother often confirmed that for Emily.

She often commented to Emily that she was the apple of Joe's eye. Emily now thought about this comment yet she couldn't quite get a handle on why her step-grandmother thought that.

That feeling of being special was lost to Emily. She did however, remember how that particular day she felt privileged at having been asked to go with him because he only asked her. He didn't ask any of her siblings to go. But any positive feeling that evening ended swiftly.

As if it were yesterday, Emily clearly remembered the details as they unfolded.

While driving down the highway, Joe asked her to sit next to him. She recalled protesting, but he then told her that if she sat next to him, everyone would think she was his girlfriend. Emily felt a twinge of guilt as she recalled that she moved closer. She felt humiliated as she thought *I don't know why I did that. I think he made me feel special; but now I'm not sure. I hate that I moved over!* Then Emily remembered how fast she no longer felt special as her dad put his hand on her knee and began rubbing her thigh. Then, as Joe parked the car in the store lot, he didn't get out right away. Instead, he said something to her which, for the life of her, she just couldn't recall; but, she fully remembered what happened next.

He pulled her closer to him then slipped his hand down the front of her pants and down into her underwear. They sat there in the lot for what seemed like a long, long time as he rubbed her tiny part. She remembered how her private part stung. Then he abruptly stopped, pushed her and angrily commanded her to move back over to the passenger side as he disappeared out the door.

The Door: when he slammed it shut, in her mind Emily heard an extremely loud cracking sound. She now thought about that explosion only to realize it sounded as if the entire world had broken in two.

On the way home, they didn't speak at all; but, just as they turned down their street, Joe stopped the car which caused Emily to tremble. She was convinced he was extremely angry at her.

With both hands gripping the steering wheel, Joe sat very still for what seemed like an eternity. Then he slowly turned and looked over at her and said, "Emily, look at me."

When she looked at him he continued, "I'm so sorry I did that. But, Emily, you have to promise me you'll never, ever tell anyone, especially your mom. Please, please promise me that you'll act very normal and will never let anyone even suspect that happened. Can you do that? Can you promise me that, Emily? If you tell, Daddy will get into a lot of trouble. So, it's really important that this be our secret. Can you do that for me, honey? Can you make sure Daddy doesn't get into trouble?"

Emily recalled how wretched and sorry her father sounded and how it not only made her feel sad for him but it made her feel very ashamed.

She also recalled how she's never been able to figure out what it was she did or does to make her dad want to do those things to her. The thought of all that always made her feel very depressed and dirty; as if it was all her fault.

Suddenly a loud car horn sounded jolting Emily back to the present. She looked around and realized she was no longer walking home.

Instead, she was sitting on a rock to the right side of the sidewalk. Then she remembered how she began thinking of all of that. She also realized she was crying.

Her dad was coming home in a few days and the wonderful freedom from fear and guilt she had been able to experience those last several months would all go away.

Emily got up, wiped away her tears, brushed herself off, then brushed off the dirt that was all over her painting and walked the rest of the way home.

When she entered her house, she tried very hard to act cheerful.

I could act in a movie, Emily resigned as she recognized how she could turn sadness into cheerfulness in a split second at least on the outside that is.

She showed her mom the painting with the bright red tulips in the cobalt blue vase. Sarah made a big deal of the painting and told her she was going to find a very special place to hang it. She then told Emily to hurry up and get ready for dinner.

"We're having mashed potatoes, hamburger and peas mashed together."

It was one of Emily's favorite meals. For Sarah, it was an easy and cheap means of feeding her mother and kids while Joe was away.

As Emily came back down and sat at the table she noticed her mom wasn't eating. "Where's your plate, Mom?"

"Oh, I'm not eating tonight, Emily. I just managed to lose 40 pounds for your dad. I even bought a new dress to go meet him in. I want to make sure it still fits Saturday when we all drive up to Boston to pick him up at the pier."

"Well, Mom, I've been meaning to tell you that you look great. I think Dad will be proud of how you look when he sees you."

"You're very kind, Emily. Now eat your dinner. You still need to do your homework before you go to bed."

That Saturday morning Sarah got all the kids up early and urged them to hurry up. "It's a two hour ride into Boston and the ship anchors at 1 p.m."

As they all came down the stairs Emily ran to her Grandma's room and noticed that Bertie was still dressed in her nightgown. She came back out to the kitchen where Sarah was standing and asked Sarah why Grandma wasn't dressed.

Grabbing her purse, "It's a long drive even for your Grandma, Emily. I've asked Martha to keep an eye on her for us."

"Well, you're probably right. Grandma does get antsy on long trips. By the way, Mom, you look beautiful. You look like a movie star in that dress."

"Well, Emily Callaway, thank you so much. You just made my day!"

Just as they all piled into the car, Martha ran out of her house frantically waving at Sarah. "Oh, Sarah, I'm glad I caught you before you left. You forgot to give me the key to your house. I've decided to just spend the day there while you're gone. Would that be ok with you? I would just feel more comfortable if I could be there rather than here and worrying if your mom has fallen or something terrible."

"That would be lovely, Martha. Here's the key. We should be back around four or five. Ok, kids, we're off," Sarah said as she waved to Martha.

Several hours later, they were all back in the car. Joe was driving and talking only about his trip and bragging about his accomplishments while away.

This time, Emily was sitting in the back seat on the driver's side. She could see her mother's face and watched her expressions.

Mom seems really sad. I think she feels hurt. Dad didn't even say anything about how she looks. Emily continued watching her mother the entire trip home. Joe went on and on bragging about himself while Sarah sat staring ahead and didn't say much the entire trip home. Emily could tell that Sarah felt totally defeated and dejected and it made Emily sad. *Dad's so selfish. Mom tried hard to lose her weight. All he had to do was tell her she looked beautiful; but all he wants to talk about is his own stupid self.*

Later that evening, after dinner and the kitchen was clean, Emily went into the living room where Sarah was sitting to kiss her mom goodnight. As she did she hugged Sarah.

"Mom, I just want you to know that you really looked beautiful today. I'm proud of you!"

Sarah was taken completely off guard as she looked at Emily with a puzzled expression. Then she hugged Emily very hard and said, "Thanks, sweetie. That's very kind of you to say that. I love you, Emily. I'm proud of you as well!"

"I love you too, Mom."

As she pulled back from Sarah she thought she could see tears in Sarah's eyes. She intuitively knew her mom felt totally let down.

Chapter Eight

Over the next two months, Emily's dad only bothered her once. It was a week night.

The other children had all gone to bed. Emily sat a while longer on the floor in front of the TV putting a handful of curlers in her hair. Joe was sound asleep in his Lazy Boy chair so Emily thought for sure she could finish and then sneak upstairs without waking him.

Sarah was in the living room. She had been reading and fell asleep. Emily finished clipping the last curler, quietly picked up her brush and mirror and slipped past Joe's chair. She thought she was home free when she felt something grab her arm. She turned to see Joe wide awake and staring at her.

"Where are you going, Emily?" asked Joe. "You can go to bed in a few minutes. Sit on my lap for a while."

Emily protested with a lie, "Dad, I have a big test tomorrow. I really need to get some sleep."

"Emily, you've probably studied enough to pass the test with flying colors, now sit on your dad's lap and give me a nice kiss," he cajoled as he pulled her to his lap. "You know, Emily, I wish I were twenty years younger. Then I could be your boyfriend," Joe said as he slipped his hand down her pajama bottoms. "Now kiss me and stick your tongue in my mouth. I want you to give me a passionate kiss."

Emily felt sick to her stomach. She hated how his tongue felt in her mouth; and she had no idea what passionate even meant. But she obliged thinking that if she just did it, let him do what he wanted, she could be done and in bed in a few minutes. Suddenly Joe stopped, and literally pushed Emily off his lap as Paul bounded down the stairs.

Emily fell to the floor, her brush flew across the room and her mirror broke into several pieces on the floor. As she climbed to her feet, she cut the bottom of her foot on a piece of glass and began crying. All the commotion woke Sarah, who came running into the room and asked Emily what happened.

Through tears Emily lied. "I was about to go upstairs when I slipped and fell and broke my mirror, Mom. I'm sorry I woke you up."

Seeing the blood, Sarah scooped Emily up and carried her to the bathroom. Just as Sarah turned her back on Joe, he put his finger to his lips indicating to Emily to hush and keep their secret.

Joe then yelled at Paul, "What are you doing, Paul? I thought I told you to go to bed."

"I was in bed, Dad, but I remembered I forgot to get something from the garage to bring to school."

"Well, hurry up!"

All bandaged up, Emily came back to the TV room and began picking up the broken glass which her dad didn't even bother to pick up for her.

As she got back up, Joe whispered, "Just remember, Emily. This is our secret."

Emily didn't say a word. She dutifully nodded her head. What else could she do? She was trapped in his web.

As she climbed into bed Joe's words resonated in her head. *If he were twenty years younger, it would mean he wouldn't be married to Mom. I don't want to take him away from Mom. I love Mom. He should love Mom. I wish I could just disappear. If I could just disappear, everyone would be happy. I wouldn't be here, and Dad would love Mom and she would be happy.* Emily fell asleep that night asking God to help her disappear from the world. She didn't want to be in the world anymore.

The following morning Emily woke from a dream. She dreamed she was riding the bus with her grandmother and they were going downtown to shop for new shoes for Emily. She and her grandmother didn't live with Joe and Sarah. They lived in a house all by themselves and they were happy.

Emily lay in bed trying really hard to fall back to sleep so she could go back into the dream. When she realized she couldn't she thought about the night before and about the nights her dad would crawl into her bed. She never knew when she would be trapped in his snare. She only knew she had to figure out how to stay out of his way; how to hide from him. Then, one evening she came up with what she thought was an ingenious plan.

To help make the girls room seem larger, Sarah convinced Joe to let her buy a set of bunk beds for the two youngest girls. Now, instead of three beds, there were basically only two. That allowed Sarah to also purchase a special study desk for Emily. Emily helped Sarah paint the walls of the room purple which Emily proclaimed to be her second favorite color.

Sarah didn't know why, nor did she stop long enough to analyze her feelings, but deep inside she was feeling more and more like she needed to be extra nice to Emily. She rationalized she was rewarding her for the way she was always so thoughtful toward her mother.

The other children stayed away from their grandma and complained whenever they were asked to help her; but not Emily. She was *always* willing and ready to do whatever was needed to make her grandma more comfortable; and that made Sarah feel appreciative of her young daughter.

When Sarah told Katie to make her bed one morning, Katie made a huge fuss. Emily felt bad for her youngest sister and offered to make the bed for her. Of course Katie accepted the offer and answered ok to Emily when Emily called after her, "Just remember though, Katie, you owe me one."

That evening, as the three girls got ready for bed, Emily said to Katie. "Hey, Katie, I have an idea. You hate making your bed and I sure don't want to have to make two beds every morning so, how about this. You sleep with me every night and you won't have to ever make another bed again. Too, I'll now only have to make one bed. What do you say?"

Katie looked at Emily skeptically. "I can sleep with you and never make my bed? What if Mom asks? She'll get mad."

"No she won't. Besides she doesn't have to know. It can be our secret. How does that sound to you?"

"Sure," Katie nodded.

So Emily crawled into bed first and Katie crawled in next to her. Emily fell asleep satisfied that she had solved the late night visits from her father. *Now I only have to stay out of his way while I'm awake.* For the first time Emily could ever remember she felt safe falling asleep.

Chapter Nine

It was Christmas Eve and Emily was filled with excitement and anticipation. It was her favorite time of the year.

Unlike the rest of the year, Emily felt that *everyone* in the world seemed nicer to each other. She also felt it was a magical time. She quit believing in Santa Clause a long time ago, but, with all her heart, she still wished there was a Santa Clause somewhere in the world. Just knowing there was would make life more bearable. It would mean that anything and everything was possible.

****

She was so excited because Sean, his mom and her new husband were coming to spend Christmas Eve with Martha. Sean was scheduled to stay through the entire Christmas break while Beth and Bill Haskell went to Europe for a late honeymoon.

Emily was beside herself with excitement about the Christmas present she bought Sean. She did a few extra chores for her mom who she bargained with for enough to buy a beautiful Swiss Army Knife with all sorts of gadgets attached.

Sean told her about the one his dad bought him a couple of months prior to the terrible crash. Sean lost the knife one day when he was on a Cub Scout camping trip two years ago. He told Emily he cried for several days when he couldn't find it.

Emily couldn't wait to give him the knife, so she rushed to her dresser pulled out the box, and ran down the stairs to ask her mom for wrapping paper and ribbon. She wrapped it up, tied the ribbon around the box and had Sarah make the biggest, prettiest bow, red of course.

Emily didn't want to use one of the impersonal to/from gift tags, so she went back upstairs to find a blank piece of white paper with which she could make her own personal card.

She drew a big red heart on one side of the paper and in the middle drew and colored a Christmas tree full of red, blue and gold ornaments. At the top tip of the tree she drew a big gold star then drew several bright yellow lines originating at the tips of the star and running all the way up to the top of the heart. *They look like beams of light going straight up to heaven; to Sean's dad,* Emily reasoned.

Emily then turned the paper over and wrote, "To Sean. May this gift fill you with the joy of your dad and make you forever close to him. I know he watches down on you from the middle of the Little Bear with so much love in his heart. Love forever and ever, Em."

She carefully and lovingly folded it, kissed the card then the present and tucked them into her top dresser drawer. Next she ran to the window to see if Beth's car was at Martha's yet, thinking *I can't wait, I can't wait, I can't wait to see Sean and give him his present!* Beth's car wasn't there yet as she wondered if she should give him his present tonight or tomorrow after she got home from Mass. After much thought, *I'll bring it with me and give it to him when everything feels special. I hope, hope, hope he loves the knife; cuz I love, love, love him!*

Emily ran down the stairs, put on her coat and hat, ran by the Christmas tree and turned it on and then ran outside. Katie was sitting in the dirt digging when Emily realized she was using one of her baby turtles as a shovel.

"Katie! What are you doing? You could kill Marvin!" Emily screamed as she grabbed the poor turtle from Katie.

There was dirt all down in the shell, so Emily dashed in the house and ran the water on the turtle. Katie stood behind Emily crying. Sarah rushed into the kitchen and asked Emily what all the commotion was about.

Emily explained then said, "Thank God. She must have just started digging with Marvin because he's still alive."

Katie stopped crying and said, "I'm sorry, Emily. Is he really still alive? Can I see?"

Emily picked up Marvin, crouched down to her knees and showed Katie that Marvin was still alive then said, "But you have to promise me, Katie that you'll never do something like that again. It would be the same if someone picked you up, turned you upside down and started using your head as a shovel. That would hurt, don't you think?"

"Yes," Katie answered through a few more tears and sniffles. Emily put Marvin on the floor and hugged Katie telling her it was ok and reminded her that Christmas was almost here and now it was time to just be happy. That's all Katie needed as she bent down and petted Marvin. "Ok, Emily. Can I help you put him back in his home?"

"Sure. Come on, Katie. I'll lift you up so you can personally put Marvin back in his home."

Sarah watched this whole episode from the doorway as she remarked to herself that she was very fortunate to have such a loving daughter in Emily.

As Emily and Katie finished putting poor Marvin back in his home, Emily heard the phone ring. She went to the top of the stairs so she could hear who it was.

She heard Sarah say, "Ok, Martha. I'll tell Emily and send her right over."

Emily's heart quickened as her mom called her name. She ran over to her drawer and grabbed the box with the red ribbon and card and practically flew down the stairs. Sarah had her coat, hat and mittens all ready when she reached the kitchen.

Sarah buttoned Emily's coat and kissed her forehead. "Now, Emily. It's Christmas Eve. It's 5:00 right now. Martha's invited you for dinner. I do want you back in the house by 8:00…ok?"

"Yes, Mom. I'll let Martha know to help me watch my time. Thanks for letting me go. I just hope Sean likes his present."

"I'm sure he will, Emily. Have a good time."

Emily ran across the street and rang the front door bell. Sean answered the door almost immediately.

As Emily walked in, Beth laughed. "Well, hi Emily. Sean's been standing at the door for over five minutes just waiting for you to ring."

Sean moaned with protest. "Mom, you don't have to embarrass me!"

Bill then said, "Sean, I don't know why you feel embarrassed. If I were you and I knew Emily was as pretty as she is, I'd be waiting at the door too just as anxious."

Emily giggled and Sean laughed as well. Emily thought she

was going to have a wonderful time that evening as Sean took her coat, hat and mittens.

Martha came out from the kitchen and announced that dinner was ready. They all went in and sat at a beautifully set dining room table.

"Umm," Emily called. "Everything smells so good, Martha. Can I help with anything?"

"No, dear. I just have one more bowl to fix then I'll sit down as well," Martha said as she stuck her head around the corner. "Now everyone start eating...please!"

Minding his manners, Sean picked up the bowl of mashed potatoes and offered it to Emily before he took some for himself.

As soon as her plate was full, Emily looked at Beth and asked, "When do you leave for Europe?"

"Our plane leaves at 1 p.m. tomorrow."

"I'll bet you're excited," exclaimed Emily. "I've never been to Europe. The only place I've ever been outside America is Canada. One time, we drove up to Maine and then into Canada. It was summer. I think we were in a place called New Brunswick. We stopped at a lighthouse and I got to walk out on the rocks that looked out over the ocean. It was exciting for me because I realized I was standing on the edge of the world."

Beth couldn't help but marvel at how mature Emily seemed. *After all,* she silently remarked, *what young child could have such deep yet romantic thoughts?* She felt very thankful that Sean had found a friend in such a sweet young girl.

They had a wonderful dinner. When they were all done, Martha got up and began clearing the table. Beth jumped up to help as did Bill. Emily picked up her plate and carried it to the kitchen as did Sean.

She then began to go back to clear more when Martha asked, "Emily, what time does your mom expect you home?"

"Oh...I'm glad you mentioned that. Eight o'clock," answered Emily.

"Well, it's seven o'clock right now. Listen you kids go and have some fun. Bill, Beth and I will finish cleaning up."

Then Beth looked at Sean and said, "Emily, Sean has a gift for you. Sean, why don't you go get it and give it to Emily."

"Ok," responded Sean, "But, Mom, do you mind if we go out

back to the slant tree? I'd like to give it to her there. Is that ok with you, Em?

"Yes, Sean. I like that idea."

She then ran to get her coat, taking her card and present for Sean out of her pockets. She put on her coat and mittens and waited for him at the back door. He came down the stairs and out they went.

She slipped a little as she began climbing the tree. She had her good shoes on. Unlike her tennis shoes, the soles were slick.

Sean caught her and said, "Let's just sit down here, Em. I sure don't want you to fall. I never thought about your shoes. Mine too, probably. We're always in tennis shoes when we climb."

Emily laughed as they sat on the bottom portion of the tree. The moon was full and the sky was clear; just perfect for such a romantic evening. Sean looked at Emily and gave her a small box wrapped in red with a white bow around it.

As he handed Emily her gift, she handed him his along with the card and said, "You open your present first, ok?"

He opened the card first and remarked how nice it was that she made it special for him.

He pulled out a small flashlight from his coat pocket. "A boy scout is *always* prepared!"

They both laughed as he could now see the star at the top of the tree Emily drew and then he read the words out loud, "To Sean. May this gift fill you with the joy of your dad and make you forever close to him. I know he watches down on you from the middle of the Little Bear with so much love in his heart. Love forever and ever, Em."

Sean got a little choked up and told Emily how much he appreciated her thinking of his dad. He then opened his gift trying hard not to rip the paper. As he opened the box he gasped at the shiny red knife with the white Swiss cross on it. The knife seemed to shimmer in the moonlight. He began crying and then apologized that he was even crying.

Emily put her arm around him and told him it was ok for him to cry. "In fact, I kind of like it. Boys are always told they can't cry, and I just think that's wrong. Everybody has a reason to cry now and then."

He hugged her and told her how much such a wonderful gift meant to him. He also told her how much she meant to him. Then he asked her if he could kiss her. She said yes and they kissed sweetly.

Then excitedly Sean begged, "Emily, open your present now, please."

She began unravelling the ribbon and, as did Sean, tried very hard not to rip the paper as she took it apart. She opened the box. Sean was holding the flashlight so Emily could see. Inside the box was a beautiful gold heart locket on a gold chain.

"I hope you don't mind, Em, but I put my picture on one side of it. Maybe you could put your picture on the other side. The locket belonged to Grandma. My grandpa gave it to her when they were very young. When I was trying to decide what to get you, Grandma showed me the locket. It's old and it isn't store bought...."

Emily put her finger to his lips so he would stop making excuses. "Sean, it's beautiful. I can't tell you how much this means to me that you and your grandma think so much of me. I'll wear it forever; and I love that your picture is in it because, Sean, I love you."

They kissed again and hugged very tightly and she asked if he would put it around her neck. He did and they kissed again. Then, they heard Martha calling them in. They got up, held hands and went in the house.

"It's almost 8:00, Emily. We don't want you to be late." Then she smiled, "Oh, dear, the locket looks so pretty on you."

"Thank you so much, Martha. I can't tell you what a special gift this is. I've never had a present so beautiful or so precious. I will cherish it forever," said Emily as she hugged Martha.

Then Sean produced the Swiss knife and showed Martha.

Martha gasped and remarked, "Sean, I could tell from the first time I met Emily that she is very special. What a wonderful and thoughtful gift."

She hugged Emily again and then again after she read the card Emily made for him.

Later, when Emily was gone, Sean showed his mom the knife and the card and Beth cried a little as she hugged Sean. "Sean, your dad would be so very proud of you. I am extremely proud and so happy you're my little boy."

Chapter Ten

Christmas and New Year's came and went. With it came the first big snow of the season as Emily and her siblings learned what it was like to live in New England. They also learned the benefit of living midway down a steep hill.

It had become a tradition on their street for the parents to rally for the children by petitioning the city to plow and salt only half their street, leaving the other half intact so the children were able to sled to their heart's content.

Emily's parents eagerly joined the other neighbors especially since they bought each of their four kids a brand new American Flyer sled for Christmas.

All four children gathered around the TV the night before to hear the weather forecast. Ten inches of snow was scheduled to start blanketing the neighborhood at around 1 a.m. and, if that happened, there would be no school the next day.

Plus, those American Flyers would be primed and ready to fly down the road. Paul soaped the bottoms of all the red rungs after he learned it helped cancel out the newness of the rungs and readied them for a smooth and speedy glide on the newly fallen snow. The children were ecstatic when Joe burst their bubble by telling them to go up to bed.

"But Dad," Lily complained, "There's no school tomorrow. Can't we stay up just a little longer?"

"No," barked Joe, "It hasn't even begun to snow which means school is a go until it does start to snow. We'll turn on the TV first thing in the morning. Now, everyone, get up the stairs. I want to see lights out in ten; and I better hear you all snoring in twenty."

Katie giggled, as she kissed her dad goodnight and made a snoring noise on her way up the stairs.

Once in the bedroom, Emily climbed into bed and Katie

climbed in next to her. It was cold in the room so they pulled all the covers up to the tops of their necks to get warm. Katie giggled again as she nestled up to Emily. They were all sound asleep in a matter of minutes.

Later that evening Emily, who was asleep and facing the wall heard the bedroom door creak. She woke to the noise, turned slowly and lifted her head up a little to see what was making the sound. She saw a dark figure enter the room and cross the floor to her bed. It stood at the side of the bed for a few seconds and then it was gone. The door creaked again as the figure closed the door. Emily fell back to sleep with the comfort of knowing her plan of having Katie sleep with her worked. *I'm safe,* she thought as she drifted back to sleep.

The next morning, Emily woke to the gleeful cackles of her two sisters who were out of bed and peering out the front window.

Emily sat up, rubbed her eyes and asked the million dollar question, "Did it snow?"

Lily called back with tons of excitement in her voice. "It sure did! Come look Emily. It's beautiful!"

Emily climbed out of bed and joined her sisters as they all looked in wonder at this stuff called snow that had transformed their formerly bleak looking neighborhood into a wondrous winter park.

"Wow," exclaimed Emily. "It looks just like it does in the movies! Let's hurry up and eat so we can go out and play."

There was a lot of commotion and scrambling in the household that morning as the children dressed, put on their new boots and rushed down the stairs. Sarah was standing at the kitchen sink looking haggard as she filled the Mr. Coffee pot so her husband had a fresh cup of coffee before he headed out to work.

"Mom," Lily protested, "Dad can't go to work. How's he gonna get up the street with all the snow on it?"

"Well, Lily, you forget. Your father grew up in Rhode Island. He knows how to drive in it. There may be no school for all of you, but Dad's work never stops for anything, not even snow!"

Just as Sarah finished educating Lily and the other children on the fine art of driving in the white stuff, Joe walked down the hall toward the kitchen. He looked handsome in his starched khaki uniform.

Emily noticed how sharp he looked as Katie ran to her dad and screamed with glee, "Daddy, daddy. It snowed; and we don't have to go to school."

Joe laughed as he raised Katie up in his arms and gave her a big kiss. "Sarah thanks for picking up my long sleeve shirt last week. I didn't think I'd need it for at least another week. Is the coffee ready?"

"You're welcomed; and, yes the coffee is ready. Have a seat; I have your soft-boiled egg just about ready for you to eat. Here are a few pieces of wheat toast. It's a good thing you bought those snow tires last week. Hopefully they'll help you climb that hill. The plows haven't bladed off the street yet; at least not since the last time I looked out."

Joe bit off a corner of toast. "Yea, the snow tires should help a great deal with the traction. It'll still be a challenge to get up the hill. It drizzled a little last night before it began to snow, so I'm sure there's a thin layer of ice under all that snow."

Just as he said the word snow, Paul ran into the kitchen laughing. "You should see that old codger, from the bottom of hill. Mr. Parker has been trying to get his car up the hill. He just slid back down. His car stopped just at the edge of our yard. He's out there cussing all the neighbors and kicking his tires. What a lush!" laughed Paul.

"Paul!" Sarah admonished. "Don't call him a lush."

"Well he is, Mom. I saw one of the bottles he tossed in Henry's bushes last week."

"Well, you don't know what that man has had to go through in his life. Be respectful. Joe, do you think you should help Mr. Parker get his car unstuck?"

Lily ran back into the kitchen and heard Sarah's question to which she giggled. "No need, Mom. I just watched him fish tail all the way up the hill. Wow, that was something to watch. I can't wait to fish tail down the street on my new sled!"

Joe pushed his chair away from the table. "I better get going, Sarah. There's no telling how long it will take me to get to the base."

"Ok, hon. Be careful and call me once you get there."

As Joe pecked Sarah on the cheek, "I will."

Of course, Sarah knew he wouldn't. He never follows through on requests like that leaving her to fret the entire day about his safety.

"Ok, kids," Joe called out. "Give your dad a kiss. Mind your mom and have fun in the snow today. This should be a real treat for all of you."

One by one, they all kissed him. When Emily was about to kiss him, he looked at her with a question on his face and a lot of disappointment as well. At least that was what Emily imagined she saw. Although she was guarding against her own pain, she couldn't help but regret disappointing her dad.

Joe left as all the children sat around the table loaded down with four different boxes of cereal, milk, sugar and a big gallon jug of orange juice. Emily grabbed her box, Cap'n Crunch, her favorite cereal and poured a big bowl. Once they were all done, one by one, they got up and ran up the stairs to finish getting ready for their big day.

Sarah called after Emily, just as she was about to leave the kitchen area, "Emily, would you mind helping to clear the table and load the dishwasher before you go out? I'd really appreciate it. I have a big load of wash to do and it would help me out a lot."

"Sure, mom. Then can I go out as well?" Emily asked, anticipating, *I'll probably get stuck folding clothes. I knew it was too good to be true!*

To her amazement and delight, however, Sarah answered, "Yes. Clothes folding can wait till later in the day. I want you to go out with the other kids and get your first taste of what it's like to live in Rhode Island. Thanks, dear. Oh, and put on your leotards under your jeans. It's cold out there," as Sarah disappeared around the corner.

Emily hurriedly cleared the table and loaded the dishwasher. She was about to quit when she realized the mess her mom left on the shelf.

Better clean that up too, thought Emily. *It's either do it now or later; might as well get it over with.*

Emily finally made it out the door.

****

Her sisters were standing on the other side of the street. The plow and salt truck had just bladed and salted the one side of the street.

Katie ran over to Emily, "Whoa, Emily. This is so much fun. We've already been down the street twice."

Emily looked down the hill to the house on the downside of Martha's house and asked, "What are Paul and the other boys doing down there?"

Katie answered. "They're building an ice ramp. Once they pour water on it we can sled over it."

Then Lily spoke up, "I don't know. The boys are saying that they won't let any of us girls go over the ramp."

"Well, we'll see about that!" Emily barked.

"Are you going to try it, Emily?" asked Katie.

"You bet I am. The boys can't have all the fun now can they?"

"Well, if you're going to do it, then I will too," said Lily.

"Let's be careful though," exclaimed Emily. "Don't do anything until the boys go over the ramp a few times. That way we'll know if it's ready, then, watch out, right Lily?"

"I'll be right behind you, Emily. But you'll have to go first, cuz I don't want any boys beating me up!"

"Ok, now let's go have fun!" Emily exclaimed as she grabbed Katie's hand and began trudging up the hill.

The neighborhood kids had fun all day long sledding down the street and walking back up to the top. An hour after stepping outdoors, Emily redirected her sled and aimed for the ramp as the lookout boy, Bobby, tried to block her. He jumped out of the way at the last minute and landed in the snow next to the ramp.

Up in the air Emily flew. She and her sled landed about ten feet from the ramp. BAM! She glided the rest of the way down the hill acknowledging the punch such a stunt gave her stomach as she and her sled smacked back down on the street.

But she grinned with glee at her bold accomplishment when she heard Bobby yell, "Whoa, good job Emily! Hey, Paul, your sister's cool!"

The rest of the day, most of the girls as well as the boys flew one by one over the ramp. Lily crashed on her second try, but Emily flew over the ramp with sureness and grace every time.

By the next weekend, the snow on the street had melted to the point of creating so many patches of asphalt that the kids were no longer sledding.

"But…" Jeanie said, "We drove by the golf course last night. You know, the one about half a mile down the highway. It's still covered in snow. All sorts of people were there sledding. That hill's nearly as long as our street. And…" Jeanie continued, "There's supposed to be another 3 inches of snow fall tonight. I heard my dad tell my mom that this morning."

"Oh, I hope so. Sean will be here tonight and I so wanted to go sledding with him," exclaimed Emily.

"Well, my dear," Jeannie grinned. "You just might get the chance to do that very thing. Now I better skedaddle. It's nearly 5 and we eat at 5:30. See you in the morning."

"It's a deal!" Emily called over her shoulder as she turned to go in her own house.

Sure enough, the next morning, Saturday, there was a new dusting of snow. It wasn't enough to cover the street's bare patches, but it was enough to give the hill at the golf course enough thickness promising a joyful day of sledding.

****

Emily was finishing up the dishes when the phone rang. She answered, "Callaway residence. This is Emily speaking."

"Hey, Em," said a familiar voice.

"Hi Sean! What time did you get to your grandma's last night?"

"I think it was about 9:30. Mom and Bill had to work late. They're working on a big case together. I knew it was too late to call you, so I waited till this morning,"

"I'm glad you did, Sean. Dad wouldn't have allowed me to talk to you last night anyway. I'm not allowed on the phone after 8:00. But I'm so, so happy you called me this morning. Do you want to go sledding today?"

"Sure; but the street is pretty melted from what I could tell last night."

"Oh, I'm not talking about the street, but I've gotta tell you about sledding down it this past week when there was no school. I went over the ice ramp a bunch of times."

"Well," Sean asked, "Where can we go sledding?"

"Jeannie told me about the golf course hill which is about half a mile up the main highway. It must be a little farther than my school cuz I don't remember ever seeing the place. Do you think Martha will let you go? I haven't asked my mom yet, but since I already walk most of that to school I don't see why she wouldn't let me walk a little farther to the golf course."

"Let me go ask Grandma and I'll call you back in a little while."

"Ok. I'll go ask Mom too. Keep your fingers crossed. I can't wait to see you, Sean!"

"Go ask your mom what?" asked Sarah as she walked out into the kitchen.

Startled, Emily whipped around to see her mother standing by the refrigerator.

"Oh, Jeannie was telling me about a golf course just a little farther up the highway from school. She said when she rode by it last night there was still lots of snow and people were sledding down the big hill. That was Sean on the phone. We all want to take our sleds up there, especially since it snowed again last night. Can I go, Mom?"

"Well, I guess you can as long as it's not too much farther than school; but you have to promise me that you'll be careful. Is it on the same side as the school?"

"I'm not sure, but there's a traffic light just beyond the school. I promise I'll make sure we cross there, ok?"

"Ok. Are you finished in here?"

"Yes, I just finished loading the dishwasher. Can I go get...?" Emily stopped just as the phone rang. She grabbed it and said, "Hey, Sean. You can. Oh, that's great; so can I! I'll call Jeannie. Let's meet out front in half an hour, ok?"

She hung up and then called Jeannie and arranged for Jeannie and Phillip to meet Sean and her in front of her house in a half hour. Then she ran up the stairs to get ready. As she did, she asked her mom if she would braid her hair. "Sean likes my hair in braids."

"Ok, just bring everything down when you're ready."

Emily got dressed. She pulled on her pink sweater over her turtle neck, grabbed her pink knit hat and mittens. Then she put her brush, two pink hair bands and her pink barrettes in her hat and ran down the stairs. It was almost time to meet everyone out front.

She was antsy as Sarah began brushing her hair to which Sarah complained, "Stop wiggling, Emily. I'll never finish braiding your hair with you wiggling so much."

Emily giggled. "Ok...I'm sorry. I'm just anxious to go sledding."

Lily overheard the conversation and mocked. "Oh, Emily, I'm sure you're anxious to go sledding. I *know* you're really anxious to see Sean." Then Lily started chanting, "Sean and Emily sitting in a tree, K-I-S-S-I-N-G. First comes love, then comes marriage, then comes Emily with a baby carriage."

"Ok, Ok, young lady," Sarah insisted. "Leave your sister alone and go watch TV with Katie."

Lily quietly repeated the chant as she walked from the kitchen to the TV room.

****

Jeannie and Sean were in the middle of a snowball fight when Emily walked out her front door. SMASH! Jeannie got Emily with one big ball on the back of her head. Some of it went down her coat and she screamed from the cold.

"Ahh... I'll get you for that, Jeannie. You just wait. When you're least expecting it, I'll get you," Emily called with great laughter.

She then ran to the garage and grabbed her sled. All three of them started up the street. "Where's Phillip?" asked Emily.

"Oh, he decided to play with the boys today. What does he know anyway? He'll miss out on all the fun. You guys are gonna love this. You think sledding down this street is fun; wait till you slide down the hill at the course," exclaimed an excited Jeannie.

"Oh...Jeannie, what side of the highway is it on? If it's on the other side from the school I promised my mom we'd cross at the traffic light just beyond the school," stated Emily.

"No prob. It's on the other side and the light is right there at the entrance to the golf course; so that's where we'll cross."

"Hmm," said Emily, "I don't know why I've never noticed a golf course across the street from the school."

"Ahh...probably cuz you don't golf, Emily, ya think!" giggled Jeannie.

Emily giggled as well and then looked at Sean. "Sean," she asked, "You're awfully quiet. Are you ok?"

"Sure," answered Sean. "I'm just listening to you two jabber away. Who can get a word in edge wise when you two are talking?"

Emily dropped the rope to her sled, stopped, put her hands on her hips and scowled at Sean, to which Sean rolled his eyes in sarcasm and remarked, "What can I say?"

They all had a good laugh at that.

As they got to the traffic light, they stood and waited for it to change. It did, but when they started to cross the highway a black car seemed to come out of nowhere and ran the red light.

"Whoa," yelled Jeannie. "He could have hit us. God that scared the stink outta me!"

"Well, he isn't going too far," said Sean excitedly. "A cop just pulled out of the street down there."

They could see the blue lights flashing and heard the siren.

"Good. I hope the cop saw he nearly ran us over and throws the book at him!" exclaimed Jeannie.

The three friends spent the better part of three hours sledding down the hill, throwing snowballs at each other, eating snow and making snow angels. By the time they started home, they were tired, hungry and exhausted.

"Man, I could eat a cow! Let's stop at Grandmas. I think she'll fix us some sandwiches and hot chocolate."

Jennie licked her lips. "Umm, hot chocolate. That's one of my favorite parts of winter. Can I call my mom from your grandma's?"

"Me too," asked Emily. "I'm afraid if I go home to ask I'll get stuck doing more chores."

"Sure," said Sean.

They arrived at Martha's house but she was way ahead of them. She had a whole platter loaded with peanut butter and jelly sandwiches and cookies on the table and hot chocolate was warming on the stove.

"How'd you know we'd be back in time, grandma?" Sean asked.

"Oh, just a hunch. Girls why don't you take your wet coats off and give your moms a call?"

"Ok, Martha," both girls said in unison.

Chapter Eleven

The following spring through most of the summer Sean didn't visit his grandmother as often but he and Emily wrote endless letters to each other and, took turns calling, talking almost every night for the 30 minutes she was allowed. A few times, she and Sean managed to talk longer; and, one evening, when her father had all night watch duty at the Naval base and wasn't home, Sarah fell asleep watching TV and Emily got to talk for a good 2 hours. When Sarah woke, she looked for Emily and got extremely upset with her.

"Emily, what were you thinking? That's a long distance call to Quincy. Your dad's going to be very upset with you and with me when he sees the bill."

Emily quickly said good-bye to Sean and hung up the phone. She then apologized to Sarah who seemed livid with her. Sarah told her to go to bed and also told her that she wouldn't be allowed to talk to Sean for the next full week.

Emily was hurt by this, but part of her understood because she knew she had taken advantage of her mother especially since that call was at her parents' expense.

She knew Sarah was asleep in the TV room. Yet, Emily just didn't understand why her mom feared her husband like a child fears their father, so just as she was about to go to bed, she came to her mom, kissed her good night and asked a question she would never have dreamed of asking in the past.

"Mom, don't get mad at me, but why are you afraid of Dad?"

Sarah looked stunned then growled, "What? I'm not afraid of your dad. What kind of a question is that?"

"I don't know," answered Emily now using a slightly more timid tone. "It's just that, when Dad isn't here, you're so different. You take over and do a great job taking care of all of us; and, you do things with us you never do when Dad's around."

Sarah, now somewhat embarrassed but getting angrier by the second, yelled, "That's enough, Emily. I don't know what's gotten into you. You're getting too big for your britches young lady. Perhaps I should ban you from seeing or talking to Sean all together!"

"No, no, Mom, please don't do that. I didn't mean it. I just love you so much and want you to be happy," begged Emily who now didn't know how to get herself out of the hole she just dug.

"Well, I think it's time for you to go to bed. You march yourself right up to your room; and, I don't ever want to hear that kind of surliness from your mouth again. Your dad is a good man, husband and father. If it weren't for him there's no telling where any of us would be! Go to bed. NOW!"

Emily kissed Sarah and hugged her. For a second Sarah didn't hug her back, but just as Emily began to pull away, Sarah grabbed Emily and hugged her very tight.

"I'm sorry for yelling at you, Emily. You're just growing up so fast."

"I'm sorry too, Mom, I didn't mean to make you mad," Emily said as she now cried.

Sarah looked at Emily, took her face into her hands and affectionately answered, "I know, I know. Now, go wash your face and go to bed; ok? You have a big day tomorrow, don't you?"

"Oh my gosh, yes! I almost forgot what day it was. It's Jeannie's birthday party and Sean will be here. Gosh…I can't believe Halloween's almost here either. I've gotta figure out what I want to be. See ya, Mom. Love you!"

Emily trotted off to bed as Sarah watched her little girl take a side trip to go kiss her grandma. Five minutes later, she watched Emily as she climbed the stairs.

Emily sat at her desk looking at her reflection in the standing mirror she bought at a garage sale one of the neighbor's held that past summer. She brushed her hair as she dreamed of Sean and thought about Jeannie's party. She was determined that she and Sean would have their first dance and had given Jeannie her Neil Young CD for safe keeping until the night was perfect for what she decided was their song. Staring at her reflection, she thought, *you're going to get to dance with Sean. God, I can't wait.* She then hugged herself and went to bed imagining what their first dance would be like.

****

Later that same night, Sarah lay in her bed thinking about what Emily said to her earlier that evening. Sometimes she forgot just how young Emily was. Sarah noted that Emily was way too perceptive for a 12 year old girl. Then she wondered if Emily was right about how she allows Joe to dominate her. Her mom was anything but submissive even when Sarah's dad was alive.

Her mom, not her dad ran their household; but her dad seemed to like it that way. He had more of a carefree personality than did Sarah's mom. Not having to wear the pants in the family also gave him the freedom to do traditional female things like cook and garden.

For a moment Sarah got totally lost in her memories of her father and the year she was fourteen.

The two of them planted red and white tulips, Jonquil daffodils, purple iris and chrysanthemums in the fall and her favorite, delphiniums and fox glove as well as pink and white coneflowers in the spring. By the following year the garden was in bloom from early spring right up to the first hard frost. Her dad just loved all sorts of flowers and ferns.

In fact, the year before he fell ill and died he won the Norfolk, Virginia (where she grew up) Garden Club's blue ribbon for most beautiful garden. She recalled the local newspaper made a huge deal because the garden was planted and cared for by a male versus a female.

She also remembered how angry it made Mrs. Taylor down the street from them because Mrs. Taylor was absolutely convinced she was going to win the honor for a third year in a row. Mrs. Taylor even planned a big party in her garden that year expecting the club officers and the press would show up and present her with the coveted blue ribbon. Mrs. Taylor was not only crushed but she was furious when she won honorable mention instead.

But Sarah and her mom forgave Mrs. Taylor the following

year when she sent a magnificent plethora of flowers to the funeral and then personally apologized to both Sarah and her mom for being what she called a horse's ass that last summer.

How strange life can turn out, Sarah pondered as she also recalled how her mom and Mrs. Taylor became best of friends after her dad died.

Then, as Sarah began drifting off she determined that when Joe came home in the morning she would tell him, not ask him, that she planned to take the children and her mom for a long weekend ride up the Mohawk Trail the weekend after Halloween when the leaves would be at their peak color.

He had a flight to Maine that weekend and Sarah was determined that she was going to live up to that person in charge Emily referred to. She wanted her daughter to look up to her. Then she thought how ironic it was that here she was sandwiched between two strong females, her mom on one end and her little Emily on the other.

What happened to me? Sarah asked herself. Before she could consider that question she drifted off to sleep.

****

Joe walked in the door the next morning in an absolutely rotten mood. There had been a helicopter crash at the base during his watch and with the cleanup and the ensuing investigation he was now charged with orchestrating, he got absolutely no sleep.

In fact, he told Sarah he came home only for a fresh change of uniform since he had to turn around and go right back to the base.

Sarah felt the heat of his mood when he discovered she hadn't picked up his spare khaki uniform from the cleaners.

He started slamming doors when he realized he would have to wear his dark Navy blue uniform. He became even angrier when he considered having to poke around the crash site in the white shirt that went with the uniform. By the time he was dressed and ready to walk back out the door, Sarah was in the kitchen trying to think what she could do to make up for her negligence. She literally jumped a few inches off the floor as he slammed one of the kitchen cabinet doors.

Emily and the other children were sitting at the kitchen table. They were all quiet as could be. None of them wanted to become the target of their dad's wrath. Just as Joe slammed the cabinet door, Katie and Lily were tugging at a rag doll they both had been bickering over.

Emily glared at both girls and mouthed, "Stop it!" They did as the doll dropped to the floor.

Emily then watched out the corner of her eye. It made her very sad to watch her mom cower.

Then she thought, *why didn't he pick it up himself? He drives right past the cleaners.* That thought startled her as she then thought, *what the heck is getting into me?*

She had, after all, always been right there with her mother, absolutely fearful of her dad, especially when he displayed his anger tantrums. But, lately, she was just losing all her patience with his bully type behavior. *I just wish with all my heart Mom would stand up to Dad and just yell, that's enough! He needs to be yelled at. He needs to be treated like the spoiled brat he is,* as she lowered her head trying hard not to have such…what was it her mom called her behavior last night? *Surly,* Emily now recalled.

****

Before she knew it, her dad was gone and her mom was now acting calm and unafraid. Emily felt guilty for having such surly thoughts about her dad.

At the same time Sarah was cussing herself for being such a coward in front of her children. As a result, she was now even more determined that she would take her mom and the kids on that long weekend trip.

We'll pack a picnic lunch and stay at the Mohawk Cabins in Williamstown, Massachusetts, determined Sarah.

Emily finished her breakfast, jumped up from the table and began cleaning up the kitchen. Sarah thanked her for doing it without having to be told.

Emily said, "Sure mom. Now why don't you take your cup of coffee in the TV room and watch TV for a while. I'll take care of everything out here."

Sarah pulled Emily close to her side, bent down and kissed her on the head, "I think I'll do just that, Emily. I think I'll also make a nice cup of tea for your grandma so she can sit with me in the TV room."

Sarah was beginning to feel quite defiant by the time she brought her mother out of her room and into the TV room. In fact, she had Bertie sit in Joe's Lazy-Boy chair. Then Sarah blushed to herself as she thought, *and, if you pee while we're sitting here, well so be it!* Of course she really hoped her mom didn't pee because she'd just have to clean it up; but the thought made her giggle to herself.

Soon Emily was finished in the kitchen. She walked into the TV room where her mom and grandma were sitting and asked, "Mom, do you mind if I go down to Jeannie's so I can help her decorate for her party? I've finished the dishes and the kitchen is sparkly clean."

"Go ahead, but before you leave, why don't you lay out what you plan to wear tonight. I'll take a look at what you're going to wear and I'll run the iron over it if it needs a little pressing."

Emily so liked when her mom was thoughtful and behaved kindly toward her. It made her feel like the special little girl she dreamed of being.

Emily finished dressing and called Jeannie to tell her she was on her way.

"Great," Jeannie responded. "Phew, I sure could use the help. My mom bought so many party decorations I don't know where to begin."

Soon the girls were having the time of their lives putting up hot pink and black streamers, blowing up balloons and hanging Happy Birthday signs on the basement walls. They blocked off a 10 x 10 area, where the party goers could dance.

"How many people did you invite?" asked Emily.

"I think it was about 20 but I know 5 of them can't come because they have other plans. I'm hoping at least 10 people show up. This should be fun. I think the last birthday party I had was when I was five or six," recalled Jeannie.

"I've never had a birthday party where I could invite people outside my family," Emily explained, "But, I'm hoping Mom will let me have one this year for my 13th birthday as well. Boy, I sure got my head bit off last night by my mom."

"What happened?" asked Jeannie.

Emily then recounted the conversation she and her mom had and then stopped hanging the streamer, and got a pensive look on her face. "Honestly, Jeannie, I don't know what got into me last night. I'm going to have to watch myself because I thought Mom was going to go through the roof she was so mad!"

"Well, at least she didn't smack you. The last time I sassed back to my mom, she waited till my dad came home to tell him. I got the lickin' of my life and then was grounded for a whole week."

"Wow, I'm definitely glad Mom didn't tell my dad this morning because he was in one of the absolutely most rotten moods I've seen him in for a while. He was slamming doors, and stomping around like one of those grizzly bears I saw on a nature special last week. I had to tell Lily and Katie to stop fighting over a stupid rag doll that doesn't even belong to either of them so Dad wouldn't turn his anger on us. But, let's not think about any of that stuff. We're going to have an absolutely glorious time tonight and I can't wait."

"Me either. Maybe Phillip will even kiss me tonight. Oooo, I've been waiting so long for him to kiss me. He's so cute!"

"And I'm going to have my first dance with Sean. We've gotta work out some type of signal so you can pop in the "We Never Danced" song. I think I'm just going to faint thinking about dancing close with Sean. He's an absolute doll!" said Emily as they both now giggled. Then they began planning their signal for Emily and Sean's song.

Chapter Twelve

Sarah curled Emily's hair then she tied a pink ribbon, head band around her hair. Emily ran up to her bedroom where she slipped into her favorite purple dress with tiny pink hearts on it, put on a pair of matching pink socks with lace around the fold and her shiny black, patent leather Mary Jane's. She ran downstairs to look at herself in her mother's stand up mirror.

She stood in front of the mirror, adjusted the pink ribbon head band and said out loud, "Sean Mahoney, you don't stand a chance!"

She had no idea Sarah was standing in the doorway until Sarah burst with laughter as she admired her young daughter.

As Sarah stopped laughing, she said proudly, "You knocked that one out of the ballpark, Emily. Sean doesn't have a prayer. You look stunning!"

"Thanks, Mom," said Emily now a little embarrassed that her mom even heard her give herself such a compliment, but then they both sat on the bed and laughed out loud.

"I just wish your dad were home to see how beautiful his oldest daughter is. Let's take a couple of pictures with my Kodak before you head out the door."

Sarah took a few pictures. The camera was one of those instant picture cameras which popped the picture out almost immediately. Sarah laid them on the living room coffee table so they could dry.

Then she went to the front closet, pulled out Emily's spring coat she got for Easter.

"Let's put this on you. It's getting a bit chilly outside and this will be just enough to prevent you from catching a cold."

Just as Sarah took the coat off the hanger, the front doorbell rang and Emily's eyes got really wide.

She made an excited huh-like sound and then almost

whispered, "That must be Sean, Mom."

Sarah went over to the door and opened it.

She invited Sean in and exclaimed, "Why Sean, you look so handsome. I don't think I've ever seen you in a suit. Come in. I just took a couple of pictures of Emily. Let's take a couple more of you and Emily."

Sean turned red and said, "Thanks Mrs. Callaway." Then he saw Emily and couldn't contain himself. "Em, you look beautiful!"

Emily blushed from ear to ear as Sean pulled a small white box from behind his back and produced a small wrist corsage made with pink carnations.

"I hope you don't think this is stupid, Em. Grandma thought it would be nice to get this for you. She knew you'd have at least some pink on tonight."

With delight Emily smiled. "Sean, don't you know girls love flowers? I love the corsage. It's so grown up too!"

"Ok you two," said Sarah as she held the camera.

"Sean, why don't you put the corsage on Emily's wrist and I'll snap a few pictures as you do, then we can take a few more of the two of you in front of the fireplace."

Sean fumbled with the box and finally managed to get the corsage out. He looked around trying to decide where to put the box when Emily said, "Here, I'll take it. I want to keep it as a memory."

She handed the box to her mother for safe keeping and Sarah took the shot as Sean clumsily put the elastic band around Emily's wrist. He accidently snapped the elastic band and Emily said with a smile, "Ouch."

Sean apologized and Emily giggled as Sarah took another picture. Then she had the couple stand in front of the fireplace and took a few more pictures.

"I'll have reproductions of these made at the drugstore, Sean, so you can have a set. Would you like that?"

"Oh yes, Mrs. Callaway. Grandma and Mom would never forgive me if I didn't have a set to show them."

They then got ready to walk out the door when Sarah kissed Emily.

"Be a good girl, Emily. You take care of her, Sean; and both of you have a wonderful time."

"Yes, ma'am. I'll take really good care of Emily."

Outside the door and once they got to the corner of Emily's yard, Sean presented his arm as his step-dad instructed him to. Emily put her hand through his arm and they both walked down the street talking and laughing all the way to the party.

They arrived at Jeannie's house along with several other children, some of whom neither Emily nor Sean recognized. They were all chattering making each other's acquaintance when Jeannie's mom, Gladys Chandler opened the front door.

In they all went and were led to the basement stairs where they hurried down to the party area. Jeannie was downstairs with Phillip and about five other kids, three girls and two boys. Jeannie introduced everyone to each other then went over to her dad's CD player he set up for the party. She popped in a John Melencamp CD and the party began. Some of the kids got up and started dancing just as Gladys came down the stairs with a camera to take a few photos.

The party was about fifteen minutes in progress when Gladys said she'd be back down in a half hour with Jeannie's birthday cake. That was Jeannie's cue which she coached her mom on to pop in Emily and Sean's song.

The song, "We Never Danced" began and Emily took Sean's hand and whispered, "This is our song."

She led him to the dance floor and he clumsily took her hand while putting his other hand around her back.

He blushed and said, "I hope I don't step on your toes, Em. Both Mom and Grandma did their best trying to teach me how to slow dance."

Emily smiled sweetly and said, "Sean, you can step all over my toes. I don't care. I'm just in heaven that we're finally going to dance. This is such a special song that I wanted it to be our first slow dance song."

They began dancing. Sean surprised himself at how not clumsy he was.

"See, Sean, I think you had two very good teachers," said Emily as she pressed her cheek to his.

She melted in his arms and floated away feeling his sweet

breathe against her ear as she listened to his heart beat.

When the song was over Sean whispered, "Emily, I've never heard that song before but it's perfect. It is our song. I love you, Emily Callaway," he said as he then kissed her.

When she opened her eyes, she saw Jeannie and Phillip also locked in a caress. He was kissing Jeannie. Jeannie looked over at Emily as Emily waved a few fingers. Both girls had died and gone to paradise.

Almost exactly a half hour later, both Jeannie's dad, Phil and Gladys descended the stairs. Phil was carrying a beautiful cake with 13 pink candles all lit up. He was trying very hard to walk down the stairs without tripping as Gladys followed with her camera all ready to shoot pictures of Jeannie blowing out the candles.

Phil put the cake on the card table where the plates and utensils were and said to Jeannie, "Give your dad a big kiss, sweetheart."

Jeannie kissed her dad then, closed her eyes tight, made a wish and blew out the candles.

Everyone then sang Happy Birthday after which one of Jeannie's female classmates called out, "Jeannie, what did you wish for?" to which Jeannie answered, "Well, if I tell everyone my wish it won't come true."

They all laughed and then Gladys began cutting the cake.

Everyone had such a great time that, when, at 9:00, Gladys flipped the overhead light on and off a few times marking the end of the party there was a universal, "Ohhhhh!"

As Sean helped Emily with her coat, Emily told Jeannie she'd be down around 9 a.m. the next morning to help her clean up the mess. She and Sean left the Chandlers and walked up the street.

It was chilly but the moon was full and Emily's head was full of wonderful memories, especially the one of their first dance. Sean walked Emily to the front door and they kissed once more. They held hands and extended their hands as he moved back and began walking down the stairs backward. He almost fell making them both laugh. Then he turned around and walked across the street to his grandma's house.

As he reached the front door, he was illuminated by the two front stoop lamps on either side of the door. He turned and they both waved. Emily blew him a kiss as he made a gesture of catching it then put it in his pocket next to his heart.

****

Emily went in her house and immediately felt foreboding as her father emerged from the darkness of the dining room. From the dining room window he had been watching her and Sean as they said goodnight.

"Where's mom?" Emily anxiously asked.

"She wasn't feeling well, so she went to bed early. Did you have a nice evening with Sean?" His tone was extremely sarcastic.

"Yes, Daddy I did," she responded as she began climbing the stairs.

"Wait a minute. Take off your coat. I want to see how pretty you look. I only got to see pictures."

He crouched down to a bended knee position and began unbuttoning her coat. He slid it off her shoulders and said, "The pictures don't do you justice. You look all grown up and beautiful. Turn around."

She did and as she turned back to face him, he slid his hand up her dress. But she pulled away, looked at him and *told* him she was going to bed, then coldly pointed a finger at him almost touching his nose. "And, *don't* follow me up there!"

Joe looked stunned as he lost his balance and fell backward to the floor.

As Emily climbed the stairs, Joe commanded, "Come back down here!"

But Emily just waved her arm and hand in a go away manner. She didn't even turn back around but continued climbing the stairs as she thought, *he is not going to ruin the best night of my life!*

She climbed into bed between Katie and the wall knowing that he wouldn't dare try to do anything with Katie next to her. She managed to put the image of her vile father out of her mind and replaced it with the sweet, innocent and so loving image of Sean.

She hugged herself and in her mind, *I love you Emily because*

Sean loves you. He sees you for who you really are.

She fell asleep and dreamed happy dreams as she once again danced with Sean.

Chapter Thirteen

The following morning, a Sunday, Emily remembered Sarah wanted to go to an early mass.

I'll have to call Jeannie to let her know I'll be down later than I told her I would, she thought to herself as she climbed down the stairs.

Her mom was sitting at the kitchen table looking really bad.

"What's the matter, Mom?"

"Honey, I'm sicker than a dog. Don't kiss me because I don't want you to get whatever it is I have," moaned Sarah. "Your dad's going to take you to church this morning."

"Where's Paul and the girls?"

"Katie and Lily are in the TV room and Paul went to church with Henry and his family. Now go on upstairs and get ready for church. Your dad wants to go to the 9:00 mass."

In her mind, o*h, Go*d! Then she asked, "Mom, should I go tell the girls to get dressed too?"

"No. We're not going to make them go this morning. They're both complaining of sore throats. Now hurry up, sweetie. You need to be ready to go in twenty minutes."

Emily's mind spun out of control at this turn of events.

As she climbed the stairs, a dreadful feeling churned in the pit of her stomach. *Oh God...I can't believe this is happening. I was so disrespectful to him last night. I don't know what he's going to do to me.*

She began trembling and her head began to pound as she got dressed and feared, *what will he do to me when we're alone in the car?*

She sobbed as she thought, *God, please help me. I just want to run back down and beg Mom to let me stay home. I'll tell her my throat is sore too.* Then she realized that wouldn't work because her mom would know she was lying and then wonder

79

why she was lying. She'd ask Emily what was going on. *I can't tell her the truth. I have to protect Mom from knowing what Dad is doing to me. It would break Mom's heart. I don't want Mom to hate me.* So, she wiped her eyes and blew her nose, then finished dressing not know what was about to happen.

Her head began pounding even more. Then, she heard Joe calling her. She had been sitting on the bed for several minutes trying hard to prolong not going down the stairs.

His brusque voice bellowed up the stairs, "Emily, get a move on. We're going to be late!"

Emily slowly descended the stairs, went out through the kitchen, kissed her mother's cheek and went out to the car. Joe was sitting on the driver's side watching the door for her to come out.

She opened the passenger side of the car, climbed in but clung to the door and never once looked at her father. He backed out of the driveway, put the car in drive and began the climb up the street.

As the car approached the end of the street and they sat at the stop sign ready to turn right onto the main highway, Joe sneered, "I did *not* at all *appreciate* your attitude last night, young lady! I was just trying to *show you* how pretty I thought you looked."

Emily didn't say a word as tears trickled down her cheeks. She sat with her head turned to the window and prayed to God the morning would end.

But it didn't.

Instead of pulling into the church parking lot, Joe drove right past it.

"Where are we going, Daddy?" whimpered Emily.

Snot rolled off his tongue. "You'll see!"

He soon drove down a side street and then down a dirt road and Emily began crying very loudly. She wretchedly plead, "I want to go home, Daddy. Please, let's go home."

"Not yet," spat Joe, "This is a special place. It's where lovers go to make out. Do you know what making out means, Emily?"

She could barely speak. "I...I...I think it's kissing."

Creepily..."Well, you're half right, Emily."

The car came to a clearing and Joe stopped the car. Emily was trembling ferociously as Joe slid across the front seat.

He put his hand on her leg. "Now, be a good little girl. Let's take your dress off, honey," The words seemed to slither off his tongue and down his chin.

"No, Daddy, I don't want to."

Emily had been fidgeting with a pencil she found in the pocket of the door as her father began sliding his hand up her leg.

Suddenly, clutching the pencil, Emily raised her arm and with all her might thrust it into her father's hand nearly making a through and through puncture.

He screamed as he pulled his hand away. "You fucking little brat. You made my hand bleed!"

He pulled the pencil out of his fresh wound again screaming with anger and pain then grabbed his clean handkerchief and began wrapping it around his hand.

But before he could do anything else, Emily was out of the car and standing next to it screaming.

"I don't care. I hope I hurt you as much as you've always hurt me!"

Tears were gushing down her cheeks.

He desperately tried to calm down and regain control. "Ok, honey. I'm sorry I yelled at you. Now, come on and get back in the car."

Emily stopped crying. She gazed at the ground; both fists clenched red tight.

Again Joe plead, "Please Emily, get back in the car."

Then she slowly raised her head and glared at him with an expression on her face he'd never seen on anyone's face let alone his own young daughter. But before he could say another word she spoke.

"No. I will not get back in that car. You are never, ever going to touch me again. Do you understand what I just said?"

She was yelling in a voice that seemed to roar. "This stops right now, today. You will never, ever put your hands on me again. Do you understand what I'm telling you?"

Now, it was Joe who was trembling. "Ye, ye, yes, Emily. I u, understand what you're t, telling me."

But before he could say anything else she spoke with the certainty of the adult he was trying to force her to be.

"If you ever lay another hand on me again I will tell Mom and I will also tell Admiral James! Do you *fucking* understand what I'm saying?"

"Ye, yes, yes, Emily I p, promise I understand. Now, p, please, get back in the car and we'll go home."

Convinced she now had the upper hand, she got back in the car and barked, "Now turn this car around and drive me home."

He didn't say another word. Instead he did exactly what she told him to do.

When they arrived home, she got out of the car and went in the house. Sarah was no longer sitting in the kitchen, so Emily walked right past her two sisters who were watching TV and ascended the stairs to her room, shut the door and locked it.

Joe went into the bathroom and tried his best to clean up his hand and bandage it as he concocted the story of how his hand got hurt. Fortunately for him Sarah had gone back to bed.

He tip toed down the hall and peeked through the crack in the door and saw she was sound asleep. He sighed relief, as he walked back down to the bathroom.

Emily changed her clothes. She put on a pair of jeans, a red pullover sweatshirt and her tennis shoes. She looked in her mirror and could hardly believe what had just happened. She was half way laughing and trembling all at once.

Then in a low whisper, "I can't believe I said fucking."

Then to her reflection, she spoke. "I can't believe I stood up to him. I swear he will never ever touch me again!"

She brushed her hair as she recounted how she was able to turn her father into a blubbering idiot. She was still trembling as she walked out the front door. She crossed the street and went to the slant tree, walked up the tree and sat with her legs dangling in the air.

She had no idea what would happen next and couldn't even imagine what she was going to do next; but she couldn't help feeling very powerful and proud of herself for telling him no as she thought, *it's what I wanted Mom to say; but I'm the one who said it!*

She was deep in thought when she heard, "Hey Em, why didn't you knock on my door?"

She turned to see her sweet Sean standing behind the tree.

She was shivering as she asked him to come up. He sensed something wasn't quite right, so he put his hand on hers and they sat silent for a very long time.

Then finally, "What's the matter, Emily? Something's the matter. I can feel it. Did I do something wrong?"

Emily looked at him and now the tears were streaming down her face again. "No, Sean. You haven't done anything wrong. You're the one person in this world who has done everything right."

Relieved yet still very concerned, he took her delicate hand in his and began caressing it with his other hand. They sat there again in total silence. He looked at her and she looked at him as he pulled down the sleeve of his T-shirt and grabbed the end with his hand. He gently began wiping the tears from her face. He didn't press her because he trusted that she would tell him what was wrong when and if she was ready to.

She lay her head on his shoulder and said, "I said fucking to my dad today."

"You said what?" asked a confused Sean.

"I said fucking," she repeated.

"Why?" asked Sean now completely lost, yet something in his gut told him nothing was good right now. "What happened, Emily?"

"Oh, God!" She sat straight up, folded her hands in her lap and stared out over the meadow.

"Emily, you can tell me. I won't tell anyone if you tell me not to. Please, tell me what's going on. You have me scared right now."

"Well, there's actually nothing to be scared of ever again. I've been thinking that my dad will never ever tell anything because they'd kick him out of the Navy if he did. That's the power I now know I have over him. So he better watch out!"

Her tone was strange and seemed to echo miles away from where they currently sat.

"Emily, what happened? Please tell me. I'm really worried." He plead as he took her chin in his hand and turned her head so he could look into her eyes.

Then Emily sighed the biggest and longest sigh anyone could ever express. She turned her entire body sideways and continued to look him in the eye. "You have to promise that you will never, ever tell anyone what I'm going to tell you right now. Do you promise with all your heart?"

"I promise, Emily. I'm your best friend. I would never, ever do anything to make that change, honest to God!"

"Ok, where's Martha?"

"She went to church and won't be back for at least an hour. Now, please, please tell me what's going on." He sounded desperate.

With Martha gone, Emily knew she was safe to talk. No one would bother them and she had to tell someone.

"There's no one else in this world I would trust to tell this to except you, Sean. You're my best friend. You're the only real friend I've ever had in my life; and, I think it's because you are my friend that I did something today that was, well, braver than I ever thought I could be. Scary brave." Emily was beginning to completely grasp the depth of her bravery.

Again there was a long silence.

Then Emily took a huge breathe and as she breathed out…"Sean, my dad has been doing sexual things to me ever since I was six years old and no one knows about what he's been doing, not even my mom. You're the first person in this entire world I've told and that's why it's so important for you to never, ever tell anyone."

Sean sat there totally dumfounded. He was having a difficult time grasping what she just told him. He had never heard of anything like that before.

They were both silent for a very long time, then Sean asked, "Emily, what do you mean he's been doing sexual things to you?"

She looked at him and spoke. Pain and shame resonated in her tone. "He puts his hands on my private parts and does dirty things to me."

She began crying again and sounded unspeakably pitiful. "Do you think I'm a bad girl?"

"No, Emily. I would never think you're a bad girl. You're the best girl I've ever known in my life besides my mom and grandma. You could never be bad. You're a good girl." He then cradled his words in soothing love. "You're my good girl, Emily. Please don't cry."

Sean felt fresh tears running down his own cheeks. He didn't know what to say or do. He just knew he wanted Emily to stop hurting.

Emily finally growled. "I hate my father. I've tried everything to stay away from him and to avoid him. I even bribed Katie to sleep with me. She actually has her own bed, but she sleeps with me. It's the only thing I could think to do to keep my dad from climbing in my bed at night.

The last time he climbed in my bed, he pressed up against me and I felt something very hard pushing into my back. It scared me so much I just started crying. I don't know what it was that was pressing into me, but, when I started crying he left my room. The next morning I woke up trapped between my bed and the wall. I've wanted so much to tell my mom, but I can't. I think she will hate me if I tell her. I think she would blame me if I tell her.

He tells me all the time that he wishes he was twenty years younger so he could be my boyfriend. But, if he was twenty years younger, he wouldn't be my mom's husband and that would hurt my mom. So I can't tell her. I can't tell anyone; and, I never have until today. I just couldn't take it anymore.

He was going to do stuff to me last night.

He was hiding in the dining room when I came in. But, I told him no and went up-stairs to bed and told him not to follow me up the stairs. I was trying so hard to hold onto the best night of my entire life; and, I didn't want him to take that away from me. He's taken *everything…everything else* away from me.

I've been so unhappy for so long I can't even remember if I was ever happy until I met you. I've been so happy since I met you that I think it's what made me brave last night and today. I never thought I could ever, ever be brave.

I was supposed to go to church with Mom this morning; but she was really sick and told me my dad would take me. When I asked her if the girls were going with us she told me no that they both had sore throats and she and Dad decided to let them stay home. After I told my dad last night not to bother me, I just knew it was going to be really, really bad and there wasn't anything I could do about it.

We went to church, but he drove right past the church. I

didn't know where we were going and he wouldn't tell me. Then we pulled down a dirt road and he told me it was a lover's lane where lovers go to make out. Then he asked me if I knew what making out was and I told him I thought it was kissing and then he told me that I was half right. Then he stopped the car and we were in the middle of nowhere and I was so, so scared. He slid over to me on the front seat and was sitting so close I could feel his smelly liquor breath.

When I was fidgeting with the door I found a pencil in the pocket of the door. I had no idea what I was going to do with it but when he started to put his hand on my leg and told me he was going to take my dress off, I just got so, so scared. He's never taken my clothes off before. I just got so scared. I just didn't know what he was going to do so I jabbed the pencil into his hand as hard as I could, then I jumped out of the car and started yelling at him. I told him he was never going to be allowed to touch me ever again and that if he did, I was going to tell Mom and Admiral James. He got really scared and then I knew. I just knew I could make him take me home so I got back in the car and he drove me home.

I don't know where he is right now; probably somewhere in the house. I don't know what he's going to tell my mom; but he better not tell her it's my fault because it's not. It's not my fault. I never, ever wanted him to do any of those things to me. All I've ever wanted in my entire life was for him to love me like he loves Lily and Katie. I don't want him to love me like he loves my mom. I don't want him to love me like a girlfriend so I said fucking to him and I'll say it again, and again. I'll jab a knife in his hand the next time if he ever tries to touch me again I swear to God I will. I hate him. I hate him. I wish he would just die."

Then she fell absolutely silent. She was totally exhausted and almost fell off the tree. Sean caught her and she readjusted her sitting position.

Then Sean asked, "Do you want to tell Grandma when she gets home? She will know what to do."

"No! We can't tell Martha. We can't tell anyone; not anyone. I have to figure this out for myself. You have to promise me, Sean. You just have to promise me that you will keep this secret. Right now I know I'm safe. I don't know how I know it but I just know it. I have a way of knowing in my gut about things and I *know* I'll be ok.

My dad's job is the most important thing to him in the whole world. It's more important than my mom or any of us. It's what makes him feel like a big shot. As long as he's afraid I will tell he won't come near me. So, please, please, give me time to think about all this and to figure out what I'm going to do. Maybe if I can just keep him scared of me like I've always been scared of him, he'll stay away from me. I don't want to leave home. I don't want anyone to take me away or even take my father away. I love my mom with all my heart and I don't want her to be sad or unhappy."

Just as she finished, they heard a car, turned around and saw Martha getting out of her car. Martha waved at the kids and they waved back. Martha called Sean to come in and eat as she held up a bag from their favorite deli.

He said, "Emily, I've gotta go. I'll come knock on your door in a while."

As he started to get up, she grabbed his arm, looked at him and said, "You promised me you won't tell. You have to keep your promise."

He shook his head yes, then got up and walked down the tree. She also got up and walked down the tree, crossed the street and sat on her front stoop before going in.

Chapter Fourteen

Sean walked in through the side door. Martha was pouring him a glass of milk and making herself a cup of coffee. He sat down and started picking at the egg, bacon and cheese sandwiched between two thick slices of grilled Texas toast. Martha sat down and noticed how unenthusiastic he was. He was usually thrilled to have his favorite breakfast treat.

"What's wrong, Sean?"

"Nothin."

"Is everything ok between you and Emily?"

"Oh yea, we're fine…" he trailed off.

"Well, did you two have a good time last night? I was sound asleep when you got home and by the time I woke up you were sound asleep. Tell me all about it."

"It was great, Grandma. It was probably one of the best nights of my life. I did a really good job dancing with Emily and she looked so pretty. Her mom took pictures of us and is going to have reproductions so I can have a set."

"That's nice, dear. I can't wait to see them."

Watching Sean, Martha realized something was not right. She decided to ask one more time but promised herself she wouldn't press him if he didn't want to talk.

"Sean, something seems wrong. What is it? Is Emily ok? Did something happen to Emily at home? Please tell me. I might be able to help."

"Something did happen, Grandma; but I promised Emily I wouldn't tell anyone until she decides what to do herself. Please don't ask me again cuz I don't want to lie to you; but I just can't tell you. I love you Grandma, and I don't want you to be mad at me; but it's really, really important that I don't tell you or anyone else right now." He sounded pathetic.

"Ok, dear. I trust you. I know you would tell me if you

thought Emily was in danger. But, Seanie, promise me you'll come talk to me if you have to. I love you dear and I've come to love Emily as if she were my granddaughter."

It took everything Martha could muster to go without pressuring her grandson; but she did refrain as she watched him. He was clearly disturbed but she knew he was determined to protect the trust of his friend.

****

Sean had so many questions regarding exactly what Emily told him her dad had been doing to her. He clearly felt her sadness and desperation and also sensed that she had done something extremely brave that morning. He wanted to ask Martha questions, but he didn't want to raise alarm regarding why he was asking the questions; so he waited for the right moment.

That moment came the following week.

One evening as Sean sat in his kitchen, Beth was preparing dinner and the small counter top TV was on. Beth was chopping fresh vegetables when she turned up the volume as the local evening news came on. Sean played with a model airplane his Uncle Peter had given him when he heard the news anchor say the words, *known sex offender*. He stopped, sat up and began listening to the news story.

That morning a man had been arrested in Cambridge and it was alleged that he had molested several neighborhood girls. Sean sat listening attentively. His gut told him this story was related to what Emily told him her dad had done to her.

When the story ended, Sean asked Beth, "Mom, what was that man doing to those girls?"

Beth turned the sound on the TV down, looked at Sean and asked, "I'm sorry sweetie. What did you ask me?"

Then Sean, trying hard to act nonchalant asked again, "What was that man in the news story doing to those girls?"

Beth tried her best to explain it to Sean so he could not only understand but so he would know that all children, including him, needed to be vigilant about adults who behaved in an overly friendly manner. She made Sean promise never to go into any adult's home or car without asking her permission. Without scaring him she told him that the world simply wasn't as safe as it seemed to be.

Sean promised his mom and went back to what he was doing prior to the news story; but he now wasn't paying as much attention to the plane as he had been. Now he was thinking about the words Emily used to describe what her dad had been doing to her since she was six; how she's had to be so inventive with strategies for staying safe and then, how incredibly brave she was for fighting back.

In his head Sean kept going over that conversation with Emily on the slant tree. In fact, he thought about it every day. He also thought about Emily's mother and father. He interacted with Sarah more than with Joe. When he did interact with Joe he realized he had always felt afraid of him. *He's never been very nice to me.* Then he began to realize that Emily never interacted much with her father when he was around the two of them. *She doesn't act like she likes her father like I liked mine. She never talks about him or about her mom. She talks about her grandmother a lot. I know she loved her grandmother and her grandmother loved her before she got sick. What's life been like for Emily?*

The more Sean thought about Emily's situation and about Joe, the angrier he became until one day he promised himself that if he ever thought Emily was in danger from her father again, he would personally beat her dad up. Sean thought about how wonderful his father had been to him and how unfair it was that his father had to die while Emily's father lived. His new understanding of Emily's situation angered him but also saddened him. At the same time he began to acknowledge how he now intuitively felt closer as well as very protective of his young, red headed friend.

Chapter Fifteen

Emily sat on her front stoop for a very long time. Then she finally mustered enough courage to go in the house. She had no idea what was waiting for her in there, but she knew she had to face whatever was about to happen. She pondered how much she had endured during her short life. Yet, she realized that she would just have to gather enough guts to keep going; guts for herself and for her mom.

She got up, opened the front door and walked in. She stood in the foyer for several minutes listening intently to see if she could detect anything or anyone. Then, rather than retreating to her room, she bravely walked out into the kitchen. As she did Sarah called to her from her bedroom.

Sarah was sitting up eating toast and drinking a glass of orange juice.

"Emily, are you ok? I heard what happened and how your dad broke a bottle and cut his hand. He's gone to the base infirmary to get a tetanus shot since the bottle was full of dirt and who knows what else. You didn't pick up that filthy bottle did you?"

As Emily answered, she walked down the hall and into her mother's bedroom. "No Mom. I'm ok. I was just visiting with Sean. How do you feel?"

"I feel a little better. I have a slight temperature but I think it's just a touch of virus. I think I'm going to stay in the bed the rest of the day. Could you make sure your two sisters are behaving themselves, and look in on your grandma?" asked Sarah as she now slid down under the covers.

"Sure, Mom, now you get some good rest. I'll make sure everything is ok."

Emily stroked Sarah's head, then walked over to the window and pulled the shade down. Next she walked out into the hallway and closed the door behind her.

Life as usual, thought Emily; but, then, she would rather have life as usual, without the stuff her dad does than any other life.

She couldn't even imagine life without her family, especially her mom. She knew in her heart that her mom was a good mom. She felt sorry for her mother. *She's always been afraid of him just like me. I want Mom to be happy. I just have to be brave, stand up to Dad and protect Mom from ever knowing the truth.* Then, with a lot of conviction she resolved, *He better do everything I tell him to do because if he doesn't he'll be the one sorry, not me.*

Everything was quiet in the house, so Emily called Jeannie and apologized for not helping with the cleanup. She told her how sick her mom was and that her dad had to go get a tetanus shot because he cut his hand on a dirty, broken bottle. Emily was amazed at how cool and collected she was. She could really take control of her emotions and her situation. *Boy, I am in charge. He better be afraid of me now!* She was beginning to understand just how grown up she really was.

She went into the kitchen got a cold glass of milk and four Oreo cookies. She then went into the TV room to watch TV while she waited until her dad came home.

Just remember, she said to herself, *he's now scared of you. Don't let him know you're anything else but in charge."*

She watched TV for about an hour without even knowing what she was watching. She jumped every time she heard a car drive down the street. Soon she heard Joe's car pull into the driveway. She sat straight up and didn't even look up when he came in.

He walked right past her, into the kitchen and down the hallway to his bedroom. Finally she realized she was holding her breath so she relaxed and breathed deeply. Then she heard his footsteps. The hairs on the back of her neck stood straight up as she gripped the arms of the chair and told herself to calm down and act brave.

Joe came out into the TV room, sat in the chair positioned at a 90 degree angle to Emily. He put his face in his hands as he rested his elbows on his knees. She could see him from the corner of her eye but she purposely made believe she didn't even notice him. She was becoming braver by the second as she mentally repeated, *I am in charge! I am in charge!*

Then he spoke, "Emily, I am so, so sorry for everything. I've been a terrible father to you for a lot of years. I promise you things will be different from now on."

Emily looked over at him and for the first time in her life she wasn't the least bit concerned with how he felt as she said, "All I will say is that I meant every word I said earlier. If you ever...."

"Shhh," pled Joe. "I promise. I don't want the family to break up because of this. I love your mom. I really do; and I love all you kids. I want things to go back to the way they were before I started doing any of this. Can we do that, Emily?"

He slid forward on the chair and almost knelt on the floor. He looked pitiful, but she didn't care. She knew how he tried to make her feel responsible for everything when it was him that was responsible.

Emily waved her hand as if to say enough and spoke.

"I know about the lie you told Mom about how you cut your hand. I don't care what you told her. I'm not going to tell her how it really happened; but it's *not* to protect you."

She paused and glared daggers at him.

"I'm not going to tell her because I love Mom and I don't want her to hurt. I'm also doing it for myself."

She then pointed her finger at him and roared using a low but forceful tone. "Nothing is for you."

He put his hand on his forehead as if he was relieved and simply said, "Thank you."

He then got up and walked out of the room. It was one of the last times he and she would talk about this again for a very long time. It was also the last time she feared being in his presence.

Her bravery had put her in total control of *everything*.

Chapter Sixteen

Several weeks went by. Emily and Sean spoke nothing of their slant tree conversation. They also didn't call every night like they used to and Sean only visited his grandma a few times. When Sean did visit the weekend prior to Thanksgiving, he knocked on Emily's front door and they went for a walk.

They walked up the street and down the main road to the mom and pop drugstore that still had one of those old fashioned soda shop counters. It was one of their favorite spots.

When they sat down, Sean asked if Emily wanted an ice cream sundae. She looked at him, crossed her arms and began hugging herself while making a burrrr sound.

Sean laughed. "Ok, how about some hot chocolate?"

"That's more like it." She giggled approvingly.

Just then, the male owner, Mr. Hogan, walked around from the store side to the back of the counter and asked for their order. He was dressed in a Norman Rockwell like outfit, complete with the hat, bowtie and apron.

"We'll both have some hot chocolate," to which Emily added, "And I'll have some whipped cream and a cherry on top."

"Coming right up," said Mr. Hogan in such a cheerful voice that Emily smiled to herself and thought Mr. Hogan must like playing the part of the old time soda jerk as she recalled the Normal Rockwell painting.

She liked corny older people. *They seem so...well, real*, she thought.

Sean and Emily sat in silence for several minutes, then Sean, put down his mug and looked at Emily.

"Em, are you ok. We haven't talked about *it* since that day. I've been worried, but I didn't want to bring it up unless you did first; but I've just gotta ask."

Emily looked at Sean and smiled.

"That's one thing I like about you, Sean. You respect people's privacy; but you're also caring. I'm fine…honest. My dad and I had a short conversation when I went in the house that day and he tried to convince me that he was sorry. I don't know, maybe he was trying to convince himself because I didn't buy any of it. I just told him I meant what I said about never touching me again. I then told him I wouldn't contradict his lie about how he injured his hand not because I cared about him, but because I cared about my mom and about myself. That was about it. We've been polite enough to each other so that no one in the house seems to suspect anything; but I will say this. He's much nicer and more respectful to my mom and kinder to Paul, Lily, Katie and even Grandma if you can believe that. I don't know, but I think I scared the bejesus out of him. So, yes, I'm really fine and much happier when I'm home because I no longer have to fear my dad. Katie has even gone back to sleeping in her own bed."

When Emily finished, Sean sighed such a huge sigh that his whole body seemed to melt.

"God, Em. I've been sick worrying about you. I've wanted so much to go over to your house and just beat your dad up. But after what you said and did that day, something told me you'd be ok. I can't explain it."

Then he looked at Emily and got a very serious look on his face.

"Emily Callaway *you* are the bravest person I've ever met in my life! If I'm ever in a fight I want you there with me because I believe you'd knock out the ones I don't knock out."

To this they both started laughing out loud. Mr. Hogan heard them laughing, came back, walked to the back of the soda fountain and asked, "Well, is there anything else I can get you two fine people?"

"No thank you. We're ready to close out," said Sean speaking like he's heard Bill speak whenever Bill and his mom took him out to dinner with them.

"Coming right up," said Mr. Hogan as he handed Sean the tab.

Emily watched Sean as he sat up, reached in his back pocket, pulled out a wallet and produced a five dollar bill.

Mr. Hogan took the five, then returned the change to Sean to which Sean pulled out a one dollar bill, handed it to Mr. Hogan and said, "And this is for you."

Mr. Hogan smiled, took the bill and said, "Well, thank you my fine man. Thank you very much."

Emily and Sean got down off their stools, put on their coats and began walking toward the door.

When they got to the door Sean said, "Excuse me miss, but allow me." He opened the door for her to leave first.

Emily smiled, curtsied and said, "Well, thank you so much kind sir."

On the way home Sean promised Emily that he intended to help keep her safe.

"I *never* want you to be in danger ever again and I will do whatever I need to do to keep you safe!"

Then he looked very serious and added, "Em, I also want you to promise me that if you ever feel you're in danger again from your dad or anyone else and I'm not around to help you that you'll run over to Grandma's house and tell her. Will you promise me that, Emily? I want you to be safe," he said as he held her hand and squeezed it tightly.

Emily was so touched by Sean's caring words that she told him she would love him for the rest of her life.

"No one in this entire world has ever cared about me as much as you do. Sean, I was so very alone in this world before I met you; and I know too your grandma also cares a lot about me and my safety. I promise with all my heart that if I ever do feel in danger again and you're not around I will run over to your grandma's house as fast as I can because I never, ever want to be in that kind of danger ever again."

As they walked down the hill of their street Sean asked Emily to come in so his grandma could say hi to her.

Emily agreed. "Let me just stick my head in my door and tell my mom."

She ran over to her house and did just that. When she came back out, Sean was waiting for her on his grandma's front stoop.

They both went in as Martha walked out from the kitchen. "I thought that might be the two of you. How are you dear?" she asked Emily as she hugged her.

"I'm very well, Martha. Thanks for asking. How are you?"

"Why don't you two come on out to the kitchen? I've been getting a jump on the holidays and was in the middle of making some Christmas cookies. I'm going to freeze most of them, but I've made some that look like turkeys for Thanksgiving. We can all have a couple of cookies and milk or hot chocolate."

Martha then pulled down a plate from the top of the refrigerator.

"I thought I smelled cookies" remarked Emily. "And Christmas style cookies are some of my favorites. Oooo…And you've even frosted them which makes them even yummier!"

As the three sat at the table Martha asked, "Do you have big plans for Thanksgiving, Emily?"

"Well, we always have a huge turkey, lots of pies and other stuff. My grandma's sister is coming over with my Aunt May, Uncle Tim and cousins. It should be a nice day; and, of course I *always* eat way too much. You're going home with Sean and Beth and Bill are cooking - right Martha?"

"That's right dear. This will be the first Thanksgiving in…well I don't remember how many years that I won't have to cook; and, believe me I am going to be a lady of leisure," exclaimed Martha as she waved her arm in a la-di-da fashion.

They all had a good laugh.

"Emily," Sean interjected. "Mom and Bill are having a big Christmas Party three Saturdays from now and they would like you to come. Err, so would I. You could ride up with Grandma and stay the night in the spare bedroom Grandma stays in. What do you think?"

"Well, of course I'll have to clear it with Mom, but I don't think she will say no. I'm pretty sure I'll be able to."

"That would be great, Em. We could even dance again. I've been learning a few other steps; and, must say, I'm not bad," smiled Sean.

The three of them laughed and started jabbering about the upcoming party, Christmas and New Years.

Soon, Emily looked at the clock. "Oh…I better get home. My Uncle Bart is coming over for dinner. I haven't seen him in a long time. I'm really excited. I love Uncle Bart!"

She then got up, kissed Martha on the cheek as Martha

handed her a few cookies wrapped in tin foil and said, "A few for the road, dear."

Sean walked Emily to the door. "I've had a great time today, Em. I'm so happy everything is so much better. Just remember, though, if ever you feel afraid again to let me or Grandma know."

He took her hands, leaned close and kissed her. Then he said, "I love you so much, Emily."

"I love you too, Sean. I also promise you with all my heart." Then she said, "Oh…that reminds me."

She pulled her locket out from under her turtle neck sweater, "I wear this *all* the time." Then she lovingly opened the locket, "But now, the locket's complete."

She showed him there was now a picture of her on the opposite side of him.

"Mom bribed the guy who took our class pictures into making a small enough copy so she could put it in my locket. Now, we're always together, right here next to my heart."

They kissed again and she was gone.

Sean slowly shuffled back out to the kitchen.

Martha stood at the sink with her back to him. "Sean," she turned her head slightly. "Emily seems happier than I've seen her in a while. Did you two talk about the family situation?"

"Yes, Grandma, we did," responded Sean. "Emily is sure she has everything under control, and I believe her."

Then Martha turned around, wiped her hands on a paper towel and walked over to the table where Sean was now seated. She sat down and folded her hands in front of her as she rested them on the table.

"Sean, I know in my heart that something terrible happened to Emily. But I also sense that whatever it was the danger has passed and Emily feels safe now. I promise you I will not press you to tell me what actually happened that day; but I hope you will one day feel comfortable enough to tell me because there may come a time that I will need to know the entire story."

With his hands also folded on top of the kitchen table, Sean sat intently listening to every word his grandma spoke.

Then finally…"I know you know Grandma. I think what happened to Emily kind of made me grow up a little. I want to tell you the truth because I want you to know if there is ever a time Emily has to come to you for help. It's painful to tell you Grandma. It's painful for a lot of reasons. The biggest reason is because I promised Emily I wouldn't tell anyone, even you. I think she was a little ashamed that day; but I also think that she's had a lot of time to think about this and she knows nothing was her fault. I don't want to tell Mom or Bill because they're lawyers. I don't want to cause trouble for Emily. So, Grandma, I need to know that you will keep this a secret between you and me."

Sean sat there very silent then he looked up at his grandma and tears began running down his face.

Martha moved closer to Sean and drew him close to her.

"Sean, honey, I promise you I will not mention anything to anyone unless it's to help Emily. I've become very close to Sarah and I sense something isn't quite right in that household. I also promise you that I will do nothing to harm Emily even if it means I must keep my mouth shut. But, if you can just trust me to know the truth, then we can both keep watch on Emily in order to make sure she remains safe. I know how much you love Emily, and, Sean, I do too. I don't want her to suffer anymore because in my soul I know she has suffered. If you can trust me it could help ease your burden as well."

The rest of that evening Sean and Martha talked about that day he and Emily sat on the slant tree. They also talked about how he figured out everything that Emily had told him. It felt good to unburden his heart and he knew he could trust his grandma to not only help him keep a watchful eye over Emily but to also keep quiet in order to protect Emily from any more emotional pain.

"Grandma, Emily has had a really hard life. She's told me several times that she's never had anyone she trusted enough to tell her secret to. I want Emily to be happy, Grandma. I don't want her to ever suffer again. But I also want her to be able to trust me."

That night Martha promised Sean she would not tell a soul, not even Beth. She too wanted to not only protect Emily from danger but she also knew how they both needed to help Emily learn to trust. That trust begins with us she told Sean.

When they were exhausted from talking, Sean kissed his grandma and went to bed. Martha lay in her bed that night thinking about the entire situation and the new information she now possessed. She feared for Emily and the other Callaway children. She vowed to herself that she would watch the family and especially Joe like a hawk. If there was any indication at all that something was not right, she would take action.

****

A few weeks later, Martha bumped into Joe in the parking lot of the new CVS store in East Providence. He was getting in his car as she was getting out of hers. Joe waved to Martha as she got out of her car. She shut her door and stood at her car for a few seconds then, walked over to his car. He opened his window and said, "Well, hello Martha."

She was trembling but managed to gather enough courage to look him in the eye and say, "I want you to know I know what you've been doing to your daughter for many years."

He was stunned at first, then fear took over. He was white as a sheet so Martha could tell she had his attention.

"I am not going to report you but it is not to protect you. If there weren't going to be horrendous consequences for Emily, Sarah and the rest of your precious family I would report you in a heartbeat. Do you fully comprehend what I am saying to you, Joe?"

All Joe could do was nod that he understood.

So she continued, "If I *ever* hear of or even *suspect* you of hurting Emily again, or any other child for that matter, I will not hesitate to have you dragged off to jail. Do you understand me, Joe?"

All Joe could do was again nod his head vigorously. Then, Martha stepped back from his car and said, "You can leave now."

Joe started his car and sped off so fast he almost hit one of the lamp posts at the corner of the parking lot. Martha stood there watching him drive away. Her legs felt like jello. They were shaking so fiercely all she could do was walk back to her own car and get in until she calmed down.

That was the last day she and Joe ever spoke to each other again. He avoided her like the plague. Whenever she came over to his house to visit with Sarah he would disappear.

Chapter Seventeen

It was Christmas day. Sean, Beth, Bill and his two children were having dinner with Martha.

Two weeks prior Emily spent the afternoon with Martha helping her decorate a small tree she purchased from the new CVS in East Providence. Martha invited Emily to eat with all of them Christmas day and, to her amazement, Joe and Sarah gave her the ok rather than go with the family to eat dinner with her relatives.

It was 5 a.m. when she woke up to Katie shaking her, "Emily, Emily, it's Christmas morning. I peaked and Santa Claus came. Let's get up and go see what he left us."

Katie was so excited she had a case of the hiccups and could barely get each word out without hiccupping.

Lily, who was sound asleep turned to see the two of them and said as she sat up in her bed, "What's going on? You just woke me up from a really good dream."

Katie tried to tell her but she was hiccupping so much she couldn't so Emily said, "It's Christmas morning and Katie wants to see what Santa got all of us."

Now up, Lily's eyes got as big as saucers. Then she looked out the window.

"God, I forgot what day it was; and, look it snowed! We have a white Christmas!"

Now the three girls were looking out the window as the snow began falling again.

"Let's go get Paul, Mom and Dad," exclaimed Emily. "Now Katie, no opening any presents until everyone is in the living room, promise?"

"Ok, I promise," Katie now said as she hiccupped then burped robustly.

They all laughed as they put on their slippers and bathrobes.

Emily was the first one out the door. She crossed the hall and knocked on Paul's door. He opened it looking like he was sleep walking. She told him to hurry. He shook his head and shut the door.

Emily tip toed down the stairs as Katie and Lily followed. Just as she reached the stair where the wall and banister connected, she turned, put her finger to her lips and said, "Shhh…wait here, I'll go get Mom and Dad."

Katie and Lily both nodded. Emily tip toed down the rest of the stairs and was about to turn the corner when she heard Katie.

"I got a bike!"

Emily turned and looked through the spindles, put her finger to her lips again, and said, "Shhh!"

Katie covered her mouth with her two hands, vigorously nodded then hiccupped again. They all started giggling as Emily tried to compose herself and tip toed the rest of the distance to her parents' bedroom door.

She was about two feet from the door when Joe opened it. Sarah was right behind him with her camera.

Joe said, "Gather your brother and sisters in the living room then go wake your grandma, I'll get a big trash bag for the wrapping paper and ribbon."

"Ok Daddy," Emily said as she went to get Bertie while Sarah walked to the living room.

Once Sarah was in the living room, she looked toward the stairs and saw the two girls crouched down peeking through the spindles as their brother stood behind them rubbing his eyes. She couldn't resist the opportunity, so she aimed her camera and snapped a picture, then motioned for them all to come down and sit.

Soon Joe returned with a huge green trash bag while Emily helped Bertie to the couch. It was obvious to Sarah that her mom didn't have a clue what was going on, but as she covered her with a blanket she thanked God for her family and for the gift of having her mom with them for one more Christmas.

As Lily and Katie started grabbing at presents, Sarah admonished them.

"Girls. Remember the tradition? Paul, start handing your dad presents."

Full of anticipation, they all gathered around.

Katie tugged at Sarah's bathrobe. "Mommy, Mommy, is that pink bicycle – hiccup – mine?"

Sarah laughed. "Well, Katie, I'm guessing it's yours since you were *very specific* with Santa that you wanted a *pink* bike. Go see if there's a tag on it."

Katie navigated the wrapped packages as she made her way back to the bike, then exclaimed, "It is, it is!" She then hiccupped all the way back to her seat.

Joe said to Lily, "Go get your sister a glass of water."

Since Lily didn't want to miss any of the action, she got up, rolled her eyes, made a huffing sound and started walking to the kitchen as Sarah remarked.

"Don't worry we won't start until you get back."

While Lily was gone, Paul built a very large stack of wrapped gifts making sure everyone was represented. When Lily returned with the water, she handed it to Katie and sat down.

The festivities began.

Once the last present was unwrapped, Katie and Lily counted their presents making sure they had the same number. Joe motioned to Paul and Emily to help him gather all the trash in order to fill the trash bag. Sarah snapped away with her camera.

She so loved Christmas as she watched her family. Even her mother appeared to enjoy herself as she put on her new gloves.

Emily went over to help Bertie. "No, Grandma, they go on like this." Then Bertie began rubbing her face with her gloved hands and everyone laughed joyously.

Once all the trash was picked up and the presents were neatly placed back under and around the tree, Joe said, "Ok, now let's all go out into the kitchen. I'm cooking breakfast this morning."

The kids squealed with glee. They loved when their dad made breakfast. It was an event just like those nights when he would gather his children to make fudge.

When everyone was stuffed with pancakes, scrambled eggs and bacon, Emily looked around and realized that, as usual, Joe had made the biggest mess. *God, he made a mess just like he always does. Looks like he used every single pan in the house. What a jerk!* She sighed as she got up resigned that it was now her job to clean up his mess; but something miraculous happened.

Joe, reached for her arm, and said, "Sit down, Emily. It's Christmas and your brother and sisters are giving you their present. Paul, girls it's about time the three of you started chipping in around here."

There was a unison, "Awe, do we have to?" to which Sarah said, "Yes, your dad's right. Emily's been picking up all your slack for long enough. It's time the three of you and especially you, Paul and Lily start sharing in the chores. Katie, you can help as much as possible. Now, what do you all say?"

Katie spoke first, "Yes, Mommy and Daddy. I'll help. Emily's always been the bestest sister."

Then Paul, looked down at the floor and said, "Yea, ok," as did Lily.

"Great," said Sarah, "Your dad and I are proud of you. Now, Emily, go do whatever you want to do. This is your day off as is the rest of this week through your birthday!"

Emily was dumbfounded and didn't know what to say. The only thing her now swirling brain could think to produce was a very weak, "Thanks Mom and Dad."

As she got up to go collect some of her presents in order to bring them to her room, her dad looked at her and winked. This made Emily feel extremely uncomfortable and even a little angry. She had no idea if this was just his way of wheedling his way back into his old behavior. She didn't make one facial expression. She just left.

Up in her room, she marveled at her fantastic Christmas booty. She'd never received such a plunder of gifts and, for the first time ever, didn't feel slighted because her birthday was only three days away.

Usually her parents held aside a few Christmas presents and gave them to her for her birthday, but not this year.

Now she felt even more suspicious of her father's intentions as she remarked to herself. *I'm going to keep my eye on him. If I even think he's up to no good, he will be very, very sorry.*

She walked to the door of the attic space which hid behind her dresser, slid her dresser away from the wall and door and slipped into the narrow room with the slanted ceiling, turned on the light and hung her beautiful brand new white figure skates on a hook just inside the door. She looked at them with admiration.

She only learned how to skate last year.

Both Sean and Jeannie spent hours helping her overcome the fear of at first just standing on the two narrow blades and then learning how to glide, turn and stop. It was a huge accomplishment for her to be propped up on those blades on a slick surface with gusts of wind moving her when she never intended to move at all. It was such an out of control feeling in the beginning and, if she's learned anything from being molested by her dad, she neither liked the feeling of being out of control, nor she vowed to never allow herself to be caught in an out of control situation ever again.

Now she proudly looked at the skates, stroked them like they were a favorite pet and kissed them. "I can't wait until I get to skate with Sean this year," she said out loud as she turned off the light and shut the door to the attic space.

She was about to slide her dresser back against the wall when she felt a presence in the room. She turned around to see her dad standing in the doorway. It startled her and conjured up all her old fears as she stood there with clenched fists.

She finally demanded, "What do you want?"

"Emily, I just wanted to come see if you were all right. Your mom and I tried very hard to make this a special Christmas for you. That's really all I wanted to tell you. Everything's ok. I promise. I am determined to change my behavior. Because I've been trying so hard lately I've seen what a pleasant atmosphere exists in the house and I want to keep it that way. I swear to you that's how I feel."

"Well, Dad, I've really enjoyed how everything feels in our house now as well. Mom seems to be a lot happier; but, you're not out of the woods yet. I can't help but feel I need to be on my guard. I have decided that no one will ever hurt me like you did ever again; and, that includes you!"

She stood with her fists still clenched but not quite so tight.

"I know, Emily; and, I will never blame you for that. I just hope over time I can earn your trust and, even one day your love. I've come to realize what a wonderful young woman you've turned out to be and I know that's all your mom's, grandma's and your own doing. I'm just a very lucky father that I didn't ruin your life. That's all. Merry Christmas, Emily."

Joe turned around and left her room.

Emily slid down to the floor and sat on the cold wood floor. She wondered if she would ever be able to trust her father again. She used to think she loved her father regardless of what he was doing to her; but, now she wasn't so sure. She asked herself, *How could I love him now or ever? He's always been mean to me? I think I hate him. I wish I didn't but I can't help myself. I can't even remember if he was ever kind to me. I'll just have to do my best and hide my new feelings for him. I've always kept the other secret. This secret should be easier to keep especially from Mom.*

Then as she thought of all of that, especially in the context of her father's visit, she decided it didn't matter. What mattered was that *I love myself by taking care of myself. I promise with all my heart that I will never, ever let anyone in this entire world hurt me ever again.*

She also resolved to be very vigilant about paying attention to everything that went on in the household. After all, she had two younger, vulnerable sisters. She worried mostly about Katie because of how innocent and trusting Katie was.

Kind of like me, when I was her age, thought Emily.

The rest of the day was quiet in the Callaway household. Paul brought all his presents to his room, closed the door and didn't emerge again until it was time to go to his cousins' house. Lily and Katie played with their dolls for most of the morning. Around noon, Katie begged her dad to carry her new pink bicycle down to the basement so she could ride it. It was still snowing outside which meant no outside riding till the snow melted.

Bertie went back to bed and Sarah fell asleep in front of the TV. Joe sat in the living room reading his new book, RUNAWAY JURY. He read all of Grisham's books and was anxiously waiting for A TIME TO KILL to come to the theaters.

Emily had been in her room all morning. She started writing in her new diary.

She wrote: **Dear diary, I've never owned a diary before; but I know how important they are. That's why I asked for one for Christmas. I read THE DIARY OF ANNE FRANK over the summer and just can't stop thinking about Anne. I** feel as if I know her. She was so brave. I wish she were still alive and realize that at least I am. She had so much more to bear in her life – so much more than me.

My dad came to my room this morning and I really got scared. Things have been so much better since the day I had to stab his hand with that pencil; but I've just been waiting for everything to go back to the way it used to be. So, when I turned around to see him standing in my doorway I just got so darned scared. I thought I was going to have to be brave all over again. It's Christmas and I just want this Christmas to be free from any trouble from him. I don't even remember the last Christmas I wasn't afraid of what he would do to me. But, he said he just wanted to wish me a Merry Christmas and let me know how hard he's been trying to be a good father. I just can't trust him; but, for today I think I will have a peaceful Christmas. I'll just have to wait and see.

Diary, I'm going over to eat with Martha, Sean (I so love him), Beth, Bill and Bill's two kids who he has for the day. I didn't know what to get Sean. It was hard to think of what could top the Swiss Army knife I got him last year to make up for the one he lost that his dad gave him before he died. I remember how happy and amazed Sean was when he opened his present. I also remember how he cried and then got embarrassed. I loved being able to hug him and tell him it was ok for him to cry. God, why are boys always told they can't cry? I think it's very unfair. I know from knowing Sean that boys have the same deep feelings girls have but they're always being forced to hide them. It just doesn't make any sense. Since I couldn't figure out what to get him, I got him a really nice carrying case for his knife and even had it engraved with his name, Sean Mahoney. I sure hope he likes it, Diary. I just want him to be as happy as he makes me.

Life has changed so much for me since I met him. I just know that I was brave that day with my father because of how Sean loves me for myself. When I met Sean and his grandma, Martha, I don't know. Everything inside me changed. For the first time in my life I felt as if I *really* mattered. I like that feeling and never want to lose it. I know that's part of where my bravery came from. I just think it's

**important for a person to feel important because it gives a
person courage to believe they are important.**

****

Emily fell asleep and woke about three hours later. She
looked at the new red banded watch she got from her grandma
and realized she needed to hurry up and get dressed. She didn't
want to be late for dinner at Martha's.

She ran down the stairs and almost ran smack into her mom
who was coming out of the bathroom where Emily was headed.

"Whoa, Emily what's your hurry?"

"Mom, I have to be over at Martha's in less than two hours
and I have to wash and dry my hair and you know how long it
takes to dry this thick mop of mine!"

"Ok, you just take care of showering and drying your hair.
Tell me what you want to wear today and I'll go up and make
sure it's all laid out on your bed."

Emily thanked her mom, went in the bathroom, closed and
locked the door, then looked in the mirror and felt panicked as
she thought about what she wrote in her diary. Then, she
remembered she shoved the diary way under her mattress until
she could come up with a better place to hide it.

Phew, she thought. *God that was scary!* She then mentally
patted herself on her back for thinking about hiding it. She was
in such a panic when she woke it would have been easy to
carelessly leave it somewhere Sarah could have found it.

Emily showered, brushed her teeth then dried her hair. She
heated up the curling iron and put a few extra curls in the ends of
her hair. Satisfied, she emerged from the bathroom to find her
mom standing at the door about to knock.

Startled she thought, *I did hide it, didn't I? I wasn't dreaming
was I?*

Then she sighed relief as Sarah offered to let her put on just a
little of her Channel No. 5 cologne.

"I think you're old enough for just a little," said Sarah as she
brushed Emily's hair to one side and dabbed her skin with the
stem of the bottle top.

"Umm. That smells so good. I sure hope Sean thinks so too."

"Ok, hurry up and go get dressed. I want to make sure you're safely inside Martha's house before we leave for Uncle Bart's."

"Ok, Mom, thanks so much," Emily said as she turned to go up to her room, then she stopped and turned back around.

"Oh, and Mom, thanks too for this morning when you asked Paul and the girls to clean up the kitchen. And thanks for just a very wonderful Christmas. It's honestly the best Christmas I've ever had. I love you, Mom."

Sarah smiled bursting with love. "You're welcomed, Emily. I love you too, sweetie."

Emily was ready to go. She put on her rubber snow boots over her shoes, put on her coat, hat and gloves and picked up the wrapped present still sitting under the Christmas tree. She went out into the kitchen where Sarah and Joe sat waiting for the rest of their children to come down so they could leave for Bart's.

Emily said, "Merry Christmas, Mom and Dad."

"Merry Christmas," said Joe in a very sweet way Emily's never heard before.

"Here, Emily. I made an extra pumpkin pie for you to take over to Martha's. I know she was making an apple pie so I thought it'd be nice to have another choice."

Sarah put the pie in a pie box she got from the bakery last week, then dropped it into a big paper bag with handles and put it on her daughter's arm.

Sarah then kissed Emily. "Have a wonderful time today, sweetie."

"I will Mom. Merry Christmas Mom and Dad. I love you."

She then turned and went out the front door.

She rang the doorbell and Sean immediately opened the door.

"Em, I was getting worried. I was about to call to make sure you were still coming."

"Oh," Emily laughed, "We've had such a nice Christmas day that I fell asleep in my bedroom while I was writing in my new diary I got."

As she put everything down and started taking off her coat, hat, gloves and boots, Martha, Beth and Bill came out into the living room next to the foyer.

"Merry Christmas," said all three at once.

They all laughed and Emily said, "Merry Christmas to all of

110

you and thanks so much for inviting me. Oh, Mom made a pumpkin pie. She knew you were making an apple pie, Martha."

Just then two children about seven and ten ran up from the basement. It was the first time she had ever seen Bill's children so Bill introduced them. Emily began to say, "Nice to meet you," when the two rambunctious children just disappeared from site.

They all retired to the living room where the Christmas tree was lit up.

"Oh, Martha, the tree is so beautiful!" exclaimed Emily. "But, where's the little one I helped you decorate?"

"I put it in the dining room. I just had an urge to have a real tree. This is the first year in a very long time I've had a real tree, especially one this big. It took me forever to rummage through the attic to find all the ornaments. I forgot how many ornaments I even had. Some of them could probably be regarded as antiques."

Emily walked closer to the tree so she could see all the beautiful ornaments. She was holding her present for Sean, so she bent down and put it under the tree.

Martha gestured to Beth and Bill. "Oh, my. I better go check the turkey. It's just about time to take it out of the oven."

Beth said, "Martha, I'll mash the potatoes, Bill can you help me out?"

They left and Sean said to Emily, "You know they're doing that so we can be alone."

"Yea, I kinda thought so," smiled Emily. "Do you want to open your present now? It's not much, but...."

This time it was Sean who put his finger to her lips. "I'll love whatever you got for me. You're my present, Emily, and you're the best present anyone could ever ask for. Now, this year you have to open your present first."

He handed her a sizeable gift. They sat down on the floor and Emily began unwrapping it. She finally pulled all the wrapping paper off and folded it neatly, placed it and the bow on the floor and opened the box. Inside was a beautiful red velvet jewelry box.

"Oh, Sean, it's beautiful."

"That's not all, open it up."

She looked at him inquisitively. Once open, a small ballerina

111

dressed in red, purple and pink popped up and began twirling to the Nutcracker Suite.

"Oh my. It's a musical jewelry box; and I've never seen a ballerina with these wonderful colors; all my favorite! I love it. Now I have someplace special to put my locket."

"That's not all, Emily," said Sean. "Lift up the drawer. There's a secret compartment."

She did and on the bottom of the box was a small Wonder Woman doll. Looking puzzled, she put the box down and picked up the doll.

"What? I don't get it."

"I told you, if I ever get in a fight I want you to be with me, cuz I know you'll be fighting right there with me just like Wonder Woman would. You're my Wonder Woman, Emily!"

They both laughed out loud then Emily hugged Sean.

"Now, you," said Emily as she handed him her gift. He opened it up and folded the wrapping paper then laid it on Emily's pile knowing she would want to keep both wrapping paper and ribbons.

He opened the box and exclaimed, "Oh, Em. This is wonderful. Now I have somewhere to keep my knife. It fell through a hole in my pocket last week and I got so scared I lost it, but luckily it got hung up on a loose thread inside my pants leg. This is great!"

Again they hugged. Then Sean grabbed a glass dish off one of the end tables and said, "Your favorite, Christmas cookies with buttermilk frosting."

They sat on the floor a while longer and recounted all the presents they got for Christmas. Emily told him how Paul and the girls had to clean up the kitchen.

"God, Sean, this was the best Christmas I can ever remember. I cleaned up on presents and then didn't even have to lift a finger to do chores. It's too amazing."

Then she told him about her father's visit to her room. Sean looked visibly angry so she put her hand on his arm.

"It's ok. I'm still in charge. He told me he just wanted me to know that he's trying to change. He even said he hoped that one day I would learn to love him." She then laughed in a sarcastic manner. "Fat chance of that ever happening. I told him that I was watching him and would continue to watch him like a hawk. I'm pretty sure he is still afraid of me and that's a good thing because he has no idea what I could do to him. But, let's not think about him now. This is our special day, Sean."

"Em, I was scared for a minute there. I pretty much hate your father for what he did to you. But, I trust you. You are wonder woman, Emily! She's not real; but you are. I love you wonder woman!"

Just as he finished Beth stuck her head in and told them dinner was being put on the table. They both jumped up, looked at each other and spontaneously hugged each other very tightly. Then they walked hand in hand to the table holding their presents in their free hands. Once seated and grace was said, they each showed the adults what the other one got each other. When dinner was finished, and the dishes were cleaned up they all retired to the living room where they turned off all the lights except those on the tree, and turned on the stereo to listen to Christmas music. Both Emily and Sean with their heads resting on each other fell fast asleep.

Bill put his arm around Beth. "Oh, to be young and innocent again."

He, Beth and Martha quietly laughed.

Chapter Eighteen

The winter of 1996 was a winter to remember in Rhode Island.

On January 7th, it started snowing and didn't stop until there was two feet of snow with *huge* snow drifts. The wind blew so fiercely that night that Emily's dad had difficulty shoveling all the snow from the front of the garage door the next morning. The winter was a frigid one too. It didn't start warming up until almost mid-April.

Emily, Sean, Jeannie and Philip were inseparable. Sean came down to visit practically every weekend and if they weren't all sledding down their street or the hill at the golf course, they were ice skating on the pond in the new park up the street, across the highway and halfway down to the drugstore.

They had a wonderful winter and by the end, Jeannie told Emily she ought to try out for the Ice Follies. Jeannie and Emily just watched the 60th anniversary reunion of the Ice Follies on TV; and they were both more than impressed!

It was the end of March when Emily, Sean, Jeannie and Phillip decided to go up to the pond for one last skate. They knew the ice would be gone in a few weeks. Their parents and Martha made them promise not to skate on the ice if any of it was beginning to melt. They promised and off they went.

When they got to the pond there must have been ten other kids putting on their skates or out on the pond. They were all having the time of their lives skating when a boy from Emily's class showed up with two other friends. Emily knew him as a bully and tried her best to ignore him. But, he wouldn't leave her alone.

Finally, when he realized Emily didn't want to have anything to do with him he pushed her down on the ice and called her a whore. Sean wasn't far away when he saw what happened and heard the kid yell at her.

He skated over to the kid and pushed him yelling, "What did you call her?"

The kid looked stunned as he turned around then yelled back, "I called her a whore. What are you going to do about it weenie?"

Then the bully pushed Sean who fell down on the ice. Sean got up angrier than before and punched the kid in the face. The kid fell down on the ice as well, but as the bully got back up the two boys began throwing punches.

Emily was horrified as she rushed over to try and stop them, but one of the bully's friends grabbed her arm and held her back.

"Get back here, bitch."

But the bully's friend was no match for Emily because she hauled off and punched him right smack in the balls. BAM! He buckled over in pain and Emily skated away.

Sean and the bully scuffled as Phillip and the third friend began scuffling as well. Sean skated after the bully who seemed to have had enough, but just as he reached the bully, he pushed Sean. Then a huge gust of wind popped up and blew Sean even further.

Emily and Jeannie were skating toward Sean when he got a terrified look on his face. Sean realized he was standing on melting ice as he heard the ice cracking beneath his feet. Emily yelled and kept skating toward him but Sean yelled at her to go back. Then the unthinkable happened. Sean disappeared into the pond.

Emily was more than horrified. She skated over to the hole as both Jeannie and Phillip tried to pull her back. But she yelled, "No!" and jumped into the pond.

She swam to the bottom and grabbed Sean, but she couldn't get him to swim up with her. He gestured to his foot. She swam down further and saw his skate was caught between two concrete blocks. She tried to free it, but couldn't. Then she realized she needed to go up for air, and did.

As she popped her head out of the water Jeannie yelled for her to take her hand. She ignored Jeannie, took a deep breath and went back under. She swam down to the bottom and saw that Sean was now limp, but she refused to give up.

She found a piece of rebar at the bottom of the pond and pried the two blocks apart. Sean was free.

She grabbed his coat by the neck and pulled him up with her.

When she got to the surface, a policeman was there waiting for them.

He pulled Emily and Sean out of the pond and over to the land portion just a few feet from where Sean had fallen in. Emily was shivering and crying as she watched the policeman lay Sean's limp body on the ground and begin to administer CPR. He had already called dispatch for an ambulance. It arrived within a few short minutes.

The EMTs rushed over to Sean, put an oxygen mask over his mouth, lifted him up and laid him on a stretcher. Emily was crying as she begged the EMTs to let her go to the hospital with Sean.

She lied and said she was his sister remembering that on all the hospital shows she had watched no one but immediate relatives were allowed in to accompany the patient. The EMTs said ok and as she climbed into the back of the ambulance she told Jeannie and Phillip to hurry home to tell Martha and her parents.

Once the ambulance was on its way, she watched the one EMT work on Sean. She heard him talking to someone in the Emergency Room at Bradley Hospital in East Providence.

The EMT told the person he was talking to that Sean was breathing but his breathing was very shallow. His blood pressure was critically low.

Emily was shaking all over and praying as hard as she could, *God, please don't let Sean die. Please God, just let him live. I can't live without him. Please, please God.*

They arrived at the hospital and a team of doctors went to work on Sean.

One of the nurses took Emily by the arm and said, "Sweetie, I need to take you to the waiting room. We need to give the doctors all the space they need to save your brother."

Emily nodded and followed the nurse out.

She was sitting in the waiting room crying when Martha, her parents, Jeannie and Phillip rushed in. Emily told Martha what the EMT said. Martha told Emily that Beth and Bill were on their way. As Sarah sat in the chair next to Emily she realized Emily was soaking wet. She then ran over to the nurses' desk and asked them for towels and warm blankets. Martha was sitting in a chair in complete shock. It was about an hour before anyone came out to talk to them.

Doctor Sweeny, the senior emergency room doctor came out. He sat down with Martha once she identified herself.

"We've stabilized your grandson. We won't know for a few days if he'll be alright. He suffered extreme hypothermia from being in the icy water for so long. We've got him resting comfortably in ICU. It's now just a matter of time."

"Can I go up to see him?" asked Martha.

"Yes, but only you and your granddaughter. No one but family is allowed in the room; and only for a few minutes."

Martha was shaking like a leaf when Emily took her hand and said, "Martha, I'm sorry but I lied and told the EMTs I was Sean's sister. I'm the granddaughter the doctor referred to."

They both walked up to ICU together, entered the room and clutched each other as they both cried. Soon Beth and Bill were in the room asking how it happened when the nurse came in and told them they all needed to leave.

"But he's my son," exclaimed a desperate Beth.

Then Sean's machines began to sound an alarm and the nurse insisted they leave the room. As they left they heard a call over the intercom system calling doctors to Sean's room for a Code Blue.

Beth knew what code blue meant from when Davie was in the hospital. She panicked and fainted as Bill caught her. A nurse rushed over to help.

Once Beth regained consciousness, the commotion in Sean's room had subsided. The doctor assured them that Sean was again stable but told them they needed to go down to the general waiting room. Someone would be down to get them if there was a change.

They went down and Sarah and Joe were still there with Jeannie and Phillip. They went over to join them. After about an hour Sarah announced she and Joe had to get home to their other children.

Gladys had come up to watch their other three kids. Sarah kissed Emily while Joe patted her head. They both told her how brave but stupid she was for jumping in the pond.

"You could have drown, Emily!" said Sarah.

"I know, Mom, but I had to try."

Knowing Emily was in good hands, she and Joe walked toward the door. Jeannie and Phillip got up and followed when Jeannie stopped, turned around and ran back to Emily.

"Oh, Emily; I was so scared. I thought you were going to drown. But I absolutely loved when you punched that rotten kid. You are my all-time hero!"

Emily hugged Jeannie and as she rubbed Jeannie's back she said, "It's going to ok, Jeannie. I have to believe it is."

Martha, Beth, Bill and Emily sat huddled together. Emily's clothes were finally dry. It was 8 p.m. when the four trekked down to the hospital cafeteria to get something to eat. Emily hadn't eaten since breakfast and was starving.

As they began eating, they joined hands and prayed for Sean. At the end Emily said, "He'll make it through. I just know he will. I'm no longer afraid."

Chapter Nineteen

Sean was comatose for more than three weeks. The doctors were concerned and already suspected there was severe damage to Sean's frontal lobe, and temporal lobe and possibly minor damage to his parietal lobe.

Dr. Jenkins, Head of Neurology, scheduled a sit down with Beth, Bill and Martha. Martha begged for Emily to be present and after some resistance, Dr. Jenkins agreed.

They sat around a conference table. On the table in front of him, Dr. Jenkins placed a model of a human head with all its brain parts exposed. When Beth saw this she uttered a terrible moan and Bill tightly clasped her hand. Beth's reaction terrified Emily which Martha immediately picked up on as she pulled Emily close to her, clutching her tightly.

Dr. Jenkins explained that preliminary brain scans and diagnosis indicated that it was likely that there was severe damage to both the frontal and temporal lobes. He then, using the model, pointed to each of the three lobes and described what each of them controlled.

"This portion of the brain, the frontal lobe, is responsible for decision making, problem solving, and control of purposeful behaviors, consciousness and emotions. This portion, the temporal lobe, regulates memory, emotions, hearing, language and learning. These are the two areas of Sean's brain which we consider may have sustained severe damage. In addition, this portion of the brain, the parietal lobe, is responsible for receiving and processing sensory information from the body. Its major job is to regulate speech and thought. We suspect there is some damage to the parietal lobe as well. Although it's difficult to be certain or even to predict what Sean's mental capacity will be once he awakens, it's also important that I inform you that, the longer he is in a comatose state, the worse the odds are for a healthy recovery."

Beth sobbed and Emily shivered. Bill and Martha, although on the verge of tears, hung tight knowing they needed to be strong for Beth and Emily.

119

Emily asked, "Doctor, is there anything we can do to help Sean come out of his coma?"

Dr. Jenkins pushed his chair back away from the table, crossed his arms and breathed heavily. "Dear, from what the staff is telling me you are doing everything right. Someone is with him all day long and you have been talking to him which is an excellent thing to do. It's hard to know if he can hear you, so just keep doing what you've been doing. I'm also told the night staff has been extremely attentive to his needs. Jose, one of our night nurses sits with him during the night playing his guitar and singing to him. Right now it's a waiting game. So, just hang in there, Emily and let your brother know how much you love and miss him."

With that said, Dr. Jenkins stood up, shook their hands and bid them all, "Be well."

He then excused himself and told them they were welcomed to remain in the room for as long as they needed to be. He quietly left the room and gently closed the door behind him.

Emily began sobbing uncontrollably as she choked on her words. "I didn't do enough. If only I didn't come up for air."

Beth's heart sank as she got up, walked over to Emily, grabbed her and hugged her tight. "Emily, none of this is your fault."

She then sat down and, holding Emily's chin, looked her directly in the eye. "If it weren't for your bravery, we may not even be sitting here right now. We would have already lost our sweet, little boy. *You* and you alone are the reason we are here and Sean is lying in a hospital bed and not a coffin, so, please Emily, put all those terrible thoughts out of your mind right now."

Emily stopped crying as Beth begged, "Do you promise me that, Emily?"

"Yes, Beth, I promise."

Beth grabbed a tissue from the box of Kleenex which was sitting in the middle of the table and wiped Emily's eyes and nose.

Beth then stood up, crossed her arms in an authoritative manner.

"*Now* let's all go back to thinking and behaving positively.

You heard Dr. Jenkins. We need Sean to hear positive reinforcement. Emily, I want you to continue to read books to him and Martha, you keep singing all his favorite childhood songs and reciting all his favorite childhood rhymes and I'll do the same. Our little Seanie is going to wake up and when he does, he's going to be just like he was before this happened. Are we all in agreement?"

They all vigorously shook their heads yes.

****

Two weeks later and almost five weeks after the accident, nearly to the minute, Sean opened his eyes.

Emily was reading out loud Tolkien's LORD OF THE RINGS, when she paused to get some water. She was holding the book with one hand and holding Sean's hand with her other. She put the book down and reached for the bottle of water she brought from home when she heard, "Don't stop reading, Emily."

She dropped the bottle on the floor and looked at Sean who seemed to be wide awake.

"Sean, you're awake!"

"Well, of course I'm awake. I was only taking a nap after all; but I love how you read and don't want you to stop."

He spoke with absolute clarity and perfect diction.

Just then, Beth and Martha came into the room and Emily shouted. "He's awake!"

Beth and Martha rushed over to the bed. Beth leaned over and hugged Sean. "Oh, baby, we thought we lost you."

"Mom, I've been here the whole time, but, I still can't figure out what happened to me. I kept trying to ask all of you but nobody seemed to hear me. What did happen to me?"

As Beth and Emily tried to explain, Martha ran out to the nurse's station. Soon several nurses and a doctor came rushing in. They asked all three women to step out for a few minutes while they checked Sean's vitals.

Beth, Martha and Emily stood at the side of the hallway opposite to Sean's room hugging each other and crying tears of absolute joy.

"Our little boy is back," cried Beth with so much conviction and elation that they all began laughing joyfully.

Soon the doctor came out of the room and, scratching his head, walked over to the three women.

"This is remarkable. I've only seen this one other time in my life. From preliminary examination, Sean seems to have made a complete recovery. All his vital signs are normal and he's talking up a storm. He's even asked one of the nurses for his guitar."

"His guitar?" asked Beth with a most perplexed look.

"Yes, his guitar," repeated the doctor.

He then told Beth that they were taking Sean down for tests and CT scans which meant that he would be out of his room for the better part of the day.

He smiled and advised the ladies. "Go home and get some much needed rest and we'll see you all in the morning."

As Sean was wheeled from his room, the three women kissed and hugged him telling him they'd be back before he even realized they were gone. Sean raised his arm and waved as he was rolled down the hall to the elevator.

The three women sat down in the chairs that lined the windowed side of the hall. They were dumfounded and totally exhausted.

Then Beth tilted her head. "What on earth was the doctor talking about regarding the guitar?"

Emily and Martha both shrugged their shoulders.

Then, suddenly Emily jumped up from her chair and gasped excitedly. "Jose! Remember when Dr. Jenkins told us that Nurse Jose plays his guitar and sings to Sean every night?"

"That's got to be it!" exclaimed Martha.

Then Beth frowned not sure about that answer. "But Jose was playing his own guitar. Sean wasn't playing it."

They were all quite perplexed, yet Emily secretly had a premonition that Sean actually believed he could play Jose's guitar.

On the ride home there was an abundance of emotions being expressed; joy, giddiness, hopefulness and questions about the damned guitar.

When they got home, Beth hugged Emily tightly. "I love you, Emily. Thank you for saving my little boy. Now we can all get a good night sleep. Martha and I will be over to pick you up tomorrow morning at 9 a.m., ok?"

"I love you too, Beth. I can't wait to see Sean again in the morning. I'm going to bring him my CD player and all the CDs he loves!"

Martha took Emily by the hand and walked her home. They both went inside to tell Emily's family the wonderful news.

That night before going to bed, Emily called Jeannie and exclaimed, "Jeannie, Jeannie, Sean is awake and talking like he doesn't even realize he's been asleep."

They were jabbering ferociously when Emily exclaimed, "And I've gotta tell you something strange. This nurse named Jose; remember I told you he has been playing his guitar and singing to Sean almost every night? Well, Sean thinks it's his guitar and he also thinks he's been playing it. He asked where his guitar was." Then she said, "I know. I can't believe it either. But I've gotta tell ya, Jeannie, I think Sean can actually play a guitar. It's just a very strange but certain feeling I have. I can't explain it but I'm going to try and find out if I'm right tomorrow when I see Sean! Now, gosh, I think I'm about to collapse on this floor. I can't remember the last time I was this tired."

Jeannie and Emily said goodnight, then Emily went to the kitchen to kiss her mom. Her dad wasn't home. He had been gone for over a week. He was in Iceland this time.

Sarah hugged her little girl and told her how proud she was of her.

"Go to sleep honey and dream happy dreams tonight. You deserve all the happy dreams there are to have."

Before she turned off her light, Emily wrote almost verbatim what she just told Jeannie over the phone.

She ended with these words, **Diary please tell all the angels in heaven that I really appreciate everything they've done. Also, if God isn't too busy, please tell him thanks for saving my best friend and letting me have him back.**

The next morning Emily carried a bag full of books, a CD player and several CDs including Neil Young's CRAZY HORSE. She couldn't wait to ask Sean about the guitar. She actually dreamed Sean was sitting on the slant tree next to her strumming on a guitar. She didn't have to wait very long to ask him however because as she, Beth and Martha entered Sean's room he was sitting in the chair next to the bed playing a guitar. All their jaws dropped when they entered his room and saw this display.

Beth asked as she hugged and kissed Sean, "Where on earth and when did you learn to play a guitar?"

"God, Sean," said Emily, "You sound like you've been playing one for a long time."

Martha simply didn't know what to say as she also hugged and kissed her grandson.

"Jose came back to my room last night to see me. I asked him if I could try his guitar and I just started playing it. Jose told me I was playing all the songs he played for me while I was sleeping. I have no idea because I know now that I've been asleep for over five weeks. Strange isn't it," laughed Sean.

"It certainly is!" exclaimed Beth.

Then Sean looked at Emily. "Listen to this, Em!"

He picked the guitar back up and started playing "We Never Danced." Emily literally fell into the chair next to Sean and listened as he not only played the piece perfectly but sang the words perfectly as well.

When he was done, she laughed. "Well, I think I'd keep my day job, Sean. A singer you are not, but you play like a musician!"

Sean, lowered the guitar, looked at her and frowned. "Thanks for the insult about my singing, Em," to which he began laughing hardily as did the three women.

Sean spent two additional weeks in the hospital for observation before he was released; and Emily went back to school. With Martha and Beth's help she had been trying to keep up with her work which the school had been sending home for the last five weeks.

On the Thursday before Sean was released a reporter from the WPRI-TV, Providence contacted Beth and asked if she could come interview Sean and his sister, Emily who she heard was responsible for saving her brother's life. She also heard an uncanny rumor that when Sean woke up he could play the guitar.

"Is it true that Sean has never played a musical instrument in his life?" asked Melody Rogers.

"Yes, that's absolutely true. Never, not even the piano let

alone a guitar."

"Well," Melody responded, "My news producer handed me a brand new, absolutely beautiful Les Paul Standard Gibson guitar which has been signed by Neil Young with a special note that reads, "Sean, and Emily, We Never Danced, forever Neil" and shipped overnight to us from California. I don't know what the story is with the We Never Danced because I thought Emily was your daughter, but I guess I'll find all that out if you are willing to give me permission to come talk to Sean and Emily tomorrow."

Beth fell to the back of her chair as she listened. "Wow. Yes, by all means. Sean and Emily will be thrilled. Emily has school tomorrow but I'm sure we can arrange for another day off. We'll all be there. What time tomorrow?"

They arranged for the meeting to take place at 1 p.m.

Melody explained that "As we speak, my producer is arranging with the hospital to do the interview in an area of the hospital where we can set up with a camera crew."

Beth hung up the phone, sat in the chair looking at the now silent phone in her hand and shook her head in disbelief. She then called Martha and told her to go tell Sarah so Emily would be available and dressed for the big day.

When Emily came home from school Sarah was waiting for her at the door. She told Emily she was taking her to Macy's in Providence so she could get a brand new outfit. Emily didn't understand and asked why.

When Sarah explained the entire scenario to Emily she got excited; then she became very serious.

"Well, Mom, I guess it's time to tell the hospital the truth that I'm not Sean's sister. Boy, I hope the doctors and nurses don't get mad at me for fibbing to them all this time."

"Emily," Sarah laughed, "I think the doctors and nurses have probably already figured out that you're not his sister but his best girlfriend. That's the last thing we need to be concerned with. Right now, you and I are going shopping, and, we're also going to have dinner downtown as well; just you and me. "

"Can we also get a coffee cabinet Mom?"

"You bet we can, sweetie! You can have anything you want tonight. Oh, here comes Martha. She's going to stay with your brother and sisters. Are you ready?"

"I sure am!" said Emily as they walk out the door to greet Martha.

"Martha, have you heard the news? Sean is going to get a guitar signed by Neil Young tomorrow. Isn't that simply amazing?"

"It certainly is, dear. What's also amazing is that you're going to be interviewed as the brave young woman who jumped in the icy water to save Sean. How about them apples, Emily?"

They hugged and Emily and Sarah were off waving to Martha as Sarah backed the car out of the driveway.

The following morning Sarah and Emily got ready for the big day. Sarah arranged for Gladys to stay with her mother and to also be there when Paul, Lily and Katie came home from school.

Emily looked positively stunning. She didn't want to wear a dress. Instead she wanted to dress like someone who was hip so she chose a brand new pair of jeans, a purple top, a denim vest and a pair of boots. She managed to tuck her jeans into her new Western style boots for a very sophisticated, trendy look. Sarah helped curl and fix her hair. Emily wore it down and parted to the side.

As they walked out the door, Martha walked across the street. The plan was to meet Beth and Bill at the hospital. Just as they were about to get in the car, Gladys pulled her car up to the front of their house. Jeannie and Phillip both jumped out of the car and ran over to Sarah's car.

Sarah got out and greeted Gladys. "Hi Gladys! We were about to drive down to pick Jeannie and Phillip up."

"I thought I'd save you the trip. I was on my way up anyway. I don't want your mom to be alone even for a minute. I know what it's like to worry about a disabled parent."

Sarah and Gladys went in the house, then, shortly Sarah reemerged and they all left for the hospital.

Jeannie was beside herself with excitement for her two friends. "God, Em. This is exciting beyond words, isn't it Phillip?"

Phillip wasn't paying a bit of attention so Jeannie poked him in his side.

"Uh…Yea, yes it is. I can't believe you guys are going to be interviewed by the TV station. I called several of my friends from school and told them that they needed to watch the news tonight."

There was so much chatter in the car for the forty-five minute drive to the hospital that Sarah almost missed the turn. As they arrive in the front Lobby, they were greeted by the Executive Vice President of Public Relations and Marketing for Bradley Hospital.

"Hi, my name is Bruce Williams. Sean, Beth and Bill are already in our cafeteria where the TV crew will be conducting the interview." He vigorously shook Emily's hand. "You must be our hero, Emily!" She nodded; then Bruce said, "Follow me please."

They walked down the hall and took the elevator up one floor. Emily couldn't believe the crowd that was gathered in one whole half of the cafeteria. They even had an audience as staff going and coming from lunch and other people using the cafeteria were gathered around the perimeter the news crew had established. A tall, stunning red headed woman walked over to greet Martha, Emily and the rest of the group.

She introduced herself as Melody Rogers. "I'll be conducting the interview. So you're Emily," she said as she shook Emily's hand. "I should have realized you were a red head. We red heads get things done. Isn't that right, Emily?"

"Yes, we do," agreed Emily looking all around. Then she spotted Sean sitting in a wheel chair next to a 30 something male holding a guitar. She waved then said to Melody, "I have a confession to make before we get started."

Melody tilted her head and laughed. "Emily we all already know you're not really Sean's sister but his girlfriend. We also know you convinced the EMTs and hospital staff that you were his sister so they'd let you be by Sean's side the whole time. Pretty darned clever on your part! We were all just talking about that. The hospital staff loves that twist to this story. Now let's all go over so we can prep for the interview."

"Phew, Mom," said Emily as she took Sarah's hand.

Sarah squeezed Emily's hand then smiled at her sweet, innocent daughter.

"See, honey, I told you it wouldn't be a problem. You worry

too much. Now let's go have some fun. Sean is waving for you to come over."

Sarah, Martha, Emily, Jeannie and Phillip all walked over. Emily broke away, ran over to Sean and gave him a big hug.

"Are you just too excited?" she asked him.

"Yea, but I'm a lot scared too. What if I mess up on the guitar?"

"Shoot, Sean that should be the least of your worries. Just start playing like you did the other day for me. No one will ever know you made a mistake. And, besides, if you do, they'll fix it at the station before they put it on TV."

"Yea, you're right. I'll just look at you the entire time I'm playing. That way I won't mess up. I'll just make believe no one else but you and I are here. That should work!"

Then he grabbed Emily's hand. "Hey, Em, have I told you lately that I really love you?"

Emily hugged Sean tightly and kissed him to which the entire crowd cheered and a young man standing in hearing distance yelled, "Hey Sean, that sounds like the lyrics to a song!" Sean and Emily turned red as beets and laughed as did everyone in the immediate vicinity.

Then Sean looked at the man sitting beside him, "Oh my God, Em. I forgot to introduce you. This is Jose."

Emily hugged Jose tightly, "Jose, thanks so much for helping Sean come back to us. This is amazing beyond belief isn't it?"

Jose smiled bashfully, "Yes, it is. But, the whole time I played and sang I just knew Sean could hear me. I had no idea though that I was teaching him to actually play the guitar. That has totally blown me away."

Just then Melody came over and began prepping all three with questions she planned to ask and described some of the shots the camera crew would be taking.

Melody instructed, "Just act very natural and don't pay attention to the lights and all the people. Just look at me and the camera folks will do all the rest of the work. Ok?" said Melody.

For the next several minutes, Melody asked Sean, Emily and Jose her questions then she invited Jose and Sean to play together with Jose stopping in the middle as Sean continued to play. When they were finished and the camera crew turned off the camera lights the room exploded with applause and cheers.

"See, that wasn't so bad, was it?" asked Melody.

"No," said both Sean and Emily simultaneously. Jose smiled and patted Sean on the back. He was extremely proud of his student.

Sean asked, "Will this be on the six o'clock news?"

"Yes and the 11 o'clock news as well so be sure to watch tonight. Emily and Sean you're both about to become celebrities! I've heard the TODAY SHOW and Oprah Winfrey have already called the station. You two are about to have a lot of fun. Oh, and, Neil Young is scheduled to be in New York City in a few weeks for a concert. There's a rumor he's going to have you both come out on stage. Sean, he wants you to play with him," smiled Melody.

"Holy cow!" both Emily and Sean said as they looked at each other with eyes wider than saucers.

That evening Sean, Emily, Martha, Beth and Bill sat in Sean's room waiting for the six o'clock news broadcast to come on. Jose, who was about to begin his shift, came into the room to watch with them.

The phone in Sean's room rang off the hook with friends and classmates telling Sean they would be watching the news. Sarah was at home with her mother and children. Jeannie and Phillip were there as well. At about 5:45, Sarah called the room and told Emily they were all in front of the TV waiting for her big debut.

Emily laughed and said, "Awe, Mom, it's just the news."

She and Sarah talked a little longer then Sarah told her she would see her in a couple of hours. Emily hung up and the room became totally silent as Sean turned the volume up on the TV. It was a big TV which Bruce Williams, the public relations guy had rolled into his room.

"You can't watch such an important broadcast on a small hospital TV. You two need to get the full effect!" Bruce remarked.

Soon, the news anchor cut to Melody Rogers. Melody asked the question, "What would you do if your best friend fell through the ice and into an icy pond? Would you jump in to save your friend knowing you too could drown? Well, this young lady did just that. She didn't give it a second thought but jumped in to save her young friend, Sean. Emily, tell us what went through your mind when you jumped in the water?"

"Well," said Emily, "I didn't think anything. I just did it."

"And tell me what happened next."

"When I got down to Sean, his skate was stuck. I tried to free it but couldn't. Then I had to come up for air and went back down. I found a piece of metal on the bottom, freed Sean's foot and swam back up pulling Sean with me. But Sean was unconscious."

"And, that's not the end of the story is it Sean. You were in a coma for five weeks and when you woke up you began playing the guitar? When did you learn to play the guitar?"

"Well," answered Sean, "When I was in a coma, Jose played and sang to me every night. When I woke up, I could just play."

Then Melody turned her attention to Jose, "Jose, did you ever dream that you were actually teaching Sean to play?"

"No, not at all. I did, however, feel certain that Sean could hear me and that my music was helping to keep him connected to what we call reality."

"And, Sean, can you play a little bit for us now. I understand you and Emily have a favorite song by Neil Young. In fact, Neil Young sent you this beautiful Gibson guitar with a message written on the guitar to you and Emily. It reads, "Sean, and Emily, We Never Danced, forever Neil.""

Jose and Sean played several chords of the song We Never Danced, then Jose lowered his guitar and Sean continued to play solo, just long enough for the viewers to understand how remarkable Sean's playing truly was. "Back to you Tom."

"Melody, that's quite a remarkable story," said the anchor.

"Yes it is Tom, and the story continues because both Sean and Emily will be special guests of Neil Young in three weeks at Neil's concert in New York City where he will invite Sean to play guitar with him on stage." A few additional comments were made and the story ended.

"Wow," exclaimed Bill. "Little did I know I was marrying into such a remarkable family? I'm blown away, Sean!"

Just as Melody predicted the next several weeks were a whirlwind. Sean was released from the hospital and within a few days Beth, Sean and Emily flew up to New York City to appear on the TODAY SHOW. Katie Couric, who Emily just adored, interviewed them, and then they were shuttled over to another morning show for yet another interview.

The next day it was on to Chicago to appear on the Oprah Winfrey show. Finally they flew back up to New York City to meet Neil Young.

Neil introduced the two of them to his audience, recounted the story and then told the audience of the song that Emily and Sean declared to be their own special song, "We Never Danced." He then, had three chairs brought out on stage; one for Emily the second for Sean and the third for him. As Sean and Neil faced Emily, Sean picked up his special Gibson guitar and he and Neil began playing "We Never Danced" to which Neil sang the lyrics.

When they were finished, the entire audience jumped up clapping, cheering and raising brightly lit lighters. It was a night these two young adults would not forget for a very long time.

Once they returned home, life settled back to normal. The media had gone on to the next big story. Sean and Emily were just as happy it had. They were becoming quite annoyed with all the media attention and wanted to go back to their simpler life.

Chapter Twenty

Two years went by. It was Sunday, December 27, 1998. The following day was Emily's 15th birthday.

With the help of Gladys, Martha, Sarah, Jeannie, Phillip and Sean had been secretly planning a surprise birthday party. It was Christmas break, so rather than waiting to hold a belated birthday, they decided it was a safe bet that all the invitees would be able to attend provided they were spending the holidays in town.

They all had tons of joint friends at the time many of whom resulted from Sean and Emily's brief stardom. Since the party was being held in Jeannie's basement, Gladys instructed the three teens to pare down the list of party goers which was up to a whopping 50 names.

"That's just not going to work! Between the three of you figure out who would mean the most to Emily. The rest have got to go!" demanded Gladys.

They edited the list numerous times, occasionally squabbling with each other. Soon, however, the list had been chopped in half and Gladys gave her approval.

The morning of December 27th Martha picked Sean up from his mom's and drove him down to stay with Phillip. Emily thought Sean wouldn't be back to his grandma's house until Friday which was New Year's Day. The three still had last minute planning to do and they also needed to decorate Jeannie's basement.

Jeannie told Emily a white lie when Emily called her that morning to ask her to go down to the drugstore with her to have hot chocolate and a piece of pie. When Jeannie explained she had to go with her parents to see a relative, Emily decided to just stay home in her room and paint all day.

She got a beautiful French style wooden easel for Christmas and a basket full of acrylic paints along with several different styles of brushes. Sean gave her several canvases for Christmas and a thick sketch book telling her he never wanted her to stop painting. She thought of Sean and sketched a picture of him and her sitting on the slant tree as viewed from behind. She wanted to capture all the emotions she had for Sean from the first time they met up through the present.

After five attempts and five crumbled pieces of sketch paper strewn on the floor she stepped back and looked at her sixth attempt and finally felt satisfied. She recaptured the sketch on the 30 x 30 inch canvas Sean bought her, which she prepped with gesso the day prior.

She stepped back and looked at the canvas and said out loud, "That's it. It's even better than the sketch."

She then put on her red smock with a yellow tulip pattern dotting the smock. Martha sewed it for her and gave it to her for Christmas to compliment Sean's gifts and the French easel.

Next she ran downstairs to fill her metal water cup with fresh water for cleaning the brushes in between. Before she went back up to her room, she stopped by the linen closet and pulled out a scrappy looking towel and asked Sarah if she could use it while she painted. Since it was old, Sarah told her she could. Emily spent the entire day into the evening painting.

It was about 8 p.m. when she heard the phone ring. She stopped, walked over to her bedroom door, opened it and listened. Her heart skipped several beats when she heard the words, "Emily, it's Sean."

She dropped everything almost spilling her water on the floor, but managed a save, put her paint brush in the water and ran down the stairs.

She was out of breath when she picked up the phone.

"Hi Sean. I was hoping you would call me tonight. You'll never guess what I'm painting."

"Hey Em. You sound out of breath. I'm about to go to dinner with Mom, Bill and his kids, but I wanted to call and wish you an early happy birthday especially since I won't see you till Friday."

He covered the phone with his hand as he waved Jeannie and Phillip away. They were laughing at his ability to lie through his teeth. Jeannie and Phillip both covered their mouths and tip toed to the other side of the basement where they continued to laugh quietly as they heard more of Sean's lie.

133

"Thanks, Sean. What's all that noise? It sounded like people laughing."

"Oh, it's just Bill's kids. They were bugging the heck out of me so I shooed them out of the room. So, what are you painting?"

Emily told him what she was painting and that she wanted to give it to him when she was done.

They talked a little while longer then Sean said, "Em, I gotta go now. Bill just motioned to me to get a move on. Happy Birthday, Em. I love you."

"I love you too, Sean. I can't wait till next Friday. I'm going to die several times between now and then waiting to see you."

They said good-bye and hung up the phones.

Sean feigned irritation with Jeannie and Phillip. "God, guys. You nearly gave me away. I thought I was going to burst out laughing and spill the beans to Emily!"

Jeannie was still laughing as both she and Phillip walked back over to where Sean was sitting. "God, Sean. You're an awfully good liar. You had me convinced you weren't here."

Now they were all laughing as they resumed decorating.

The following day the three planners put the final touches on the basement.

All the party goers had been given explicit instructions that Emily would arrive at exactly 7 p.m.; and that, if they were running late, to simply wait until 7:15 or later to arrive. They would just have to miss out on the surprise portion. The instructions on the invitations were printed using **bold** letters and were highlighted in yellow.

It was approximately 1 p.m. and the three were going crazy waiting around. Gladys suggested they head up to the TV room and watch movies until it was time to get ready for the party. They did and all of three fell asleep around 4 p.m.

At 5:45 p.m. Gladys came into the room with a spoon and pan. She stood in front of the TV and started banging on the pan.

They all jumped as Jeannie exclaimed, "Geez, Mom. You scared the crap out of us."

Gladys frowned. "Watch your language young lady. I just thought I'd have a little fun."

They all scrambled. Since Sean stayed with Phillip, he and

Phillip left to go get dressed as Jeannie ran up the stairs to her room.

At 6:30 Phillip and Sean rang Jeannie's door bell.

She ran down the stairs and opened the door.

"I thought I was going to have to send out a search party for you two. Come on. Hurry up. We only have a few minutes till people start arriving."

Then she began barking orders. "Sean, you stay here and answer the door. Phillip you show everyone to the basement stairs."

Phillip rolled his eyes and asked sarcastically, "And what are you going to be doing while we're doing all the work?"

Jeannie rolled her eyes back at him and answered with just as much sarcasm in her voice. "Geez, I'll be in the basement getting everyone positioned. What do you think? So, when you see Sarah's car, you two run down into the basement and hide and I'll run up to greet Emily."

Everything was going smoothly. All 22 attendees were hiding in various spots in the basement.

At 7 p.m. sharp the doorbell rang and Jeannie ran up the stairs as the two boys ran down to the basement. Once she saw the boys hit the bottom step, she flipped off the light and ran to the door.

She opened the door. "Hey Emily! Hi Sarah! Mom will be right down."

The ruse was that Emily thought she was being taken to dinner. The two women walked in the house.

Jeannie put her arm around Emily. "Em, before we leave I've got to show you something. Come on."

Sarah said, "Go ahead, dear. I'll wait for Gladys."

Emily followed by Jeannie started descending the basement stairs.

Emily stopped half way down and looked at Jeannie. "Aren't you going to turn on the lights?"

Jeannie waved her arm. "Oh, the overhead is burned out, but I have a table lamp at the bottom of the stairs I'll turn on."

As they made it down to the basement, Sarah was peeking at them around the corner. Once the two girls reached the bottom step, Sarah flipped on the overhead and 24 kids jumped out from

135

everywhere yelling "SURPRISE!"

Emily just stood there with her eyes bulging out of her head and her mouth gaping. "Oh my God; Jeannie, you tricked me. Sean, you little turd. You were here last night when you called weren't you?"

"Yea, I was and that was Jeannie and Phillip you heard laughing. They almost gave everything away."

Everyone started laughing and the party began. About ten minutes later the last two guests arrived.

Sarah came down the stairs and, Pricilla Connors walked over and handed Sarah her camera. "Hi Mrs. Callaway. I think I got some good shots of Emily with her mouth down to her knees."

"Thanks, dear," laughed Sarah. "Emily, you have a wonderful time and happy birthday! I'll be upstairs helping Gladys."

The music began and they all started dancing. The third dance slowed down as "We Never Danced" began playing.

Sean drew Emily close and whispered, "Happy Birthday my favorite birthday girl."

He kissed her on the ear and they melted into each other's arms.

At 8 p.m. Sarah flicked the lights on and off to signal the cake was coming down. As Emily turned she saw that not only her mom was climbing down the stairs holding the cake lit with 15 candles but her dad was also descending the stairs and was carrying a huge wrapped present.

"Dad, I didn't think you'd be back home till tomorrow!" exclaimed Emily trying to feel delighted he was there, as she thought, *geez, I thought he'd be home tomorrow. Smile, Emily.*

Joe smiled. "Emily, I wouldn't miss this birthday for the world!"

Then Sarah put the cake on the table and everyone told Emily to make a wish and blow out the candles.

She closed her eyes as tight as she could and, in her mind, made her wish. *When I grow up I want to marry Sean.*

Then she opened her eyes and blew out all the candles. Everyone clapped as they sang Happy Birthday.

When they were finished singing the same girl who yelled out at Jeannie's birthday party two years earlier yelled, "What did you wish for, Emily?"

Emily looked up and said, "Carol, just like Jeannie told you two years ago, I can't tell you what I wished for. I want it to come true."

All the kids laughed as did Carol.

Sarah began cutting the cake as Emily said excitedly, "Oh, Mom, you baked a tomato soup cake...my favorite."

Sarah handed Emily the first piece and asked, "Well, Emily, what other kind of cake would I bake for you?"

"When did you sneak that in?" asked Emily.

"When I was baking for Christmas; you couldn't tell the difference between the smell of the cake cooking from the smell of the pumpkin pies."

"Good one, Mom!" said Emily taking a huge bite of cake.

It was time to open the presents as Joe brought over the big box.

"Open this one first, Emily," he said.

She did. Her eyes got really big when she realized it was a beautiful white knee length parka with white faux fur around the hood.

"Oh, Mom, Dad; I love it!" She kissed both of them then went back to opening more presents. She opened Sean's gift next. It was a new CD player.

He laughed. "I think your old one is about worn out from playing it so much, Em."

The rest of the gifts were opened and they all went back to partying till 9 p.m. as the adults walked back up the stairs.

Sarah turned to Sean. "Joe and I are going to go back to the house. Would you make sure our daughter makes it home in one piece?"

"Yes, ma'am. I'll take really good care of her."

When it was time to leave, Emily said, "Jeannie, can we come back down tomorrow to collect my presents. We'll also be down to help clean up...promise!"

"Absolutely, I'll see you in the morning." The two girls hugged and Jeannie whispered, "Don't do anything I wouldn't do."

Sean helped Emily put on her new white parka and they left hand in hand and began climbing the street to her house.

Half-way up the hill, Sean pulled her over to the side of the street and they kissed.

"Happy birthday, Em! Can you tell *me* what you wished for?" asked Sean.

She shyly looked down at the ground. "Do you promise not to think it's stupid?"

"Nothing you could say would ever seem stupid, Em." He kissed her again.

As she began to turn red as a beat in the light of the street lamp she again looked down at the ground and whispered, "That we get married someday."

"Oh, Em, you know that's going to happen. Who the heck else would I marry? You're my girl!" He lifted her head by her chin and kissed her again.

They hugged and finished walking up the street chattering all the way to her door.

Sean kissed her once more. "Good night, Emily Callaway; or, I should say, future Mrs. Mahoney."

Emily giggled. "I love you Mr. Mahoney."

They kiss one last time and Emily went inside.

Sean hesitated as she shut the door remembering the last time they walked up the hill from Jeannie's birthday party. At the same time, Emily, now standing on the other side of the closed door stood and reflected on that same night which now seemed eons ago. She was about to turn off the outside light when something told her to open the door again. She did as Sean asked, "Are you ok? I just wanted to make sure."

She stuck her head out the door and said, "Kiss me once more. I'm ok." Then she said, "God that must have been mental telepathy because I had the same thought. I love you, Sean." He kissed her once more and said, "Goodnight, Em. I love you with all my heart. Happy Birthday." They smiled sweetly as she shut the door. Then she walked to the window in the dining room and watched as Sean crossed the street and went inside. She walked back to the foyer, turned off the two lights and walked up the stairs to her room. Just as she climbed into bed she said a short prayer. *Thank you God for changing my life. Thank you for Sean and allowing me to be happy.*

Chapter Twenty-One

One year passed. With its siren blasting, an ambulance turned a quick, hard left off the main highway and began racing down the street.

Emily was walking home from school when she heard it, jumped from fright then turned to see it was headed right for her. Like a seasoned athlete, she leapt over to the side of the street just in time for it to pass. She watched it disappear down the hill and heard the siren wind down as she realized its destination was either her house or an immediate neighbor's. Her heart began beating rapidly as she started running. She was terrified it was Bertie or Martha.

She reached the crest of the hill and saw the ambulance backed up to her front door. Flinging her back pack at the closest yard she began running down the hill as fast as she could.

"Grandma, grandma," she's cried out loud. She rushed through the front door.

Sarah was walking next to the stretcher as one of the EMTs held a drip bag high in the air and the other two EMTs wheeled the stretcher through the living room.

She yelled, "Grandma!" But, when she got close enough to see, she realized it was her father.

Martha was standing in the living room and rushed over to Emily. "Step back, dear so the EMTs can get through."

"What happened?" Emily cried.

"Your dad had a heart attack," Martha whispered.

Then Martha instructed Emily to sit down on the sofa as she walked over to Sarah. "Go on with Joe, Sarah. I'll gather the children, let them know what's happened and we'll follow you to the hospital as soon as Gladys arrives."

Sarah nodded but it was obvious to Martha that she was in a complete daze as she walked out with her husband and the EMTs. Martha closed the door behind them and Emily heard the screech of the siren as it dissolved up the street.

"Is he going to make it?" cried Emily.

139

"I don't know, dear. It was a pretty bad one. Wait here a minute. I'll go look in on your grandma. Your brother and sisters should be home any minute."

Emily sat there wringing her hands feeling a glut of mixed emotions. She felt incredibly sad, confused and numb all at once. She also felt guilt. She kept thinking of the many times she wished her father dead. Now, it could actually happen. She said a prayer in her head, *God, I didn't mean all those wishes. I don't want my dad to die. I want him to live. If he dies Mom will be broken hearted. Please, please forgive me for being so hateful.* She was sobbing as the front door flew open.

It was Paul and he was carrying his back pack and hers as well. "Emily, what the heck's going on? I found this up the street. Dad's going to kill you."

Just as he said the word kill, Emily burst out in tears and cried ferociously.

"What's the matter," asked Paul as he came over to the couch and sat down.

"Dad's been taken to the hospital. He had a heart attack."

Paul fell against the back of the couch. "How?"

Just then, Martha came back in the room as the two girls ran in the house. Paul was crying causing the girls to stop dead in their tracks.

Martha walked over to them and gently said, "Lily, Katie, go put your back packs in your bedroom, we need to go to the hospital."

"Why?" they asked in unison.

"Cuz, Dad's in the hospital. He had a heart attack," cried Paul.

Lily was now crying and Katie was asking what a heart attack was. Martha bent down to Katie and tried to explain as Gladys arrived. Now all four children were crying as Martha took the girls' backpacks, put them on the stairs and encouraged all four to follow her across the street to her car. They did and soon she backed the car out of the driveway headed for Bradley Hospital.

They arrived at the hospital and went in through the Emergency Room door. Martha had the children sit down then walked over to the admissions desk. She was told the doctors were still working on the children's father but that they would let her know when and what to do when it was time.

Martha walked back over to the children and rearranged their chairs in a tight circle so they could all hold hands. They waited for nearly three hours, when Sarah walked into the waiting room looking like she had been through hell.

The children jumped up and ran over to Sarah.

"Shhh. Let's go back over to your chairs."

As they all sat down, Sarah also sat while Martha stood behind her.

"Daddy's in a private room right now. He's asleep. The doctors said they won't know anything until the morning."

"Is Daddy going to be alright Mommy?" asked Lily.

"I don't know sweetie. We'll know more in the morning. Right now the doctors said the best thing for all of us is to go home and come back in the morning. I'm going to stay here a while longer, but I want you to go on back home with Martha, have dinner and go to bed."

Paul cried, "But we want to stay!"

"I know you do, honey, but right now Daddy and I need you to go home. Please children, do this for Dad and me. We need you to be good right now."

They *all* nodded and the four of them left with Martha.

"I'll call you in a while, Martha. Thanks so much for all your help."

Sarah dabbed her eyes with a tissue. On the way out the door with Martha, the children waved to their mom.

Martha picked a pizza up on the way home. Once home, Paul, Lily and Katie ate; then quietly said good night.

Emily didn't eat. She couldn't.

The house was silent when Martha talked to Sarah. She then walked into the TV room to see Emily curled up in a tight ball in her father's Lazy Boy.

Martha walked over to Emily, put her hand on Emily's head and spoke. "Emily, your Mom won't be home until the morning. I'm going to run over to my house and get a few things. I'll spend the night here."

Emily barely raised her head to ask, "Is it alright if I wait up until you get back?"

"Yes, dear. Why don't you put the kettle on? I'll bring back a couple of Chamomile tea bags which will help us both sleep."

Martha wasn't gone more than fifteen minutes when she walked back into the house as the kettle began to whistle. Emily got up from the chair, walked out into the kitchen and turned off the burner. Then she reached up into a cabinet and pulled down two mugs.

"Honey, why don't you run up and put your pajamas on. I'll make the tea and when you come back down we'll talk."

Martha intuitively knew Emily needed to talk to someone she trusted right now.

As Emily walked upstairs Martha looked in on Bertie and shut her bedroom door. She then turned off all the lights in the downstairs except the ones in the kitchen and the TV room. When Emily came back down, Martha was standing in the kitchen.

"Let's go sit in the TV room, Emily where we can be comfortable."

Emily followed Martha and once again sat in the Lazy Boy. She curled up and laid her head against the back cushion. Martha placed the tray holding two cups of steaming Chamomile tea, cream and sweetener on the table beside the Lazy Boy and stood over the table.

She asked Emily if she wanted a little sweetener in her tea. Emily shook her head yes.

Then Martha asked, "Would you like a little cream Emily? I always like cream in my tea. It takes away the bite."

Emily again shook her head yes then began to cry. Martha stopped what she was doing, sat on the arm of the Lazy Boy and began stroking Emily's head. Emily just couldn't stop sobbing.

Then, in the kindest voice, Martha said, "Emily, its ok. I know you must be feeling very mixed up right now. Please don't be mad at Sean or at me, but I know what your dad used to do to you. I also know about the day you stabbed his hand with the pencil. Its ok, Emily, just cry as hard as you can. I'm here. I won't leave you."

Emily briefly stopped crying as she looked at Martha. She was stunned but deep inside she wasn't surprised. She was also now very relieved that she had a grownup she could let her heart pour out to. Looking pitiful, she leaned against the back cushion choking on her tears.

Then she raised her head and looked at Martha. "Can I sit on your lap?"

Martha whispered, "Of course, Emily."

Emily got up and Martha slid into the chair. Emily collapsed into Martha's arms and began crying hard as Martha caressed her head.

"I don't know what to think, Martha. I'm so confused. I just don't know. This is all my fault. I've wished so many times that he would die. He hasn't done anything to me for a long time. He's actually become a nice father, but I just can't forgive him. I can't stand to be around him and I feel just awful about that."

"I know, dear, I know," Martha held Emily close. "Emily, its ok. Whatever you're feeling is ok. You need to let yourself feel what you *need* to feel. There are no wrong feelings right now. There are only feelings you need to let come out. Let yourself feel what your mind knows you need to feel. But, Emily you need to understand this is not your fault. Your feelings for your dad are *his* fault. *He* did this to you and to himself. What he did to you for all those years was the most horrific thing a father could do to his child. He took away your safety and your trust. He made you feel unsafe in your own home. In the one place a child should feel absolutely safe in, you feared for your safety. What your dad did to you was not only horrendous physically but I can't even imagine the emotional trauma you've had to endure, hiding what he was doing, trying to make everyone in the world think that you had a loving father and a normal family life, and then trying to keep that painful secret from your mom. But Emily, you *have* to take care of *yourself*. You *have* to let yourself feel *everything*."

Then, Martha continued, "Look at me Emily. Look at me dear."

Emily lifted her head and looked into Martha's eyes.

"This is all on your father's soul. This is *not* on your soul. You have the purest heart and soul of any young woman I've ever known. I knew you were a very special person when Sean first talked about you; and then when I met you that following morning I could sense what a wonderful human being you were.

You are a truly remarkable individual, Emily, to have been able to endure all the unimaginable pain your father gave to you;

but, more importantly, to have grown up to be such a sweet, kind, loving individual.

That's the miracle here. *You are the miracle, Emily*! If your dad has any humanity in him he realizes what a loss he has caused himself. Look at you, such a precious human being he missed out on. Emily, whatever you feel for your dad, you need to understand this is *his* tragic loss. *You* are the jewel. Emily, you have created in yourself a tremendous gift to this world.

He tried to destroy you because of his own depravity. Yet, in all your purity of heart you rose above all his corruption to become the kind of person everyone would be blessed to know."

Martha paused for a few seconds then began again. "You know, Emily, I think when we die, especially if we have a death that we actually watch happen to ourselves, we must reflect on how we've lived that life. Unless your dad is a pure monster which I hope for his sake he isn't, I can only imagine the absolute regret he must feel for what he did to you and to himself. He has a wonderful family, but he has especially a truly magnificent daughter in you, Emily."

They sat for a few minutes in silence and then Martha asked, "Emily, do you think I'm a good person?"

Emily looked at her with a puzzled look and whispered. "Oh, yes. I think you're a wonderful person, Martha. I love you with all my heart."

Then Martha asked, "Do you think Sean is a good person, Emily?"

Emily looked less puzzled because she thought she knew why Martha was asking her these questions.

"Martha, from the moment I met Sean I've always known that he was one of the purest, most perfect human beings I would ever meet."

Then Martha smiled. "There, Emily. What does that tell you about yourself?"

Emily sobbed and hugged Martha tight. "That I'm a very good person?"

Martha stroked Emily's head as she answered, "Emily, you've always been a very perceptive, intelligent young woman. Now you should have the answer to all the questions that have been running through your mind today. Am I right?"

"Yes, Martha. Thank you so much for reminding me of who I am."

She and Martha sat in the chair for about a half hour just holding each other, when Emily raised her head and said, "I love you, Martha. Thank you for loving me."

Martha's heart melted and that emotion reflected on her face.

"My God, Emily, you sweet, sensitive, wonderful person, what's not to love."

Emily was getting very tired so Martha said, "Let's get you upstairs and into bed."

They walked upstairs and Martha tucked her in, leaned down and kissed her forehead.

"Sleep tonight, Emily. You deserve to just sleep. God loves you and I know in my heart that he is going to give you a wonderful rest of your life because you so deserve it. Go to sleep my little angel and let the heavens cradle you in its bosom."

She kissed Emily again and Emily fell asleep.

When Emily woke the following morning she felt better. Her talk with Martha comforted her. She couldn't recall her dream, but she felt sure that in her dream she was being forgiven for her feelings toward her dad. *Martha was right. This is not my fault. I wish with all my heart that things had been different. If only he had never done any of those things to me and loved me like he loves Lily and Katie, I'd feel so different. All I ever wanted from him was a good father I could love and trust.*

As she laid in bed, she thought about her dad and began crying, but she wasn't crying out of shame. She was crying because he took away her love for him so many years ago, and she knew there was no way for her to recapture the love she must have felt before he began hurting her. She cried for herself and all that he stole from her. She knew however that there wasn't anything she could do about that. She tried her best to be a good daughter, but it was never enough for him. *He did this to me and to himself.* She resolved that morning to hold onto that truth because it was the truth. *Martha was right. I've tried so hard to be a good person. I am a good person. He just never appreciated me for who I am.*

Chapter Twenty-Two

A few days later, the prognosis looked grim. Joe had four more heart attacks. He was in and out of consciousness. Finally, the doctors told Sarah she needed to prepare for his passing.

It was a Sunday morning when Sarah woke the children and told them to get dressed. They were going to the hospital to see their dad.

When they pulled into the parking lot of the hospital, Sarah turned off the ignition and turned around to face all four children. Her eyes welled up and tears began falling down her cheeks. The children knew that wasn't a good sign.

Then Sarah began, "Paul, Emily, Lily and Katie your dad needs you to be really strong right now. I need you to be strong right now."

There was a long pause, then, "Your dad is going to die. He's not going to make it which means he won't be coming home."

Paul, Lily and Katie began to wail as Emily leaned forward and gently touched Sarah's hand which was resting on the top portion of her seat. "It'll be alright Mom."

Sarah was momentarily puzzled by Emily's gesture but then as she put her free hand over Emily's she said, "I know it will be, sweetie."

Then Sarah looked at her other three children. "Please children. Be brave for Daddy. The doctors are doing all they can to keep him awake as long as possible so we can all say good-bye. Can you do that? Can you be very, very brave today?" sobbed Sarah.

"Yes, Mom," the three children said.

Sarah then turned back around to the front, took the key out of the ignition, gathered her purse and climbed out the door. She stood next to the car and motioned for the children to do the same.

Emily was seated next to Katie who she was cradling in her arms as she got out then helped Katie get out as well. Paul, Lily and Katie all looked like wounded birds who were trying very hard to be brave for their mom and dad as they all quietly whimpered.

Paul and Lily took Sarah's hand. Emily continued to hold Katie as they all walked.

Once they arrived at the door of Joe's room in ICU, Sarah asked them to sit down and be very, very quiet. "I'm going in to let your dad know we're here."

Shortly Sarah came out of the room and, beginning with Paul, sent the children in one by one to say good-bye.

While Paul was with his dad, Sarah sat across from Emily. She was perplexed by Emily's calm, adult like behavior. Emily sat very still and quiet as she stared at the floor. She tried hard not to let on that she was aware that Sarah was watching her.

What's wrong with her? Sarah asked herself. Emily continued to stare at the floor as she also wrung her hands. *I don't know if she's sad or worried about her last conversation with Joe.* Yet Sarah said nothing and asked no questions. Instead, she concentrated on comforting her other three children and herself. She was so overwhelmed with grief and fear about a future without her husband that, in her mind, she simply dismissed Emily's behavior. Instead, she rationalized that Emily was grieving in her own quiet way. *After all, Emily is a very private person. She rarely talks about her feelings or thoughts.*

Sarah's rationalization allowed her to ignore Emily's behavior. Instead she fell into a place where she intuited that Emily felt responsible for helping Sarah guide the other three children through this horribly painful ordeal.

Later when Emily emerged from Joe's room it was evident that Emily had been crying. Her face was stained with tears. Yet, Sarah noted in her subconscious that something was different about Emily. To Sarah, Emily looked ten years older. In addition Sarah noted that there was something almost angelic about Emily's appearance as she exited Joe's room. But Sarah didn't have time to stop and dwell on Emily. Instead she turned her attention to her two youngest children who were overcome with grief.

Joe died the following day. After all the children said goodbye to their dad, Sarah took the children home. Martha was already at the house with Bertie. She would spend the night with

Bertie and the children so Sarah could return to the hospital.

He died on a Monday. The funeral was held the following Thursday. Sarah briefly discussed Emily's behavior with Martha but Martha didn't say a word about her conversation the night Joe was taken to the hospital. She was committed to protecting Emily's trust. *In time, if Sarah is meant to find out the truth about Emily and what her husband was doing to her, then it will have been meant to happen. For now I must maintain a neutral position for both their sakes.* Martha then did all she could to emotionally comfort Sarah. She was after all a close friend. Martha was committed to both Emily and Sarah as she attended to their separate needs.

Beth, Bill and Sean attended the funeral. After the funeral many of the attendees returned to Martha's home for a buffet lunch. At one point Sean looked for Emily but couldn't find her anywhere. He was worried about her. Then, he looked out the back window and saw her sitting on the slant tree so he went out.

Emily jumped from fright when she caught a glimpse of someone walking up the tree to her. When she realized it was Sean she extended her hand to him. He took her hand and sat down next to her.

"Thank you for finding me Sean. I had to come sit here. I needed to feel safe. I was hoping you would come out and sit with me. You and the tree make me feel safe and loved. I need to know I'm loved right now."

"Oh, Em, I love you more than you will ever know. I got worried when I couldn't find you. Then, I just knew you would be up here. He paused, then asked, "Em, are you ok?

"Well…yes and no."

Before she could say anything else he said, "Grandma told me about the talk you two had. I hope you listened to Grandma. She loves you so much, Emily, but she's worried about you. I am too."

She began to cry. "I had to tell him that I didn't love him."

She sounded so wounded that Sean put his arm around her and pulled her close to him. His heart was breaking for her.

"I told him that I don't know if I will ever be able to forgive him or ever feel love for him. Oh, Sean, I just wish with all my heart I could feel the same love you have for your dad, but I just can't." There was a long pause then, as she wiped her tears with the bottom portion of her dress she said, "You know he told me that he had been molested by three grown men when he was just a little boy. I felt sad for him, but I told him that it wasn't an excuse for what he did to me. I told him he hurt me like no one in the world could ever hurt me. I know my mom is wondering what's going on with me. I know she was watching me when we were at the hospital before it was my turn to go talk to him. It makes me so sad that I can't tell her. I can never, ever tell her. It would break her heart."

"Em, don't you think she might already know?"

"NO!" Then Emily looked off into the distance and quietly said, "I don't know, Sean. Maybe she does know. I've always wondered why she never came looking for Dad. But Mom hasn't had a very easy life with Dad either. He treated her so badly. I also know she always felt sad and hurt by him. He never tried to make her feel good about herself or anything. He was a selfish man, Sean. He only ever thought about himself and that's what I had to tell him and how his selfishness makes me feel. He cried a lot when I talked to him and I think he finally felt sorry for what he did; but, I also think he was feeling sorrier for himself than for me. Like I said, he was a very selfish man. You were so lucky to have the dad you had, Sean. I would have given anything to have a dad like yours."

She began crying again as she laid her head on his shoulder. They said nothing more. They just sat quietly for the next half hour. He knew she needed to feel what she needed to feel so he did what he could to comfort her and she loved him for that.

Chapter Twenty-Three

An entire year passed.

Emily sat at her study desk preparing for her senior final history exam. She was reviewing the Vietnam War era which reminded her of her dad.

She remembered the stories he used to tell her and her three siblings regarding some of the rescue missions he flew during the last two years of that war.

Then her thoughts drifted back to the private conversation she had with her father the day prior to his death; the last day he was alert and lucid.

She approached that memory with a surge of emotions.

Emily was still unable to reconcile all her feelings and wasn't quite sure she ever would. She didn't even know, she thought if resolution was important or if it was even possible.

Life is so complex, a young yet spiritually old Emily reflected.

She thought about the pain she heard in his voice when he told her about the three separate individuals, an uncle, a trusted friend of her grandfather and an older priest who had molested him when he was just a boy. She was sure she was the first and only person he told that secret to and it pained her because she knew his pain. Then she remembered what she said to her dad.

"I'm really sorry that happened to you, Dad. But, Dad, you're a grown man and you had a choice to make when you decided to do to me what was done to you. You had a choice, Dad. You could have chosen to simply love me as a good father loves his precious daughter; and, Dad, if that had been your choice I swear to you, I would have loved and worshiped you with all my heart and soul. But instead, you chose to hurt me. You chose to steal from me the one thing that was mine and mine alone. You stole my childhood, Dad. You stole my innocence. You hurt me like no one in the world could ever do. You took away my trust. You made me feel unsafe in the one and only place a child should feel safe in. I was never safe in my own home because you took that safety away from me. You build a prison around me Dad. You made me live in hell every day of my life, and because of that you are going to have to suffer. There are consequences for the choice you made and the things you did to me knowing all the while you were destroying me. You were trying to destroy me; but I promise you, Dad, you will never, ever destroy me. If I have to live the rest of my life undoing the damage you chose to do to me, I will, because I am going to be happy, Daddy. I am determined that I will be happy because I have chosen to be a good person. I have chosen to never, ever do to anyone else what was done to me. When I am on my death bed, I will be able to look back over my life and be proud of who I became. Something you chose to take from your own self.

I don't know what happens to us when we die, Daddy. I don't know if there's really a heaven or hell. I've been reading a lot about reincarnation, so I don't know if you are going to have to come back to make up for what you've done.

All I know, Dad, is that this is yours. It's not mine. I can't forgive you; and I don't know if I will ever even want to forgive you or if it even matters. There's still a part of me that loves you, Daddy; but it's not a love that was built on trust or something you earned. You earned only my distrust and indifference; so, I guess I love you only because you are my dad; and, I wish I could have helped to take away the pain you suffered when you were just a kid. But I can't because you chose to give that pain away by giving it to me."

Then she paused and finally asked him as her voice cracked. "Now I have to ask you a very important question; and, I need you to be honest with me…and, Dad, honest with yourself. I need to know if there is anyone else that you've hurt over the years."

Joe was most awake for Emily's discussion and was crying as Emily handed him the box of Kleenex that was sitting on the stand next to his bed. She offered the box but not her sorrow for having to ask such a poignant question.

She *had to know*.

In the back of her mind, she had to know so that one day she could reach out to those children in order to help them with the pain her dad gave them as well.

She sat in her chair next to her father's death bed. He wiped his eyes but he didn't lift his head. He couldn't even look at her as he choked on his own tears and shook his head yes.

Emily recalled that she had hoped with all her heart the answer was no; but when she watched his head move up and down instead of back and forth, her heart cracked into smaller pieces than it already was. Deafening silence filled the room.

Still with his head bowed he began ripping at the wet Kleenex when Emily finally asked. "Who Daddy?"

"I can't," sobbed Joe.

"Yes you can, Dad," she insisted. "This is your chance to cleanse your soul. This could help you on your next journey. I want to help you, Daddy. I really do."

Still avoiding her gaze, he whispered two names. One was a young girl who lived next to them when they lived in Pensacola. The other Emily had to think about.

It was a boy but she couldn't quite picture him when she asked, "How did you know Peter McLain?"

Between his two fingers, Joe was twisting the blanket that covered him as he whispered, "He was one of the kids I coached when I coached the little league team. I'm so, so sorry, Emily." Then he sobbed and whispered, "I'm so, so sorry. God forgive me. I'm so sorry for the way I've lived my life."

At that moment Emily suspected her dad was really and truly sorry; probably for the first time in his life.

Then Joe raised his head, but still didn't raise his eyes. Emily could see his face was stained with tears as he asked, "Emily do you ever think you'll forgive me?"

At that moment, Emily felt the burden of having been asked to forgive him not only for what he did to her but for what he did to the other children.

She choked back her own tears and answered. "Daddy, I want to. With all my heart I want to; but, I honestly can't say I will. I just don't know that answer. I guess it will take a long time for me to be able to work through all of this. But, I think right now what you need more than anything is to forgive yourself. You're dying, Daddy. You probably won't live too much longer. You need to try and forgive yourself. It's the only way I think that you can have a little peace. I think it could help me too," she said as she began crying torrentially.

"Ohhh, Emily, please don't cry. God, I wish like hell you wouldn't cry. I wish to God I had given you the father you so deserved to have. But, I didn't and I know I will have to carry that with me now." Joe spoke with absolute resignation.

He then, for the first and last time, looked Emily in the eyes, blinked several times and asked if he could touch her hand which was lying on the bed next to him.

She cringed. She felt as if she wanted to pull her hand away, far away; but she mustered all the courage she could possibly gather and gave him permission by simply nodding her head.

Joe put his hand on her delicate hand and said, "Thank you, Emily. Thank you for being you. I only wish I wasn't so selfish because I now know how much I missed; and," he sobbed, "I never will get that chance to…"

Emily slid her hand out from under his, stood and said, "I know, Dad, I know. Now, I've got to go. Lily and Katie want to come talk to you too. Bye, Daddy," she whispered as she kissed the top of his head.

Then their eyes met and he mouthed, "I love you."

Yet all she could offer in return was a look that said, "This is the best I can do."

Then, trying hard to compose herself, she turned and left the room knowing her mom was sitting just outside.

Chapter Twenty-Four

It was the beginning of summer as the now 17 year old Emily mentally prepared herself for her entrance into adulthood.

During the course of her senior year she managed to score in the upper 10% on her SATs. She applied for and was accepted to Brown University where she would earn a bachelor's degree in environmental science. She planned to go on for her masters then her doctorate.

She was extremely excited as she stood at the dawn of the rest of her life.

This is where life truly begins, she thought.

It was a summer of great seriousness as well as giddiness as she bid farewell to her childhood. Emily who loved the dramatic considered herself somewhat of a poet without rhyme. As she visualized her future she wrote in her diary:

My Dearest Diary, as I arrive at the summit breathlessly filled with anticipation I look forward and see progress. I take those first few steps only to pause and turn 180 degrees.

I look backward toward the familiar and recognize that too was progress.

I stand frozen in time wondering whether to continue into the unknown or turn back in order to bathe in the progress of my past.

What's my hurry?

But then, in my mind I glimpse the dim light as the sun rises on that yet to be discovered future and I make my decision.

I will go forward with the knowledge and heart of my past. I trust my past to guide me forward, not cautiously, but respectfully.

I open my heart to my forward journey with all the heart and soul of the past which makes me realize that the most important lesson to take from all of this is to live in the here and now; to enjoy all I am surrounded by and savor my existence with all that is here in the present.

As she closed her diary, she tip toed over to her dresser, moved the dresser away from the wall, opened the door to the attic, slipped inside, turned on the light and walked to the end of the attic floor as she bent slightly to avoid banging her head on the slanted ceiling. When she arrived at the end, she shoved the diary into its tiny hole and covered it with the pink fiberglass insulation for safe keeping.

She then walked out into her room, closed the door and pushed her dresser back against the wall. She leaned up against the adjacent wall, slid down the wall and sat on the floor and thought about the years she had lived in this house and everything that had happened; the good, the bad and the ugly. Then she thought about the last conversation she and Sean had over a week ago.

He was scheduled to leave for Berkley, California in just a few short months. They would be separated by thousands of miles for more than four years with only occasional visits during holidays and vacations. They had had a wonderful infatuation for over seven years, but, she asked herself *are my feelings for Sean much more than just infatuation? I think they are, but I need to know before he leaves.*

They had discussed whether or not they should experiment with sex before the summer's end. They were both terrified but desperate to discover how deep their feelings went. Was it only infatuation or was it genuine love; the kind between a man and a woman.

Neither of them knew what to do.

They had both attended Catholic schools their entire lives and sex was not a topic talked about except in the framework of sin. Neither of them knew how to go about gaining access to birth control.

Emily's mother had never really talked to her about sex except in the context of marriage and she always used books written by clergy to explain anything of that nature.

Bill attempted to talk to Sean, but not being his biological father, the conversations were at best brief and awkward.

She and Jeannie broached the subject a few times but each time were interrupted by one of Emily's siblings or a parent.

Emily stood back up, put on her nightgown and crawled into

bed. It was only 8 p.m. Paul, Lily and Katie were downstairs watching TV. She craved quiet right now. She wanted to think about what she should do next.

The next morning she got up, dressed, grabbed a quick bowl of cereal and called Jeannie.

"Jeannie, can you meet me at the slant tree in a half hour?"

Jeannie was curious to know what was so urgent, but she didn't ask. She and Emily had become best of friends over the last seven years and she realized that a friend when needed should be just that...a friend.

About forty five minutes later, Jeannie walked through Martha's yard and saw that Emily was already sitting half way up the tree waiting. She walked over to the base of the tree, climbed up and walked up to where Emily was seated.

As she sat Jeannie asked, "What's so urgent?"

Emily hem hawed around for a few minutes and then stopped, sat quiet then turned to Jeannie and asked, "Have you and Phillip had sex yet?"

Jeannie looked surprised then shook her head yes.

"How are you keeping from getting pregnant?"

Jeannie looked at her with a perplexed expression then finally said with a chuckle, "Oh...wait a minute. You're Catholic. No one talks about birth control to you Catholic girls do they?"

Emily shook her head no.

"Yea, yea, they all think girls should be virgins forever until they get married. What was it your mom once said to you? Oh, yea, the only birth control a Catholic woman can use is the pill she holds between her legs."

She giggled then said, "Geez, Emily, all you have to do is go down to the Planned Parenthood facility and get set up on birth control pills!"

"Planned Parenthood?" Emily looked lost.

"Look, let's go back home, tell our moms we're going to the movies downtown but instead we'll go to the Planned Parenthood facility. We'll then grab one of the movie magazines from a store, find out what movies are in town and read all about them then pick a movie so we can come home and answer any questions our moms might ask us."

"Don't I have to have my mom with me?" asked Emily.

"Heck no! You go in, talk to a nurse and tell her you don't want to get pregnant. Then you see the doctor who examines you and they give you the pills. Then you get a prescription for additional pills. You can begin taking them immediately. But you need to wait about seven days for the pills to take effect and *then* you and Sean can start having sex till the cows come home!" Jeannie finished with a whack on Emily's back followed by a hearty laugh.

Emily looked at her. "That's it?"

"That's it. I promise. Now let's get going."

Emily felt like the weight of the world had been lifted from her shoulders. She never knew becoming an adult could be so simple.

She and Jeannie climbed down from the tree and shook hands as if to say it's a deal!

They began running toward the street when Martha stuck her head out the door. "Hey girls, wanna come in and have a cup of coffee with me?"

Jeannie simply shook her head no, but Emily stopped. She couldn't just brush Martha off so carelessly.

Jeannie said "Ok. Just go give her any lame excuse you can think of and don't take too long. I'll meet you at the top of the hill in *no more* than 45 minutes. See ya!" She waved as she continued running backward toward the street.

Jeannie felt like the big sister she's never had. "This is going to be so much fun!" She giggled to herself.

Emily walked over to Martha. "Good morning, Martha. Gosh, it's going to be a wonderful day isn't it."

Martha looked up at the bright blue sky. "Yes, I think it is dear. Come on in!"

"Gosh…I'm sorry, Martha, but I can't. Jeannie and I have big plans for today. We're going to take the bus into Providence and go see a movie and maybe walk around to all the department stores."

"Well, that sounds a heck of a lot more fun than hanging around with an old lady. You go on and have fun; but don't forget Sean comes down for the summer in two days. Now go on. It looked like Jeannie was in a big hurry."

"Ok, Martha thanks for understanding. Love you. See you

157

later," Emily called as she ran toward the street waving backward.

Approximately fifty minutes later, Emily walked to the top of the hill. Jeannie was already there at the edge of the Lombardi's yard pacing back and forth. As Emily approached, Jeannie turned around, put her hands on her hips, gave a big where have you been look, then produced a huge smile and a stem full of tiny blue flowers she handed Emily. She had snuck over to the hydrangea bushes that lined the Lombardi's driveway and picked it for Emily. She knew Emily loved the hydrangea bushes.

Emily took the stem and then the two girls held hands as they began skipping down the now level street toward the bus stop. They felt like little girls again.

As they passed old Mrs. McGillicutty's big, yellow Victorian house to the right and slightly hidden by tall bushes, Jeannie exclaimed, "I still think she's a real witch and that house is haunted!"

"Me too. She's a spooky lady." Emily shivered as if frightened.

They giggled and continued walking the rest of the way.

Once at the bus stop Jeannie pulled a round plastic looking thing out of her jeans pocket.

"What's that?" asked Emily.

"Silly," responded Jeannie. "It's my box of birth control pills. This is what the whole thing looks like; small and compact and easy to hide from everyone. See this?"

She showed Emily the small hole in the top side of the plastic. Jeannie deposited the small yellow pill into the palm of her hand, opened her mouth and popped it in. She made the funniest face as she tried to produce enough saliva to swallow the pill without it getting stuck in her throat.

Then she made a huge gesture with her hand and said, "Violas, now I can't get pregnant!"

"Let me see," an excited Emily demanded.

Jeannie placed the plastic in Emily's hand. "This is how it works. The clear plastic top turns around. There's one pill for every day. You take all these yellow pills, then while you have your friend you take these white pills."

"My what? My friend?"

"Geez, Louise, don't you know anything Emily? What have I been trying to teach you all these years? Your friend, your period for Pete's sake!"

Jeannie laughed as she shook her head and rolled her eyes at her friend.

"Ohhh, that friend!" Emily laughed. Then she banged her forehead with her right palm and said, "What was I thinking?"

"I don't have the slightest idea. Geez, you're way too serious sometimes, Em."

"Yea, I know. My mom's always telling me the same thing. So, continue explaining. Why are all these pills yellow and these white?"

"Ok, the yellow ones are the real pills; and the white ones are fake pills. They're called Plocebites, or something stupid like that."

"You mean placebos?"

"Yea, yea, that's what the nurse called them. How do I know, Plocebites, placebos, you're the brainy one here. Anyway, there's a pill for every day. The biggest thing to remember is to make sure you take one *every* day. You can't miss one single day!" Jeannie frowned.

Always so inquisitive Emily asked, "What if I miss a day? Then what?"

Jeannie rolled her eyes and sarcastically said, "What if, what if...how the heck do I know. Who do you think I am...Einstein? Just make sure you take a pill every day and everything will be fine. Have you told Sean yet? I'll bet he's peeing in his pants with excitement."

"Jeannie!" exclaimed Emily. "Don't be so crude! This is serious. I want to REALLY get to know Sean and find out what my feelings are all about."

"Yea, yea...serious, smerious. Here comes the bus. Get ready for some serious finding out and sex is the cherry on top! Uh...that is after your cherry drops out," Jeannie began laughing so hard she was buckled over.

Emily couldn't help herself, she was also laughing so hard she nearly tripped off the curb. The bus driver laid on the horn and Jeannie grabbed Emily's arm and pulled her back away from the curb.

The door to the bus opened and the driver barked, "Well…are you getting on or off? Make up your mind. I have a schedule to keep ladies!" Then he smiled and waved. "Come on."

The two climbed the three steps up, deposited their eight quarters each as the driver said, "Seriously, you two need to be more careful. It looked like you were having a lot of fun, but that would have ended badly if I hit you." Then he looked at them and with his hands gestured and exclaimed, "Splat!"

The girls jumped back and he began laughing so hard his belly bounced up and down against the horizontal steering wheel.

The girls laughed too as they walked toward the very back of the bus to sit. There were only two other people on the bus.

As the door closed with a thud, Jeannie giggled. "Did you see how his jelly belly wiggled when he laughed?"

"Yea," giggled Emily, "Just like a big bowl of jello!"

They both laughed so hard.

Then Jeannie said, "Ok, ok, stop. I'm gonna pee my pants before we even get to a place I can pee."

"Ok," Emily put her hand up to her mouth as if she was wiping the smile from her face, then gestured she was throwing the wet laugh out into the air and they both held their sides, buckled over and laughed all over again.

The woman sitting two seats in front of them turned around and glared at them then turned back forward.

Jeannie poked Emily's side. "Oooo, I think she's mad at us. What do ya think, Em?"

They both couldn't help themselves; they laughed again and again all the way into town.

****

They arrived at the front door of Planned Parenthood.

Emily paused, then took a huge gulp. "I'm kinda scared, Jeannie."

"Nothing to be scared about; besides I'm here. I'll be with you the whole time. I'll pretend we're sisters and I'm just showing you the ropes."

"Ok." She grabbed Jeannie's hand and held it tight as they walked through the door.

160

Once inside, Jeannie spotted Nurse Julie and waved.

Julie waved back and smiled. "Well, hi, Jeannie. It's nice to see you again. How've you been doing?"

"I'm well, Julie! I just got out of school. I graduated this year and am going to URI next September."

"Well, congratulations! What will you study?"

"I'm pretty sure I want to teach high school; but, I don't know. I'll just play it by ear. Julie, this is my best friend, Emily. She also just graduated. Emily *really* needs to get set up on the pill. She and her childhood boyfriend are on the verge of doing it for the first time. We can't let Emily get pregnant because she's going to Brown next year to become a scientist; and we need to make sure Emily does that because I'm convinced Emily is going to save the world one day!" said Jeannie as she winked at Emily.

"Well, that's quite an introduction. Nice to meet you Emily," exclaimed Nurse Julie as she smiled from ear to ear. "Let's go down here to the examining room and we'll get you all set up. I'll just need to ask you some important questions and fill out a little paperwork."

Emily looked apprehensive. "Is my mom going to find out? Can Jeannie please come with us? I've never done anything like this before and I'm…well… I'm scared."

"No to your mom, yes to Jeannie and there's nothing to be scared about. This is all very routine. But we want to get you on the pill right away because we, Jeannie and I, want to make sure you are out there in the world one day saving us all," Julie said as she patted Emily's hand.

She led them down the hall as Emily grabbed Jeannie's hand and pulled her along.

Julie showed Emily a skimpy green gown, instructed her to remove all her clothes, put the gown on frontward and then sit up on the table covered with a paper sheet.

As Jeannie sat in the chair close to the door, Julie excused herself. "I'll be back in a few minutes to ask you some health questions."

The door closed and Emily looked at Jeannie as if to say, what the heck am I doing here? Then she said, "What's going to happen? Why do I have to take all my clothes off? Why do I have to put this gown on so my private parts are all exposed?"

Jeannie became serious and tried her best to get Emily to calm down and relax. "Emily, it's going to be ok. I promise! The doctor's going to just check you out to make sure everything is normal. You need to get used to this. Now that we're both adults we will have to get routine checkups like this every year. You want to do this right don't you?"

"Yea, ok; but will you hold my hand when the doctor comes in, please Jeannie?"

"Of course I will, Em. Have I ever let you down? Now start undressing," counseled Jeannie sounding like a real big sister.

She helped Emily put on the ugly green gown, patted the examining table as the white paper made a crunching sound. Emily hopped up on the table, wiggled a little and then pulled the two edges of the green gown as closed together as she could.

Just as she was settled and clutching for dear life the two edges of her grown, Nurse Julie returned. She had a stethoscope around her neck and a clipboard in one hand and a pen in her other hand.

"Ok," said Julie. "I know those stupid green gowns are uncomfortable, but Dr. Harris is a female doctor so you don't have to worry that a man is going to see your body."

Emily took a deep breath as her ridged body melted in relief.

Julie pulled up a rolling stool, sat on it put the pen to the paper and began her questions as she filled out every blank on the paper and checked some of all the boxes. When the three page questionnaire was all filled out and Emily signed and dated it at the bottom, Julie put it aside.

She then walked over to a chart that diagramed the reproductive parts of the male and female body and began explaining to Emily what the pills did, how the reproductive system worked and what she should expect.

Before Julie began, Jeannie said, "Julie, Emily is Catholic, so please take your time to explain everything."

Julie nodded indicating she understood exactly what Jeannie was suggesting and began. Emily listened intently, asked questions, and acknowledged when she understood.

Just as Julie finished the quick but concise education there was a shallow tap on the door and a tall, slender dark haired woman with stylish spectacles walked in and Julie left.

Dr. Harris said in a gentle voice, "So, you're Emily. Well, Emily I'm Dr. Margaret Harris. Julie and I are going to take very good care of you today. We'll be as gentle as we can, so just relax. Ok, sweetie?"

"Yes, Dr. Harris," Emily said as she extended her hand and wiggled it for Jeannie to come hold her hand.

"Is it alright if I move my chair over to that side and hold Emily's hand, Dr. Harris?

"Yes, it is. I'll let you know if I need to have you move. Ok, let's get started."

Dr. Harris' touch was soft and motherly as she delicately slid the green gown aside and listened to Emily's heart. She took two blood pressure readings then asked Emily to scoot back on the table and lie down. Emily followed orders but then became alarmed again when she heard the clanging of metal as Dr. Harris extended the table and pulled the stirrups out of their sockets.

She asked Emily to scoot down on the table and put each of her bare feet into the two stirrups. She then pulled open Emily's gown and covered her lower half with a sheet.

Next she walked to the top side of the table and said, "Emily, I need you to lift both your arms and place them over your head. I'm going to feel your breasts for lumps."

Emily did as she was told but got a terrified look on her face.

"Don't worry dear. You're a healthy young woman. There's nothing to worry about. This is just a precaution." Dr. Harris said.

Emily again breathed a deep breath and her body began to melt as the paper sheet crunched under her.

Then Dr. Harris said, "Ok, dear, this may be a little scary, but I promise you I've done this a million times. I'm going to inspect your vaginal area. I'll put my fingers inside your vagina."

Next she held up the speculum and said, "Then I'll lubricate this speculum and insert it into your vagina. You may feel a slight pinch but I'll be as gentle as can be. I need to see way up inside you. Then I'll take this cotton swab and take a sample from the tip of your uterus. You'll feel a little pressure, and then we'll be done. Ok?"

"Yes," said Emily and squeezed Jeannie's hand she was again holding.

Jeannie smiled and assured her friend. "It's nothing, Em. Just look at me and it'll be over in a jiff."

It was.

Dr. Harris who had been sitting on the stool peeked over the top of the sheet that was draped over Emily's knees and said, "That wasn't too bad was it, Emily?"

"No," said Emily with a slight quiver in her voice.

Dr. Harris stood up, removed her gloves, reached for Emily's hand and helped her to a sitting position. "Ok, again, it was a pleasure meeting you, Emily. I hope you have a very nice day and a wonderful life. I hear you're going to save the world one day."

Emily blushed and said, "Awe, that's just Jeannie. She just always talks like my best friend. I'm just going to study the environment."

"Well, Emily, you better hold onto your best friend because I think she loves you a whole lot." Dr. Harris shook Jeannie's then Emily's hand, said good-bye and left the room.

As Dr. Harris left the room, Nurse Julie came back in, picked up the slide with the sample of Emily's tissue and said, "Ok, Emily, you can get dressed again. I'll be back in a few minutes with your first month's supply of pills and a prescription you can take to any drug store to get it filled. Just make sure you take it to a drugstore that has a branch near the campus."

Julie left the room and the girls were alone. Emily took a deep breath and let it out with a huff.

"See, it wasn't so bad... right kiddo?" smiled Jeannie.

"No," answered Emily. "But, I don't know what I would have done if the doctor was a man. I was so relieved when Julie said Dr. Harris was a girl doctor."

As she got dressed she said, "Let's get out of here as quick as we can. I need to sit down somewhere where I can breathe. I have a huge headache now."

She was tying her tennis shoes when Julie came back in the room.

"Ok, Emily, here's your first months' worth of pills. You mentioned that your period ended a few days ago...correct?"

Emily nodded.

"Perfect!" Then Julie said, "Start taking these tomorrow. Here also is your prescription. It's really been a huge pleasure meeting you. You have a really good friend here in Jeannie," said Julie as she extended her hand to shake Emily's.

Jeannie piped in, "Julie, do you have a couple of aspirins. Emily has a big headache."

"Sure. Just ask Pricilla at the front desk. I'll let her know to give Emily a couple of Tylenol."

"Thanks, Julie," responded both Jeannie and Emily in unison.

They *finally* left the clinic and walked the five blocks to the Woolworths store. They bought a couple of trash magazines for the movie reviews and a newspaper to figure out what was currently playing, then walked over to the lunch counter area and slid into one side of a booth covered in red vinyl.

They looked at a menu and ordered. As they were sitting there Jeannie asked if Emily was happy they did what they did?

Emily nodded. "Yes. But it was totally scary. I can't wait to tell Sean so we can plan our first time. I'm very excited but a little scared, but more excited than scared. I get such a tingly feeling whenever Sean touches me. I can't wait to just let myself go."

"That's my girl," exclaimed Jeannie. "But I gotta tell ya, I almost busted a gut when Nurse Julie began describing how you can get pregnant. When she said, as the penis is inserted into the vaginal cavity, I thought you were going to disappear into the table. The look on your face was hilarious. You looked mortified. I wish I had a camera so you could see just how funny you looked. I thought your eyes were going to pop out of their sockets and you were going to get lock jaw from opening your mouth too wide. I could see Nurse Julie get a little smile on her face. I think she almost busted a gut too but she was trying really hard not to embarrass you. She looked relieved as hell when the doctor walked in. Did you notice how fast Julie disappeared?"

Emily frowned. "Yea, but it wasn't that funny, was it?"

"Are you kidding? You looked like a deer in the headlights!" Jeannie was laughing.

"Ok, ok, I guess you're right; but this was all way too new for me. I admit. I did want to jump off the table and crawl under it!"

Emily cracked a smile then laughed as loud as Jeannie was laughing. "I guess it was funny."

"Funny! It was a hoot and a half, Emily; but it was sweet too. I have to admit. I was really proud to be your girlfriend today."

Then Jeannie exclaimed, "Listen, Em, after the first time you and Sean do it, you and I need to go somewhere so I can show you some pictures from a magazine Phillip gave me to look at. There are some really mind blowing pictures of couples having sex! It'll give you some ideas on how to give Sean some pleasure and how he can do the same for you, but we're getting ahead of ourselves right now. You have to do it first."

Emily got really serious again, and whispered, "Jeannie, does it hurt the first time. You know when the cherry is broken?"

Jeannie looked at Emily and said, "It hurts a little bit and there's a little blood but if Sean is as gentle as Phillip was for me, it won't hurt a lot. It is a little scary, but after that, sex is great; and, I'm not kidding!"

She stopped talking as the waitress brought their food; two cheeseburgers, French fries, one strawberry milkshake for Jeannie and a coffee ice-cream cabinet for Emily.

As Emily took the first big gulp of her drink she said, "You know, when we first moved here and Dad told us he was taking us to Friendly's Ice-cream for coffee cabinets, I thought he was outta his mind. I thought they were going to bring each of us a wooden cabinet. I didn't know what to think. But, when I realized it was just a milkshake made with coffee ice cream and tasted it I thought I died and went to heaven. This is my favorite drink in the entire world. You didn't get one. Don't you like them?"

Jeannie looked at Emily and wrinkled her nose. "Yea, they're ok. I just don't like coffee ice cream as much as strawberry or chocolate even. But I can imagine what you were thinkin. Your dad didn't tell you it was a milk shake?"

"No. He just kept repeating himself about the cabinet. You can't get coffee ice cream in Texas or even Florida. One time, Mom took us to get cabinets and little Katie piped up, "Mom, I don't want a coffee cabinet. I want a tea one. It was so cute we all couldn't help laughing."

The girls ate, then shoved the empty dishes and utensils to the other side of the table.

"Ok," said Jeannie, "Let's see what's playing right now and the times. We need to get our stories straight."

They had the movie schedule page opened up, as they began scouring the magazines.

"Ok, I think I've got it," Jeannie said with conviction. "Let's tell them we went to see A WALK TO REMEMBER with dreamy Shane West. Let's see, it's 2 p.m. now. Ok. There was a show at 12:15. Here, I'll read the plot and review. It's also got Mandy Moore in it. She's really pretty."

They both put their heads together and Jeannie started reading from the trash magazine. Once they believed they had all the needed details memorized, they left Woolworths.

As they were walking out the door, Emily said, "Oh, I want to buy some gum. You've been so generous paying for lunch, now it's my treat. Do you want anything like a candy bar for later, Jeannie?"

"No, I'm good. I'll just have a piece of what you get."

Then, as Emily pulled her wallet out of her purse, Jeannie burst with laughter.

She took Emily's wallet. "Good grief, Emily, you need to get a new wallet. This is a kid's wallet."

"Yea, I know, I've had it since I was about 8. It is kinda lame. Maybe I'll ask for one for Christmas," said Emily turning bright red.

"Well, I think you better get one before then. I wouldn't recommend pulling that thing out of your purse when you get to Brown. You'll be laughed off the campus!"

"Yea, you're right. Let's stop at Macy's before we catch the bus. I'll get one which has your stamp of approval. Ok?"

Jeannie approvingly smacked Emily on the back. "Okie-dokie-artichokie!"

They stopped by Macy's and picked up a wallet, then Jeannie grabbed Emily's arm and asked, "How much money do you have on you?"

"Oh, I don't know. Probably about $20, maybe $30. Why?"

"Because, across the street is Victoria's Secret. We ought to go over and pick out a sexy pair of underwear and bra. You don't want Sean to see a pair of tighty whitey cotton underwear and a boring white bra, do you?" asked Jeannie.

"No. I guess not. Plus, it would be nice to have something pretty on under my jeans when I take them off," responded Emily turning redder by the minute.

They picked out a pair of flame red, lace top bikini panties and a very sexy lace trimmed red bra. Jeannie went with Emily to the dressing room so Emily could try on the bra.

Emily put it on and turned around as Jeannie exclaimed, "Sean's gonna cream his pants when he sees that. You look mavalous Emily; just mavalous!"

On the ride home they recounted some of the other funny things Nurse Julie said about having sex. There were several more people on the bus ride home so they whispered and tried not to laugh too loudly.

Walking down the street, Emily stopped dead in her tracks. "Oh my God. How do I sneak in my Victoria Secret bag without my mom figuring out what's going on?"

"Here, let me see it!"

Jeannie spoke with confidence as she took the bag, removed the bra and panties and gave the bag back to Emily with verbal instructions.

"Hide it deep in the trash can in a cereal box or something."

Then Jeannie asked for Emily's purse, walked over to the side of the road, took everything out of the purse and laid it on the ground, folded the panties and bra into the most compact fold possible, put them into the bottom of Emily's purse and piled all the junk back in the purse.

"That's how. Just make sure you take your purse upstairs before you go talk to your mom. And be sure to hide it from your two snoopy sisters, especially Lily. She's a little busy body. If she finds it your goose will be cooked!"

Later that early evening, Emily and Jeannie sat on the rocks talking about their day.

Jeannie asked, "Did your mom ask about the movie? Mine grilled me. I'm just glad we got our facts down pat."

Emily answered with a note of disappointment.

"No. She didn't ask about anything. Ever since Dad died, half the time she walks around in a daze. I don't know if she'll ever stop moping. I feel really bad for her though. Mom just doesn't know what a strong person she really is. Whenever Dad was gone, she just seemed to physically grow several inches. She was the in charge lady; but when Dad would come home she'd shrink back and act like a lost kitten. I'm worried about her when I leave for school. Sure, I'll be home on the weekends, but during the week she'll be all by herself in that house with Grandma who's on a permanent vacation and the two girls who are always fighting."

Then Jeannie asked, "Is Paul home from boot camp yet?"

"Yea, he came home yesterday. But he leaves again in two weeks. I think Mom said he'll be headed to the naval base in Norfolk then he'll be stationed on the Enterprise; you know like in Star Trek but this one floats? It doesn't fly."

"I know what the USS Enterprise is you knucklehead. I'm not that out of touch with current events," Jeannie sarcastically responded.

"I know, Jeannie, that wasn't very nice of me. I'm just worried about my Mom. That's all."

"I know, I know. So when are you going to tell Sean?"

Now with animation in her voice, Emily responded, "He'll be here the day after tomorrow. I've gotta be careful and get him alone so no adult can hear us. Oooo...I'm kind of getting excited just thinking about it."

Chapter Twenty-Five

The morning Sean was scheduled to arrive Emily woke up full of excitement and anticipation.

She rubbed her eyes, got up and looked out her front window. She rubbed her eyes again as she stared at Martha's driveway. There was a brand new, hot red Mustang sitting in the driveway.

"Oh my God," she said out loud. "I hope that's Sean's car. Holy shit!"

Just then Lily walked into the room. "Oooo, I'm gonna tell Mom you said shit!"

"Oh shut up and come here and look!" exclaimed Emily.

Lily came over and stood at the window. "Yea…what? I don't see anything!"

Then Emily pointed to Martha's driveway. "I think that's Sean's brand new car. He said he was getting a new car for graduation and going away present; but I had no idea he was getting a new, new car let alone a hot Mustang!"

"Wow, do ya think he'll give me a ride?"

"I'm sure he will. He's going to be here all summer!"

"Oooo, are you and Sean gonna do the thing in the back seat?"

Emily acted dumb. "What thing?"

"You know…the thing." She raised her eyebrows up and down Groucho Marx style.

"I don't know what you're talking about, Lily. I'm going to get dressed now. Go do whatever you came up here to do." Emily pretended to be annoyed.

Lily looked hurt. "Don't be so mean, Emily!"

"Ok, ok, I'm sorry."

Soon Emily was in the bathroom brushing her teeth and combing her hair. She then headed for the kitchen to get a few pieces of toast.

Sean was sitting at the kitchen table with Sarah talking about going to Berkley in the fall.

Emily looked stunned as she rounded the corner.

"Hi, Emily. I was just telling your mom about Berkeley."

Sarah got up from the kitchen table where she and Sean sat. "It all sounds very intriguing, Sean." Then she looked at Emily. "Did you know Sean is going to study the brain, Emily?"

"Yes Mom. I know. He's going to become a Neuroscientist. Very brainy stuff...get it...brainy?" Emily laughed and rolled her eyes as if she was less than impressed.

Sean said with a big smile, "Very funny, Emily! Hey, I have something to show you."

Emily now appeared to be extremely bored and not at all interested that her Sean was sitting in her kitchen. "Your red Mustang?"

"Yea. How do you know I have a red Mustang?" he asked not yet getting her lousy mood.

"Well gosh...I don't know? Let me see?" She stroked the bottom of her chin then used a very sarcastic tone. "Duh, it's only sitting in your Grandma's driveway. I didn't figure it was Martha's, although I wouldn't put it past her to get one. She's not as old as she makes out to be."

Sean looked wounded at Emily's behavior. "Wow, what side of the bed did you get up on, Em?"

Emily made an attempt at recovering Sean's attention. "Hey, Sean, I'm only playing with you. You kinda snuck up on me here so I was just getting you back a little."

Sarah interrupted. "Ok, ok, you two. Emily here's a couple of pieces of toast. Now you two get out of here, and Sean, you drive the speed limit."

"Yes, Sarah, I will."

They walked out the door. Sean stopped as Emily continued walking. "Em, are you mad at me? Did I do something wrong? Cuz, if I did tell me so I can make up for it."

She turned around and now looked remorseful. "You didn't do anything wrong, Sean. I'm just, well, I woke up with a splitting headache. I sometimes get them the week after my period ends. I'm just a little irritable; that's all. I'm really happy to see you. I've been waiting all week to see you. Plus, later I have something to tell you."

Looking less wounded, he walked toward her. "I'm sorry, Em. Did you take anything for your headache?"

171

She nodded; so he asked, "What did you want to tell me?"

"Not now. I'll tell you later."

Sean looked frustrated. "Why can't you tell me now? Why do we have to wait?'

"Because this is kinda something special and I want to be able to tell you at the right moment"

"Ok. I guess I'll have to wait. Do you want to see my Mustang? Mom and Bill got it for me. They just finished a trial with a huge settlement. They were going to get me a Junker but decided to splurge on the Mustang. Isn't it a beauty?" He was beaming with pride.

Emily looked enthusiastic. "It is beautiful. I saw it this morning when I got up. I was actually hurrying trying to get dressed as fast as I could so I could come see it."

Then she took a nose dive right back into her former snotty behavior. "Oh, and of course...come see you too; I don't even know why."

She shrugged her shoulders and exaggerated rolling her eyes.

Again Sean looked wounded as well as confused by her behavior. "Ok. Maybe I should go back to Quincy and come back down another day."

He walked away from her.

She realized her behavior was absolutely atrocious and even schizophrenic. "Sean, I'm sorry. Wait for me...please?"

But by then, Sean had had enough of her crazy behavior. He was no longer hurt. He was pissed off! So, he gave her back her own medicine by using a nasty, high pitched complaining tone. "Ok, if I have tooooooo!"

He was about to inject some well-deserved anger into his retort when they both heard a male voice calling Sean's name.

They turned around to see Phillip running up the street.

Phillip called as he got closer, "Hey, man. I heard there was a hot GT Coupe in your grandma's driveway. Is that your ride?"

Sean knew this was his opportunity to give Emily a well-deserved figurative smack across the face so he continued walking away from her and toward his car while waving an arm to Phillip. "Yea, come on; I'll show you around."

Phillip quickly caught up to Sean as he behaved as if Emily wasn't even there at all. She instantly regretted her behavior so she quickened her step and followed them.

When she caught up, the two males were already at the car with the hood up and Sean was bragging up a storm. "It's got a 4.6 liter overhead cam with a V8 engine…260 horse power with 302 pounds of raw torque at 4,000 rpms. It'll go 0-60 in less than 6 seconds. I know cuz I tested it out. Plus…you can do donuts all day long."

Phillip looked inside. Then, with a very stupid expression, looked back at Sean and asked, "What the hell? Sean, this is a stick shift. Why did you get a standard transmission when you could have had an automatic?"

Sean chuckled and then spoke with absolute authority. "Are you kidding, Phil. Automatic in a car like this would be like kissin your sister! This car deserves nothin less than a standard. In fact, I just ordered a Hurst classic white 6 speed knob for that old school look."

Phillip got it instantly and was now almost literally drooling. Emily was standing off to the side watching this shocking display of machismo. She wasn't at all used to seeing Sean act so *male*. She was used to his softer side.

While she watched this display of masculinity she could almost envision Sean's head getting so large that he appeared to have a big orange pumpkin head and it turned her off.

Little did she know but Sean was not at all oblivious to her facial expressions and he was enjoying rubbing it in and making her even more angry than she was previously.

Sean, opened the passenger side of his car, turned to Phillip and said with as much enthusiasm as he could muster. "Want a ride?"

"Hell, ya!" exclaimed Phillip, "When?"

"Right now! Let me go tell Grandma." Then, he knew he had his chance to verbally and euphemistically shoot Emily straight through the heart for being so cruel to him.

"Em, hop in the back seat so Phillip can sit up front."

There it was!

She was shot through and through and it didn't hurt her as much as it shocked and infuriated her. In fact it was the most furious she had been in a long time. She wanted to murder Sean right then and there!

So, with all the irritable female attitude she could foam at her mouth, she said, "Naw. I'll just go sit with Martha in the women's conference room called *the kitchen* while you big macho males go off shooting your wads."

She walked right past Sean, stuck her nose in the air and made believe she was going in the side door.

Sean sensed victory and an opportunity to rub salt in the wound so he took the shot. "Ok, suit yourself. Tell Grandma I'll be back."

He pulled his keys from his jeans, walked around to the driver's side, got in and told Phillip to hop in. As soon as Phillip shut the door, Sean backed the car out of the driveway, shoved the stick into first and screeched the wheels all the way up the hill leaving a long, constant burnt rubber path in the car's wake. He felt all powerful for having put Emily in her place as he thought, *fuck her if she wants to act nasty. I will too.* Then he immediately felt guilt for reacting the way he did. *But, God, she was so rotten to me.* So he pushed his guilt feelings away and aggressively stomped on the gas pedal as he pulled onto Pawtucket Avenue. The car squealed around the corner leaving more rubber. Phillip just hit his knee and yelled, "Fucking cool, man!" Sean scanned the immediate vicinity for a cop. There were none so he calmed down.

Emily was now the one not only pissed but deeply hurt. She was totally wounded all the while knowing deep down that she deserved every ounce of pain she felt so she ignored her pain and concentrated on her anger.

Instead of going in to see Martha she stormed back to her house, walked right past her mother and went up to her bedroom. She sat up there for the hour Sean and Phillip were gone and she pouted the entire time.

About fifteen minutes into the ride, Phillip exclaimed, "Man, this is one hot car, Sean. I envy you."

"Well, don't. I just got lucky. Mom and Bill just killed it on a settlement. But, who knows it could become a famine in a few months and the car could get repossessed." Sean tried his best to act modestly humble.

Although thrilled with his car, he wanted his friends to know he was still the same old Sean.

The two boys rode a little longer with the windows down and the radio blasting with a Bruce Springsteen CD when the song, "Born to Run" played. Sean reached for the radio knob and turned up the volume. With outstretched arms, the two males thumped the outside of the car. They were in the zone; the male zone.

When the song ended, Phillip reached over and turned the volume way down.

Sean was stunned and looked over at Phillip. "What did you do that for? Don't you like Springsteen?"

"Naw, man, I love Springsteen. Especially that tune. It's perfect for your new ride. I just wanted to ask you what's up with you and Emily. I thought you two were going to bite each other's heads off." He was looking over at Sean.

Sean took his hand off the shift knob and made a gesture as he flipped his hand and wrist. "Hell, Phil, I don't know. Sometimes she can be so sarcastic. She said she's got a post period headache or something like that, so I guess that's what's going on. I don't know. It's hard sometimes. I mean, I have no idea what it's like to be a female. I guess their hormones go haywire, but, damn, we haven't seen each other for almost a month. I don't know. I guess we'll make up this afternoon."

Sean then shrugged his shoulders and slowed down to a more reasonable speed.

"Well, I just don't want to see anything happen to the two of you. You just seem right for each other," answered a sincere Phillip.

Then he smirked. "Besides, I don't think you want to be pissin' her off now anyway."

"What do ya mean?" Sean looked intrigued.

Still grinning. "Well, I'm not supposed to tell you this and you have to promise you won't let on you know. I sure don't want to have Jeannie giving me down the road for telling you, but, Emily is on the pill."

Sean looked at Phillip totally stunned. "What?" he exclaimed as he swung a hard right into a church parking lot. He stopped the car so hard they both bounce backward then forward and back again. "You're kidding?"

Phillip snickered joyfully. "Nope, you're going to get some

175

man! So you better make up with her or she might change her mind!"

Sean breathed hard, put the heel of his palm up to his forehead and ran his hand through his hair. "Damn. I shouldn't have been so hard on her. I was just pissed that she was acting so mean. Damn."

Phillip laughed again. "Hey Sean. It's ok. Everything's cool. Emily really loves you. You'd have to do a whole lot worse for her to change her mind."

"When did this happen?"

"A few days ago. Jeannie took her to Planned Parenthood. I guess you and Emily talked about it a little and she really wants it to happen."

"Damn. I feel like crap now. I know she was mad at me for telling her to hop in the back. But I was just giving her back a little of what she was dishing out. I've gotta go back," Sean said hitting the dashboard with his fist.

Phillip gasped. "Wait. I have an idea. This works with Jeannie every time. Stop just up the road at Stop and Shop and grab a dozen roses for her. That will get you in the door and back in her good graces."

Sean looked at Phillip with skepticism. "You think it will? Not that I'm thinking of the sex, even though that would be a hell of a bonus, but I really want this last summer to be special. She's really scared about my going all the way out to California. You know, she's scared I'll find someone else, which is ridiculous. Ok; sorry to cut the ride short, buddy, but let's go get those roses. Thanks for the suggestion. And I promise to act really surprised when she tells me about the pills." He had talked himself into believing the flowers were the answer.

****

From her bedroom, which now had the window opened so she could listen, Emily heard the rumble of Sean's Mustang. She peeked out through the curtains she pulled tight and watched Sean and Phillip get out of the car.

The guys waved to each other and Phillip headed down the street.

Emily pulled the curtains open just a little more. She didn't want Sean to know she was anxiously waiting for him to return. She wanted him to suffer and wonder where she was and if she was still mad at him. But then she saw something spectacular in his hands. He was carrying a bouquet of red roses.

Oh, my God, she thought. *Gosh, I hope they aren't for Martha.*

She watched him go inside and waited. A few seconds passed when he reemerged carrying the roses as he walked from his driveway and crossed the street.

Little did Emily understand how well Sean knew her because as he walked across the street, although he kept his head straight to give the appearance he was looking forward, he was actually looking up at her window. He could see that someone was peeking through a slit in the curtains which were *never* closed, but were now.

She's up there watching me, he thought as he smirked to himself.

She let go of the curtains and quickly dropped to the floor as he lifted his head to get a better look at her window. "God damn," she said out loud. "I sure hope he didn't see me."

Then she heard the doorbell ring. She got up off the floor and tip toed over to her dresser, quickly fixed her hair and waited for whoever answered the front door to call to her.

She had a million butterflies fluttering in her stomach and she felt flushed. She hated that they had a fight and just wanted to be back in his good graces and arms.

Then she heard Lily yell, "Emily, Sean's here, and he's got something for you!" She tried to compose herself as she opened her door and walked down the stairs. He was standing there at the entrance looking up at her and holding the roses in front of his face. She could barely see his beautiful eyes peeking from behind the bouquet.

As she descended the last step she said ever so sweetly, "Oh, Sean, I'm so sorry I was such an irrational witch earlier."

He couldn't help himself. "Why Emily Callaway. Did you just call yourself an irrational bitch?"

She looked at him and scowled. "No. I would never call myself a bitch. I said witch. There's a big difference!"

177

He grinned as if to say I beg to differ with you.

Then she acquiesced. "Ok, ok, uncle, uncle. Maybe just a little bitchy; but I hate that word!"

He smiled even more. "I know you do. But, I hate to say it; the word is a little more appropriate. But, ok…let's use the word witch instead."

She couldn't help herself. She poked him and laughed.

He laughed as well as he handed her the roses. "Since we're calling ourselves names, I'll admit, I was somewhat of a prick. But, I have to tell you, it sure was fun. After all you did deserve it!"

She poked him again and they both laughed as she took the roses and melted into his embrace. "Let's go put these in a vase."

As they walked to the kitchen he asked, "Do you still have a headache?'

"Just a little. The Tylenol I took earlier seems to be helping.

As they entered the kitchen holding hands, Sarah giggled to herself. "Well, I guess you two made up."

Sean and Emily laughed and answered yes simultaneously. Then Sean asked Sarah if she would mind him taking Emily for a ride in his new car.

"Of course not; but have her home in an hour. We're going to her Uncle Bart's for dinner."

"Ok, I promise," he said as the two of them walked out the front door holding hands.

They were standing next to the car, Sean reached for the door as Emily was facing him. She was leaning back against the car.

He pressed up against her and said, "Em, I really am sorry about earlier. God, Em I love you so much. I would never want to hurt you."

He kissed her like he had never kissed her before. He kissed her with his mouth open and his tongue touching hers. She got such a warm feeling in her vaginal area as she felt his now enlarged penis against her and moved so that her body rubbed it. She no longer had to worry about exciting him only to say no.

She couldn't wait for the pills to kick in because when they do she thought, *I'm going to fuck his brains out!*

Then she blushed violently to herself for being so explicit in her thoughts; but she wanted him so much. She was thinking all of this as they kissed and didn't realize how passionately she was kissing him.

He opened one eye and saw Martha peeking at them from the back door. He then moved away and said, "Let's go. We have an audience."

She whispered, "Ok."

They moved apart, he opened the door and she got in.

When he climbed in the other side she said, "I do really love your car. And it's red!!" Then she said, "Even though I was mad at you earlier, I couldn't help but realize how handsome you looked as you peeled out of the driveway. Maybe in a few minutes we can stop somewhere and I can tell you what I said I wanted to tell you."

"Ok. I know a little spot," he smiled. "You know it too."

He backed out and was careful not to burn rubber. "Sure don't want your mom getting mad at me."

His cell phone rang and he answered, "Oh, Grandma. No. I'll be back in a few minutes I just wanted to give Emily a ride in my new car. (Pause) Yea, I promise. Love ya."

"What was that about?" she asked.

"Awe, she was worried about us. She knew we had a fight and just wanted to make sure we were ok. I know too she's a little concerned. She doesn't want us to get into trouble," he said as he shifted gears.

"What do you mean trouble?" she asked, knowing exactly what he meant.

He looked over at her. "She's very nervous that now that we're adults and know we'll be separated soon that we'll have sex unprotected. She's never really come right out and said it but I can tell she's worried." He pulled into the park and said, "Remember this place?"

Emily breathed deeply and answered, "How could I ever forget it? I was so scared that day I would never see you again. I've never been back here since. Oh..." She turned to look at him. "...And that brings me to what I said we needed to talk about."

He pretended ignorance. "Ok. I'm listening."

"Sean, I'm on the pill." She watched his facial expression trying to gauge his reaction.

He made a face full of resignation. "Look Em, I can't lie to you. Phillip told me earlier. Please don't tell Jeannie. She'll eat his lunch!"

Emily was actually relieved. "I won't. Besides, I kind of had a feeling you knew by the way you kissed me back there. I'm glad you know. It makes it a lot easier to talk about. But I have to ask you a question, because I have to know the truth. When we do this, will you think any less of me?"

He looked at her with all the love he felt for her. "Emily. What kind of a question is that?"

"I don't know," she almost apologized. "I think that's the Catholic in me speaking. You know how they're always trying to make us feel guilty. The big, fat mortal sin! I'm so sick of all that garbage. Do you know when I was in 9th grade, I cried myself to sleep one night because of a story Sister Mary Dominic told us?"

He sat with his back against the door. He loved how she elaborated about…*well, everything,* he thought.

She was still jabbering. "She told us about a very wealthy girl who wanted to become a nun, but her father didn't want her to because he felt she would miss out on the pleasures of life. She was supposedly beautiful by the way. Well, she joined and about a year later, he showed up at the convent with a new mink coat for her and a beautiful white Jaguar convertible. He was trying to bribe her to leave before taking her final vows. The daughter wanted to become a nun so bad, she didn't take the bribe. The moral of that story was that, when you're being called to the convent or to priesthood, you should sacrifice everything and go. That night, I was so convinced I was being called, but because I didn't want to go I cried myself to sleep. Disgusting, don't you think."

"Yes, absolutely," he smiled. "I'm sure glad you didn't let them talk you into becoming a nun."

She laughed. "Me too. Look at ALL the pleasures of life I would have missed out on."

She looked at him adoringly and moved closer to the middle, then looked at her watch. "There's no way up here to put my arms around you. We have exactly twenty minutes before you need to take me home. Do you want to go in the back and just kiss?"

He didn't utter a word. Instead he got out of the car and climbed in the back. She did the same. She moved over to him and they kissed.

Then she asked pleadingly, "Sean, kiss me again like you did back in the driveway. I want to be able to dream about what's waiting for us."

He put his arm around her so that she was leaning back against the window and kissed her deeply. "God, Em, I love you."

"I love you too, Sean."

They kissed several more times and were moving around so much, she found herself lying on the seat under him.

"We've gotta be careful," Emily whispered.

"I know," he said as he moved back, sat up and then helped her back up. "That's why I'm taking you home a few minutes early. I can't take this. I want you too much."

She brushed her hair back from her face. "Ok. I think that's a good choice. Because I'm on the verge of throwing caution to the wind and I don't want either of us to regret anything."

He bent the front seat forward, reached for the door handle and opened the door, got out, extended his hand and helped her out.

"Phew," she said. "We have (she counts on her fingers) five more days to avoid doing anything stupid."

Emily walked around to the other side of the car when he exclaimed, "I have an idea. Since both Phillip and Jeannie know what our plan is and what our timetable is, let's get them to help us stay in control."

"That's a great idea! We'll talk to them tomorrow. Let's go home before either of us changes our minds."

They went home.

****

Martha was totally relieved when she heard the rumble of the car. She ran to the living room window and watched Sean walk Emily to her front door where he kissed her one more time.

He walked back home thinking about how he could plan a special first time with Emily.

As he walked into the kitchen, Martha was sitting at the table.

She spoke, "Sean, I don't mean to pry, but can we have a really serious talk right now?"

"Sure Grandma," he said.

He sat down and folded his hands on the table top like he used to do when he was a kid and his grandma asked to have a serious talk.

She smiled as she put her hands on his. "Sean, have you and Emily been intimate yet? Please be honest with me."

Sean looked directly at Martha. He had learned a long time ago that honesty was his *only* option for communicating with his grandma in serious situations such as this. She had a way of knowing when he wasn't being completely honest.

He answered looking her directly in the eye. He didn't flinch. "No Grandma, not yet. But I know what you're thinking and I know you're worried so I'm going to tell you the truth, ok?"

As Martha nodded her head, he continued, "Emily and I really think we love each other and we do want to be intimate. In fact we feel it's important that we allow ourselves to be intimate especially since we're going to be worlds apart in a few months for a long, long time. Grandma, Emily just started taking the pill yesterday. Jeannie took her down to Planned Parenthood a couple of days ago. We have five more days before it's safe to have sex. I'm telling you this because I know you won't judge either of us. This is a good thing, Grandma."

Martha sat looking at Sean for a few minutes and then she sighed a huge sigh. "Thank God! I was so scared for both of you. Then I was scared to ask you because I didn't want you to think I was prying. I've watched you two from the first day you met on the slant tree; and, I also believe you have a real love for one another. You know, I married your Grandfather when I was just 18. I know what real love is and I feel it between the two of you. I'm proud of both of you for making a very adult decision. You have my blessing. Now what are we going to do for the next five days?"

"That's going to be the tough part, but we've decided that since Phillip and Jeannie know, we're going to ask them to help us get through these next five days. I promise you, Grandma, I want to do this right. I *have* to do this right. I respect and love

Emily too much. She's been through a lot in her life; and I want to remain what she calls the one right thing."

"I love you, Seanie," she said as she brushed his hair with her hand.

Sean felt utter relief for choosing honesty. "I love you too, Grandma. Thanks for being so understanding. Now I think I'm going to watch a little TV."

"Ok, sweetheart," she stood, kissed him on the forehead and walked out of the room.

Chapter Twenty-Six

The next morning, Sean knocked on Emily's door.

Paul was in his pajamas watching TV. He went to the window, saw Sean, then ran to the bottom of the stairs and yelled, "Emily, Sean's at the back door!"

"Could you please let him in, Paul?" She yelled back. "Tell him I'll be right down. I'm looking for my tennis shoe."

Paul went back to the TV room, walked over to the door, opened it and said, "Hey, Sean, come on in. She's looking for her stupid tennis shoe or something. Hey, that's a really fine car." Paul went back over to the TV and fell into the huge Lazy Boy which used to belong to his dad. "Mind if we go for a ride later?"

"Sure, Paul. Just say when and we'll go. I may even let you drive it. You ever drive a stick?" Sean asked Paul as he sat in one of the other chairs.

"Shit, yea. Most of my buddies drive sticks. My goal is to own a Corvette. Maybe when I get out of the service. Who knows, maybe before," Paul said. Then he laughed, "I heard what you told Phil about an automatic transmission. That's a good one, it's like kissin your sister. I'm gonna remember that one." Then he made a noise and gesture as if he were spitting. "Kissin your sister. Good one. Hey, do you want something to drink?"

"Naw. Thanks though. How long are you home for?" asked Sean.

Paul answered then they began talking about cars and Paul's experiences at boot camp.

They were laughing when Emily rounded the corner carrying her tennis shoe, walked over to Sean and kissed him. Then she sat down on the ottoman next to the chair. "God, I thought I'd never find this damned shoe. It was way under Katie's bed behind a bunch of stuffed animals. I can't wait to live in a dorm room where I only have to contend with one other female,"

She finished tying her shoe laces, jumped up and exclaimed, "Ready! Where to?"

"I have something to show you and then we'll go pick up Jeannie and Phil," he said.

"What do you want to show me?" she asked as she follows him out the back door.

He ignored her question and said to Paul, "Hey man, good seeing you. I'll be here all summer so, just say the word and we'll go for that ride!"

Paul, waved his arm as he continued watching TV. "Sure, Sean. Good to see you again. We'll get together."

Sean and Emily walked out the door and down the step. They began walking toward the street when Emily abruptly stopped.

"Oh, wait a minute. Let me just go tell Mom."

"Ok. I'll wait out here, go ahead." He said as he walked back to the door and sat on the concrete stair.

Emily went back inside, walked down the hall and knocked on her mother's door. Sarah opened the door. She was actually dressed in a nice pair of cargo pants and a print blouse.

"Wow, Mom, you look nice. Where you going?" asked Emily.

"Martha's been bugging me to go down into Providence with her and I finally agreed. Paul's staying with your grandma all day since we figured you and Sean probably want to spend a little time together," answered Sarah.

"Wow, Paul offered to do that?" exclaimed Emily.

"Yes he did; but I think there's a method to his madness. I think he's hoping it will get him a ride in Sean's car. Now, I've gotta go. Martha wants to leave in fifteen minutes."

Sarah was putting her shoe on when Emily bent over and kissed Sarah on the cheek. "Well, have a great time, Mom. You really deserve it. And don't worry about getting back for dinner. I'll fix us all something or we'll call for a pizza."

As Emily walked back through the TV room she said, "Thanks, Paul for taking care of Grandma today."

"Sure. Have a good one, Em." Paul waved his arm.

Emily walked out the door as Sean stood up. "Sean, did you know Mom and Martha are going downtown?"

"Yea, I think I remember Grandma mentioning it. She said something about wanting to get your mom out of her stupor; or something like that. Now let's go look at what I want you to see."

He took her hand as they walked across the street, down the driveway, past the garage and into the back yard.

Emily asked, "Does this have something to do with the slant tree?"

"It might," Sean said using a rather curious tone.

They walked around to the side that faced away from his house. There on the side of the tree about as far up as the very first time they sat on the tree together were five slashes.

She looked at Sean and asked, "Did you do that?"

"Yea, I did, with my Swiss Army knife some sweet young girl gave me several years ago. Never did get her name, but I love the knife. The slashes mark the number of days till…"

Emily walked close to him, took his arm and put it over her shoulder. "I know what they mark off. Let's come back here every night and cross each of them off till there are no more to cross off."

He wrapped his arms around her and they kissed. As they kissed several more times, he backed her up against the tree and kissed her neck. She made a little pleasure squeal as he ran his tongue up her neck to her ear and bit it ever so lightly.

She felt his manhood pressing hard against her and sighed to herself. *God help me. I'm going to die a zillion times between now and the last slashed off mark.*

He reached down to her behind, cupped it and pulled her even closer so she could feel him more. "Oh, Emily I can't wait to devour you." His voice cracked.

Then they heard a car horn. It was Martha and Sarah. Martha was backing out of the driveway and was waving out the window. They pulled away from each other slightly and waved back.

"Grandma knows," said Sean.

Emily gulped so hard she made a noise. "She does. "How?"

"It's ok, Em." He kissed her again. "Grandma's pretty cool when she wants to be. She saw us kissing by the car yesterday and became alarmed. She made me sit at the kitchen table when I came in and asked if we've been intimate. She was totally relieved to know that we're protected. You know, she married Grandpa when she wasn't much older than you. She was 18. So she knows what we feel."

Emily looked amazed. "Wow, Sean. That's pretty cool. I don't know what my mom would say if she knew. She's never been cool that way. She's by the book Catholic."

"Well, at least this conversation has cooled us down. Let's go pick up Phil and Jeannie and figure out what we're going to do today." He patted her behind and she smiled.

They walked back to his car. He opened the door for her and then said, "I'll be right back. Gotta get my keys."

Emily got in the car. She had a pretty red button down blouse on. She unbuttoned three buttons so you could glimpse her red bra. But when she saw Sean come back out, she hurriedly buttoned them back up. *God, this is going to be torture*, she thought.

He climbed into the car and looked at her. She looked flushed. "You ok?"

"Yea; just dying here." She fanned herself with a map she found in the side pocket.

"This is going to be pretty tough, Em. It might get to the point where we'll have to take a break from each other. I'm trying really hard; but, it's tough," he said.

He started the car and turned on the radio and smiled. "A little distraction is needed."

As Phil and Jeannie jumped in the car Jeannie gave them a lot of distraction because she was jabbering a mile a minute. Then she suddenly stopped. "Wait a minute. Em, did you tell him?"

Emily smiled coyly. "Yea, I told him."

Then Sean turned around and looked at Jeannie then Phil. "We have four more days till D-day; and Emily and I are asking you guys to kind of chaperone us so we can keep our cool."

Jeannie laughed. "We can do that; but what's the D stand for?"

Sean smirked. "D as in DO it."

They all laughed joyfully.

"Where we going?" asked Phillip.

Jeannie excitedly asked, "Hey, who wants to go to the zoo? I haven't been there in ages and I heard they've done some renovating, especially in the elephant house. Emily, you love elephants, right?"

Emily vigorously shook her head yes. "They're my favorite

land animal! Let's go, Sean, please?"

He turned back around, reached over, patted her thigh, started the Mustang and revved the engine. "Ok, Roger Williams Park it is."

Emily got very excited. "Peel up the street like you did yesterday!"

"Roger that. Your mom's not home to tear me a new asshole," said Sean as he put it into first gear, popped the clutch and stomped on the gas leaving a long trail of burned rubber half way up the hill."

"Goddamn," squealed Phillip.

"Weeee," screamed Jeannie loving every minute of it.

Then Sean slowed down considerably. "I better not do that too much. Sure don't want the stupid neighbors complaining to Grandma or callin the cops; but that was a hell of a rush!!"

He looked over to Emily and she was giggling like a little girl.

The zoo was an hour away. They opened all the windows and Sean turned the radio up as loud as he could. They all laughed and bobbed their heads to the music then jabbered excitedly during the few commercial breaks.

When they arrived, Jeannie yelled excitedly. "Let's go to the elephant house first and see how they hang!" Then she covered her mouth and laughed.

Emily cackled. "Jeannie, that's what I love about you, you're so dirty."

"Someone has to be!" giggled Jeannie as she bumped Emily with her hip causing her to sail across the concrete path. The two girls held hands and almost skipped along.

The guys looked at each other rolled their eyes and Phillip remarked, "Let's hang back a little. This could get downright embarrassing."

He and Sean ambled along while the girls ran from house to house and cage to cage. Jeannie was finding sexual images everywhere and she was making Emily buckle over with laughter.

On the other hand, the boys were talking the fine art of muscle cars, past and present. About an hour into the day, they broke for lunch and headed for one of the refreshment stands that dotted the park.

Before they arrived, however, there was a cage sitting outside the ape house. Inside the cage were two chimps. There was a crowd gathered around the cage because the male chimp was jacking off.

The four friends got closer as the chimp came and shot his wad toward this man who had been harassing the chimps. The man was eating an ice cream cone and that was exactly where the semen landed. BULLSEYE...right on the top of the ice cream!

The man yelled, "Son of a bitch!" to which his wife loudly admonished him.

The man disgustedly threw his cone into the trash can next to the cage as the crowd roared with laughter.

Emily smirked gleefully. "Serves the ass right for harassing the chimps!"

Jeannie sneered with speculation. "I'll bet that's why these two chimps are out here instead of inside. The keepers want the male to jack off at assholes. I love it! Let's get some ice cream and make mine vanilla!"

Emily looked at her, made a squeamish face and said, "Jeannie - eww!"

Then Jeannie jumped up and down squealing. "Look, look, I told you so! The male's name is Dick as in Dick loves his prick!"

The four of them buckled over with laughter as they stumbled over to the refreshment stand.

They then walked around for about another half hour when Sean asked. "Who wants to learn how to drive a stick shift?"

Phillip shouted robustly. "Shit yea!" Then he slapped his leg. "Hot damn!"

Jeannie yelped, "I do I do!"

Emily didn't say a word; she just grinned like she was ready for the next show.

As they pulled out of the zoo parking lot, Phillip yelled with excitement. "Hey, make a right here. There's a huge church down the road on the left with a big empty parking lot!"

They arrived at the parking lot and it was totally vacant. Phillip was the first student.

Emily graciously and willingly relinquished her front seat to

Sean so he could give blow by blow instructions. She got out, pulled the seat forward and began climbing in the back. Sean grabbed her ass and she paused a few seconds making it obvious she liked it.

When she was settled in the back, Jeannie looked at her then nudged her. "I caught that! What is it four more days?"

Emily held up two fingers from both hands and then crossed them. They both giggle.

As Phillip jerked the car forward then killed the engine, he shouted. "Hey, quit laughing,"

"We're not laughin at you silly. We're laughin at girl stuff," giggled Jeannie.

He killed the engine a few times before he got the hang of it.

Then Sean said, "Ok, wanna learn how to burn some rubber?"

Phil was ecstatic. "Hell yea!"

Sean instructed him to drive all the way to the far end of the parking lot.

Once at the far end, Sean reached over and turned off the traction. Then he said, "Ok, Phil, put your clutch in and shift into first."

"Ok...ready."

"Ok, now release the clutch a little, apply a little gas, then slide your left heel over to the break, apply gas like a normal take off then take your foot off the clutch and the break."

Phil did, stalled it out, but on the second try accomplished a great burn out.

"That's what's called poppin the clutch," said Sean.

"Fuck, can I do it again?" begged Phillip.

"Ok, one more time. Can't do it too much though because Bill will kill me if I need new tires too soon. We've already had that conversation."

Phillip did it one more time and burned a little more rubber. "What a rush, thanks man!" exclaimed Phillip.

Sean turned to look at the two girls. "Ok, who's next, Jeannie?"

"No, but thanks. I think I'll stick to an automatic transmission,"

Then Emily said, "I think I'll wait for a private lesson, maybe next week."

Sean and Phillip changed seating positions. Sean got behind the wheel and adjusted the rearview mirror. "What's next?"

Jeannie said, "I'm pooped."

"Me too," claimed Phillip.

Sean looked at Emily. "Em?"

She said. "Maybe we should go home. It is getting late and I promised Mom I'd fix dinner for everyone. Wanna come eat with us, Sean?"

"Sure, baby," he said.

Jeannie nudged Emily, looked at her, winked then did an exaggerated imitation of two people kissing using the back of her hand. Emily nudged her back, then, she slipped her hand under her blouse and flapped her hand making it look like her heart was beating fast. They laughed and Sean looked in the rear view at Emily.

She smiled then mouthed, "I love you."

Jeannie was sound asleep when they arrived home.

Phillip jumped out of the car and Emily woke Jeannie. They both climbed out, then Emily and Jeannie hugged.

"That was fun," said Jeannie.

Phillip walked around the front of the car to the driver's side and Sean and he bumped fists.

"Thanks, man," said Phillip.

"Anytime," said Sean.

Then Jeannie asked, "What are we going to do tomorrow, day three till D-day?"

Emily suggested, "Let's watch the forecast. If it's going to be nice, let's go down to the shore."

"Sounds like a plan," exclaimed Jeannie. "Besides, I just bought a new bikini; and it is (she sang) sexyyyy!"

They all said good-bye, Emily hopped in and Sean drove up the street.

He pulled into his driveway, put the car in first gear and turned off the ignition. "Looks like Grandma and your mom aren't home yet. Wanna come in?"

"No, better not. They could be home anytime. Let's go mark off one of those slashes then go over to my house and call for a pizza. I know where Mom keeps her funny money," she smiled.

They both got out and as they walked to the front of the car,

191

Sean smacked Emily on the ass. She jumped forward and laughed with delight. "Hey, buddy!" then laughed again.

Emily got to mark off the slash which gave her a thrill. Then they held hands and walked back over to her house.

As they were about to open the front door, she turned to him and put her hand on the front of his pants. "Just three more days little fella!" she said lovingly then squeezed a little.

Sean frowned, then asked in a high pitched voice, "Hey, who're you callin little?"

They laughed and went in.

They ordered pizza, everyone ate then Emily cleaned the kitchen. Sean was right by her side helping.

When they finished, he put his arm around her. "Paul and the girls are in the TV room, let's go in the living room."

She loved that idea.

They turned off all the living room lights except one which Emily turned down to the dimmest setting, then they snuggled on the sofa.

They were French kissing. He had his knee between her legs, rubbing her as she moved in rhythm.

Suddenly she put her head back against the sofa while her eyes moved to the top of her head as she moaned with pleasure. He watched her facial expressions.

Then she looked at him with the biggest smile he'd ever seen and whispered, "Oh my God. You just gave me an orgasm." She moved close to his knee again and pled, "Hurry, do it again."

He began stroking her again with his knee when they heard Sarah's voice.

They both leapt up from the couch. Emily hurriedly fumbled with the light switch nearly pulling the lamp off the table but managed to turn the lamp up to the brightest setting as they both fell back down at opposite ends of the sofa.

As Sarah walked past the living room, she heard them laughing and stuck her head in.

"Hi, Mom. Did you and Martha have a good time?" asked Emily. "We've all eaten. I ordered a couple of pizzas."

"Oh, thanks, Emily. Yes, I really did have a lovely time." Then she looked at Sean. "All I can say is your grandma loves to shop!"

He snickered. "Tell me about it. She used to drag me all over downtown when I was a kid."

Then Sarah lifted her leg and took the shoe off one of her feet. "Honey, I think I'm just going to go lie down. I'm pooped and my feet are killing me from walking around all day."

"Sure, Mom. We're going to call it a night too."

Sarah disappeared and Emily exaggerated wiping her forehead. They both grinned like two cats that just got away with eating *all* the mice.

Sean moved closer, put his hand between her legs and asked, "Did you really have an orgasm?" She rolled her eyes back and said, "Oh, yes; and it was scrumptious."

"I can't wait to give you an orgasm with my hand touching your naked skin," Sean whispered.

"I can't either."

They kissed again as Lily rounded the corner making a kissing noise to which Sean and Emily decided they better call it a day.

The house was alive again!

The next two days went about the same. Jeannie was having a great time teasing them with sexual innuendos and Sean and Emily were having a harder time keeping their hands off each other.

On the last night before the fifth day, Emily and Sean went back to the slant tree and marked off another slash leaving only one.

Sean kissed Emily. "I have a special surprise for our D-day!"

She plead with him to tell her; but he only said, "I know where there's a small cabin in a forest just outside Cranston where we won't be bothered."

"Is it safe?" she asked.

"Yea, my uncle owns the land and the cabin. I used to go hunting with him years ago. It's very secluded," said Sean as he moved even closer to her.

"What are we going to do tomorrow, Sean?"

"Em, I was thinking that maybe tomorrow we should meet here in the morning, mark off the last slash and then just stay away from each other. That way we won't be tempted and it will make our D-day even more intense."

193

"I like that idea," she said, "But it's going to kill me," as she slid her hand down to his groin. "I'm looking forward to meeting my new friend." Then she stepped back, pointed to her vaginal area and said in a tiny yet high pitched voice, "So am I!"

They laughed very loudly, kissed again then walk back to the driveway.

"I'll see you in the morning. Till then, take excellent care of my good new friend," he said.

She patted his ass. "You take care of my good new friend too."

Chapter Twenty-Seven

D-DAY!

Emily got up around 6 a.m. She couldn't sleep another wink. She was meeting Sean in two hours.

Trying not to wake her sisters, she tip toed over to her dresser and quietly moved the dresser, went in and got her diary. She looked for a pen then went over to her bed, climbed back in and propped herself up with pillows against the head board.

She wrote. **"Dear Diary, It's *finally*, *finally* D-day. I have two hours to go before I meet Sean. He called yesterday and told me everything was set. I think he drove to Cranston to check out the cabin. God help me I can't wait. I love that guy with all my heart and soul and just can't wait until he's inside me. I can't wait till he gives me a billion orgasms, one after another. I can't wait to watch his face as he comes inside me. God, Diary, keep this as our secret. Stay hidden safely in your hiding place. I'll tell you all about it tomorrow. For now, wish me a wonderful first time with the man I love. Love, Em"**

She tip toed back to the attic and hid her diary, slid the dresser back, put on her bathrobe and slippers and tip toed downstairs after grabbing her clothes with the red panties and bra tucked inside.

In the kitchen, she placed her belongings on the chair at the backside of the table and fixed herself a bowl of cereal and a glass of orange juice. She ate twirling her hair around her fingers as she dreamed about Sean.

When she was finished, she washed her bowl, glass and spoon and looked at the clock. It was 7 a.m. *Just one hour to go.*

She picked up her belongings and tip toed to the bathroom, closed the door and took a shower.

She stood under the shower soaping herself. Closing her eyes, she ran her hands over her breasts imagining that they were Sean's hands. Then she slid her right hand down across her belly till she reached her vulva. She soaped her vulva and between her

195

legs, then dropped the bar on the bathtub floor and stuck one of her fingers inside herself. She stroked her finger in and out as she rubbed her breast with her other hand. Then she began rubbing her clitoris and gave herself an orgasm, a second and a third. When she was spent she opened her eyes, then her mouth and drank in the water as it rushed into her mouth. She was so ready!

At eight o'clock she walked back into the kitchen. Sarah was standing at the stove. "Want something to eat, Emily?"

"No thanks, Mom. I grabbed a bowl of cereal a while ago. I'm going to meet Sean. Is that ok?"

"Yes, sweetie. What are you two going to do today?" yawned Sarah.

"A bunch of things. He's going to try and teach me how to drive a stick shift. Then we're going into Providence to see MEN IN BLACK II, then just walk around and have lunch. Jeannie and Phillip are supposed to meet us there later in the afternoon and, if it's ok, we're all going to dinner. Is that ok with you, Mom?"

"That'll be fine. You be careful driving that car. It's not like driving a regular car. Do you have your new cell phone on you? Make sure it's charged so you can call me later this afternoon so I won't be worried about you."

"Ok, Mom. I'll call you before we meet up with Jeannie and Phil. Love you, Mom." She kissed her mother.

Sean was standing at his car when she walked over.

Emily laughed, "Holy cow! I just told Mom the biggest lie of my life and she totally bought it. Don't let me forget to call her around 5. Phil and Jeannie did say they'd meet us downtown didn't they?"

"Yea, we'll give them a call later and make sure." He extended his hand to her and whispered, "But now…it's our day."

"Our D-day," smiled Emily as she took his hand.

He opened the door for her and they kissed before she got in.

Sean got in on the other side, started the car, backed it out and gently drove up the hill and down to the main highway. At the stop sign, he turned on the radio. He had the CD player cued so that the first song to play was "We Never Danced." He looked over at her and smiled.

She smiled back and said, "I love you, Sean."

"I love you too, sweetie."

Sean turned right onto Pawtucket Avenue and headed toward Veterans Memorial Parkway. They held hands when he wasn't shifting. They barely talked all the way. There didn't seem any reason to talk. They both felt very connected to each other.

It was the most wonderful ride as a warm breeze rustled their hair and the sun smiled down from the bluest sky.

They were headed to heaven; their heaven.

As Sean drove through downtown Cranston, he hung a left down a sparsely populated black top and said as he squeezed her hand, "We're almost there."

He then slowed down and lifted his hand so he could shift. There was a white rural mailbox at the end of a gravel road which he turned onto. They drove slowly for about a half mile and as they arrived in a clearing there was the cutest little log cabin Emily had ever seen. It had an inviting front porch with two rocking chairs sitting on it.

"Is there a chance someone will come out here today?" asked Emily.

"No, Em. I talked to Uncle Peter a few days ago after I thought of this place and asked him if I could bring a couple of buddies out. He told me where the key was and asked that I make sure it was cleaned up when we left. Then he told me to have a good time." Sean smiled sweetly.

They both got out. As Sean walked around the car, Emily stood staring at the cabin. She wanted to remember every tiny detail. Sean extended his hand and she took it.

He had a patchwork blanket under his other arm. "This is a gift from Grandma. She wants this day to be as special for you as I do. Come on, baby."

They walked up to the cabin and onto the porch. He reached under a small wooden barrel next to the door, unlocked the door, and pushed it open, then returned the key to its original spot.

She looked at him and whispered, "I'm kind of scared, Sean."

He gently said, "I am too, baby. This is my first time as well. We'll just take everything really slow. We have *all* day long."

He caressed her face as a tear rolled down her cheek. He wiped the tear away, put his arm around her and they walked inside.

The cabin had one room with a sofa and chair, a table and a small kitchen area. Over in the far corner was a double bed.

He said, "Let's just sit on the sofa for a while. Would that be ok, Em?"

"Yes. I'd like that, Sean," she whispered.

They walked over and sat next to each other. He put his arm around her as she turned slowly so she could nuzzle her face into his chest. She felt like a delicate bird in his arms.

He whispered, "This is all for you Emily. We'll go slow and at your pace. I'm not in a hurry to rush anything. I want this to be a day we both remember for the rest of our lives. I love you so much."

They sat in silence for about fifteen minutes when she finally looked up at him and sat up so her face was close to his. He gently put his hands on her cheeks and pulled her close. They kissed sweetly.

Then she said, "I want to go over to the bed and just lay next to you. Would that be ok?"

"Yes, baby, yes. That would be wonderful."

They got up and walked hand in hand over to the side of the bed. There were no bed linens so he spread the quilt on the bed. She sat down on the side of the bed, then watched him as he walked over to the night stand on the other side. He pulled out a lighter from his pocket and lit several candles he had placed there the day before. He also left a bottle of wine with two glasses on the stand. He removed the cork and poured the wine. He walked back and handed Emily a glass.

He sat next to her and said, "Here's to the rest of our lives, Em."

They clinked glasses and she took a sip.

Then she asked, "Will you take my blouse and jeans off me, Sean?"

He didn't say a word. He simply stood up, took her glass and placed it along with his on the floor far enough away that they wouldn't get kicked over. He looked at her and sat down as she turned toward him. He brushed her hair away from her face and over her shoulder.

"You're beautiful, Emily." He kissed her ever so gently. He then reached down and began unbuttoning her blouse. When he unbuttoned the last button, he pushed the blouse back off her shoulders and kissed each shoulder.

He took her blouse, folded it and placed it on the chair about a foot from the bed. Then she laid down on the bed and he moved close to her, took off her sandals and placed them on the chair.

Then he reached for her jeans and asked, "Ok?"

She shook her head yes as he unbuttoned her jeans, slid the zipper down and slid her jeans off as she lifted up. He folded her jeans and placed them on the chair.

Then he pushed his own shoes off with his feet and said, "Scoot over, Em."

She did as he laid next to her. He brushed a strand of red hair from the corner of her mouth, bent down and kissed her. "I love your red bra and panties. They look wonderful against your milky skin."

That excited her as she put her tongue in his mouth and they kissed passionately.

He caressed her breasts as she begged, "You can take off my bra. I want you to."

He moved one of the shoulder straps off her shoulder, then the other as he kissed her hard. He then slid his hands onto her bare breasts and moved the bra so that her breasts were fully exposed.

Next he leaned over and kissed her breasts one after the other. "God, Emily, I can't believe you're really here with me."

"I am Sean. I am. Forever," she whispered.

Then she took his hand and slid it down to her panties. He slipped his hand underneath and down to her mound and stroked her.

She pled, "Please take them off me."

He raised up a little and slid them off as she lifted up. She then turned toward the opposite direction so he could also unhook her bra. He gently folded her bra and panties and put both of them on the chair.

She was lying on her back as he drank in her vision. He thought of how she almost appeared illuminated by the sun that first time he ever saw her and marveled at what a stunning woman she had become. He felt like the luckiest man alive as he ran his hand lightly over her breasts, then down her stomach and onto her vulva. He stroked her gently as she parted her legs.

She was moist and getting moister by the second. Then he traced her slit with his finger as she reached down and put her hand over his and implored, "Put it inside me, Sean."

He did and her eyes roll to the back of her head. As he pushed his finger in and out, he was rubbing her clitoris with the heel of his hand. He watched all her facial expressions. This lasted for several minutes; then she arched her back and buckled in pleasure. He kept rubbing as she arched three more times moaning with utter pleasure.

The fourth time she was about to come she opened her eyes and begged, "Kiss me."

He put his mouth on hers and she opened to receive his warm, delicious tongue. She kissed him as hard as she could as her back arched one more time and her body almost vibrated with absolute, splendid ecstasy. They laid there in silence for several minutes.

Then she said, "I want to take your clothes off you."

He smiled and stood up as she sat on the side of the bed. She pulled his black T-shirt out from his pants and then his white undershirt. He reached down and pulled them over his head. He wasn't so neat and careful with his clothes. He simply dropped them on the floor.

Then she reached down and unbuttoned his jeans and slid the zipper down. As she slid his jeans off, she also slid off his briefs.

She sat there looking at his magnificent specimen of manhood and put her hand around it and said "It's beautiful, Sean."

She then laid down and motioned for him to lie next to her.

As he did, she touched him again and asked, "What do I do?"

He lifted her hand and spat into her palm and said, "Now caress it gently."

She did as he put his hand over hers and showed her how. They kissed again with their tongues fully in each other's mouth.

He then said, "I don't have to come inside this time if you're scared."

She whispered, "I am scared, Sean, but I want you inside me just be gentle."

He kissed her cheek. "I will Em. I promise."

He felt her vagina to make sure it was nice and moist. "Let me play with you for a while so you're wet."

She laid back and closed her eyes as he rubbed her gently. He stuck two fingers inside and stroked in and out.

She was extremely wet. "I think you're ready."

She pulled him toward her and she felt him getting hard again. She spread her legs as wide as she could and helped him put his penis into the opening of her waiting vagina. He pressed in, watching her face. He didn't want to hurt her.

She winced a few times and he asked, "Do you want me to stop?"

She said, "No, God, no. I want all of you."

She winced once more then pushed on his back for him to go as deep as he could. He did. Then he began moving in and out. She wrapped her legs around him and fell into his rhythm. They glided gently back and forth for several minutes and then the pace picked up.

She sensed all of him and melted into him with the rhythm. Then he moaned loudly and held his breath as he came. When he had deposited every last drop of love juice into her, he stopped and laid down on top of her. They were both breathing heavily and wringing with sweat…wonderful, delectable sweat.

A few minutes passed and he lifted up his head and kissed her. Tears were now streaming down her cheeks as he asked, "What's the matter, Emily?"

She sobbed, "I just feel so safe with you. I never knew sex could be so wonderful. I love you so much, Sean for teaching me the beauty of sex."

He smiled as he kissed her tears. "My sweet Emily. I thank my lucky stars I found you sitting out there on that slant tree six years ago. I think the angels and my dad were smiling down on me that day and now they're smiling down on both of us today."

He kissed her one last time, rolled off and grabbed his white undershirt off the floor. He began wiping her and then himself.

She gasped. "That's your shirt, Sean!"

He laughed. "I never wear undershirts. I bought this just for today. I know how you like to keep everything so I thought you just might want to keep this."

She giggled like a delighted little girl. "Yes, I want to keep it. When I'm a wrinkled old lady I'll be able to take it out from its safe keeping, hold it to my heart and remember the day I was taken to heaven."

Sean then pulled her over to him and she laid her head on his chest. "I love you, Emily. I love you so, so much."

"I love you Sean, with all my being."

They fell sound asleep.

When they woke, it was nearly 3 p.m. They still had an hour before they needed to head into Providence to meet Jeannie and Phillip.

They made love again and if it was even possible they both felt it was better than the first time.

Chapter Twenty-Eight

On their way to meet up with Jeannie and Phil, Emily checked in with her mom.

"How was the movie, Emily?" asked Sarah.

"It was good, but not nearly as good as the first movie."

Sean looked at her as she put her fingers to her mouth and made a face like she was laughing because she was getting away with it.

He smiled as Emily answered the next question, "Well, Sean got a little impatient with me cuz I kept killing the engine; so, we're going to try again in a few days. I was having a hard time coordinating my feet; but it was fun anyway." Then she said, "Well, Mom, I've got to go. We just pulled up in the parking lot where we're meeting Jeannie and Phillip. Jeannie just jumped out of the car and is waving like a fool. Yea, I know. She just cracks me up all the time. Love you too, Mom. We'll be careful...promise. Bye!"

She hung her cell phone up and looked at Sean and laughed.

"Damn, Em, you're a hell of a liar when you want to be."

She made a face and shrugged her shoulders. "What can I say?"

They both laughed.

Soon they pulled into the meet up parking lot and there Jeannie was.

She jumped out of the car and was waving her arms like she was directing traffic. She made huge sweeps with her arms indicating Sean should park in the space adjacent to where Phillip was parked.

"You know her like a book, don't you?" Sean snickered.

"Awe, she's just one of those free spirits who just can't get enough fun. I love it."

"Well, I love it too. She sure keeps things interesting." He chuckled as he obeyed Jeannie and parked right next to Phillip's car.

Sean killed the engine and Emily got out first as Jeannie ran around to her side, grabbed her two hands and began jumping up and down like a little kid in a school yard, "How was it? How was it, Em?"

Emily, always more serious said, just loud enough for Sean to hear, "I think I've died and gone to heaven and I hope I never come back."

Sean smiled to himself as Phillip patted him on the back.

While talking up a storm the entire way, Jeannie and Emily walked toward the main street as the boys followed.

Phillip was excited. "Hey, Sean, my cousin told me about a muscle car show tomorrow over in Woonsocket. Do you want to go check out the cars? He went last year and said they have a ton of the classics there?"

"Sure, Phil. What time does it start?"

"It starts around 10 and lasts till around 4."

"I'll ask Em if she wants to go."

Phillip made a huffing sound. "Awe, I thought we could go by ourselves. You know…guy stuff. I already mentioned it to Jeannie and she didn't act at all interested. Why don't we let the girls hang out together tomorrow? If we get there around 10, we can leave around noon and be back by 1. I know you and Em just got together but, hell Sean, you don't want to get apron tied. Besides we'll be back before they even miss us. It should be fun. What do you say?"

"It sounds good, Phil. Let's plan on it."

Just as the four of them were about to walk into the restaurant, Sean told Emily he needed to ask her something.

Then he suggested that Phillip and Jeannie should find them all a table. "We'll be right in."

Sean and Emily stood on the sidewalk for a few minutes. He braced himself, expecting that the game had changed for him and Emily. He heard stuff like that all the time from other guys who complained their girlfriends became so possessive. This was all so fresh for him and, although he knew in his heart that Emily was different than most girls, still, he just wasn't 100% confident. He remembered how mad she got when he asked her to sit in the back seat while Phillip sat up front several days ago.

To his utter amazement, however, she told him, "That'd be nice, Sean. I know Phil likes you a lot and now that he's driven your stick shift…. Sure, you and Phil go have a good time. Jeannie and I will find something to do."

Then she looked at him, closed one eye and curled the corner of her mouth. "I'll bet you thought I was going to get mad, didn't you?"

"Well, to be honest, I wasn't sure. You got so mad at me the other day when I gave Phil that ride."

"That was different. You were acting like a male jerk and it…well, it pissed me off. Look, I don't want us to get to the point where one of us thinks the other shouldn't have a life. I love you Sean. I don't want to own you or even control you. We need to respect each other's space. There's plenty for us to do together; but, tomorrow you and Phil need to just be two guys hanging out together without your girlfriends in tow."

He looked delightfully amazed. "Wow, Em. You're full of surprises!"

"Hell, Sean, you'd do the same if I told you Jeannie and I were going shopping or something like that. Go have fun tomorrow…ok? And don't worry thinking you have to cut the day short. Tomorrow has an evening as well."

Sean laughed, then shook his head. "Thanks, Emily. God I love you a lot. And, you're right, tomorrow does have an evening."

She put her hand on his arm. "Now, let's just relax, enjoy each other's company and the company of our two friends. I love you too, Sean; and I want to keep it that way."

Then, she looked serious. "You know, I really think that's where couples go wrong in a relationship; and this is a relationship; a really amazing one. Neither of us wants to live in a prison. Now kiss me!"

Emily put her arms around his neck. Overwhelmed, Sean pulled her close and kissed her. "Let's go find them."

The four friends had a great evening. After dinner they walked around the city for a while.

The girls were looking at all the store windows when Phillip asked Sean, "So what did she say?"

"What do you mean?"

Phillip smirked. "Hell, Sean, I'm not that dumb. I know you were getting her permission for tomorrow; so, what'd she say?"

Sean scratched his head. "You're right, I did ask her; and, damn, basically all she said was go have a good time being guys. It was pretty amazing. Oh, and we don't have to watch our time because she reminded me that tomorrow has an evening as well as a day."

"Hot damn! That's about what Jeannie told me. I think I could get used to this."

They both laughed as they caught up to the girls.

While the guys were hanging back, Jeannie nudged Emily and said, "Em, with the guys going to that muscular car show tomorrow, let's pack a picnic lunch and go back in the fields behind my house. There's an old abandoned house back there. Remember that sex magazine I told you Phil gave me?"

Emily nodded. "Yea. I remember."

Jeannie winked. "Tomorrow would be the perfect time for me to show it to you. We've tried a few of the positions and some of them are pretty freaky awesome!"

"That sounds like fun, Jeannie. But don't get pissed at me because I want to save you from Phillip laughing at you."

Jeannie looked perplexed. "What are you talking about?"

"Jeannie, it's called muscle car show, not muscular car show."

Jeannie laughed loudly. "How the hell should I know what those stupid cars are called? Muscular, muscle, dick, prick, schmick; they're cars for Pete's sake."

Both girls laughed joyously as Emily patted her friend's back. "Jeannie, you're crazy; but, damn I sure love that you are. You make me laugh all the time."

They put their arms around each other and walked down the street laughing the entire time.

Suddenly Jeannie stopped and looked at her watch. It was 10 p.m. "Shit, we need to go home. I'm supposed to be home in a half hour. Mom's going to kill me."

"Call her on the way home and tell her you got caught in a traffic jam where an accident was being cleaned up. Crap, embellish, embellish, embellish; if you can't do anything else, Jeannie Chandler, do your thing. I've learned how to do that myself because (pointing her finger at Jeannie) I learned from a pro!" laughed Emily.

The girls turned around, yelled to the guys and quickly walked back to them.

Jeannie grabbed Phillip's arm and the two of them started running as Jeannie yelled back, "See you tomorrow, Emily. I'll call you!"

Emily and Sean began walking back to his car. She didn't have to be home until 11.

"Did you tell Phil you were ok to go with him tomorrow?"

"Yea and it's funny. When we first talked about going, he tried acting like the guy who was determined he wasn't going to be tied to an apron. In truth, Jeannie acted just as you did. She simply told him to go have fun at the (Sean laughed) muscular car show."

Emily giggled. "Poor Jeannie, I told her it was called muscle and not muscular but I guess she already used the term muscular. She's a trip!"

"Yea," he laughed, "But so is he."

Chapter Twenty-Nine

The following morning Sean called Emily around 8:30 a.m. She answered her cell phone but it was obvious she was half asleep.

"Hey, Em, sorry I woke you. Go on back to sleep. I just wanted to let you know Phil and I will be leaving in about a half hour. Do you want to go see "Men in Black II" for real tonight?"

She sounded a bit groggy. "That would be great." Then she laughed. "Oh, and have fun at the muscular car show today, Sean."

He laughed as well. "You have a good time looking at that dirty magazine and get some good ideas for us, ok? Love you Em."

"Love you too, Sean."

He hung up the phone and remarked to himself that life was pretty damn good right now. She hung up, fell back to her pillow, looked over at her two sisters who were fast asleep in their own beds and slid her hand under the covers, thought about Sean and the cabin and began rubbing herself.

At about 10:00 Jeannie called. Emily had been up for about an hour, eaten breakfast and cleaned up the kitchen. She was dressing when the phone rang. They arranged to meet at Jeannie's house in an hour. Emily told her she would bring a few bottled waters and a couple of Diet Pepsi's. Emily checked with Sarah to see if there was anything else she needed to do before she left. Sarah was watching TV while folding a load of laundry. She looked up and said no then told her to have a good time.

Emily was at the door ready to walk out when she turned. "Oh, and, Mom is it ok if Sean and I go to the movies again tonight?"

"Sure. I think Martha is coming over to watch a DVD with me anyway. What are you going to see?"

"Well, believe it or not, we're going to see Men in Black II again."

"You are? I thought you didn't like the movie?"

"I didn't, but Sean loved it; and, well, shoot, I agreed to suffer through it a second time. Is it ok if I go?"

"Sure, that's fine. Have fun today with Jeannie."

Emily walked down the street and saw Jeannie coming out her front door with a big wicker picnic basket on her arm. Emily was carrying a small ice chest full of ice and the two waters and Pepsi's. She waved to Jeannie as she approached her house and Jeannie walked to the left toward her driveway then waited for Emily.

The two girls were walking toward the field when Emily asked excitedly, "Do you have it?"

Jeannie looked at her with a sarcastic expression. "Well, duh, of course I do?"

"Where is it?"

"I can't show you now. My mom could be looking out the window. Let's walk a little farther."

Soon, Jeannie looked back toward her house and believing the coast was clear, flipped up the lid of the basket. "See, it's right on top."

"Boy, that's a scrappy looking magazine, Jeannie,"

Jeannie giggled. "You haven't seen the half of it, Em. This magazine has been well used. I couldn't get Phil to tell me who gave it to him. He just said a friend, but I'll tell you, this thing has been around the block who knows how many times."

"I can't wait to see it!" exclaimed Emily.

They walked for about 20 minutes when Jeannie pointed. "There; up there; do you see the house?"

Emily shuddered. "Yea. Looks scary. There aren't any snakes are there?"

"Don't think so; I've been here a bunch of times and have only seen a few harmless spiders. Let's go!" Jeannie began running with Emily right behind.

They moved aside a few boards that were blocking the entrance and walked in. It was a mess, but at least it was private, and there was even a few concrete blocks sitting under a hole in the roof where light was filtering in. They walked over and sat. Emily asked Jeannie if she wanted a water or Pepsi.

"Water please. Let's save the Pepsi's for lunch. I have a couple of turkey sandwiches in here."

Then she pulled the magazine out of the basket and Emily grabbed it. Her eyes got as big as saucers as she flipped it over and looked at the front cover and then, as she opened to the first page she gasped, "Oh, my God. Is that even possible?"

They both laughed loudly, then Jeannie took the magazine, flipped the pages and said, "Look at this. I don't even know what's on the next page because it's stuck to this page. Well used I would say! Maybe the original owner was Dick the chimp!"

They both giggled so hard they nearly fell off their concrete seats.

Jeannie composed herself and flipped to the back of the magazine to show Emily a much older guy playing secretary with a much younger woman.

"Phillip and I have played this game; only I was the older woman and he was my office boy. That was off the hook sex!" Jeannie roared with laughter.

But then, Emily clammed up. She felt as if she were going to throw up.

In a few short seconds, her eyes and mind scanned the pictures and what she saw was a young, small girl wearing a plaid uniform-like short skirt sitting on this old man's lap. He had his hand down her underwear and the look on his face was far too familiar. Her brain screamed but her mouth remained mute. Jeannie's laughter suddenly became piercingly loud.

Emily slid off the concrete block, and began pushing herself with her feet along the dirty floor until she was propped up against a wall. Jeannie was still laughing when she noticed Emily was no longer sitting beside her but was instead tucked away in the darkness of the wall several feet away. She watched this action not knowing what had happened or even why.

She stared at the now seemingly tiny Emily, and thought. *Emily's basically a serious girl but she's never this serious. She at least always laughs at all my stupid comments, sarcasms and jokes.*

There was absolute silence between the two best friends for several minutes as Jeannie tried to assess what the heck had just happened. Emily looked terribly distraught and now sat with her knees bent, her arms crossed resting on the tops of her knees and her head was buried in her arms.

More silence; then Jeannie quietly put the magazine back inside the basket, closed the lid and got up. She crossed the room and sat on the floor in front of Emily and stared at her friend. Then, she put her hand on Emily's head.

Emily jumped as Jeannie said in a soft, caring voice, "What's going on kiddo?"

With her head still buried in her arms Emily took a huge breathe and let it out. Then she mumbled, "I thought I was done with all of this."

Jeannie begged her friend. "Em, I can't hear you. You're mumbling. Look at me, please. Tell me what you just said…please!"

Emily lifted her head. Tears filled her eyes and she choked as she spoke. "I just thought I was done with all of this."

"Done with what, Em?" Please, Emily, I'm your best friend. We've been through a lot in the last several years. Talk to me. I'm listening."

Emily looked at Jeannie with the most serious look Jeannie had ever seen from her young friend. She felt a little scared. She had no idea what to expect.

Then, she asked, "Is it something to do with Sean?"

"God, no! He's the good in my life. You're the good in my life."

Then she cleared her throat and with her right hand pulled her hair back as she ran her hand from the top of her forehead to the back of her head. "I'm going to tell you something, but it's not good. It's not at all good; but you *have* to promise me something."

"What? Anything…I'll promise anything. I'm your friend. I'm the one who loves you with all my heart. You're my hero, Emily; don't you know that by now?"

"Well, I may not be your hero anymore once I've told you what I'm going to tell you," Emily's face was contorted and full of pain. "But, first, you have to promise me you will never tell anyone, especially your parents and Phillip. I'm not kidding about Phillip. I never want Phillip to look at me different. I always want him to know me as the Emily he's always thought he's known. Promise me Jeannie. Promise me! Please!!"

Jeannie was holding Emily's hands, stroking them as she

tried to convince her friend she was with her all the way.

"I promise. With all my heart, I promise. And, just so you know, I do care a lot about Phillip. After all, he was my first; but, I'm not ready to open a checking account with him yet. I have a lot of youth in front of me. Hell, I'm going to URI in a few months. I'll be living in a dorm. There are so many good looking guys there; my head is spinning just thinking about how much fun I'm going to have. Oh, and of course, I want to get my degree because I do want to teach. So, don't worry about me opening my big mouth to Phillip; and, God forbid, my parents are the last people I'd tell a guarded secret to. So, now, I'm all ears; and I promise to try and keep my big yap shut so you can tell me everything you want to tell me. Just talk to me, Emily…please talk to me."

Emily took another huge breath and let it out. "My childhood hasn't been like yours."

Jeannie tried to inject a little humor hoping to get at least a smile from Emily. "Ok…I'm an only child and you're one of several. I'm Protestant, thank God and you're Catholic, poor thing. I've got that."

"No, Jeannie, that's not what I mean. You have a truly loving dad who's always been a great dad to you. And you've got a mom who obviously loves your dad but doesn't take any crap from him. My family's not like that."

Then, as Jeannie was about to try a little more humor, Emily blurted, "My father began molesting me when I was six years old and he continued until I stabbed him in the hand with a pencil one day."

Jeannie was dumbfounded and perhaps for the first time in her entire life she was speechless. She just sat watching Emily's face and listened. It was just what Emily needed. She needed Jeannie to be quiet and listen before she lost her nerve; so, she told her the entire story.

She told Jeannie about the first time and the many times he would trick her and pull her to his lap when all the other kids were in bed and her mom was asleep in another room. She talked about the night after night, he would come into the bedroom and climb into her bed. Then she talked about the night of Jeannie's birthday party when he wanted to ruin her evening and about the following day when she knew with all her heart he intended to penetrate her, so she stabbed his hand with a filthy pencil causing him to go to the infirmary to get a tetanus shot. Then she told Jeannie about her conversation with Martha and what she said to her dad just before he died.

Emily was totally spent and out of breath when she finished. She buried her head back into her arms. She felt alone. She felt defeated.

Still lost for words, Jeannie slid back against the wall and next to Emily. She purposely let her shoulder touch Emily's.

Sadly resigned, Emily lifted her head, looked forward and pathetically said, "Guess I'm no longer your hero."

After a few more seconds Jeannie exclaimed, "God, Emily, I never, ever expected this. I don't know what to say except I'm so, so sorry. But I also want you to know that you're still my hero, only more so. Now I know where that punch to that jerk's balls came from."

Emily looked at Jeannie not knowing what she meant.

"God, Em, the day Sean fell through the ice. You hit that kid in the balls. I'll bet he was singing Alto for days!"

Emily looked at Jeannie who was making a funny face as she sang one very high note, then laughed softly. She managed to get a little laugh from Emily.

Then Jeannie looked at Emily, put her hand on hers and spoke with absolute conviction. "That took guts to stab your dad, Em. Then, my God, you took charge! You're my hero alright...big time!"

Then there was a long pause. "Does your mom know any of this?"

"No!" Emily said emphatically, choking on her words. "She will never know! Mom's not like your mom. Dad had her completely under his thumb. She was scared of him and felt small around him except, and this is the strange part, except when he was gone for weeks or months. Then, she became transformed. I loved my mom when she was like that; but it would only last as long as Dad was gone. Toward the end though, and after I stabbed him and then threatened him with his career, he was nice to her and to everyone. He even tried to get back in my good graces the right way; but it was too late for that.

He had already destroyed everything inside me. I couldn't let him get close to me, even if he just wanted to be a good dad. We were way beyond that ever being possible. So, I just remained cordial toward him even to the end."

"Didn't your mom ever notice any of that?" asked Jeannie.

"No," I don't think anything ever registered with her. Jeannie, over the years, I guess you could say I've become an excellent actress. Hell, if there was an academy award for best molested daughter, I'd get the award or at least be in the final running for it. That's how I had to live my life; in secrecy. But, I decided months ago and now, after today and how I reacted to those pictures of the older man with the young girl, I guess I'm more determined now than ever to seek counseling once I'm in school. I found out psychological counseling is free to students. I really thought I was bigger than all of this. And I honestly thought I was long past all of it too, especially with Dad out of my life."

Then Jeannie asked, "Em, you share a bedroom with your two sisters. Didn't they ever wake up?"

"No. Lily and Katie sleep like logs. They never woke up; and I never made any noises. I was so ashamed that I tried so hard to keep what he was doing a secret." Then she stopped and thought. "Except this one time. I recall waking up the following morning stuck between my bed and the wall. I had the hardest time getting unstuck. The night before he climbed into my bed. I was facing the wall when I felt something hard poking me in my back." She paused and looked like she was remembering something. "My God!" she exclaimed. "It was his penis!" Then she sobbed. "I've never made that connection before. I just always remembered that I was more scared than ever before. I knew something was different that night so I began crying so hard and loudly that he quickly got up and left the room. I guess he was afraid of my waking someone else up."

She put her hands on her face and cried hard as Jeannie lovingly rubbed her back.

Then, when she composed herself again, Jeannie asked one more pointed question. "Emily do you think there's a chance he did the same things to Lily or Katie?"

Emily looked up and shook her head back and forth rapidly and fresh tears rolled down her face. "No, Dad always loved them and showed them only love. They knew nothing. They knew a different father and they have only love for him; and, that's how I want to leave it. I've just always wished with my entire being he could have loved me; but he didn't and I will have to live with that knowledge for the rest of my life. That's another reason for promising myself to seek counseling. I need to figure out how to deal with this knowledge and pain so that it doesn't affect the rest of my life. I want to be happy. I deserve to be happy. I know that now!"

She and Jeannie talked for several hours longer when they looked at their watches and realized how late it was.

"The boys must be back by now," said Jeannie.

"Yea, they probably are. I'm supposed to go to a movie with Sean. I fibbed to Mom about going to see Men in Black yesterday and now Sean wants to see it."

"See, Em, I've taught you a thing or two over the years, even how to fool the parents."

Emily stoked Jeannie's face. "Yea, you have Jeannie. You've been the best girlfriend I could have ever hoped for. Between you and Sean, outside my house, life has been, well…sane. I love you for that, Jeannie. I really do."

Jeannie put her arm around Emily and they both sat there for a while longer. Then they got up and left.

As they walked Jeannie paused. "Hang on a minute."

She put the picnic basket on the ground, opened the top, took the two wrapped turkey sandwiches out, removed the wrappers and dumped the sandwiches on the ground. "Might as well give a few critters a good meal."

They held hands and went home.

Emily made up her mind that day that she would seek counseling. She had no idea how deep her wounds went. She had no clue how long her healing would take. She will spend about three years talking to a counselor; most of her years as an undergraduate.

For the most part, she will be able to get through the conscious scars. She'll be able to put all the conscious pain and results of that pain in perspective so that she can have a normal life; but, the unconscious scars will have to wait.

She won't even know there are unconscious scars to deal with. Her dysfunctional behaviors such as striving for perfection and impatience and intolerance of other people's imperfections for example will have to wait. Then there are behaviors which have not yet surfaced or even become evident because they've become so much a part of who she is. It will take her years before she even recognizes these behaviors as being dysfunctional. One day, however, in the distant future she will come face to face with that realization and she'll have to figure out how to deal with them.

Emily has something significant going for her however. She not only wants to be but is determined to be happy. She's also determined that she will *never* allow herself to be in a place similar to her mom. She's determined to be economically independent as well as emotionally so. Still, she will need help now and later in order to finally realize her desire to be truly happy. It will take a lot of work and it will take a very long time to accomplish; most of her adult life.

Chapter Thirty

As Emily and Jeannie walked out of the field into Jeannie's back yard, Emily's cell phone rang.

She pulled it from her pocket. "Hello,"

It was Sean. "Hey, Em, where've you been? I went over to your house and your mom said you weren't home yet. You still want to go to the movie tonight, don't you?"

"Hi Sean. Yes. Jeannie and I just got back. I'll be up in a while. What time did you want to go?"

"You ok? You sound funny. Let's see, it's 4:15 right now. Can you be ready in about an hour? We'll catch the 6 p.m. show." Then he said, "Stay there, I just hopped in my car. I'm on my way down. That'll cut down on time for you."

She and Jeannie heard the rumble of his car as it came down the hill.

Jeannie touched Emily's elbow. "You ok, Emily?"

"Yes. I feel like a burden's been lifted off my shoulders. I guess there's a lot of burdens balanced on my shoulders. I'll only know they're there when they begin to feel like burdens I guess. I know now that I have a lot of work ahead of me...a lot of healing."

Jeannie smiled a huge smile. "Well, Emily Callaway, if anyone can work through all those burdens it's you. Of that I have no doubt whatsoever! Now, go have a great evening with Sean; and make sure you spank him on his bottom when he's a bad little boy!"

They laughed, hugged and, just as Sean pulled up, Emily got in and Jeannie waved, turned and went in her house.

Emily got out of the car, and started walking across the street when Sean called to her. As she turned, Sean was standing right behind her.

"Emily is everything ok?"

"Well, yes and no; but let me go change and we'll talk about it, ok?"

"Yea, I guess. Am I in trouble?" he asked.

She walked closer, put her hand on his cheek and lovingly said, "No. But if we start talking right now we'll never go anywhere; and I want to be with you tonight. I need to be with you tonight, Sean."

He was so relieved it showed. "Ok. I'll meet you back over here in a half hour."

Emily smiled, turned and walked across the street. She went in her front door and managed to avoid any long conversations with Sarah. She changed into a clean pair of jeans, changed her bra to the red one, slipped on a red T-shirt with white owls on the front, put on a pair of sandals, went downstairs, said hi and bye to Sarah and walked out the front door.

Sean wasn't outside yet, so she knocked on the side door and Martha answered. "Hi sweetie."

"Hi Martha."

"Sean's almost ready. How are you doing dear?"

Emily tried hard to sound convincing. "I'm ok."

"Are you sure, Emily? Sean mentioned you seemed a little sad. Anything you want to talk about?" Martha asked looking very concerned.

"I'm ok, Martha, really. I just had an event happen today that made me emotionally crash a little. That's all."

"Well, Em, I know you and Sean are going to talk about it; and since I know you're in good hands, I'll butt out. However, if you need to talk to someone else, or even someone older you know where I am."

"I know that, Martha. I love you for that. I'll be ok. Honest," she said just as Sean walked out into the kitchen looking all fresh and delectably handsome.

"You ready Em?"

Emily nodded her head yes. Sean kissed Martha and they began to walk out the door.

Emily hesitated, looked at Sean and said, "Hang on a minute."

He lifted his hand higher on the door so she could duck under his arm. She walked over to Martha who was standing there watching them, gave her a huge hug and said, "Thanks for being you."

Martha hugged her tightly and Sean and Emily left.

She and Sean got in the car. He started the engine, backed the car out of the driveway, put it into first and they drove up the hill toward the end of the street.

He looked over at her. "We don't have to go to the movie tonight, Em. Do you want to just go somewhere and talk?"

Emily shook her head yes.

He then said, "Tell you what. Men in Black is actually showing at a drive-in. Phil and I passed by it this morning. I didn't even know drive-ins were still around. It would accomplish several things. We'd be able to talk, watch the movie, get something to eat from the snack bar and go from there. What do you say?"

She slightly smiled. "I like that idea."

They settled into the drive and a little small talk. She asked him how the muscular car show was and they both laughed. He turned on the radio, grabbed her hand and just drove. He liked where they were at in their relationship. She hoped it would never end.

Once they arrived at the drive-in Sean paid at the entrance, found out how they were able to listen to the movie through the car radio then pulled to the very back lane and parked. He asked Emily if the location was ok to which she answered it was perfect. Then they walked to the snack bar and got a couple of hamburgers, fries and diet cokes.

They got in the back seat of the car and ate. It wasn't quite dark yet so they had plenty of time to talk before the movie started so Sean asked about the afternoon with Jeannie. She told him they were having a lot of fun looking at some of the most outrageous pictures she had ever seen and then about the two pages that were stuck together and the comment about Dick the chimp Jeannie made.

She was laughing especially at Jeannie's antics when Sean pulled her close, put his arm around her and said, "That sounds like fun; but something else happened, baby. Tell me what happened,"

Emily became very serious as she described the surprise reaction she had to the pictures showing the older man with the younger woman.

"I just wasn't expecting anything to hit me like that, Sean. I can't even explain how it felt except that it felt horrible and I just wanted to crawl into a corner and disappear. Jeannie was so concerned, understanding and incredibly kind. She even made me laugh when she told me that I punched a kid in the balls the day of your accident. I never even remembered that, but she did. She told me I punched him so hard she bet he was talking in an alto voice for several days later. Then I told her everything.

I don't know, I guess I was a little scared I'd disappoint her; but then she told me I was a bigger hero to her now than ever before. She has no idea how much of a hero she is to me. Look how she took care of me when I needed to get protection and didn't know how to go about it; and now, she made me feel so safe, accepted and, well, normal. I just feel so lucky to have both of you in my life."

There was a long pause as Sean pulled her close and waited. He wanted to give her all the space and time she needed. Then she pulled back slightly and looked up at him. Her expression was pitiful and full of pain. She was remembering so much of how she felt when her dad was alive.

Her voice cracked a little as she began to speak again. Her eyes were slightly glassed over. Sean watched her facial expressions as he listened.

"It was like I was living in an insane asylum before I met the two of you. I remember being in my house. The house *itself* felt schizophrenic with its delusions of normalcy, yet I always knew that utter chaos and danger was lurking just around the next corner ready to jump out, grab me and send my mind to a place where I was convinced *I* was the one that was insane and schizophrenic. I'd feel so alone in that house *surrounded* by lots of people, yet *entirely* alone and isolated. Then, when my dad would actually do things to me I'd feel as if I was so out of control that I feared I would lose myself. I even remember one time he grabbed me as I was walking upstairs and pulled me down to the stairs and I couldn't get away. Then, I wasn't even attached to my body anymore. I couldn't feel *anything*. I was floating in the air above my body. As I looked down I could see Emily, but she didn't even feel like me because I was no longer attached to her. It was the most frightening feeling I've ever had in my life. But then, I'd physically step outside my house and would feel utter freedom and safety. I never wanted to go back inside my house after I met the two of you and especially you, Sean. I felt as if, for the *first time* in my life I was safe and cared for. I needed to feel cherished and not used. That's how he made me feel. He made me feel used and worthless. I never felt safe when he was around until the day I fought back and stabbed him.

I actually *enjoyed* stabbing him. It felt *good* to hear him cry in pain and then it felt so empowering to see the *absolute fear* in his eyes when I told him I would ruin his life. I guess that's how he always felt toward me; *all-powerful*. I was his little trapped bunny rabbit he could torture whenever it fancied him. But that day I turned the tables and he was now the one afraid. I thought after I took control all the fears and paranoia would go away, but today, when I saw those pictures I *knew* they were still there hiding behind the veil and it sent me to a place in my mind that made me feel as if I was suffocating. I couldn't breathe and Jeannie gave me back my breath."

His heart broke as he listened to her, watched her facial expressions and felt her excruciating pain.

Then he said, "Em, do you remember what we talked about that you should immediately make an appointment with a counselor when you get to school this fall? I want you to promise me you'll do that. I need to know that you're not going to convince yourself that everything is ok and that all you have to do is tough it out. This is not something you can tough out. God, Emily, I feel like *crap* that I'm not going to Brown with you. I wish like *hell* I had tried to go to school somewhere where we were just a short drive from each other."

Tears were now streaming down Sean's face.

Emily looked up at him as she felt one of his tears drip on her face. "Oh, Sean, please don't cry."

"I *want* to cry Emily. I've wanted to cry about this for a long, long time, ever since we sat on the tree that day and you told me about stabbing your dad. I can't hold it in anymore. My heart is just breaking for you and I'm going away and *it just isn't right or fair*!"

Now they were both crying and neither of them had any Kleenex. Sean had a light jacket in the trunk.

He said, "Hang on a minute, Em," as he got out.

He was back in a flash, took his T shirt off and said, "I think we could both use this."

As he wiped the snot from her nose, she laughed just a little. "This is not a shirt I want to keep!"

She made him laugh as well as he hugged her tight.

Then she said with conviction. "Sean, you don't have to worry about me not going to a counselor. That shook my world so much today that I told Jeannie I was looking forward to going to school because I would be able to get counseling for free and my mom would never know. I know I need help. I'm not going to fool myself anymore thinking that I'm done with this or even that I can do this on my own. I need a trained person to help me get through all of this."

He was hugging her hard. "I never want to let go of you, Emily."

The movie had already started but neither of them were paying attention. In fact the sound wasn't even on.

"Can we just stay back here until the movie lets out?" she asked as she nuzzled him.

"We're not going anywhere, baby. That's why I chose the last lane. Do you want to fall asleep, Em?"

"No Sean. I don't want to fall asleep ever again, unless it's next to you."

She slid down a little and cuddled into him as he kissed her head. "Make love to me, Sean?"

"Here? Are you sure?"

"Yes, I want you to take me to that place you took me to yesterday. I want to feel attached to you. I want you inside me so I know you're real and I'm real. Please make love to me?" she begged.

It was completely dark outside, the space on the left side was vacant and the car on the right was occupied by a single couple and the windows were tinted so he lifted her up so she was sitting on his lap facing him and they kissed.

He caressed her. "Oh Emily, I love you with all my heart. God how I love you."

Soon, he pulled her shirt from out of her jeans and lifted it over her head. As they were kissing, he un-hooked her bra. Then they both wiggled out of their jeans and underwear.

She sat back on his lap and took him into her. "Oh, Sean, you feel like you belong inside me. I want to do this so much before you have to leave that I never forget how you feel attached to me."

They fell into a rhythm that swept them both away. As he began to come, his body buckled several times and he moaned, "Emily, Emily."

Then they just held each other and kissed. As he felt himself growing small, he grabbed his shirt, slid it between his legs and under her. She slid off his lap and back onto the seat as he gently wiped her.

Then he looked at her. "Emily I want to do something but I need to know if it's ok."

"What, Sean?"

"I want to give you an orgasm with my tongue. Is that ok?"

"Yes. I think I would like that."

As he scooted down, he looked up at her. "Are you sure? I want you to tell me if you *ever* feel uncomfortable with anything I do or ask to do. Promise me that, Em. It's so important to me that you love everything I do to you sexually."

She put her hand on his head, and whispered, "I promise you, Sean. I want this."

He put his mouth close and breathed in the sweet scent of her vaginal area. Then he spread her slit and searched for her clitoris with his tongue. He felt the swell of her sweet button. As she began to move her hips with his tongue, he reached for her breast with his right hand and cupped it. He had her hard nipple between his fingers as he kneaded her breast. He felt the untamed passion in his groin as she writhed with excruciating pleasure. He knew he could give her yet another orgasm even more torrential than the first so he lathered her with his tongue harder and she bucked a second and a third time till her body collapsed under his tongue. He felt her body breathe as it was absolutely spent. As he came back up, he kissed her stomach, then each of her breasts and then her mouth. She couldn't believe that in all the chaos that happened that day something so good and right became of it. She caressed his head.

Chapter Thirty-One

It was their last night together before Sean left for Berkley. He would go home to his mom's the next afternoon, and then the following day, he would fly to California.

Martha had been working on Sarah trying to get her to understand that her young daughter was no longer a child but a young woman in love and she was about to be separated from the only male she'd ever had feelings for. Emily didn't realize her mom knew she was now taking the pill; but Sarah's world view had been gradually changing since Joe died over a year ago. So, when Martha suggested to Sarah that she stay the night at Sarah's house in order to allow Sean and Emily to spend their last night together at her house, Sarah had a difficult time with it.

She was torn between her Catholicism and what she'd always believed and the world that Martha was trying to introduce her to; the modern world. She finally capitulated knowing deep in her heart that it was the right thing to do for these two young people. She decided to have a talk with Emily.

She and Emily sat on the side of Sarah's bed.

"Am I in trouble Mom?"

"No, Emily. But I do need to talk to you right now."

Sarah got up, walked over to the door and closed it. Then she came back over to the bed, sat down and took Emily's hands in hers. There were several unbearable seconds of silence.

Then, she said, "Emily, I want you to know that I know you are taking the pill and have been having sex with Sean for a few months."

Emily gasped, pulled her hands away, crossed her arms around her body as she held her sides in pain; emotional pain. She wasn't sure what to say to her mom.

So in a soft, calm, soothing voice Sarah spoke. "It's ok, Emily. It's ok. I'll admit I had a tough time digesting all of this at first. You know how religious I am and how I believe in abstaining until a woman is married; but after much thought, and many conversations with Martha who I consider to be an incredibly perceptive and wise woman, I've come to change my mind at least in this instance where you and Sean are concerned.

You two have grown up together and have been through a lot with each other. I am now very convinced that what the two of you feel for each other is genuine; and, I believe it is good.

I've asked myself over and over the last several days since Martha told me. I've asked myself if a love can be so special and well, as innocent as the love I believe you and Sean have for each other then how could it be anything other than right that you are able to fully express that love outside the boundaries of marriage. With all my heart, Emily, I want you to be happy; and if being with Sean sexually makes you happy then you should be with him that way."

Emily had been sitting on the bed listening to this woman talk to her and trying to connect in her mind that the woman talking to her and her mother were the same person.

She never expected this. She never expected that her mother was capable of thinking so far outside the limitations of where she had existed all these years that she would be able to understand as profoundly as she seemed to understand right now.

Emily had such a bewildered look on her face that Sarah couldn't help but continue.

"Emily, tonight is the last time you'll see Sean for several months; and I know the two of you will only see each other occasionally over the next several years. These next several years will test your love to the edges of the earth. I don't know if in the end you will be able to hold onto each other; but, for right now I want you to be able to hold on to what you have.

Martha is going to spend the night over here. I'm sure she's telling Sean the very same thing right now. So, before it gets too late, what I want you to do is go upstairs and gather what you need for tonight and tomorrow and then go to Sean with my love and my blessing."

Emily began to cry.

Sarah moved closer to her daughter, put her arm around her and said, "It's ok, Emily."

Emily grabbed her mom and hugged her hard.

"Thank you, Mom. I just don't know what to say, except that my heart is just splitting apart into so many pieces right now. I can't even imagine my life without Sean; and I'm so scared of losing him. If I lose him now it might be forever. I just pray that we can hold onto what we have because, Mom, it's the most beautiful love imaginable. I feel so much a part of him as if we are part of each other and I ache in my heart and in my soul for him. Thank you so much, Mom for giving me this gift. I love you so much, Mom. This is the most precious gift a mother could give her daughter and I'll love you forever for this."

They sat there for several minutes just hugging each other and crying together.

Then they heard a shallow tap on the door and Lily's voice.

"Mom, Emily, Martha and Sean are here."

Sarah grabbed a few Kleenex from the box on her night stand. She began wiping Emily's tears and her nose. Then they hugged very tight one more time. Sarah stood and reached for Emily's hand and they left the room.

****

Overwhelmed by the generosity of understanding that had just come into their world, Emily and Sean walked across the street. They didn't say a word. They simply held hands while Sean carried Sarah's overnight bag filled with Emily's belongings.

As they approached the side door of the house, Emily asked, "Sean, before we go in, can we go sit on the tree one more time? It would mean so much to me if we could."

"Yes, baby. I'd like that a lot!"

He laid the bag on the concrete step, as they walked toward the tree. They climbed the slant tree to the first big branch and sat down. Sean put his arm around her and pulled her close.

"It's a full moon, Emily, just like that first Christmas we sat on this tree together. Do you remember?"

"Oh, Sean. How could I ever forget? We have so many beautiful memories together I just hope with all my heart that we can hold onto those memories not as memories but as prophecies of what lies ahead for both of us together."

She began to cry.

Sean raised himself off the tree, pulled out a huge cotton rag

226

from his pocket, shook it out and then chuckled.

"I came prepared tonight."

Emily laughed and cried at the same time.

"You could always make me laugh Sean Mahoney. I'm going to miss that."

She wiped her eyes and blew her nose making a low honking noise. They both laughed again.

"I know it's going to be hard being apart, sweetie, but we'll just wear out the phones with texting and calling and emailing. I'll be home every holiday and summer. It won't be that hard. I promise Emily, cuz, Em, you're always right here (he patted his jeans) in my back pocket."

Emily held the locket that was hanging around her neck.

"And you'll always be right here resting next to my heart."

They kissed. As Emily's face glowed from the radiance of the moon, Sean was overwhelmed by her sweetness and beauty. They sat there with their heads touching for several more minutes. As they climbed down off the tree, they walked around to the back side and traced the slash marks with their hands.

Martha made a pot of beef stew for them and it was warming on the stove. She also baked some homemade rolls for them to heat up in the microwave which were sitting next to the stove.

Emily walked over and tasted the stew.

"Your grandma is such a good cook."

"Are you hungry, Em? We could eat a little something now."

"Not right now, Sean. What I want to do is go upstairs to your room and snuggle; maybe later. Is that ok?"

"I was hoping you'd say that. Right now I just want to hold you."

He cupped her face in his hands and kissed her in such a sweet, gentle, loving manner.

"Oh, Sean, you always take my breath away."

"Mine too, baby," he said as he kissed her again.

Emily turned off the stove burner as they left the kitchen and walked through the living room to the bottom of the stairs.

"Do you remember the first time I kissed you?"

Emily smiled as she envisioned the kiss.

"Always. It was that time Mom took you with us to the beach and I brought your bag to you."

"Do you remember what you said to me when I apologized?"

"I told you I wasn't going to wash my face for several days; and I didn't."

They both laughed.

"We were quite a pair weren't we, Em?"

"Sean I think I've loved you from the moment I turned around and saw you standing behind the tree staring up at me. I remember how you shook my hand that day and again a few days later. I thought you were a curiously interesting person. I had never in my life met such a polite individual, especially being you were a boy. It just endeared you to me instantly."

Emily became flushed as she reminisced.

"Em, I know this is so cliché but I get butterflies in my stomach whenever you blush. So please don't ever stop."

He then picked her up in his arms and carried her up the stairs.

The door to his room was open, the curtains were drawn and there was a small lamp next to his bed which was lit but draped with a scarf. There was a sweet perfume smell in the room that was wafting from the scarf as the lamp heated it. It was almost delirious as Sean laid Emily on the bed, then sat down next to her.

Her heart was filled as she looked at the scarf.

"Your grandma has taught you so much about how to find your way to a woman's heart."

He bent down and kissed her.

"Your heart, Emily, your heart."

"Oh Sean, take me to paradise. Please take me to paradise."

He did. They made exquisite, intense love. When they were finished, they tried so hard not to fall asleep, but they couldn't help themselves.

They woke a half hour later and went down and ate. When they were finished and had cleaned up the kitchen they went into the living room and sat all tucked into each other.

Emily asked, "Sean, tell me more about your dad. I loved the story you told me about how he used to take you hiking. I just love how your dad loved you. Martha showed me a picture of him when he was about your age. You look a lot like him."

Sean looked off and with the sweetest expression on his face he spoke.

"Oh, Emily, my dad was a special man. I used to watch him around Mom. He treated her like she was royalty.

I used to listen to other kids in school complain about how their parents were always fighting or how they seemed as if they didn't like each other; but not mine. Dad would always remember birthdays, Valentine's Day and their anniversary.

I remember especially Valentine's Day and their anniversary. They were like little kids falling in love for the first time. Each of them would spend a lot of time looking for just that right card. I know because it didn't matter whether I was with Mom or Dad when they would search. I'd just go across the aisle and sit on the floor because I knew I'd be there forever. Then they'd give each other their special card at the island in the kitchen. I'd always manage to be in the kitchen so I could just watch them. As they read their cards out loud, they'd both get choked up at the card and then at what they'd each handwrite to each other. They taught me how important a good relationship is. They taught me how to love.

Mom was devastated when Dad died. I wasn't sure she'd ever recover; and that scared me. Then over time, she got better but she'd say to me, especially on Valentine's Day and their anniversary day, "Sean, honey, I lost my best friend. I hope with all my heart you find your best friend one day." Mom loves you, Emily. When she knew we were going to spend tonight together she said, "Sean, honey, I think you found your best friend. Hold onto her for dear life; and don't ever let her slip through your fingers because there's just nothing like the love you experience with a soul mate. That's what she called Dad and now that's what she calls you for me."

They talked for several more hours before going back up where they slept in each other's arms.

When they woke around 9, they went into the bathroom and shower together. As they lathered each other's bodies they whispered to each other how much they loved one another. They promised to never lose touch with that. Then Sean picked Emily up, she wrapped her arms and legs around him and buried her head in his shoulder. When he came he cried. She was so overwhelmed by the love she knew he had for her as she lovingly caressed his head and kissed his tears.

Then, he turned off the shower and carried her soaking wet to the living room. He laid her on the couch and began kissing her body all over. He looked at her as his mouth was close to her vulva and asked her if he could taste her one last time before they parted. She didn't speak a word. She simply closed her eyes, arched her head back and covered her mouth with her hand preparing herself for ecstasy which came several minutes later as her body bucked numerous times. Then they kiss passionately for several more minutes.

Sean finally whispered, "Just stay here. I'll go get a towel and will be right back."

When he returned he had his bathrobe on and was not only holding a towel but a bathrobe for her as well. Then he asked her if she was hungry. She confessed that she was famished, so they decided to get dressed, got in his car and went to a nice breakfast café a few miles down the road.

"Grandma said we have the house to ourselves until 2 p.m. I'll have to leave shortly after that, Em. I've still got packing to do and I need to drop my car off. Bill has arranged for a service to drive my car out to Berkley for me. It's 11 now, so let's go back and just hold each other, ok?"

They did; and, when it was time for him to leave they started crying. He was still crying as he backed out of the driveway. In fact, twice he stalled his car. Then, as he shifted into first gear, Emily's phone rang. It was Sean.

"At least we can talk to each other on my ride to the drop off point."

"Oh, Sean, you truly are my heart."

They talked until his phone ran out of battery.

They talked to each other the next morning as Beth drove him to the airport and he called as soon as his flight landed and again while he rode in a cab to his new dorm. They talked almost every day and texted through that first week. This was how they spent the next several months until Christmas break.

Chapter Thirty-Two

The following week Emily prepared to leave for Brown.

As long as she doesn't have exams to prepare for or papers to write, she will live at the dorm during the week and come home on weekends. The day prior to leaving she had dinner with Martha and Jeannie.

Phillip had already left for Tufts University in Massachusetts where he planned to follow in his father's footsteps and work toward a degree in mechanical engineering. It won't be long before Phillip and Jeannie drift apart; but Emily and Jeannie will remain best of friends for the rest of their lives. Also, since URI and Brown were only an hour away they will see each other frequently.

Before Jeannie arrived at Martha's, Emily and Martha had a long conversation about Sarah.

"I'm still reeling over how Mom let me spend the night here with Sean. How on earth did you pull that one off, Martha; because I know you had a lot to do with it? Mom said you did."

Martha smiled like a Cheshire cat. "Do you recall how you used to tell me how different your mom was when your dad was gone?" Emily nodded. "Well, you evidently said something to your mom several years ago that stuck in the back of her mind."

"I remember. I thought Mom was going to bite my head off that night," laughed Emily.

"Well, all I can say is that between what you said to her, watching you grow up, your relationship with Sean and the friendship that she and I have been developing, your mom has come a long way; and I don't think she's done yet."

"What do you mean?"

"Emily, I think your mom is beginning to realize some of the life she missed out on while married to your dad. Oh, don't get me wrong, she loved your dad and she's extremely grateful for you four kids, but, I think she's finally beginning to develop a self-confidence that was stymied by your father. And even though she tries hard not to think your dad held her back, I

231

believe deep in her mind she realizes he did. Has she ever mentioned the name Mattie Collins?"

Emily appeared pensive for a few seconds. "You know, Martha, I do seem to remember that name. I'm not sure if I heard Mom say the name or I read the name somewhere. Who was she?"

Martha chuckled. "Mattie wasn't a female, dear. Mattie was a male who your mom was convinced she was in love with before she met your dad. You know, we've had our own girl conversations and evidently he was a sweetheart of a man unlike the man we both know she married. I don't know, but in talking to your mom I get the uncanny feeling that she doesn't know why but that she regrets her life took the turn it did. She still talks fondly of Mattie; and it's a fondness I've *never* heard in her voice when she mentions your dad. Quite frankly I think your mom is about to change directions in her life in a very dramatic way and I'm going to do everything in my power to help that along. Your mom is a really special person, Emily; in fact, I think you get a lot of your sweetness from her. She just got so beaten down by your dad that she never questioned her life or her choices until now."

"Oh, Martha, I so hope you're right. I love my mom so much and I ache for her to be happy. She really deserves that. Maybe you and she could come up together to the campus for a weekend. We could all stay in a hotel and shop and go to several restaurants. Mom always did like going out to eat. She wasn't much of a shopper, at least for herself, but I would treasure watching her treat herself."

Then Emily looked sad. "You know, I recall the time Dad was coming home from a Mediterranean cruise. She dieted for the entire time he was gone; four months. She so wanted to please him and have him well, faint over her when he got back. I even recall the dress she bought to meet him in. It was a sleeveless white with navy blue striped dress with a pencil skirt. It had a cute red sailor like tie around the V-neck and a wide red patent leather belt. She looked so beautiful and I remember telling her she looked like a movie star. Then I remember how Dad never even seemed to notice and how she tried so hard to hide that she felt crushed. It wasn't long after that she gained weight. He just never appreciated all that she was and all she could be. I always knew Mom was far more than she let on when he was home. I could see it as plain as day when he was gone. She could have been so much more than what she allowed herself to settle for.

You know…you never know which parent is going to go first; but, I'm so happy it was him. I'm happy for her because she's still young and can have the happiness she missed out on."

Just as Emily finished, Jeannie knocked at the back door. Martha stayed seated and waved come in to Jeannie, who had her face plastered against the door window pane, making the silliest face. She came in like a sonic boom from a jet fighter plane. Jeannie always liked making dramatic entrances.

"Well, ladies, what's going on? The air in here feels so heavy; I think I'm shrinking." She crouched down as if she were shrinking. "Auntie Em, Auntie Em, Help me, help me. I'm melting, I'm melting."

Martha was buckled over with laughter.

Emily jumped up and gave Jeannie a huge hug. "God, Jeannie, you're going to knock them all out at URI. They're not going to know what hit them; and when they finally figure it out they'll be crying for more of the same Jeannie humor. I just wish you and I were going to the same school."

"Well, kiddo, we didn't when we were in grade school or high school so why start now? At least you were smart enough to stay clear of another suck the life out of you Catholic school. Now you'll get a normal education with people who have thinking brains rather than smothered grey matter!" Jeannie laughed loudly. "What's for dinner, Martha?"

"Well, Jeannie, I was going to cook an elaborate meal but time just got away from me so I thought we'd try the Madeira. Beth and Bill stopped there one evening on their way back to Quincy and just raved about it. How does that sound?"

"Oooo, sexy!" exclaimed Jeannie. "I've read the reviews. Pricey too. I've read those reviews as well!"

"Well, there's nothing too pricey for two of my favorite young women. I'm going to miss both of you terribly!

See, Emily, that's another reason for me to give your mom a swift kick in the butt. I can't allow myself to just wither away here on this street. She needs to get her heart in the game because I intend for us to have some fun! In fact, I'm looking at splurging on a Mustang for myself. Of course I don't mind kissing *my* sister. I want the convenience of an automatic transmission."

Emily got very excited. "I love it, Martha! What color are you looking at? Wait. Let me guess…yellow."

Martha shook her head yes to the yellow when Jeannie chimed in, "Hmm. Now I think I better switch my major to biology or something like that so I can figure out how to transform myself into that fly on the wall. I'd love to see Emily's mom kickin' up her heels. You go mama with that yellow Mustang…err…*muscular* car!"

They all laughed; then Martha got up and said, "Well, ladies, we better scoot. We have a reservation at 8 and it's 7:15 now."

****

The next day, Jeannie stopped off at Emily's house. Emily was in the driveway inspecting the roof of her 2000 red Beetle. Jeannie drove up in a black 2002 Ford Focus her dad managed to squeeze his dealer brother on the price tag. She jumped out of her car and came over to help Emily load the last two bags.

"Who on earth jerry rigged this luggage carrier on your roof?" asked Jeannie with a laugh and a big smack on Emily's back.

"Henry did last weekend before he left for boot camp. I was going to try and squeeze one more bag up there but I'm nervous as it is that everything will stay put. I'd hate to be picking up bags off the highway."

"Here, let me see how secure all this feels." Jeannie inspected all the straps to make sure everything was snug. "Well, it feels pretty secure but I don't think it can take another bag. Let's try and squeeze it inside."

Jeannie opened the passenger door only to have two bags fall to the ground. "Gosh, Em, do you think you have enough stuff? Are you going on a lifelong safari or something?"

"Yea, I know I guess I over packed, but at least I have everything and lots of choices. Let's go in and say good-bye to my mom. I want to get to the campus before it gets dark. You too, Jeannie."

Sarah was sitting at the kitchen table drinking a diet soda.

Emily walked over to hug Sarah. "Mom, I think I'm all set."

"Wow, I guess my little girl is finally all grown up." Sarah gave her daughter a big hug. "You be careful and don't drive too fast. Call me when you get to the campus. And let me know if you need anything. I can always put it in my car and bring it to you."

Jeannie couldn't resist being sarcastic. "Well, Sarah if she does she better get an off-campus room because she'll squeeze her new roommate out of the dorm room. Did you see how loaded down that car is?"

"Emily always did pack too much even when we'd go on vacation." Sarah said making them all laugh. "Go kiss your grandma, Emily. I'll be out in a minute to wave good-bye." Sarah hugged Jeannie. "Good luck, sweetie!"

Emily went by her grandma's room. She was lying in bed. She hadn't been doing well for about a month and the doctors didn't expect her to live much longer.

Emily bent down to kiss her forehead and quietly whispered, "Grandma."

Bertie turned over to see Emily's face and said, "Why Emily, it's so nice to see you. I've missed you so much."

Emily jumped back as Jeannie watched. This is the only time in several years that her grandma recognized her.

"Grandma, I'm going away to college. I wanted to kiss you good-bye and tell you I love you," said Emily as she stroked Bertie's head.

"Well, you have a wonderful time, dear. I've just been sitting here talking to Walter. He says he's so glad to see you again."

Emily didn't know what to make of this, but she was grateful that at least she got to say good-bye to her grandma and that her grandma recognized her. She kissed her grandma again, hugged her and said, "I love you so much, Grandma. Tell Grandpa I love him too. You be good."

On the way out the door Jeannie exclaimed, "That was strange!"

"It was. That's the first time since I was a little girl she's

235

called me by my name. She usually calls me Sarah if she calls me anything. I don't think Grandma is going to be around too much longer."

Jeannie asked, "Who's Walter?"

Looking a bit sad, "That's my grandpa, her husband. He died when Mom was a young girl. That's what I mean about her not being around much longer. Who knows, maybe she can actually see him. I don't know. Weird stuff happens just before and during death. When she goes she'll be a lot happier. That I'm pretty sure of."

The two girls hugged, Jeannie got in her car and left promising to text a bunch.

Emily was walking around her car one more time tugging and pulling at bungee cords and straps to make sure everything was snug when Sarah walked out.

"You all set, Emily?"

"Yep, I think so Mom. Grandma just called me by my name. She was also saying she was having a conversation with Walter, your dad. I don't think Grandma is going to be here much longer, Mom."

"I think you're right, Emily. She's had a good life for the most part. I'm sure she's ready to leave. You take it easy, Emily; and drive safely. Call me once you're settled in, ok?"

"I love you, Mom."

Emily smiled as she got in her car, started the engine, backed out and waved as she drove up the street. *Gosh, I wonder what happens next in my life*, she thought just as her cell phone rang. It was Sean.

Sean told Emily he felt a big hole in his heart knowing how far away she was. She told him the same. On the other hand he was adjusting and was very excited about his curriculum and future career. She also felt the same about her future.

Then Sean said, "Hey, Em, Mom mentioned something to me the other day. She and Bill are flying out here for Christmas break rather than having me fly back there. I was heartbroken at the time until she told me they planned to book both you and Grandma on the same flight. Their joint practice is taking off like gang busters and they feel so affluent right now they are throwing caution to the wind. They both bought new cars. I know Christmas vacation is still several months away, but can you imagine?"

"Wow Sean! They'd do that for us?"

"Yes they would and will."

"That's amazing! I'll mention it to Mom when I talk to her but God yes! My life just seems to continue to get better and better. Sure helps to overshadow my past family situation. Which, speaking of, I'm already scheduled to fill out the paperwork for my first counseling session. When I went for orientation, I found out from talking to several upper classmates that there's a phenomenal female psychologist who comes highly recommended."

"Oh, baby, that's wonderful. I'm so proud of you. You took command of your situation when you stuck your dad and you're doing that again. You're my girl, Emily!" he said tenderly.

"Well, Sean. I better get off the phone. It's starting to rain and I'm having a hard time seeing. I need to get these damned wipers changed this week."

"Ok, sweetie. Drive carefully and call me later, ok? Love you, Em."

She got goose bumps whenever he called her baby, sweetie or Em. "I love you too, Sean. I'm going to dream about you tonight and start marking off my calendar till Christmas break. Talk to you in a while."

They hung up as Emily gripped the steering wheel with her two hands, scooted forward so she could see a little better and drove.

Chapter Thirty-Three

September and October flew by.

Emily went home several weekends in a row. When she didn't go home she and Jeannie got together at least one night per weekend.

It was the first weekend of November when Jeannie managed to encourage her friend to get totally wasted on beer while at the Prowler, a local URI pub.

Emily hadn't yet developed a taste for any form of liquor especially *hard* liquor. The memory of her father's stinking breath was still too close for that. Yet, since starting school and seeing as it was the preferred drink of college students she wanted to learn to like beer but just couldn't get past the taste.

She told Jeannie that night that to her it tasted like piss. Of course good ole optimistic yet sarcastic Jeannie challenged Emily to reveal when she actually drank piss. Needless to say Emily couldn't tell Jeannie that she had ever actually drank it.

"It's what I *imagine* beer tastes like," explained Emily.

However, Jeannie just wouldn't let up so she began feeding Emily beer after beer until Emily couldn't even get up from the chair she was sitting in. On the last attempt to stand, Jeannie grabbed Emily's arm and got her up on her feet; *but* when Jeannie let go in order to grab her purse, Emily plopped back down to the chair. She was like dead weight at that point!

A determined Jeannie then hailed her friend, Tom, who had just arrived at the pub to grab Emily's other arm and they both escorted her out the door. As the three arrived at Jeannie's dorm building, Emily said with an extreme slur that she had to drive back to her dorm.

"Oh no you don't, Miss I Don't Like Beer. You're not going anywhere. You're coming up stairs with me where you can either cram into my bed with me or sleep on the floor whichever suits you when we get there. Tomorrow's Sunday and I'm not letting you go anywhere."

Emily made a sorry yet hilarious attempt at saluting Jeannie as she stumbled onto the curb. "Ooooki dooooki artichoookie!"

Laughing all the way up the stairs and down the hallway, Tom helped Jeannie get Emily safely into her room. They both momentarily let go of Emily who then stood in the middle of the room with her shoulders slumped and her head pointed down to the floor as she swayed back and forth. Tom and Jeannie chuckled at the spectacle, then hugged. On his way out the door, Tom wished Jeannie luck and told her he was headed back to the pub to get his Emily on.

Jeannie tried to guide Emily over to the bed, but just as they got a hair away, Emily melted to the floor. Jeannie tried her best to get her friend up on the bed, but without the strength of Tom, her efforts were fruitless. Emily was glued to the floor.

Jeannie knew from experience that Emily wouldn't feel the hardness of the floor until the next morning when she would also experience the thunder of a hangover. Veteran Jeannie, however, knew how hard a floor could feel when waking up, so she not only covered Emily, she put a pillow under her head. Then she parked a huge pot next to Emily's head. Drawn on one side of the pot was a sad face with the word PUKESTER written above the sad face!!!

Jeannie hung a sign on the outside of the door for her roommate in case she came home before morning, propped a chair up under the doorknob and scattered several objects in Emily's path to the door knowing Emily just might wake up later, convinced she was capable of driving home.

I wouldn't put it past her, Jeannie thought.

When Jeannie was finished rigging the room against escape, with her arms folded and feeling like a seasoned general, she looked around the room, then mentally patted herself on the back for being such a clever guard, climbed into bed and immediately fell asleep.

The roommate never made it back to the room that night; but when Jeannie woke up to a loud human groaning sound, she turned over and saw Emily sitting up with her head in one hand and the pot in her other and the PUKESTER was getting quite full.

"You ok, Emily?" Jeannie asked.

"Oooo!" is all Emily could manage.

239

"You have your first hangover, kiddo," Jeannie replied as she got up, walked over to her small refrigerator and grabbed a bottle of water.

"Here, drink this and I'll get you another one when you're done. Hangovers are largely due to severe dehydration. You'll probably puke the first one right back up but we need to get you hydrated."

Emily took the bottle and as her hand and the bottle wobbled drank three fourths of it then asked, "Why am I dehydrated when I drank like a fish last...."

Emily bowed her head down and emptied more stinky liquid into the pot. Jeannie quickly exchanged the pot for a fresh one and took the "official" Pukester down the hall to empty it. When she came back Emily was collapsed back on the floor and asleep while still holding the unused pot. Jeannie laughed hardily while she helped Emily up onto the bed where she collapsed again and began snoring.

Jeannie's roommate came in for a change of clothes, looked at the guest in Jeannie's bed and asked, "Is that Emily?"

"Yea, she really tied one on last night. It's her first episode with any kind of alcohol."

Both girls laughed knowing they had both been there, done that numerous times.

The roommate changed her shirt and jeans to a fresh pair of jeans and clean shirt, said bye and left. After grabbing a bowl of cereal, Jeannie went over to her small sofa, turned on the small TV which sat on the coffee table in front of the sofa and watched a sappy women's movie then fell back to sleep while Emily slept off the rest of her hangover.

About 1 p.m. Emily woke up with a splitting headache. She startled Jeannie as she stumbled around looking for aspirin, Excedrin or Tylenol. She wasn't particular. She just wanted to get rid of the *damned jackhammer* between her ears. Jeannie got her a few tablets but she also urged Emily to drink more water which she did. She drank three bottles.

Emily sat on one end of the hot pink colored sofa and was totally silent for almost two hours. Then...she bolted to life, said she felt a whole lot better and was starving. By that time Jeannie was also starving so she helped Emily get cleaned up and they went out for something to eat. Later that day, Emily profusely thanked her good friend, left the dorm room, got in her red Beetle and drove back to her own campus and dorm room.

The girls didn't plan on seeing each other again for the next few weekends. They planned a Christmas shopping spree the weekend following Thanksgiving when they would both be home.

Chapter Thirty-Four

While Jeannie and Emily were experiencing college life, Sarah and Martha spent all sorts of time together.

Sarah's mom died in her sleep on the 28th of September. Sarah held a small funeral for her the following week and Emily went home to attend.

Paul was coming home for Thanksgiving. He told Sarah he'd be home through the following week when he would have to leave again for Norfolk then back out to sea for four months. Sarah was trying to get the house ready for her family's reunion.

She repainted Bertie's room purple and with Martha's help also redecorated it.

She bought a new mattress and box spring and, since the room smelled like piss, she hired a fumigator. Once it was fumigated Sarah decided to give her mom's furniture to Goodwill and buy a new, more contemporary suite as well as have the old carpeting ripped up and new carpeting installed.

She was eager to surprise Emily with her own new room when she came home for Thanksgiving. It was hard keeping the secret from Emily and the times she was home the room was locked as Sarah used the excuse she was trying to decide what to do with it.

It was the Saturday before Thanksgiving.

Sarah had a box of her mother's belongings in the closet of the room and decided it was time to take it to the attic. Except for the box, the room was ready for Emily and she wanted it to be perfect when her oldest daughter saw it for the first time.

As Sarah carefully laid the box on the floor at the far end of the attic she bumped something causing some of the pink fiber glass insulation including a small piece to fall to the floor. As she picked up the fiber glass and began stuffing it back in its place, she saw something that had been shoved into the space where the small piece of insulation belonged. Sarah squinted in the dim light and saw what appeared to be a book. She reached in, pulled it out and realized it was the diary she and Joe bought

Emily for Christmas when Emily was twelve.

Sarah looked at the diary, smiled and stuffed it into the pocket of the long smock she was wearing. She forgot about it until it was time to turn in.

As she removed the smock she felt the weight of the diary and remembered it was in her pocket. She took it out and thought, *Hmm...Emily will never know. I think I'll just sneak a peek then put it back in its hiding place.*

Sarah walked into the TV room and told Lily and Katie it was bedtime. The girls protested but then surrendered knowing their mom meant business. Sarah was once again the in-charge lady. So the girls kissed their mom and went to bed.

Sarah turned off all the downstairs lights, turned on the dishwasher, grabbed a bottled water from the fridge and walked down the hall to her bedroom. She changed into her pajamas then propped up a few pillows against the bed headboard and climbed in. She put on her reading glasses and began reading Emily's diary. When she opened the diary she didn't realize that she had flipped a few pages ahead.

She smiled and, with a tender heart for her oldest daughter, hugged the diary as she read Emily's description of the moment Sean opened his Christmas present and found Emily had gotten him a Swiss Army knife replacing the lost one his father had given him before he died.

She put the diary down, opened her bottle of water and took a sip. Then she picked the diary back up and flipped back to the first page; Emily's first entry.

Sarah was still smiling when she read, **"Dear diary, I've never owned a diary before; but I know how important they are. That's why I asked for one for Christmas. I read THE DIARY OF ANNE FRANK over the summer and just can't stop thinking about Anne. I feel as if I know her. She was so brave."** Sarah grabbed the bottle of water and took another sip then began reading again.

In a split second, life changed for Sarah as her eyes captured the words, **"My dad came to my room this morning and I really got scared."**

Sarah's hand began trembling causing the book to shake so hard she was having difficulty reading. She gripped her one hand with her other hand trying to steady the book.

Her stomach turned inside out as she read, **"Things have been so much better since the day I had to stab his hand with that pencil; but I've been waiting for everything to go back to the way it used to be. So when I turned around to see him standing in my doorway I just got so darned scared...."**

Sarah dropped the diary. Her conscious mind spun out of control as her unconscious mind connected the dots. *The broken bottle!*

Sarah sat in the bed for a long, long time not even moving. She was frozen.

When she finally came back to the moment she realized she had pissed herself.

In an almost robotic state, Sarah got out of bed and pulled the soaked sheet off the bed. She removed her equally soaked pajama bottoms, ran out of the room clutching the sheets and her bottoms, then ran down the stairs to the basement. She threw everything into the washing machine, put laundry soap in the soap dispenser, closed the lid and started the machine.

She then walked back up the stairs stepping on a jack dropped by one of the girls when the two were playing jacks earlier that day. The pain jolted her back to reality as she collapsed on the stair and began rubbing her foot.

She didn't know what to do next. She just wanted to die; but she couldn't. She had responsibilities; lots of responsibilities.

Then, with the burden of resignation she got back up and went back into her bedroom, closed and locked the door, sat on the bed but away from the wet side and began reading the diary again.

She was compelled to read the entire diary. She already knew what she had to know.

Sarah read how after Joe took Emily to lover's lane she made Sean promise never to tell anyone. She also read how her daughter threatened Joe with his career; how she watched Joe become a better father and husband then try to become a good father to Emily but Emily rejected him because it was too late. She then read how, before the lover's lane incident, Emily conned Katie into sleeping with her by bribing her with the promise that she'd never have to make another bed. She did this just to protect herself from her dad sliding into her bed at night. Emily wrote about her last conversation with Joe and how she encouraged Joe to confess about the other two children. Then she wrote about how Martha comforted her as she tried to convince Emily she wasn't a bad person.

"Martha told me I was a miracle and that everything Dad did to me was on his soul and not mine. Oh, God, I hope she's right because not being able to tell Dad I loved him hurts me so deeply I don't know if I will ever recover."

In between the insanity Emily wrote about the tenderness and love she had for Sean and he had for her. She talked about how Sean took her to paradise every time they had sex.

Then the entries would turn back to the suffering Emily would periodically endure resulting from situations that would remind her of what Joe did to her from the age of six.

There's mention of how Joe would tell Emily he wished he were twenty years younger and how traumatized Emily was because she felt guilty for taking her dad away from the mother whom she deeply loved and wanted to protect. The last entry in Emily's diary was the day after she and Jeannie looked through the dirty magazine. It was the day after Emily realized that, although her dad was now dead, he still haunted her from his grave.

When Sarah finished reading the last entry she realized it was now 3 a.m. She put the diary on her night stand, laid down, pulled the bedspread from the bottom of the bed, covered herself and silently cried.

Her heart was completely demolished!!

How could I miss all of this? How could I live in this house and not know what was happening to my little girl? Why didn't I get up to search for Joe? Why did I ALWAYS assume that he got up because he couldn't stomach lying next me? In her mind, these were the questions that Sarah asked herself over and over again.

Then she couldn't think anymore. She had to shut down and did.

Chapter Thirty-Five

Sarah didn't wake up until Katie banged on her door.

When Sarah opened the door to see what the racket was she saw Katie sitting in the hall crying. Katie looked pathetic.

She hadn't had any breakfast and she was terrified something had happened to her mom who wouldn't open her door.

It was 11 a.m. when Sarah scooped the small but heavy Katie up off the floor, went into the kitchen, sat down and just held her tight. Sarah didn't know how, but sometime between 3 a.m. and now she must have gotten up and put on a fresh pajama bottom because she was fully clothed and not half naked as she remembered she was when she went to sleep.

Once Katie calmed down, Sarah got up, placed Katie back down on the chair and got her a bowl of cereal. "Where's your sister, Katie?"

Katie sniffled. "She's upstairs reading. I tried to get her to bring me a bowl of cereal when she came down for one for herself; but she wouldn't do it. I got scared when you wouldn't come to the door. I kept knocking and knocking but your door was locked. Are you ok, Mommy?"

"Yes, Katie, Mommy's ok. Why don't you be a good girl and go back upstairs, get dressed, tell Lily to also get dressed and the two of you go out back and play. Can you do that for Mommy, Katie?"

Katie jumped off the chair and hugged Sarah tightly as Sarah stroked Katie's head. "Yes, Mommy."

Sarah cleaned up the empty cereal bowl and went back into the bedroom and got dressed. She then came back out into the kitchen, picked up the land line and called Martha. Martha answered in a cheery voice; but could instantly intuit something was terribly wrong with Sarah.

Sarah asked her to please come over. "I need to talk to you."

Martha hung up the phone. She had a foreboding feeling in the pit of her stomach. When Martha walked in Sarah was sitting at the kitchen table with her head in her hands. Emily's diary was lying next to Sarah's elbow on the table.

Martha instantly felt sick to her stomach and began trembling. Her instinct was to turn around and walk right back out the door as fast as she could; but instead, she managed to shake off the feeling as she quietly slid out a chair and sat. "Do you want something to drink, Sarah?"

"NO!" screamed Sarah. "I want to know how you know about this and I don't."

"Is that Emily's diary, Sarah?" asked Martha.

"You know damned well it is, Martha. How could you do this to me? How could you know all of this and keep it from me? Oh, God, how could I have not known? How could I have lived in this house with that man and not known he was torturing my little baby? My precious baby girl who lived with this all by herself for so long and I was never there to make it right. I am her mother for Christ sake. I should have been there. I should have been the one she came to. I knew that day in the hospital when Emily came out of Joe's room that something was wrong. I knew when we got out of the car at the hospital that something was wrong. All three children were crying ferociously but Emily was strangely indifferent and unmoved. I knew then something was wrong but I put it out of my head to comfort the other children and myself for losing a father and husband. I comforted myself when I should have been comforting Emily. Oh, Martha, I've failed my Emily! I've failed myself. I *let this* happen all those years right under my nose and I didn't question anything. I didn't do anything. I just acted selfish and blamed myself for Joe's coldness toward me."

Sarah stopped talking, put her head on the table and cried painfully for what seemed like an eternity to Martha. She felt completely helpless and totally out of her realm.

It was easy to comfort Emily because she was a wounded sparrow who Martha knew had the will to survive anything. But she just wasn't sure about Sarah.

Sarah had been beaten down for so long and never showed much spirit for fighting back; but Martha was Sarah's best friend. She was the only person in the entire world Sarah had right now. Martha knew she had to find the will and the way to help Sarah with her devastation.

She moved closer to Sarah and put her hand on Sarah's head. "Cry, Sarah. Just cry. We'll all get through this. We have to for each other."

Sarah lifted her head. She wanted to scream. She wanted to hit Martha. She wanted to stab herself. But something; she didn't know what wouldn't let her do any of that.

She just sobbed. "What am I going to do? How can I ever face Emily again? She must hate me. She has to hate me. I would. It's the only feeling I could have for me. It's the feeling I have for myself. I hate myself. I JUST WANT TO DIE!"

Then, something deep inside Sarah snapped. She could almost hear the change inside herself.

Sarah stood up and wiped her eyes. "I have to go see Emily. I have to talk to her. I have to tell her I'm sorry I was so stupid and never there for her. I have to just hold my sweet little baby."

"Shhh, Sarah. You're not being rational right now. Just calm down we'll figure this out. Emily will be home in a few days and we'll all figure this out," said Martha; but she didn't feel sure of anything. She was just mouthing stupid words.

Then Martha said, "Sarah, I have to run back to my house for a minute. I left a pot of water on the stove. I need to go turn off the stove; but I'll be right back."

"Do you promise?" cried Sarah.

"Of course I promise, Sarah. I'll never leave you. I'm your friend and I love you with all my heart. Why don't you just get cleaned up while I'm gone and I'll be back before you know it?"

Sarah shook her head up and down as she got up from the table.

Martha rushed out the door shouting, "I'll be right back, Sarah."

When Martha opened the door to her house she felt faint. There was no boiling water on the stove. She just had to get out of there for a few minutes before she suffocated.

She closed the door and walked over to her table and sat down. She knew she had to muster the courage to go back over to Sarah's in a few minutes; but right now she just wanted to sit motionless. She had to think.

Then Martha saw her cell phone on the shelf and went over and got it. She walked back to the table and sat.

She had no idea what to do next; but, as if on auto pilot, she called Jeannie. "Jeannie, it's Martha."

"Oh, hi, Martha," answered a groggy Jeannie.

"I'm sorry dear, did I wake you?" apologized Martha.

"Yea, but that's ok. I studied last night till 2. I have a big exam tomorrow and I have to pass the exam so I can pass the course. What's going on? It's Sunday?" She said as she tried to remember what day it actually was.

"Yes, Jeannie, I know it's Sunday, but I have a really big favor to ask of you."

"Ok. What is it? Is everything alright? Did something happen?" asked a now fully awake Jeannie.

Without even trying to mince her words, Martha blurted, "Sarah found Emily's diary last night."

"Oh my God, Martha!" Jeannie was utterly stunned. "Does Emily know? She must be devastated right now. I need to call her."

"Wait, Jeannie, wait. Just listen to me right now. Can you do that?"

"Yes. I'm shutting up. Tell me what to do."

"Emily doesn't know. That's why I'm calling you. I can't leave Sarah right now, so you're going to have to do this. So, just listen because this is what I need you to do. I want you to drive over to Emily's campus and bring her home. I don't want you to tell her what's going on until you see her. I don't want her driving home by herself. Do you think you can do that, Jeannie?"

"Yes, yes, Martha, I can do that. I'm putting on my jeans right now. Keep talking to me. I have you on speaker," she said as she stumbled to put her shoes on.

"Ok. When you get over there you can tell her; but you have to promise me that you'll bring her here. We don't want Emily driving right now."

"Of course, Martha. I know how serious this is and how bull headed Emily is. I'll pull this off. Don't worry, please. What are you going to do?"

"I'm at my house right now. I had to leave Sarah's for a few minutes just to try and collect my thoughts. I feel so out of my comfort zone right now, but we all have to pull together so Sarah and Emily can get through this. Sarah is convinced she's failed

Emily. I think the best thing for both of them is to face this head on together right now and not wait until Wednesday. I may be wrong about all of this, but I'm just going with my gut and that's what my gut's telling me right now." Martha was out of breath.

"Ok, Martha. I'm in my car right now. I'll just go over and call her just before I get there and tell her I'm coming over for breakfast. She'll believe me. She knows I'm a fruit cake."

"Oh, honey, you're anything but a fruit cake. You're an extremely perceptive woman and a wonderful friend to Emily. You're exactly the medicine she needs right now so she can come home and deal with all of this. I'm hanging up now, Jeannie. God bless you for being you, sweetie."

Martha hung up, put her cell phone in her pocket and walked back across the street.

When she walked in the house, the two girls were in the TV room bickering about what channel they wanted to watch. They both jumped when they saw Martha.

Before Martha looked for Sarah she asked. "Girls. Your mom isn't feeling well today. Do you think you could behave for the day, not fight and just give your mom a little peace and quiet? I'm going to spend the day here trying to take care of her. Can you do that Lily and Katie?"

"Yes ma'am," They responded in unison.

Martha felt confident she got through to the girls because they *never* used the word ma'am.

Martha walked out into the kitchen and didn't see Sarah. She then walked down the hall to Sarah's bedroom but didn't find her there either. As she walked back toward the TV room she noticed the basement door was cracked open. She opened it and called Sarah's name. Sarah answered so she descended the stairs. Sarah was putting the wet sheets in the dryer when she turned to see Martha.

Sarah looked mortified. "I peed myself last night after I read part of Emily's diary."

"That's ok, Sarah. Hell, I pee myself a lot, but that's just my age rearing its ugly head. Come on, sweetie, let me help you," offered Martha.

"No, it's all done. They just have to dry. Could you help me turn the mattress over and make the bed?" asked Sarah.

"Of course." She answered as she sensed optimism that Sarah was doing routine chores and was now asking for help.

Everything will be ok Martha told herself, not yet convinced she was right.

The two women went upstairs and into the bedroom.

Sarah was complaining of a sore back. She wasn't sure when she hurt her back.

"Maybe it was when I picked up Katie which I shouldn't have done, but she looked so pitiful sitting in the darkened hallway crying."

"Here Sarah, let me do the bulk of turning the mattress, you just give me as much support as you can. Ready? Turn. Ok, now push it toward me."

The mattress fell toward Martha as she stumbled back against the wall. The mattress made a thud when it fell and was now halfway on the frame and halfway on the floor.

"Ok, let's change places. I'll pull from that side and you just try to lift the mattress so it's level with the bed. Lift with your legs, Sarah. Don't push it because you'll strain your back more. Just steady it. I'll do all the heavy work."

Martha and Sarah changed positions. The mattress was back on the bed.

"Sarah, do you have a clean pair of sheets? Just tell me where they are and I'll make the bed. You sit here in the chair."

Sarah told her which shelf in the linen closet *her* spare sheets were. She didn't protest. She simply sat in the chair, folded her hands on her lap and bowed her head.

Martha made the bed, dusted off Sarah's night stand and collected all the used Kleenex that were strewn on the floor.

She then walked over to Sarah and took her by the arm. "Let's go out back on the patio. It's nice out there. The sun's out and it's fairly warm. Put a light jacket on, Sarah."

Again Sarah didn't protest at all. In her heart she was happy to have a motherly figure with her. She felt she needed a mother right now just as much as Emily did; so she simply obeyed as she put on her light black jacket and zipped it up. Martha and she walked out through the kitchen and TV room.

Lily looked up from the TV. "Mom, are you ok? Can I get you something, Mom?"

"No, sweetie. Thanks for asking and thank you, Lily and Katie for being good right now. Mommy loves both of you so much."

Sarah bent down and kissed both of them. She stood back up a little too fast and felt a jolt of sharp pain in her back. "Damn it!" Then looked at her two girls. "It's ok girls, I just hurt my back. I'll be ok. Martha and I are going to sit outside in the sun for a while."

The two women went out and Sarah sat in one of the two Adirondack chairs; the bright red one. In the back of her mind it made her feel close to Emily.

Martha patted Sarah on the arm. "I'm going back in to get us both something to drink. Is there anything in particular you'd like, Sarah? Would you like something to eat? You probably haven't eaten since early last night."

"Yes please, Martha. Maybe a bottle of water and I think there's a banana on the counter and maybe some grapes in the fridge. I am a little hungry."

As Martha turned to go in Sarah grabbed her wrist. As she tilted her head toward Martha, she looked pitiful. "Thank you, Martha, for being my friend."

"My God, who wouldn't want to be your friend, Sarah? You're the person your sweet Emily modeled herself after. She's got your heart, Sarah."

"Thanks for that." responded Sarah as a fresh tear fell to her cheek.

Martha went inside, thanked the girls for being so well behaved, and got two bottles of water, a banana and the bowl of green grapes from the refrigerator. She walked back out and sat in the bright yellow chair Emily painted last summer.

"This is your tulip chair, Martha," said Emily when she brought Martha out to see the chair.

The two women sat in silence and soaked up the healing rays of the sun. They talked but they were mostly silent as they held each other's hand.

Chapter Thirty-Six

While Martha was comforting Sarah, Jeannie was driving the hour drive to pick Emily up.

She was having a conversation in her head trying to figure out how she would convince Emily to go home with her. She didn't want to call her too much in advance because she didn't trust Emily to think rationally right now.

Hell, she was having a difficult time thinking rationally; and this wasn't even about her. Then a light bulb went off in her head.

She put her turn signal on, began to cautiously cross over the three lanes of the highway then pulled over onto the shoulder and stopped the car. She flipped on her emergency lights just in case, fiddled with her phone and called Sean.

He answered, "Hey Jeannie. What's up?" Everything ok?"

"Well, yes and no, Sean; but don't get alarmed. I'm handling it but you need to do something important. I think this is best that you do this for everyone."

He felt trepidation. "Sure. Just tell me what's going on. I'm all ears."

She told him everything. Then she said, "I think its best that you call Emily and tell her about this and also tell her to stay put till I get there. I guess you have my number keyed into your phone because you knew it was me. When I'm almost to the campus I'll dial your number again and hang up. That'll be your cue to call Emily and tell her to go down to the dorm parking lot and wait for me. If she's in her room, she should be out there when I get there. If not, it should give her enough time to walk back. Hopefully she's not somewhere in her car. Sean, I can't think of anyone else that can get Emily to behave rationally right now. If I call her she's going to press me to tell her what's going on and then I'm afraid she won't wait for me but get in her car and drive like a maniac home. I'm afraid for her right now."

"Don't worry, Jeannie, I'll handle this. You did the right thing. You're right she'll listen to me. Plus, my gut tells me

253

she'll be, and this sounds bizarre, ok with all of this. She's been seeing her counselor on a regular basis and is making a lot of progress. We both know how strong Emily is."

"Oh Sean, thanks for that. I feel so much better. Now I can slow down a bit. I've been driving way over the speed limit and Dad would strangle me if I got a speeding ticket. Thanks, Sean. I love you man. I'll call with the signal in a little while."

They hung up. Jeannie opened the back right window and cracked her window for some much needed fresh air then turned on the radio for some distraction. She then flipped on her left signal, but just as she was about to cautiously pull back out onto the highway, she heard a siren and looked in her rear view mirror.

"Damn," she said as she killed the motor and began searching for her license and registration.

The officer called to her from the back left side of her car. He had his hand on his holster. His partner was out of the car as well and standing to the rear right also with his hand on his holster.

She opened her window all the way, put her hands on the steering wheel just as her dad instructed her to do in such a situation and said, "I'm ok, officer."

He then cautiously walked toward her window. He still had his hand on his holster; but when he saw that she was gripping the steering wheel he relaxed and waved to his partner that everything was ok. "Are you alright, miss? You have your emergency lights on."

"Oh, I forgot I turned them on. I'm sorry, officer. I'll flip them off and be on my way,"

"Hold on. Hold on. Let me see your license and registration and tell me why you pulled over," instructed the very good looking officer.

Once she saw his gorgeous face, Jeannie was no longer in a hurry. "Absolutely, officer."

She gleefully and dutifully handed him her license and registration making absolutely sure he touched her hand at the same time.

Oooo, she thought. *That was a rush! Jeannie, what the hell are you doing? This is a cop!'* Then she thought, Ye*a; but he's a yummy cop.*

As she looked up at him she felt her nipples getting very hard. He asked, "Ok, so why are you on the shoulder?"

"Well, officer, I just had this strange feeling an absolute hunk in a uniform was several cars in back of me and some little voice which I have no idea where it was coming from told me to pull over and wait."

She was now blushing from ear to ear that she was being so cavalier.

Then she said before he got mad at her, "Seriously though. I pulled over to call a friend. I'm on my way to help another friend and needed to call him to have him call her. I was just trying to be a safe driver. Sorry I got so stupid with my answer, sir. Can I be on my way now? I won't take up any more of your time, I promise."

The officer was the one now blushing. "Well, miss, I commend you for being a responsible citizen. If you don't mind, however, and this is completely off the books; I'm not being very professional at all right now. Would you mind writing your name and phone number on this sheet? I could look you up using your license but I'd rather you give me those things voluntarily."

Jeannie smiled sweetly at the officer. "I'd love to, officer. My name is Jeannie by the way. Jeannie Chandler. What's yours? I can't see the name on your badge for the sun."

She was writing as he answered, "It's John. John Bertram, Jeannie. Thanks for asking."

"Ok. Here's all the information you need. Now I better be on my way. By the way, are you married? I have a mission to complete. You will call me won't you, John. I don't want to call your superior to report a pervert you know. Just kidding. Call me, ok?"

She flipped off the emergency signal and flipped on her turn signal.

"No ma'am, I'm not married and yes, ma'am I'll call you. I'll be off in four hours. I'll call you then if that's ok."

She started her car and said, "That would be perfect. Now move your sexy body so I can pull back out onto the highway. Thanks," as he moved away from the car.

John stood on the shoulder for a few minutes scratching his head as he watched her disappear down the highway. He laughed with delight then walked back to his car shaking his head in disbelief.

Jeannie left her window down and began singing to the Bruce Springsteen song that was currently playing. She laughed and said out loud. "She's the one. "Perfect timing, Bruce! But you have it all wrong Bruce, baby, you should be singing he's the one. Oooo...am I nuts or something? Hmm, maybe not...we'll see."

She tapped the steering wheel to the beat and felt a warm, tingly feeling in her sweet spot as she spoke his name, "John Bertram. You better call me or I'll become a stalker; and, I'll be the stalker from hell!"

She laughed loudly as she pulled onto the ramp. She was about ten minutes from Emily's when she called Sean and hung up. She continued to drive as her phone rang. It was Sean.

"Are you ok, Jeannie? You took a long time to call me back."

"Yes. I'm fine. In fact I'm better than fine. I think I just met my Sean; and he's a stupid cop. He stopped to make sure I wasn't broke down. But I'm almost there so call her now."

They hung up.

Sean called Emily. She was in her dorm studying.

She answered the phone and lovingly said, "Is this my Seanie?"

He said, "Yes, baby. Where are you?"

She sensed something was up. "I'm in my room. What's going on? Are you ok?"

"Yea, yea. I'm fine. Listen baby, now just listen and don't panic. Your mom found your diary and she's freaking out. But it's ok, Grandma's with her and Jeannie's on her way to pick you up to take you home. You stay there till Jeannie gets there. Do you promise me, Em?"

"Yes, I promise you, Sean. I'm fine. I had a dream several days ago. I think I've been waiting for this. I'm ok. Now I have to go help Mom with this."

Emily spoke with such calmness it scared Sean. "Are you sure, Em? I'm worried about you right now."

"I'm ok. I promise you Sean. The counselor and I talked about this yesterday when I told her about my dream and told her I remembered I left my diary in its hiding place but would get it this next week when I am home for Thanksgiving."

"What dream," he asked.

Emily told Sean about a very strange but vivid dream she had where her grandma came to her and told her that Sarah was going to accidently find her diary. "It was such a strange dream, Sean that it almost seemed real. I can't explain it. But, that's beside the point. The cat's just out of the bag a little sooner than expected and it's probably clawing Mom to death right now. I need to go home and get the fucking cat off my mom. The asshole is my dad and her husband. She needs to know that. Listen, I just got outside and see Jeannie pulling into the parking lot. Don't worry about anything. Just wish me luck and I'll call you tonight. I promise. I love you so much, Sean. Oh, and…guess what? There are only 25 more days until I get to attack your delicious body. Gotta go." She hung up, waved to Jeannie and hopped in the car.

Sean sensed the phone go dead, put it out in front of him, looked at it and shook his head in disbelief. She was constantly surprising him with her grit and grip on reality. He stopped worrying and went back to his own studying. He had a major exam in a few days and didn't feel quite prepared.

Jeannie looked at Emily with concern. "Emily…," to which Emily immediately said, "It's ok, Jeannie. I had a gut feeling and even a premonition this was about to happen. I'm fine. I talked to my counselor about a dream I had and we both feel confident I'm ready to face this head on." She gave Jeannie a short synopsis of her dream.

Jeannie looked at her and said, "Damn, girl that was a very strange dream. You're right it does sound like a premonition. Then she asked, "Sean did call you, didn't he?"

"Yea, we just hung up. Actually I think I hung up on him when I saw you pull in. He was freaking out a little, but I convinced him I was ok with this. Now let's just get home to my mom. She's the injured puppy right now. I'm just glad Martha is there for her; and you're here for me. Martha called you…right?"

"Yea, Martha's been there all day with her. She took a breather, went back to her house and called me. Then I called Sean because I didn't want to set off the fire alarm and have you hop in your car and plow into a guard rail or something horrible like that. Phew. I'm so fucking relieved. I don't know Em. At what age did you grow such big cojones; because they're hanging down to your knees? You're amazing! I don't know how I could have been able to handle everything you have over all these years. Damn!!!"

Emily just smiled. "Don't sell yourself so short Miss Fancy Pants. You're a little bit of a spitfire yourself. I know you'd be right here where I'm at if all this was happening to you. Thanks for being my best damned girlfriend in the whole world. I love you so much!"

"I love you too, kiddo," said Jeannie. "Now let me tell you something amazing that happened to me on my way here. This will blow your mind. It has mine! I think I just met my own personal Sean!"

Jeannie laughed joyfully, then began recounting blow for blow what happened.

An hour and fifteen minutes later they pulled into Emily's driveway.

Lily looked out the window then ran out back and yelled, "Jeannie and Emily just drove up. What're they doing here?"

Sarah looked at Martha with a scared rabbit look as Martha put her hand on Sarah's. "It's going to be alright, Sarah. I called Jeannie and asked her to go bring Emily home. Don't worry. You've got one hell of an amazing daughter. She's going to help *you* begin to heal. She's been seeing a counselor at school and is well on her way to healing herself. This is something the two of you need to do together. It's time."

Katie ran out and hugged Emily tight. "I've missed you so much, Emily. I didn't think you'd be home till Wednesday though. Are you staying?"

"I've missed you too, squirt. Where's Mom and Martha?"

"They're out on the patio. Mom doesn't feel good. She locked her bedroom door last night and I was scared and was crying in the hall when she finally came out." Katie was looking down at the ground and shuffling her feet.

Emily could tell the episode alarmed Katie. "Awe, Katie. Mom's going to be alright. She's a strong woman; stronger than she knows. I'm going to go look after her now. Ok, Katie? You just go back to what you were doing and everything will be fine."

Emily bent down on one knee and hugged Katie. "Ok, I was watching a good movie; and that little turd Lily better not have changed the channel!"

Jeannie watched this interaction and realized what she missed out on being an only child. *But then again,* she thought, *I got all the presents!*

As they walked through the TV room, Lily looked up. "Hey, Emily. You're home early."

"What are you watching?" Emily was determined to champion Katie.

"Awe, Beauty and the Beast again for the umpteenth time. Katie wants to watch it and I've got to admit, it's one of my favorites so I'm watching it with her."

Satisfied she didn't have to intervene for Katie, Emily smiled opened the back door and walked out onto the patio with Jeannie.

Martha had already moved the chairs from the patio table, placed one next to Sarah's chair and the other next to her chair but across from Sarah. Martha got up, but Sarah was too damned scared to get up. She was bracing herself for the worst.

She began sobbing when her lovely daughter bent down on her knees, reached for her hand and said, "Mom, I love you with all my heart. Everything's going to be ok. I promise. I'm here now. We'll get through this together. You have no idea just how tough you are; but I do. I got all my best qualities from you and that's the God's honest truth!"

Emily was now sobbing herself as she and Sarah hugged tightly for the longest time.

Martha and Jeannie sat holding hands with tears running down their cheeks. They both felt so miraculously fortunate to witness such an implausible yet beautiful drama as it unfolded right before their eyes.

It was only 3 p.m. so the four women sat on the patio for almost two more hours. Emily and Sarah were doing all the talking.

At first, Emily did a lot of the talking while Sarah interjected from time to time as she said over and over. "I'm so stupid, stupid, stupid!"

She finally stopped denigrating herself as Emily convinced Sarah how cunning her husband was to have fooled them both.

"He snuck up on both of us, Mom! But, deep down and a long, long time ago I think he was a good person. I think he started out that way but got sidetracked and made terrible choices while he was trying to cope with what happened to him."

She then told Sarah how Joe was molested by three different pedophiles when he was just an innocent child.

"That day in his hospital room he told me about that. I told him I wished I could have made it better, but that he was the one who chose the way he coped with it by giving me all his pain; and, that's not the worst of it, Mom. You need to know all of it.

I've been doing a lot of reading about this sort of thing. It wasn't until sometime in the 1970's that the term pedophilia began appearing in psychiatric journals. It was in the 70's that it was first understood to be prevalent; and, since then there's been a lot of studies done. I've been reading a self-help book called THE COURAGE TO HEAL written by two female authors who compiled recorded stories specifically about females like me. The book's helped me a lot Mom. I meant to grab it today but walked out without it. I'll bring it home Wednesday because I think it will help you as well.

I also would like so much for you to go to a few of my counseling sessions. Dr. Wells who is a professor of psychology at the college has been guiding me through all of this. She'd be utterly delighted to have you accompany me a few times. Then, maybe you could find someone like her locally to talk to. Neither of us can do this on our own. This really does require a professional guardian angel. Will you at least think about it, Mom," Emily begged.

"Yes, Emily, I will. If you think this is what we should do I will do it too. I trust you being my guardian right now. I love you so much, Emily. I don't know why God blessed me so much but he did which says something about me I guess."

"Mom, it says everything. I love you so much."

Emily then got up. Her knees were killing her from kneeling for so long on the concrete. She backed up, sat down and began rubbing her knees.

Finally Martha spoke. "Listen everyone. It's nearly 5:00.

Katie and Lily are probably starving. I know I am. Let's call it a day for right now and go get something to eat; my treat!"

With a shit eating grin on her face Jeannie said, "I'm expecting a very important phone call this evening. I better get back. I still have a little studying to do."

Then Emily asked, "But how will I get back?"

Sarah put her hand on Emily's. "I'll drive you back in the morning, honey. I'd like for you to stay here tonight. You can sleep with me in my bed. Is that ok?"

"Yes, Mom. I don't have anything to do tonight anyway." Then she looked at Jeannie. "Jeannie, you have time to stop and have dinner with us. You do have to eat so you might as well. Besides you can excuse yourself if Officer Dunkin Donuts calls. Ok?"

Jeannie laughed bawdily at the nickname and agreed to take a detour before heading back. They all stood up and Jeannie said, "Ok ladies, group hug!"

Martha told them she would be back soon. She needed to clean up and change. Jeannie went out in the TV room and watched TV with the two girls as Emily took her mom by the hand back to her bedroom and helped her change.

"Guess what, girls?" said Jeannie excitedly. "We're all going out to eat dinner. How do ya like them apples?" The two girls squealed with joy.

Chapter Thirty-Seven

Jeannie got her phone call from Officer Dunkin Donuts while they were all in the restaurant. She excused herself and walked out to the sidewalk to talk to him.

She knew full well who was calling her, but she decided to have a little fun.

"I'm sorry, I was in a noisy restaurant, this is Jeannie. Who is this, please?"

"Jeannie, this is John Bertram. I don't know if you remember me. You were in a hurry to get to your friend; but I'm the police officer who stopped while you were pulled over on the shoulder." he sounded very unsure of himself; or at least that's what Jeannie thought.

Jeannie then laughed a little. "Hi John. I knew it was you. I was just making you jump through a few hoops that's all. I wasn't sure you would call me. I think I was a little abrasive today and although I don't apologize because once you get to know me you'll only find out I have a smart mouth anyway, but I'll just say my condolences to you for actually calling me."

He laughed but then sounded even more apprehensive.

"Well, you certainly are different from any female I've ever met, but that's what intrigues me. So if it's ok, I'd like to tell you that I would like to see you again. That is out of uniform and without my hand on my pistol ready to mow you down."

She laughed loudly. "Oh, goodie. This should be fun. I'm game. When? I'm a college student at URI so, let's see. I'm going home on Wednesday for Thanksgiving. I live in East Providence. Where do you live, John?"

She was about to let go and call him Officer Dunkin Donuts but decided not to overwhelm him and restrained her urge.

"I live just across the Washington Bridge from East Providence. I have your East Providence address so, how about 7 p.m. Wednesday. I'll come pick you up. Will that work for you?"

"Yes, it should work perfectly. I'll get home from the college around 5 so that'll give me enough time to say hi and bye to my parents, shower and get ready. Where are we going?"

"Let's get some dinner. There's a few nice restaurants in Providence I like and then let's just go from there. This is my cell phone number showing on yours, so you'll have my number and I'll see you Wednesday. I won't be dressed up, so please don't make me look like an idiot by dressing up. Jeans would be great."

"I like it; and I like that you're quick on your feet. It means we should have fun at least Wednesday anyway. See you then, John Bertram," she said just to hear herself say his name.

"It's a plan Jeannie Chandler," he said as he hung up the phone then thought to himself, *What the heck am I getting myself into?*

She got off the phone ran back into the restaurant very excited, sat down and blurted, "Oh my God, Em, that was Officer Dunkin Donuts himself. We're going on our first date Wednesday and he can give me back just as much lip as I dish out. I told you my gut was telling me this is my own personal Sean."

Emily begged. "That's wonderful Jeannie, but just be cautious. You think you're all tough and everything; but you're just as vulnerable as the next person. Just take it a little slow, promise? I don't want to see you get hurt!"

"Sure, I promise; but I am excited!" Jeannie's head was spinning.

Martha was smiling when Katie asked, "Does he own Dunkin Donuts, Jeannie?"

Lily made a puffing sound as she laughed. "Don't be a moron, Katie. That's just a name they gave him because he's a cop."

Katie frowned. "Oh, but I don't get it!"

"I'll explain it later," Lily laughed again.

Sarah was quiet through this whole conversation. Emily was sitting next to her as she reached for her mother's hand under the table.

Sarah looked at Emily with an unsure glance, but Emily said, "Come on Mom. Lighten up. You like to eat out." Then she squeezed Sarah's hand. "This needs to be fun."

They ate. Jeannie hugged Emily and whispered, "Take care, Em and call me if you need a shoulder."

Jeannie left the group and swaggered out of the restaurant like she was on top of the world. Martha paid the bill and they all left.

On the way home Martha asked Sarah, "What time do you expect Paul, Sarah?"

"He's supposed to be in Wednesday afternoon. I offered to pick him up at the airport but he told me it wasn't necessary but wouldn't tell me why. Everything else is set if you know what I mean."

Of course, she was referring to Emily's room. The room would be ready for Emily when she came home on Wednesday evening. Sarah was still hoping to keep it a secret.

"Great!" said Martha. "I'll tell you what; but only if you wish. I'd like to cancel my plans to go to Quincy on Thursday. I could make a few pies this week and then either go do the Thanksgiving shopping or go with you, Sarah, then come over on Thanksgiving and help cook a nice meal for all of us."

"You'd do that, Martha?" asked a surprised Sarah.

"Of course I would. You are part of my family now and I would rather be here with you and across the street from my own bed than up in Quincy with Bill's bratty kids running around. I'll miss seeing Beth, but I'll just plan to go up there Friday evening after Bill's ex picks his kids up."

"That would be wonderful, Martha. What do you think, Emily?"

"Awe, Mom, you know how I feel about Martha; now more than ever. I think she belongs with us this Thanksgiving. We have a LOT to be thankful for."

"Oh, Emily." Sarah began to cry softly. Emily put her arm around her and Sarah buried her head against Emily. Martha looked at the two younger children in the rearview mirror and thanked God they both had their ears plugged with earphones listening to music on their brand new IPods Sarah got them for good report cards.

When they got home, Sarah was once again composed. Martha kissed everyone goodnight, backed out of their drive and pulled across the street to her own driveway. She couldn't help but be thankful that this day and night were over. She was totally exhausted and ready to crash.

Sarah and her three daughters went in the house. Once in, Sarah told Lily and Katie to go to bed.

"You have two and a half days of school this week and I don't want you falling asleep in class."

"Night Mom," said Katie. "Nite Emily. Love you both."

Lily kissed her mom and said goodnight to Emily as she also went upstairs.

Emily asked her mom if she wanted or needed anything. Sarah said no but she'd like for the two of them to just sit in the TV room. "If that's ok."

Emily answered sweetly. "Of course, Mom. First though, I need to call Sean. He was worried this afternoon. Go on and get comfortable and I'll be right in, ok?"

Sarah nodded.

Emily used her speed dial to call Sean. He picked up on the first ring. "Hi Sean. Yes, everything's fine. It'll be rough for a while; but in the end I think Mom and I will become extremely close. She's pretty traumatized right now but she'll get through it. Like I've always said, she's tougher than most people give her credit for. Yea, I know Seanne. I love you too. I'm going to get off before she gets worried again. I'll call you tomorrow when I'm back at school. Goodnight. I love you a lot."

Emily got a bottle of water and walked into the TV room. "Do you want anything, Mom?"

"No honey. I'm fine. I just want to sit here with you," she answered.

It was 9 p.m. They sat together for two hours. Sarah was still in a state of shock and felt numb; but, in the back of her mind she knew she and her daughter would get through this and would both be stronger individually and together.

As they talked, Sarah agreed to come up to the college on Tuesday to go to the counseling session with Emily. She was actually looking forward to it even though she had never been to a counselor in her life. She told Emily she once sat down with a priest with Joe; "but," Sarah said, "That wasn't legitimate counseling."

The two of them, mother and daughter sat in the TV room till

11 p.m. when they both felt so tired neither of them could keep their eyes open. So they turned off the lights, climbed into bed and fell asleep holding each other.

Monday morning Emily woke up, sat up in the bed and looked around as she remembered where she was.

Sarah wasn't in the room and the door was closed so Emily sat on the bed, remained very quiet and listened. She caught a whiff of bacon and then heard the wonderful chatter of her now small family. Sarah was getting her two sisters off to school.

Emily got out of bed and pulled her jeans on as she heard, "Bye Mom. Love you" twice indicating that Lily and Katie were gone.

She slipped her shoes on and walked down the hall and into the kitchen. Sarah had her back to her as she prepared breakfast.

Seeing Sarah at the stove filled Emily's heart full of love for her mom. She quietly tip toed across the room to Sarah and said, "Don't jump. It's just me."

She put her arms around Sarah and hugged her.

Sarah put down the spatula, turned around and hugged Emily. "Oh, sweetie. It's so good to have you home even if it is for only a few more hours. Sit down, I'm making you bacon and eggs."

Emily didn't sit right away. Instead, she started setting the table for two.

"Oh, no, Emily. I'm only making you bacon and eggs. I'll just have a couple of slices of toast."

"No, Mom. You've spent your entire life taking care of Dad, Grandma and all of us while you've let your own needs go. That changes today, please. You need to start eating right cuz I want you around for a long, long time!"

"Oh, ok." Sarah put two more slices of bacon in the fry pan.

"That's more like it." Emily said as she finished setting the table.

She looked around and thought, *Hmm. It's November. No flowers left.*

Then she looked at the wall behind the table, walked over to it and took down the painting with the red tulips and cobalt blue vase. She looked around again for something tall enough to prop it against and placed the prop and painting in the middle of the table just as Sarah turned around and brought over two plates of fried eggs and bacon.

Emily smiled at her mom. "Ok, now sit. I'm going to get a cup of coffee and freshen yours."

"Ok, sweetie." Sarah sat down as she watched her lovely daughter flit around the room.

When Emily returned with the two cups, Sarah was admiring the painting while tracing the tulips with her finger.

Then, "Oh, God, I don't know what I've done to deserve such a wonderful daughter. Where did my Emily learn to love like she does?" Tears were flowing down Sarah's face.

Now seated, Emily took her napkin and gently wiped her mom's tears. "Oh, Mom, that's an easy answer. I learned it from you and you learned it from Grandma and Grandpa and my kids will learn it from both of us." Then, with love bursting through her words, Emily pled. "Mom, tell me about Grandpa. You never really talk about him much."

Sarah was only too happy to talk about her beloved father. "Oh, Emily, your grandpa was a wonderful man. I wish you could have known him. My mom was the ruler in our family but Dad liked it that way. He was so gentle and carefree; I don't remember when he was ever angry. Oh, I'm sure he could get angry, but he never got angry with me and I only remember how kind and sweet he was. I remember the year I was fourteen.

Dad loved flowers and we had just bought our new house. It had a huge back yard which he didn't want to mow every week so he and I tore up the grass one spring and between spring and fall we planted a beautiful garden. Your painting reminds me of that garden. Your painting makes me so happy I've had two wonderful people in my life, you and my dad. Your grandma was wonderful as well, but in other ways.

That spring Dad and I planted red and white tulips, huge Jonquil daffodils, several deep purple iris and delphiniums and fox glove. He called that area of the garden "Sarah's home" because delphiniums and fox glove were my favorite summer blooms. Then in the fall we planted every color of chrysanthemums you could think of. We didn't get to enjoy the garden that year, but one early morning the following spring, Dad came into my room all excited.

He woke me up and said, "Sarah, Sarah, come look out the window!" We ran to my window which faced the garden and there they were, bright yellow Jonquils standing tall. There cones were pointed toward the sky. The sky was so blue that day and the sun was brighter than I think I ever saw it and he said, "The Jonquils are singing glory to the heavens for giving them life." Oh, I'll never forget that morning.

He and I hurried up and got dressed and went out to the garden. The tulips were starting to come up and we just sat there in our two red Adirondack chairs he and I painted that previous fall. This was our heaven he would say. Then, over the next two years as the garden matured we'd spend hours and hours weeding and mulching. We had our own compost bin and we would lovingly stick our bare hands in it and put compost around each plant. We never wore gloves because Dad thought it was a glorious thing to get our hands stained because it allowed us to be that much closer to nature and the glory of it all. That was the summer Dad won first place for most beautiful garden in the city of Norfolk. They gave the awards out during August even before the glory of fall sprung from the garden but the judges could already see the mounds of chrysanthemums that promised a fourth of July burst of color.

I remember that summer so well. It was the last summer Dad was healthy. It was also the summer that Mrs. Taylor from down the street got so angry she kicked the photographer out of her yard when he came to take pictures of her garden."

Emily was totally captivated and grinning from ear to ear. "Why was that, Mom?"

It was the first time she ever remembered her mom being so animated and talking so much and so fast and with such glorious excitement that Emily couldn't wait to hear it all.

Sarah looked at Emily's sweet face and suddenly became sad. "Oh, Emily."

Another stray tear fell to her cheek; but Emily sat up, wiped the tear away and begged, "No. I want to hear the rest of the story. I can't wait. Please Mom. There's plenty of time for everything else. This is the Mom I've always known was hiding in there. Please, please tell me more."

Sarah took a deep breath and let it out with a huge huff, "Ok. Where was I?"

"Mrs. Taylor," Emily responded.

"Oh, yes," Sarah smirked. "Mrs. Taylor. What a pip! She kicked the photographer out of her garden because he was about to take pictures for the newspaper.

She had won the best garden award for two years in a row and was absolutely certain she would win it for the third year. In fact she was in the middle of a garden party in her back yard. She had a yard full of women who were all dressed up in their Sunday best. The hats these women would wear. Why they looked like they were going to the Kentucky Derby. They were dressed to the hilt! Mrs. Taylor was expecting a multitude of people including all the flower garden judges and several photographers.

When this one lonely photographer showed up she demanded to know where the rest of the crew was. This poor guy had to break the news to her all by himself, without anyone to protect him. He told her he was sorry but he was sent over to take a few pictures of the Honorable Mention garden. She was so angry.

And this is second hand from a few other neighbors who were witnesses. She grabbed a huge bouquet of her own flowers from one of the vases sitting on one of her luncheon tables and chased him out of the yard hitting him over and over again with those damned flowers which were dripping water all over the poor man's camera. He never took any pictures but ran out of that yard as fast as he could.

I remember Mom and Dad sitting at a table in our backyard the next afternoon and Mrs. Clooney from the neighborhood, who was one of the witnesses, was telling the story. My God, the three of them were buckled over laughing. In fact, Mrs. Clooney had Dad act like the photographer and she gave a full demonstration of the whole incident. I watched from the stairs of our porch. It was a site to see.

Dad was laughing hard as he tried to protect his head from the beating and Mom was nearly on the ground laughing equally hard. When they finally all looked over at me who was also laughing, Dad waved me to come over and we all laughed for a very long time. Mrs. Taylor. I'll never forget that one.

But, two years later when Dad died, she came to the funeral. She had a terrible amount of flowers from her garden delivered to Dad's funeral so Mom invited her over to the house after the funeral for the lunch buffet. I was sitting with Mom in the dining room crying when Mrs. Taylor apologized and called herself a horse's ass for the way she acted the year Dad won the coveted prize. Mom and she became best friends after that.

I'll tell you, Emily, life is so darned strange. Whew...I can't remember the last time I talked so much."

"Mom, I just hope it's not the last time. That was the best story I think I've ever heard. Tell me something else," implored Emily.

"What's that, sweetie?"

"Tell me about someone named Mattie Collins."

"Where did you hear that name?" asked a stunned Sarah.

"Martha talked about him one day. She said you've talked to her about him a little. I thought he was a girl. I thought Mattie was a girl's name. But Martha told me that he was a he and he was someone you knew before you met Dad. Tell me about him, please Mom?"

Emily's chin was resting on her arms which were folded on the table top.

She looked so angelic and was pleading so hard that Sarah couldn't help herself.

"Mattie Collins. Oooo, what a beautiful man, or boy actually he was. We were just 19 when he and I met. I guess 19 isn't that young anymore; but it was back then. Alice Turner introduced us.

Alice and I graduated from high school together. She knew Mattie who was friends with her brother Don. Mattie and Don went to Bishop Sullivan's High School together. Anyway, Mattie and Don remained friends and I remained friends with Alice. Alice was always trying to get me to go out with Don, but he and I just didn't click so, one day I was having dinner with her family and Mattie came over to pick up Don. They were going to the movies. When Mattie walked in the door I thought my heart was going to jump out of my body and fly away.

Alice was very tuned into me so she pushed her way into us going to the movies with the boys. We did, and, Emily it was love at first sight. I think that's why I've never protested over your relationship with Sean. You two just remind me of how Mattie and I felt for one another. Of course, I was still a virgin then. I knew about the pill, but you know how the Catholic

270

Church feels about having sex before marriage. The pill wasn't even an option for me."

"Yes, Mom," Emily laughed. "I remember what you used to say to me. The only Catholic approved pill is the one a woman holds between her legs. I used to scratch my head about that because I just didn't get it for a long time. I remember one night I put an aspirin between my legs (Emily is demonstrating as she talks) and that's when I finally got what it meant. I laughed so hard that night I nearly peed my pants. But tell me more about Mattie, why didn't you and he get married?"

Sarah was laughing at the Emily's demonstration of putting the aspirin between her legs.

"Ok, ok. Well, Mattie and I dated for about six months. The Vietnam War was on at that time. Mattie had plans to go to college but postponed those plans to go fight Charlie he would say, so he broke my heart by enlisting in the army and went off to war. We wrote for over a year when I met your Dad.

I met him at a dance at the base where your dad was stationed at the time. The base held dances every Saturday night and Alice and I went one Saturday. I had no desire to go, but she insisted. She wanted to go meet the man of her dreams but wouldn't go without me; so I reluctantly went. Your dad asked me to dance and that was that. He swept me off my feet. He was the handsomest man I'd ever met. He looked like Warren Beatty. You're too young to remember Warren Beatty, the actor, but he was a heart throb; and your dad looked just like him. At least that's what Alice and I thought."

"But what happened to Mattie?" asked Emily now speaking with a sad tone.

"Well, he was gone for over two years, 1973 through 1975 when the war ended. Over time we lost touch with each other and when your dad came into the picture, well, that was the end of that. I heard Mattie met a nice Vietnamese woman in Saigon, married her and brought her back to the States. I've never seen him nor heard from him again; and you know the rest of that story." Sarah ended with a reluctant sadness in her voice.

"Mom, those were two wonderful stories. I just wish with all my heart you married Mattie. He sounds more like the man for my wonderful mom,"

"Maybe so, Emily; but, then again, I would have missed out on you and that would have been another tragedy."

"Who knows, Mom? Who knows how things happen. Maybe I would have been born to you and Mattie and I would have had a wonderful father as well, but that didn't happen; so, I'm just as thankful to have my wonderful mom."

Suddenly Sarah got very sad again. "Oh, honey, I'm so sorry for everything's that happened to you. I'm in so much pain that I never knew.

Honestly, Emily, all those years I thought it was me your dad was escaping from when he would get up in the middle of the night. We never had much of a sex life, at least for me. Oh, your dad always got his rocks off whenever it fancied him; but, for me, well, I never enjoyed sex."

"Mom, that's because you never had your own Sean who was as much, if not more concerned with your pleasure and enjoyment. Dad was sadly a very self-centered, narcissistic person. But, you're still a young woman. Who knows what love story is just around the corner for you!" Emily said lovingly.

"Oh, I doubt that, sweetie; but I guess life is full of surprises isn't it? Like the surprise I received last night when you came home to care for me. I NEVER expected that. Life is full of surprises indeed!" Sarah was smiling from ear to ear.

"Well, honey. You need to get back. Let's just leave everything here and I'll just go get dressed and then take you back to the campus, ok?"

"It's a deal, Mom." Emily got up and kissed her mom on the cheek.

Sarah got dressed and came back out to the kitchen which was now sparkling clean.

"Emily, I didn't want you to clean up the kitchen. I said we'd leave everything."

"Awe, Mom, I didn't have anything else to do. I wanted to surprise you so you wouldn't have to come home to a chore."

Emily and Sarah walked out the door arm in arm. Martha just happened to be out in her front yard as she spotted her favorite mother and daughter. They all waved to each other.

As Sarah pulled into Emily's dorm parking lot Emily said, "Mom, I'm going to run over to the Psych Department today and let Dr. Wells know you're going to be with me tomorrow. You are, right, Mom?"

"Yes, Emily. I'm terrified, but I want to do this for you, and...for me too. What time?"

"My session is at 3 p.m. sharp. I'll meet you here in the parking lot at 2:30 and we'll walk over together, ok? Don't forget!"

Emily climbed out of the car, walked around to the driver's side as Sarah opened the window and kissed her mom on the lips.

"I love you so much, Mom. I think this is the beginning of a spectacular rest of our lives together!" Emily had a sparkle in her eye.

"I think so, too, sweetie," said Sarah as she brushed a strand of red hair from the corner of her daughter's mouth. "I think so, too. You take care sweetie and I'll see you here tomorrow at 2:30 sharp!"

As Emily climbed the stairs to her room she first called Martha who had been waiting to hear the news.

"Oh, Martha. We had the most wonderful conversation this morning. I've got to tell you all about it; and I found out a lot about Mattie Collins too!"

After they talked for a good half hour she hung up and called Jeannie.

"Hey girl. What are you up to?" Emily was trying to sound hip.

"Well, I just took that damned exam." Jeannie sounded sad. Then, she had excitement in her voice as she laughed. "I think I aced it!"

"That's great. I knew you would, but you had me going there for a second!" Emily laughed. "What about Officer Dunkin Donuts?"

"He called me again today and he sounds like he's excited about our date Wednesday night. I have to control myself though. I know I can have an overbearing personality and I sure don't want to scare him away!"

"Awe, Jeannie, I think he already has an idea who he's in for, so just be your big personality self and he'll be Officer Happy Face all the way to arresting criminals next week."

"Thanks, Em. I just can't wait till Wednesday. In fact, I was going to call Mom this morning. I only have one class tomorrow and I've arranged for someone to take notes for me. I've decided to surprise Mom and go home in the morning. She's going to be blown out of the water when she meets my little hot bod officer."

They laughed and then Jeannie asked about Emily's mom. They talked a while longer and said good-bye knowing it was all good for both of them.

Emily climbed the rest of the stairs and opened the door to her dorm to see that she was thankfully alone. She walked over to her bed, kicked off her shoes and collapsed on the bed as she hit her speed dial for Sean.

"Emily, sweetie! I've been waiting all morning for you to call. How did everything go last night and this morning with your mom?"

Emily answered. "First, I've missed you. Second, I love you. Third, I can't wait to have sex with you in 24 days. Finally it was truly wonderful, Sean. Mom's going to counseling with me tomorrow. She and I had breakfast together this morning and I had her tell me stories about her father and then about a young man she should have married named Mattie Collins. Mom talked non-stop for almost two hours. I've never seen her as full of life as she recounted several stories. It was incredible, Sean. I honestly think this is the best thing in the world that could have ever happened for her and for her and me. I think my mom's going to become a changed person and she and I are going to get really, really close. I think I'm finally going to have the family I've always wanted and dreamed of. So, when's your exam, Sean. Are you ready for it?"

He answered, "It's tomorrow and I'm about as ready as I'll ever be. Tonight, I'm not going to study. A couple of guys and I are going to have a few beers, then I'm getting into bed around 9 and will take the exam tomorrow. Em, I'm so happy for you and your mom. I always liked your mom although I must admit, I've also always feared her; but it sounds like everything's going to work out. When do you go home for Thanksgiving? God, I wish like hell I wasn't so far away. I'll miss you Thursday and this weekend."

She answered, "Well, tomorrow Mom's coming back in the

afternoon for the counseling session and then Wednesday I have one class and will head home around 2. Your grandma is having Thanksgiving with us. She's become so much a part of our family now that she decided she'd rather do that so she can walk back across the street to her own house than go to Quincy. She'll go up there on Friday. She wasn't too crazy about being there for Thanksgiving with Bill's kids. They go home Thursday night. I guess they're little twerps."

"Yea, they are," said Sean. "I've only been around them a couple of times and I can't stand them, but I can't tell Bill that. I don't think Mom likes them too much either. Thank God they live with Bill's ex. Well, listen, Em, I've gotta head out the door. I'm getting my hair cut in a half hour. Call me tomorrow after counseling…ok?"

"Ok. I love you Sean."

"Baby, I love you too."

Chapter Thirty-Eight

Tuesday Jeannie arrived home unannounced.

Gladys was in the basement sewing when she heard footsteps upstairs. She felt terrified, so she grabbed her phone and ran over to the north side wall of the basement, hit something on the wall and crawled through a short tunnel into a hidden room her husband had installed in the event of a home invasion.

As Gladys closed the secret panel she thanked God Phil insisted on building it.

She protested terribly telling him he was paranoid. "Who's going to break into our house this far down a single residential street?" she complained.

She sat there in the dark, picked up her phone and began dialing 911 just as she heard her daughter calling for her. She was shaking like a leaf and had to catch her breath for a second, as she heard Jeannie calling her again, now with a hint of fear in her voice.

Gladys unlocked the inside door punched the pass code into the inside portion of the panel that separated her from the rest of the basement and crawled out.

"I'm down here, Jeannie," she yelled.

Jeannie bounded down the stairs and was totally out of breath and white as a sheet when she ran over to the crawl space, extended her hand and helped Gladys up.

"God, Jeannie, what the hell are you doing home? I thought you weren't coming home till tomorrow. I was petrified. I thought I was going to have to eat all my words for scolding your dad about this damned room."

"I'm sorry, Mom. I just never thought twice. I only had one class today which I decided to skip and came home a day early." Then she laughed nervously. "But I guess you've changed your mind about the silliness of Dad's expensive project."

"After this event, I'm never going to mention the damned money he spent ever again!" Gladys fell to her sewing chair. "I need to take a break after that little episode!"

Gladys and Jeannie climbed the stairs to the kitchen.

"I was going to stop for lunch in a half hour anyway. Now's as good a time as ever; what do you want to eat?" asked Gladys.

"I don't know. I don't even know what's in the fridge. I'll just have whatever you're having." Jeannie walked over to one of the cabinets and grabbed two clean glasses. "Want a diet cola?"

"Yes, that sounds good. So you skipped a class today. Are you going to get into trouble?"

"Heck no. People do it all the time. It wasn't going to be a very important class anyway; and, besides I have someone taking notes for me. He and I help each other that way all the time. We're in two classes together."

"He?" Gladys cocked her head. "He as in you have a new boyfriend?"

"No, Tom's just a classmate. I knew him in high school so we've gotten to know each other better. We have a beer or two together sometimes, but neither of us is attracted to one another in a romantic sense. He's just a male friend. But..." Jeannie now sounded excited. "I do have a rather unusual date tomorrow night. He's picking me up here so I wanted to tell you about him today so it won't come as a big shock."

"Ok, I'm listening," exclaimed Gladys with a twinge of concern in her voice. "You're not going to tell me he's a married man are you, because...."

"Mom!" Jeannie was now a little disgusted with her mother. "What kind of a girl do you think I am? This guy is single and gorgeous beyond gorgeous. He's a cop!"

"What?" Gladys was now the one currently sounding testy. "What did you do to have met a cop?"

"Damn, Mom, quit jumping to conclusions. This was all very innocent and legitimate. Just wait until we sit down and I'll tell you the whole story."

"Ok, ok. I'll just make us a tuna salad sandwich. There are some chips in the pantry if you want to put a few on each of our plates," Gladys resigned herself to keep her mouth shut till Jeannie had a chance to explain.

Jeannie placed two plates with a handful of chips on each on the counter next to where Gladys was preparing the sandwiches;

then she finished pouring two huge glasses of diet cola, sat down and waited for Gladys to sit down.

Jeannie took a bite of sandwich, washed it down with cola and began, "Ok, Mom, I'm going to have to tell you the background before I get to the part about John. That's his name, John Bertram. This first part, Mom, is going to be a big shocker and pretty heavy stuff; but you need to know the background so how I met John makes sense."

Jeannie first told Gladys the entire story; then as she was ready to tell her mom about John, she said, "Close your mouth, Mom. You can eat now. The rest is Jeannie stuff."

Gladys put her elbow on the table and rested her head in her one hand and said, "My God, Jeannie. How long have you known about this? Poor, poor Emily! Poor, poor Sarah! Poor, Paul, Lily and Katie. That's one of the worst stories I've heard in my entire life!"

"Mom, it's really bad; but I was there on Sunday when Emily came home to talk to Sarah. I brought her home. I'm sorry, I had to get back that night because I still had to study for that big exam I took yesterday, so I didn't stop by or even tell you I was right up the street. Mom, it was pretty amazing to watch Emily comfort Sarah. I'm still in awe of what I watched. Martha was there too. She was the one who called me. I honestly have to believe after watching the two of them that in the end it's going to be ok. Sarah's in for a long hard road, but Emily is an old pro at this now and she'll be able to help Sarah get through it."

Gladys had tears in her eyes. "Oh, honey. I'm so glad Emily has you for a friend. I guess Sarah and I have never really gotten very close except to help each other out now and then; but I'm really happy she has Martha living right across the street. My gut has always told me Martha would be the friend to have in any terrible situation. Thank God I've never had anything so traumatic in my life. I just don't know if I could handle it."

"Awe, Mom, you have no idea what you can handle until it happens. I said the same thing to Emily about me and she told me I was enough of a spitfire to be able to handle the same situation if it did happen to me. Thank God, though, it never has; and, now I'm going to have my own Officer Dunkin Donuts to back me up."

Gladys looked at Jeannie, puffed her cheeks and not only laughed uproariously, she spit out a mouthful of diet cola all over the table.

"What did you just call him?"

Jeannie was laughing hard as she wiped up the sprayed soda. "That's the make fun name Emily came up with, Officer Dunkin Donuts. You know, cops like donuts...."

"Yea, I get it," laughed Gladys. "I wouldn't call him that though until you get to know him better and are sure he won't be offended."

"I don't plan on it; although my first impression is that he'd laugh. But I'm going to save that one for a special moment. I'll know when to spill the beans! Now, let me tell you that part because it's pretty funny, I must admit. Poor guy got a crash course in Jeannie Chandler on his first introduction."

She finished telling her mom the rest of the story. "So, John is coming over tomorrow night and we're going to have dinner together. I think you and Dad will really like him. He can even dish me back a little lip and I get the impression he's up to heavier teasing."

"That sounds like fun, Jeannie; but please promise me that you won't get so tangled in a relationship that you drop out of school," begged Gladys.

"I promise, Mom. John and I are going to have a lot of fun, but I'm not in a hurry to get married for a while and I sure am not in any rush to start having kids. I want a long courtship regardless of whether we stay single or get married. I do, and I mentioned this to both Emily and Sean, think I've found my own personal Sean; but I'm smart enough to know I don't want to rush into anything until I know 100% I'm right. And that will take a long time. I want us to know each other and our histories inside and out before we get to that type of stage. So, please don't worry. Just enjoy watching me fall in love."

Gladys brushed her daughter's cheek. "Ok. I'll trust your judgment. I'm looking forward to meeting Officer Krispy Kreme. That's what you called him, right?"

"No. Dunkin Donuts, but Krispy Kreme is just as good a nickname."

They finished their lunch, cleaned up the kitchen and Jeannie followed Gladys back down to the basement to see what Gladys was working on at her sewing station.

That evening Jeannie repeated the entire story for her dad who had the same reaction but with a twist.

He confessed that he never liked Joe. "He was too full of himself. I heard him cut Gene Livingston down for having joined the Air Force vs. the Navy. And come to think of it, I also recall how he looked at Gene's 10 year old daughter when the wind blew her dress up at a July 4th picnic years ago. There was something creepy about that, but I could never really put my finger on why until now. That's disgusting!

He should be damned glad his sorry ass is dead. Who knows, he'd probably be serving time now in some prison where he'd either have to become a stone cold killer or some king pin's bitch. What an ass! Damn, Jeannie. Either way Sarah would have a hard row to hoe right now. My heart goes out to her and Emily and those other kids of hers. I'm just glad my little girl is safe." Phil hugged his Jeannie.

Chapter Thirty-Nine

Jeannie set her small alarm clock for 8 a.m. She wanted to get a jump on the day. Gladys and she were going to the mall to get Jeannie a new pair of jeans and a new top. Gladys was as excited as was Jeannie about her *hot* date.

Jeannie was rubbing the sleep from her eyes when she walked into the kitchen. "I thought I smelled bacon!"

"We need a hardy breakfast before we go shopping! I still need to pick up a few things for dinner tomorrow. Aunt Katherine and her new husband are coming for Thanksgiving so I need to pick up a few supplies. Say, why don't you ask John to come over tomorrow. That is if he has nowhere else to go and you two really hit it off tonight."

"I'll do, that, Mom. I have no idea if his family is around here or if he's even off tomorrow. All I know is he lives a little east of downtown and is single; but I'll ask him. If he isn't working or has nothing else to do, that would be great!"

Jeannie was talking as she crammed a forkful of scrambled eggs and bacon into her mouth and washed it down with a huge glass of orange juice.

"Whoa, slow down there Jeannie! You'll get sick if you eat so fast. We've got plenty of time. The stores don't open till ten."

Jeannie smiled at her mom, slowed down and even waited till Gladys was seated to eat another bite.

They chatted a bit when Gladys said, "Honey, go on and get dressed. I'll clean up down here. I just have to brush my hair and put on a little lipstick."

"You sure, Mom?"

Gladys shook her head yes. Jeannie hopped up and ran up to her room, as Gladys chuckled to herself. *Are you sure Mom? Shoot, she doesn't know how lucky she is she's never had to do many chores in her life.*

Later, Jeannie and Gladys were in the mall when John called Jeannie's cell phone.

"Hey, John. How's it hangin?"

Gladys looked at Jeannie and exaggerated a scowl.

John roared laughing. "Well, Jeannie, last time I looked it was hangin pretty well! You home yet?"

"Yes. I'm shopping with my Mom who is giving me the evil eye for my smart mouth. I came home yesterday and scared the bejesus outta her. I'll have to tell you about that tonight. We still on?"

She was crossing her fingers with her free hand and shaking the same hand next to her face.

"Sure. I just wanted to check in with you and make sure we *were* still on. Say, is it ok if I pick you up at 6 instead of 7? I thought 6 would give us a better opportunity to eat early and catch a movie if that's what we decide to do."

"Sure, that would be terrific! Say, Mom wanted me to ask you if you were doing anything for Thanksgiving. She's cooking and we're having my aunt over with her new husband."

"I'd love to, but it'd depend on what time. I have to be back at the station around 10 p.m. I have the night shift. But I could sleep a little late tomorrow so I won't need to sleep again till I get off Friday morning. I don't want to crash your family Thanksgiving though. Are you sure?"

"I'm positive. No one should be alone on Thanksgiving and I take it you don't have family here, so please plan on it. I'd love that!"

"Ok. Tell your mom thanks for the invite, now I better get off, my shift isn't over yet. See you tonight at 6."

"Roger that, Officer Bertram!" she exclaimed.

She hung up and laughed at the expression on her mom's face. "I'll bet you thought I was going to call him Officer Dunkin Donuts, didn't you." She continued laughing.

"Well," said Gladys. "I wouldn't put it past you, but I'm glad you practiced some restraint you little stinker."

They had a good laugh; put their arms around each other's shoulder and walked into the next store.

****

Right on the button, John rang the doorbell. Phil made sure he was close by the door so he could open it. He was still *very* protective of his daughter. Phil invited John in and introductions were made as Gladys walked into the foyer wiping her hands on a kitchen towel.

"I'm John Bertram, Mrs. Chandler. It smells delicious in here!" he exclaimed as he shook Gladys' hand.

"Well, thanks John. I'm just baking a few pies for tomorrow. Glad you're going to be able to celebrate Thanksgiving with us!"

Gladys guided John and her husband into the living room which was to the right of the foyer. She and Phil sat on the sofa while John sat in the armchair facing the sofa on the opposite side of the coffee table. It was obvious to Gladys that John felt a bit nervous, so she tried to put him at ease realizing that if Phil talked first John would get even more nervous.

"So, John, Jeannie tells us you're a police officer. What kind are you? She never mentioned whether you were a State Trooper or a Providence policeman."

Gladys patted Phil's hand that was sitting on the couch cushion signaling to Phil to be nice. John watched this silent interaction.

"I was a trooper but I've always wanted to work in an urban environment, so a year ago I joined the force in Providence. I'm taking a few night courses since my goal is to become a detective. I'd like to work SVU. That's Special Victims Unit like in the show Law & Order. I know this sounds lofty but my long term goal is Police Commissioner. Law enforcement runs in my family. My dad's the Chief of Police for Trenton, New Jersey and my uncle's the Police Commissioner in Newark. That's where my family hales from; New Jersey. But that's down the road."

Now, much more relaxed and glad he followed Gladys' lead, Phil said, "That's not at all lofty John. That's a wonderful ambition to have; and, if you stick to your guns...no pun intended...you'll realize your goal. Good for you."

Now confident she could leave the two males alone, Gladys excused herself. "Let me go see what's taking Jeannie so long. You know how women are. They can't fuss enough over themselves."

John chuckled. "Yes, ma'am I sure do. I have three sisters who I was constantly battling for bathroom time when we all lived at home. That's fine. She can take her time. Just tell her I have a reservation at Al Forno in Providence at 7. If you miss your call time, I'm told they won't hold the reservation."

"Al Forno," commented Phil, "One of my favorite restaurants! You have very good taste."

As Phil finished commenting Jeannie came down the stairs with Gladys behind her.

"Hi, John. Sorry I left you down in the interrogation room. I couldn't find my shoe. But I'm all set to go."

John laughed, "Awe, the grilling wasn't too bad. Your mom was kind enough to play good cop for me."

They all laughed at John's quickness as well as perceptiveness as Phil shook his hand and bid them a wonderful evening.

"Jeannie, do you have your key in your bag?" Gladys asked. "We won't wait up for you. You're way past that age."

This was another subtle suggestion to Phil to cool his engines. Jeannie produced the key, dropped it back into her purse and kissed her parents.

Once in John's car he laughed relief.

"Your mom's pretty cool. I could tell from the scowl on his face though, your Dad was about to eat my lunch. But, I can sure understand. If I had a daughter, I'd be just as protective. There are a lot of creeps in the world. I know. I arrest several every day." Then he relaxed, looked at Jeannie and smiled. "You look very nice, Jeannie; and you smell wonderful!"

"Why thank you, John. You look nice as well; and, I'm glad you're not one of those men's perfume guys because to be honest I can't stand the smell of men's colognes!"

"Well, not to worry, Jeannie. I'm just a plain man with a simple plan," responded John to which they both laugh.

They had a wonderful meal and a glorious evening. They didn't go to a movie however. Instead they drove to Lands End in Newport which was an hour away.

It was a beautiful evening. The moon was full and it was pleasantly warm for November with a light yet lovely breeze.

They parked along The Breakers. John pulled a blanket from the car trunk and they walked hand in hand out onto the rocks where he spread the blanket for them to sit. The moon lit up the bay.

"I haven't been here since I was a little kid," exclaimed Jeannie. "This used to be one of my favorite places to go. I just love the ocean and all its nooks and crannies. Thanks for thinking of this," she said as she pulled her sweater to warm her from the ocean breeze.

He looked at her and put his arm around her as she sighed, "Umm!"

The moon danced on the waves as they sat talking and looking out on the ocean. She learned all about him and his decent sized family.

"I'm glad you're going to come over tomorrow, John. I promise too I'll tell my dad to lighten up. I can already sense, though that he likes you and Mom agrees with me that you're very yummy!"

John laughed and, although she couldn't see, he also blushed robustly.

"Well, Jeannie, you're pretty yummy yourself. I'll tell you though. You took me way off guard the other day when I stopped you and I was kind of nervous about tonight. But, yea, I'm really glad we're here together."

"Well, I'm on my best behavior tonight; but I can't make any promises passed our first date. My best friend, Emily tells me I have a very big personality, so I guess you'll have to play that one by ear,"

"Well, I think I'll do just fine with your personality. It's just a gut feeling I have, but I think we'll do fine together. I know this is very forward, but may I kiss you, Jeannie?" He asked as she started to respond, "If you don't...."

He kissed her and she melted in his arms.

After several more kisses, he said, "Yea, I think I'm going to like this."

They had a wonderful first date and a delightful Thanksgiving. When John left to get dressed for his shift Thursday evening he and Phil were old buddies. Gladys was delighted for Jeannie as was Katherine and her very quirky husband, Don. They all said goodnight and Jeannie walked him out to his car.

She leaned back against the car and asked John to kiss her.

He leaned into her and kissed her passionately. She swooned with delight. When he backed off a little he asked if he could see her Saturday.

"My shift ends at 10 Saturday morning. I'll probably have to take a short nap, but can we get together later in the day?"

"Umm, I would die if you didn't ask me! What time?" Then, she scrunched her face and said, "Say, I have an idea. Why don't I go buy a few groceries and come over around 3, if that's long enough for you to sleep. I could fix us some spaghetti. I'm not the best cook in the world, but I can duplicate Mom's spaghetti alla carbonara recipe which is delicious by the way. Then maybe we can just have a quiet evening together. What time is your shift on Sunday?"

"I don't have to be at work until noon, so that sounds wonderful. I'll see you at 3 then on Saturday. Let's touch base sometime tomorrow just to make sure there's no change of plans and my shift doesn't run over, ok?"

He kissed her again.

"Ok, why don't you call me? I don't want to disturb you on your shift. Just call me when you have the opportunity. I'll keep my phone in my bra so I don't put it down anywhere." She smiled as she pointed to her right boob.

He smiled, got a warm feeling in his groin and said, "It's a deal. I'll just call your boob when I'm not arresting perverts."

She moved away from the door, smacked him on the butt and laughed. "My boob will be anxiously waiting."

They kissed one more time as he got in his car, and headed back to his apartment.

As he was driving up the hill, his best friend and partner called him.

"Hey John, how's it hangin?" laughed Sam Hendricks.

They both laughed. "Nice, Sam…nice! Really though, I think I like this girl a whole lot. She's a handful, but I think I like that she is. She makes me feel, well, alive. How was your Thanksgiving?"

"Noisy! Cindy's family is noisy. I was glad to leave. I was getting a headache from all the noise, but it was good. Cindy's mom is an excellent cook and her dad and I watched the football game in their finished basement. So, outside of all the noisy relatives and kids, we had a pretty nice one. I'm ready to hit the streets though. At least, when it's noisy out there, you expect it and are ready for it," chuckled Sam.

"Well, man, I'll see you in a few hours," said John as he hung up.

The rest of his drive home he thought about Jeannie. She wasn't at all what he expected to come into his life but he welcomed the change. Most of the women he'd dated had either been too needy or boring as hell.

She sure isn't either of those! He thought as he turned on the radio.

Chapter Forty

Saturday didn't come fast enough for Jeannie. She and her mom made a list of groceries Jeannie needed to pick up that day.

Just as they finished Gladys got up from the kitchen table and said, "Hang on a second. I just remembered something."

"Ok," said Jeannie as she folded the list and stuffed it in the side pocket of her purse.

Gladys returned with an unopened bottle of Robert Mondavi, Napa Valley Pinot Noir. She got the corkscrew out of the kitchen drawer, held it up and said, "Just in case."

"Wow, Mom, are you sure?" asked Jeannie

"Absolutely, honey. Nothin's too much for my only child!"

"Thanks, Ma! I think I have everything, I'll just go take a shower and get ready."

About 10:15 John called Jeannie as he drove home.

"Just got off and am heading home. I'm going to leave a key under the door mat just in case I'm still asleep. Just come on in and make yourself at home."

"Oooo, I like that. I hope you are still asleep. You won't shoot me though thinking I'm a burglar?" She laughed, then said, "And by the way my boob is standing at attention right now from the ring of the phone."

He laughed and shook his head. "You're a trip, Jeannie. See you after a while. Now I've gotta get some shut eye. This was a pretty intense shift. We had a wild domestic violence call."

"Ok, babe. See you soon." She hung up the phone and thought, *Oh my. I think we're going to have some savory sex today Jeannie girl.*

Jeannie left her parents' house around noon and headed to the grocery store with her list. She bought all the ingredients then looked at her watch; 2 p.m. She decided to head over to John's. She was following her handwritten directions John gave her over the phone; but had to stop a few times because she couldn't read her own writing. She finally pulled up to his address. He lived in a townhouse so no climbing upstairs she thought.

She was ready to take this relationship to the next level.

She got out of her car and carried her two grocery bags up to the stoop then went back for her purse and the bottle of wine. She looked in her purse to make sure she did drop the corkscrew into it. She then, lifted the mat, found the key and let herself in.

Once in she quietly carried everything out to the kitchen. She looked around approvingly. It was a nice townhouse but it definitely belonged to a guy she thought. It was very plain. She then explored a little as she walked up the stairs.

There was a guest bedroom to the left and another room to the right with a huge pool table in it.

"Hmm, his bedroom must be downstairs, she thought.

So she descended the stairs and found his bedroom. The door was closed. She gently opened it to see the room was dark. She could see a lump in the bed. Still asleep she assumed. She wanted so bad to go climb in his bed but decided to be good and let him sleep a while longer therefore she headed back out to the kitchen and began making the carbonara sauce.

She was in the middle of adding the remaining ingredients into a skillet when she heard a commotion behind her. She turned to see a sleepy John in a white robe standing where the kitchen floor ended and the dining/living area began.

"Smells wonderful!"

"I hope I didn't wake you with all the rattling. I was afraid I was going to have to go back out and get a skillet, but, as you can see I found one."

He walked over to her and put his arms around her as she was cooking. She turned and they kissed.

He then said, "I'll be back in a while, I'll just run and take a shower then get dressed and help."

They kissed again and she said, "Ok." Then she turned back around to the stove.

She finished cooking the sauce, then turned off the burner as she heard the shower. She washed her hands and tip toed to the bathroom door and stood there for a few minutes wanting badly to go in, but not really sure of herself.

This is a new feeling for me, she thought. *Normally, I wouldn't think twice about going in and jumping in the shower with him; but I don't want to blow this one. I really want this to become a relationship.*

Again Jeannie surprised herself as she walked back into the living room, looked over his CD collection and picked out the Born to Run - 30th Anniversary Edition Bruce Springsteen CD then put it in the player and turned it on.

About fifteen minutes later John came out. Jeannie was now sitting on the sofa sipping a glass of wine. She had a glass for him.

He sat down and kissed her then said, "I was half expecting you to jump in the shower with me."

"Damn," she said, "You have no idea how much I wanted to and was tempted. I almost did, but I just want to do this right with you. I really like you a lot."

"I like you a lot too, Jeannie."

He kissed her very passionately, after which she said, "Dinner won't be ready for a few more hours, you know. We could just work up an appetite. I know I'd like that."

They kissed passionately several more times and then he stood up and extended his hand. She blushed and took his hand as he led her to his bed. She sat on the side of the bed and he sat next to her.

He began unbuttoning her blouse and she closed her eyes just letting her mind float away. He took her blouse off then unhooked her bra. He kissed her neck, then her shoulder and finally her breast.

He looked up at her and smiled. "Is this the boob that answered the phone today?"

"It's one of them." She giggled. "They actually took turns so they probably both need attention."

He kissed her other boob as well. She put her head way back as she swooned with pleasure.

He stood and began removing his own clothes. She also stood and took off her jeans and panties. They embraced and gently glided down to the bed where they made passionate, exquisite love.

As he was stroking her clitoris she thought to herself, *so this is what love feels like.*

She buckled in absolute, glorious ecstasy as he gave her an orgasm, a second and a magnificent third.

He had been watching her face the entire time. He was definitely smitten with this beautiful but crazy girl. When she finished shuttering from her third orgasm, she opened her eyes to see him smiling at her. She smiled back but didn't say a word. She didn't want to break the spell, so she pulled him toward her and wrapped her legs around him. They kissed and fell into a rhythm.

They could hear Springsteen singing "Jungle Land" in the background and their rhythm merged with the beat of the song. As the crescendo of the street ballet played John came hard, then as the ballet slowed down and Bruce sang his poignant poetry John and Jeannie rolled back and forth on the bed in an equally beautiful ballet of emotion. Their hearts merged with the beat of Springsteen's passionate words.

As the power of the instruments came back up at the end John kissed Jeannie with such exhilaration she shed tears. Then they both collapsed from exhaustion.

John raised his head to look at Jeannie and kissed her forehead. "I could get very used to this."

"I've never felt the fire of such passion in my life," she whispered. Then she asked, "What were you smiling for when I came?"

"Jeannie, your face just looked so beautiful because you weren't faking anything. It just filled me up, that's all," he said as he kissed her again.

"John, I don't fake anything. That's not who I am. I may be pushy and maybe a little obnoxious at times, but fake I am not."

To that John smiled. "That's what I'm talking about. I could get very used to this. All I've ever wanted from a relationship is genuine honesty. That's just hard to find."

Then he looked at her as he brushed her hair from her eyes he said, "Jeannie Chandler, you make my heart dance."

Jeannie closed her eyes as her face bathed in his words.

Then she opened her eyes and said, "Oh, John. You have no idea how long I've waited to meet you. Maybe it was truly meant for you to pull up behind me that day. I sure am going to let myself believe that."

They ate dinner that evening and John told her he was impressed with her cooking.

291

"Well, please don't be. I only know how to make a few things and that's just one of them. You know I am an only child which means I've been kind of spoiled all my life; but spoiled in a good sense. My parents would never have put up with a brat. I appreciate what I have."

They finished off the wine and then did the dishes together. When they were done they decided to watch a movie. They looked through his small collection and he picked out Pearl Harbor.

"Have you seen this one yet?"

"No, I've wanted to see it since I just love Ben Affleck, but no. Have you?"

"I started watching it one night but fell asleep. I had a rough day that day but I remember it seemed like a good movie."

"Let's watch it then; but I must warn you if it turns out to be a tear jerker I will cry."

That's ok. It'll just give me another reason to kiss you and try to make you feel better." Then John blushed and said, "That sounded pretty sappy, didn't it?"

"You couldn't sound sappy if you tried. At least not in my mind."

When the movie ended it was nearly 9 p.m.

She looked at her watch. "Gosh, I guess I better get going."

"Do you have to? Would your dad have my hide if you stayed the night? I wish you would stay. I'd sure like to see what it's like to wake up next to you."

"Oh, my God, John. Mom told me not to take this too fast, but what the hell. I'm ready to throw caution to the wind if you are," exclaimed Jeannie.

"I'm game, Jeannie," said John as he kissed her again.

"Ok, let me call Mom's cell. She'll chill out my dad. Wish me luck."

"I'll get us something to drink. Do you like bourbon," he asked.

"Yes, I do with coke if you have it," she smiled.

"Coming right up."

He could hear Jeannie talking to her Mom. "Yes, mom. I know. We're not rushing anything; but, honestly Mom this feels right. Can you trust me and cool Dad at the same time? Oh, really? That's a surprise; a pleasant one. I'll see you in the morning, Mom. Love you. Bye."

"That sounded like it went well," said John as he handed her a drink.

"Yea, Mom's still concerned about me getting in over my head too fast. She doesn't want me to get hurt. Dad, on the other hand, that was a surprise! He told her he liked you so much that he hopes we get serious. No pressure, John. I'm just surprised." She said now hoping she wouldn't regret sounding so enthusiastic.

"No pressure taken, Jeannie. I also hope this gets serious. I'm a little tired of being alone all the time. But we will take your mom's advice. I don't think either of us wants to get into something that's not right."

They sat on the sofa a while longer and then turned in making glorious love again that evening and again in the morning. Jeannie was on cloud nine on her drive home around 10:30 the next day.

Chapter Forty-One

As Jeannie got ready for her first date with John, Emily and Sarah walked over to Dr. Wells' office. When they arrived it was nearly 3 p.m. so they held hands and waited.

"I'm a little nervous, Emily. I've never done anything like this in my life. I sure don't count talking to a priest as anything close to this."

Emily stroked her mom's hand. "Awe, Mom, it'll be ok. Dr. Wells is very good at what she does. Just don't be afraid to talk about whatever you want or need to talk about. Don't hold anything back. This is a process, Mom; a healing process. And, please don't worry about me. I want you to get through all of this too cuz I know how traumatic this all is. This is a lot to handle, Mom."

Just as Emily finished, the door opened and a young man walked out as did Dr. Wells. She greeted both Emily and Sarah and invited them in.

They sat in two side by side chairs across from Dr. Wells.

"Sarah, I'm sure Emily told you, my name is Dr. Amy Wells. I've been talking to Emily now for several weeks and she's doing extremely well. You have an extraordinary daughter, Sarah, so I just want you to relax and talk a little about the night you found Emily's diary. Can you do that, Sarah?"

Sarah looked terrified. "Yes, I think I can. I'm very nervous because I've never talked to anyone in my life outside the family except to a priest. I also am surprised but pleased that I don't have to lie on a couch."

Dr. Wells laughed lightly.

"Hollywood does present a scary dramatic effect with their portrayal of what we psych people do. Would you like a glass of water, Sarah?"

"No thank you, Dr. Wells. I'll be ok."

"So tell me about finding Emily's diary."

Dr. Wells sat there waiting for Sarah to begin when finally Emily said, "It's ok, Mom. Just start talking. This is very informal."

"Ok." Sarah began as a tear ran down her cheek.

Dr. Wells offered her a box of Kleenex. "It's ok Sarah. Go ahead."

"I was taking the last box of my mother's belongings to the attic. I've been fixing her bedroom for Emily, which, honey I'm sorry to tell you about that today. I was saving it as a surprise for tomorrow when you come home."

"Mom, it's a wonderful surprise. I'll be equally surprised tomorrow because I'll know how much effort you've put into it."

"Well," Sarah continued, "I took the box up to the girl's bedroom where the attic is and went in to put it all the way at the end of the small walkway. I have no idea what I did when I put the box down but I managed to knock some of the pink fiberglass insulation down, A very large piece fell and a small piece fell as well. I was trying to figure out where the small piece belonged when I saw something dark stuck in a small cubby hole so I reached in and pulled it out. I saw it was Emily's diary which her dad and I gave her for Christmas when she was just twelve and," Sarah looked at Emily, "I wasn't trying to pry, Emily. I honestly wasn't. I just got very excited because I was going to just take a little peak to see what my sweet 12 year old daughter had written in her diary.

She was smitten with the grandson of our neighbor, Martha across the street and had been for a little over a year after we moved into our house, so I just wanted to I don't know…I wanted to experience a few moments of what my daughter was feeling at the time."

Then Sarah began to cry violently. Several minutes went by until she was able to calm down.

Through tears she continued, "What I read at first was so sweet and tender but then I felt like the earth was yanked out from under me as I realized that all those years my own husband had been molesting my Emily, torturing her and I didn't even know he was!" Sarah almost screamed the words.

"That's good, Sarah," encouraged Dr. Wells, "Then what happened?"

"I felt almost comatose for a long time. I even urinated on myself when I realized that my husband never injured his hand on a dirty bottle that one Sunday but that my Emily stabbed him in the hand trying to protect herself! Emily, what was your dad going to do to you that day?"

Emily was now crying, "Mom, I know Dad was going to rape me that day. He'd been doing sexual things to me for a long, long time. The night before, I came in the house after Jeannie's party and he was hiding in the dining room when I came in from walking home with Sean. He was watching us wave at each other from our own front stoops. When I came in he took off my coat and told me he wanted to see for himself how nice I looked because all he got to see were pictures. Then he started putting his hand up my dress telling me I was all grown up. But, Mom, I just had the best night of my whole life with Sean and I didn't want him to ruin it for me.

He ruined so much of my life, Mom. So I just walked up the stairs and even when he yelled at me to come back down I just went like this with my hand as I told him not to follow me upstairs. I felt really brave that night.

But, the next morning when I found out you and the girls were sick and that I had to go to Church with him all by myself I was so scared because I had behaved so disrespectfully the night before I didn't know what was going to happen. I wanted to come down and beg you to let me stay home too; but I didn't want you to get suspicious. I remember how scared I was that he would blame me for what he was doing and that you would believe him. I didn't even know if I was to blame. I've always wondered why he chose me. I've always wondered if there was something about me that led him to believe I wanted him to do those things. I've even wondered if maybe I did want him to do those things. He always made me feel so guilty and so dirty. But I just couldn't take it anymore. I just couldn't, Mom." She was crying very hard and choking on her words.

After a few minutes Emily composed herself and continued. "Then, when he took me down that dirt road and asked me if I knew what making out was and then told me he was going to take off my dress. Mom, I just lost it. He never did that before and I just know he intended to do more to me than touch me so I stabbed him with a pencil I found in the rider side door pocket, jumped out of the car and started screaming at him that I was never going to let him touch me ever again and that if he did I was going to tell you and Admiral James. I didn't know what else to do Mom. I'm so, so sorry."

"Oh, Emily. Please don't say you're sorry, sweetie. That just breaks my heart that you feel you have something to feel sorry about. You did the right damned thing and I just wish I knew because I would have killed that son of a bitch."

Both Sarah and Emily were holding each other crying.

Once the two women stopped crying and were wiping each other's faces, Dr. Wells said, "Sarah that's an excellent beginning. Unfortunately the session is over, but I'd like you to come back again next week with Emily. Then I'd like for you to either begin seeing me by yourself or I could give you the names of some excellent counselors in the East Providence area. If you do continue to see me, unfortunately after next week I will have to charge you; but that's up to you who you want to see. Just, please, Sarah, continue seeing someone.

You've opened Pandora's Box and you won't be able to close it again or get past the shock of what you found unless you continue talking to me or someone else who is equally capable of helping you."

Sarah said, "Thank you, Dr. Wells. I will come back with Emily next week; and, I know I need to see someone on my own. I don't care what the cost is. At least that son of a bitch left a very nice insurance policy behind and I'm collecting his military pension which is very generous. The ride here isn't bad, and, if it's ok, at least for now, I'd like to continue talking to you. I think it would help both Emily and me if we were seeing the same person because you'll know what's going on with both of us."

"That would be a wise decision, Sarah. Now listen, I want you to go home and take good care of yourself. Here's my personal cell phone number. Listen too, there are medications you can take which will take a little bit of the edge off all of this and I can get you a prescription if the emotional ride gets to be too much."

"What kind of medications?" Sarah asked looking quite concerned.

"Well, let me put it this way. You've been through a horrendous shift in your world and often times, such a shift can

297

cause people to become overwhelmed with sadness. The medication would simply help you in your daily ability to function normally. We'll cross that bridge next week. You'll know if you need to take something to even you out so to speak. However, and I want you to promise me, if you feel yourself crashing before then, call me immediately and I'll have one of our medical doctors call in a prescription for you. Can you promise me that, Sarah?" asked Dr. Wells.

"Yes. Do you take anything, Emily?" Sarah looked at Emily.

"No, Mom, we haven't felt I needed anything up until now; but I'm not going to rule it out. Your finding out and how it's effecting you has been a game changer for me; so, no, I'm not going to rule it out. If I feel my studying is being effected, I will get a prescription. This shit dad gave both of us isn't anything to fool around with. I want to get through this so I can have a happy life."

"Ok, then. I'll see you both next Wednesday at 3 p.m. Have a wonderful Thanksgiving and take very good care of yourselves and each other until then," said Dr. Wells as she stood and extended her hand for Sarah to shake.

Sarah shook her hand and she and Emily left. Dr. Wells' next patient was pacing back and forth in the waiting room when they walked out.

"Mom," Emily asked. "Do you want to go back up to my dorm for a few minutes? My roommate has already left for Thanksgiving so no one will bother us."

Sarah looked extremely distraught and exhausted. "No, honey. If you don't mind, I think I want to drive home. I need to digest all of this. Is that ok? I feel like I've been hit over the head with a ball peen hammer. We'll have the next five days to talk. I'm exhausted and don't want to fall asleep driving."

"Ok, Mom; but just so you know. There are no wrong feelings here. There are no wrong thoughts; and there are no wrong actions, that is as long as you don't hurt yourself. You just have to let your gut guide you. That's exactly what I've been doing and it's been working for me. I love you, Mom. I'll see you tomorrow, ok? Oh, and one more thing. Follow Dr. Wells' advice about the medication. If you feel as if you need something to keep you from crashing emotionally, then call her. I'll probably bug you about that one; but this is serious stuff."

"Ok, Emily. I promise, now give me a kiss cuz I need to go home and lie down. I'll see you tomorrow, Ok? I love you, Emily."

Sarah got in her car and drove away. Emily was utterly concerned about Sarah and very confused by her behavior so she called Martha.

"Martha, it's Emily. Mom just left and I'm worried about her. It was pretty traumatic for her and I'm not sure where she is emotionally right now. I'm holding my breath till she gets home. Please call me the minute you see her pull in, ok?"

"I will, dear. Do you think I should call her right now?"

"I don't know. Maybe we better not disrupt her concentration right now and let her get home. But call me the instant you see her pull in?"

They hung up and Emily went up to her room where she paced back and forth for over an hour waiting. She was scared to death.

An hour and fifteen minutes passed when Sarah pulled into the driveway and stopped the car. She sat there several minutes before realizing she was home. She couldn't even remember the drive home. She felt as if she had been in a trance the whole time. As she continued to sit there she heard a tap on her window. It was Martha.

Sarah got out and asked, "Where are the girls?"

Martha said, "They're fine Sarah. They're in my bedroom watching a Disney movie. I keep a few on hand just in case. Now I'm patting myself on the back for thinking it was a good idea. They'll be fine for at least another hour. I just looked in on them and told them I was coming over to see you. Let's go in, dear, you don't look well."

Sarah walked in the door and collapsed on the floor. Martha tried her best to catch her, but she was too late. Sarah was out cold.

Martha ran to the hall, grabbed a fresh facecloth from the linen closet then ran back into the kitchen and ran cold water on the cloth. She then got down on the floor and began wiping Sarah's forehead and face.

About five minutes later Sarah woke up and was flaying her

arms like she was fighting someone. Martha was freaking out herself, but somehow she managed to get Sarah to calm down and got her back on her feet.

"Let's go lie down Sarah. I think you'll feel better if you lie down for a while."

Sarah didn't say a word, she just let Martha walk her down the hall and put her in the bed. Then Martha went back to the kitchen and got a cold bottle of water from the fridge. When Martha walked back into the bedroom Sarah was sound asleep. She closed the blinds and covered Sarah then walked out of the room, closed the door and called Emily.

"Emily, your mom's asleep now. I just put her to bed. She's not doing well, dear; but I'm going to stay here this evening and keep an eye on her."

"Oh, Martha, I feel so responsible for her reaction. I couldn't remember how much of that day I stabbed Dad I wrote in the diary. I've been trying to remember but that was six years ago and I've never reread anything I've written but now I think it wasn't much and today I told everything. I'm not sure anymore if Mom can handle this. I feel so horrible!" Emily was crying uncontrollably.

"Em, listen to me. Listen to me honey!" Martha almost yelled into the phone.

Emily stopped crying so Martha continued. "Emily, you did nothing wrong; and, honestly honey I think that's something you need to address with your counselor. You are always blaming yourself for everything that happens. You've got to learn not to do that,"

"I think I'm coming home tonight," said Emily who was crying again.

"No, Emily!" Martha said emphatically. "I don't think that's a good idea. Please promise me you'll stay there tonight, get a good night's sleep and then drive home in the morning. Please Emily, I don't know if I can handle worrying about both of you right now. Plus I have to go get your sisters. They have no idea what's happening and they're going to be asking questions. Will you promise me Emily that you will stay there for the evening?" Martha was pleading as hard as she could.

"I'll try, Martha. I'll try. I'll call you later." Emily hung up.

Martha panicked when Emily hung up. That was so out of character for her. She always at least listened and it made Martha feel petrified. She knew where Sarah was; but she had no idea what Emily might do.

She considered loading the two girls in the car and driving up to Brown but then, what if Sarah woke up and found herself all alone. Martha thought about calling Gladys but it would take too long to explain everything to her. Besides, she was totally unaware that Jeannie had already told Gladys the entire story.

She sat in the kitchen trying to decide what to do next. She was so stressed she was actually sweating. Then, she followed her instinct. She took her cell phone from her pocket and called Sean. It went to voice mail so she left a frantic message for him to call her immediately.

She didn't have to wait, he called her right back.

"Grandma. What's wrong? I couldn't pull my phone out of my pocket fast enough. I'm walking back to my dorm. Is everything ok?" He sounded desperate.

"Oh, Sean, honey, you need to call Emily right away to make sure she's ok. Call her then call me right back so I can fill you in."

"Ok, Grandma," he said as he hung up.

Sean dialed Emily and her phone went to voice mail, so he called again and again until she finally answered.

She was crying. "Oh, Sean, I'm sorry; I turned off my phone after talking to Martha."

"Where are you, Emily?" he anxiously asked.

"I'm sitting on the floor of my dorm crying. I think I hurt my mom today and I didn't mean to. She would barely talk to me when she left after our session. I just think I said too much. I'm so sad because I wasn't sensitive enough to her feelings to watch what I said. Now I'm just so scared to go home. I'm afraid Mom hates me now. This is all my fault; and I just don't know what to do."

He profoundly felt her pain to the point that he was choked up. "Oh, Emily, don't cry sweetie. Just slow down a little and think about what you just said. This is ALL new for your mom and she's having a hard time not just processing it but with the shock of it. It's like what you described to me about how it felt

301

and the thunderous noise you heard when your dad slammed the door of the car the first time he touched you. She's been through a similar earthquake. She's not even in a place where she can begin recovery. She's not even in a place where she can begin to process it. *You* are *not* the problem. Your fucking father is the problem. He caused so much pain and anguish during his lifetime.

Your mom will be alright. She just needs a little time. What she's going through right now is more than any human can withstand. She's not you, Emily. You've been a soldier throughout your entire life. You've had years to process all of this. But she just had the house fall on her and she is bound to shut down before she can even begin to climb out from under the rubble. She needs you to help her claw her way back.

Your mom loves you, Em. Her love for you is the very reason she has shut down. She's also probably feeling that she's to blame because she lived in the same house while all of this was going on. You've just got to do what you've always done, Em. You've got to stay brave for both of you. Can you do that, sweetie?"

She was no longer crying. In fact, she was totally silent. He didn't realize it but she had been listening intently to everything he said. His wisdom and insight was speaking to her and she was calming down; but there was no way he could understand that so he felt even more panicked.

"Are you there, Em? Are you there? Please say something."

Several seconds passed and they felt like an eternity to him. He took his phone away from his ear and held it in his hand trying to figure out if they were still connected.

But why isn't she talking? His brain screamed.

Then when he put the phone to his ear again he heard a faint, "Sean, I'm still here."

"Oh, sweetie, I got so scared. I thought you hung up on me. Are you ok?"

"Yes. I was just listening to what you were saying and I suddenly realized you were right. My mom is feeling exactly what I felt the first time Dad put his hand down my pants. I was a little kid, but I must have been horrendously traumatized because I remember as if it were yesterday the sound that door

302

made when he slammed it. It *was* like being in an earthquake. I was actually considering not going home tomorrow. I was thinking of getting in my car and just driving anywhere but home. But I know now that's not the answer.

My mom needs me right now; and, I need her so bad. You helped me see that. Thank you Sean. Thank you for helping me see what's right in front of my face. I love you so much. You always have a way of bringing me back down to earth. I had a shitty father but I have a saint for a boyfriend."

He chuckled as he blew his nose, "Well, I wouldn't go that far. But I'm a hell of a site better than your father ever had it in him to be; and for both of us, that's a good thing."

Now sounding calm and composed, Emily said, "I'm going to pack my stuff and go home tonight, Sean. I have a class tomorrow, but I think I'll call Dr. Wells and ask her to call my professor and explain that I have a family crisis and need to go home a day early. I know she'll do that for me. I'm also going to be proactive too and ask her to have a prescription of anti-depressants called in for my mom. I'm fine now, Sean. Why don't you call your grandma back? She's probably sick worrying about me. Tell her I'll be home in a couple of hours, ok?"

"Ok, baby. I can hear it in your voice. I know you're emotionally back where you belong. But, you know you don't have to go home right now though. You could still call Dr. Wells and just stay there tonight then drive home first thing in the morning. What do you think, Emily?"

"No, Sean. I want to go home tonight. I am calmed down now and I feel fine to drive. Honest. I promise, if I feel anything but fine on the way home, I'll pull over and call you. But, right now, I'm ok. You have to trust me on this. I'm really ok. I want to go home and be with my mom."

"Ok, sweetie. I believe you. Please, though, call me when you do get home. You may be ok to drive but there are still a lot of idiots out there. I'd just feel lots better if I knew you were ok. Promise me you'll call me. I'll also call Grandma and let her know."

"Ok. I'm going to hang up now, Sean so I can pack. When I get in my car, I'll call you back so you know I'm on my way. I don't want you to be worried about me and I promise too I will call you when I finally get home. I love you, Sean. I love you so much for being you. You are my solid ground."

"Ok, Em. I'll have my phone right here in my hand waiting for you to call. I love you too! You're my little red headed, freckled girl. Emily Callaway you make my heart sing every day of my life. I'm hanging up now, sweetie. Talk to you in a bit."

They both hung up.

Sean called Martha immediately and put her mind to ease.

Emily packed and before she left she called Dr. Wells and filled her in on the situation and asked her to call Professor Williams and let him know she was going home for Thanksgiving a day earlier. She also asked Dr. Wells to call in a prescription for her mom at the Walgreens which is on her way home and not very far down the street.

"She'll probably have you call in the prescription to the Navy Exchange the next time, but for now, this is where she shops. Thanks, Dr. Wells for everything; have a nice Thanksgiving and we'll see you next Wednesday."

Emily made one trip down to her car; came back to her room and grabbed the rest of her bags, left her room, got in the car, started it and called Sean.

Chapter Forty-Two

Sarah would sleep the rest of Tuesday and not awaken until Wednesday morning.

In the meantime, Martha was handling Sarah's small household of children. She planned to get the two girls off to school the next morning. They had a half day of school. In the meantime, Emily arrived home around 7 p.m.

When Emily came in the house she and Martha talked for a bit, then Emily called Sean to let him know she was safe. The two girls had just finished watching two Disney movies at Martha's house and were now home watching their own TV. Katie was thrilled to have her sister home a day early and both girls were behaving because they believed their mom had a fever and didn't want to be disturbed.

About an hour after Emily arrived, Martha helped Emily with her bags which were still in her car. As they walked into the TV room, they stopped at the door of the bedroom which used to belong to Bertie.

Hanging on the door was a ceramic plaque with Emily's name on it. It was white with dark blue lettering and had tiny blue flowers in each corner which were all hand painted. It had two holes at the top corners and matching blue ribbon ran through the holes which were tied in a bow at the top giving the plaque a means to hang it on the nail that had been placed in the middle of the door at eye level.

Emily was surprised and touched it as she looked at it. "Wow! Where did this come from?"

Katie ran over, jumped up and down and said, "Lily made it for you. She did it in art class!"

Emily looked over at Lily who was watching TV and not even paying attention; or that's what she was pretending at least. "Did you really make this for me, Lily?"

"Yea. I know you like blue hydrangeas and you've never had your own room, so…yea, I made it."

Emily walked over to Lily, put her hand on her head and said,

"Thanks, Lily. I really love it!" She then bent down and asked Lily for a hug.

Lily had always behaved aloof, as if she didn't care to have much of anything to do with Emily. She and Emily always seemed to rub each other the wrong way. It wasn't intentional. It simply became their way of interacting with each other.

Emily was catching onto Lily's behavior, however, and made an even bigger deal about the ceramic plaque which finally resulted in a hug. Then Emily asked her if she wanted to help her put her stuff away in her new room. Lily tried to act as if it was an imposition, but secretly, she was thrilled her oldest sister was paying so much attention to her. Little did Emily know, but Lily really looked up to her.

Martha watched the interaction, walked over to the two girls and gave Lily the key. "Lily, I think you need to do the honor of unlocking the door to Emily's new room." Trying to hide her enthusiasm, Lily got up and went over with Emily and unlocked it. Meanwhile, Martha distracted Katie so she wouldn't steal Lily's thunder.

"Katie, do you want to help me make a salad for tonight's dinner?" Katie jumped at that invitation. "We'll also call for a nice big pizza!"

As Lily opened the door, the two girls walked in.

"Wow. It smells like a new room," exclaimed Lily.

"God, it's beautiful!" said Emily. "Wanna try out the new bed with me Lily?"

"Sure."

The two girls plopped down on the bed and Emily wiggled around a bit and said, "Oooo, comfy, don't you think?"

The ice had been broken, so for the next hour Lily helped Emily unpack and they chatted up a storm. Lily was now 15 so Emily asked her about her love life. Lily was thrilled to talk about the boy in her class she thought was so hot. They had a blast for that hour and when they came out to eat, they had become best friends.

Later, when it was time to go to bed, Lily confided in Emily that she always felt left out. She just assumed that Emily loved Katie more but found out that wasn't true.

"It's just that Katie is the baby and, I don't know, Lily, you and I are closer in age so it made it awkward I guess. But, hey, I know what you go through cuz I'm only two years older than you. I'm here if you ever need to talk; and, I'm trustworthy. I won't go blabbing to Mom, cuz I know there are just things that we don't need Mom to know about."

Later that night was the first time in a very long time that Lily and Emily hugged and kissed goodnight. Lily went to bed happier than she had been in a very long time. She felt like she mattered a lot. Likewise, Emily was thrilled. As she fell asleep that night she thought about how lonely and left out she felt at 15. She vowed to get closer to Lily and provide her with as much older sister support she possibly could.

Just before dozing off she thought, *there may come a time soon that I will have to put on Jeannie's shoes and take Lily to Planned Parenthood. I need to be cautious with that though because I want to do it in a way that it doesn't appear that I'm saying go do it with anyone you want. I want Lily to know that sex is something to cherish and not waste. Hmm, I need to give that one a lot of thought.*

Once Lily and Katie turned in, Emily and Martha sat in the kitchen. They talked about the new connection Emily and Lily had developed that evening and Emily was thrilled. Then they began to talk about Sarah.

Emily looked concerned. "Martha, what are we going to do about tomorrow? Paul will be home and the girls will be asking what's wrong with Mom."

"I haven't gotten that far in my thinking yet, Emily, but your Mom's already bought everything for dinner. I'm just thankful I made the decision to stay here with all of you. Maybe you and I can work on this together. We'll just tell the girls your mom still isn't feeling well. Paul should be easy to handle. He has after all been away on his own for a while now. I think he said he'd be home around 11. He didn't want anyone picking him up at the airport either. I'm not sure, but I have a feeling he bought a new car and is driving it home. Listen, I have an idea. Why don't you and I bake pies tomorrow? Would you like that, Emily?"

"I'd love it, Martha. I'm so glad you're in our lives. Someone was watching out for all of us when we moved across the street from you and Sean," said Emily as she hugged Martha.

"I think you're right, Emily. So, it's set. We'll bake pies tomorrow. After I get the girls off to school, I'll scoot over to my house and put all the pie ingredients in a big box. We should have lots of fun. Now, let's go check out the turkey. It's been defrosting in the fridge for a few days now. Let's see if we need to take it out for the evening."

They checked out the turkey and felt it was defrosting just fine in the fridge so that's where they left it. They then got two wine glasses down and opened a bottle of merlot wine Martha had brought over a few days earlier, sat in the TV room and watched the Jay Leno show.

"Where are you sleeping tonight, Martha?"

"I told your mom earlier I would spend the night here. It may be a good idea if we stuck to that plan. I'll go lie down with her. That way neither of us will have to worry if she wakes up."

"That would be great. I sure could use a good night sleep. The last few days have been exhausting with Mom finding my diary, then our first session with Dr. Wells. I'm just wiped out."

About a half hour later, Martha, who was drifting off looked over at Emily who was sound asleep.

I'm glad I broke out that bottle of wine, thought Martha. *It's what the poor girl needed; something to knock her out.*

She got up, went over to Emily and shook her. Emily woke up, kissed Martha, went to the bathroom, went into her room, undressed, climbed into bed and was soon sound asleep.

The following morning and just prior to waking Emily had a wonderful dream about her grandmother and grandfather. Bertie was a young woman again and Walter was a very handsome, tall, slender young man with the sweetest face and smile. They seemed so happy.

Walter showed Emily the garden he and his wonderful Sarah planted with their bare hands. When Emily awakened she felt unusually safe, and totally refreshed. She got up to the smell of bacon.

She walked out into the kitchen expecting to see Martha at the stove. Instead she was utterly stunned to see it was Sarah who was cooking. As Emily stood in the doorway, Sarah, sensed her presence.

She turned around. "Oh, Emily, sweetie. Martha told me you

came home a day early. I looked in on you a little while ago and you were fast asleep. You looked like you were dreaming. Your eyelids were fluttering and you had the biggest smile on your face. Were you dreaming about Sean, honey?"

Emily was so full of joy at seeing that her mom was up and talking that she rushed over to her and hugged her so tight Sarah had to tell Emily she was hugging too tight.

"Honey, you're going to squeeze the life out of me. I'm glad you're happy to see me. I am delighted to see you too."

Emily kissed her mom's cheek and said, "Oh, Mom, thank you so very much for my beautiful room. I did have the most wonderful dream this morning. I dreamt I saw Grandma and Grandpa. They were young again and he was so handsome. He took me to see the garden his wonderful Sarah and he planted. He was so proud of that garden and of his girl; you, Mom. He even roared laughing about Mrs. Taylor; but then said she was really a good egg and that Grandma and he see her every once and a while."

"Emily, that's a beautiful dream. It's very strange because I also had a dream about Mom and Dad as well. How queer is that that we both dreamed about them?"

"Maybe, Mom, just maybe they actually did visit each of us. Wouldn't that be wonderful if it were true?"

"Oh, that would be wonderful. Let's just pretend it did happen."

They hugged again and Sarah asked Emily to set the table for three.

"Martha ran across the street to get all the ingredients for the pies. She said you and she were going to bake pies today."

"Yes, Mom, we are; and you're going to take it easy today. Ok?"

"I'd like that, Emily. But can I sit out here and watch the two of you? We could have a girl's social day. Wouldn't that be lovely?"

"That would be great! Mom. I just love what you did with Grandma's room. You even left the doily and her beautiful oyster shell mirror and brush set on the new dresser. Thanks so much, Mom!"

Just then Martha walked in carrying a loaded box. "Oh, I'm

so happy to see the two of you. This looks like old times. How fun!"

Emily finished setting the table and Sarah finished cooking breakfast. The three women sat and chatted the rest of the morning. Around 11:30 Sarah told them she thought she'd lie down for a while. The morning wore her out.

As she walked to her bedroom, Emily followed her. She had her Mom's prescription which she picked up the night prior. Emily also had a bottle of water.

Sarah climbed into bed and Emily sat on the side. "Mom, I called Dr. Wells yesterday and asked her to call in a prescription to Walgreens. I picked it up last night. I'd like for you to take one of these pills. I think this is going to help you just as Dr. Wells suggested."

"What's the name of the pill, Emily?" Sarah asked.

"It's called Zoloft. You've probably seen the commercials on TV for them. I looked them up on the internet. It's a fairly common anti-depressant. It usually takes about three weeks to saturate your body before it really begins to work, so it's important you take one pill every day," Emily handed Sarah the pill and bottle of water.

"I'm not sure, Emily. I don't like taking a lot of medications."

"Mom, let me show you what this does."

Anticipating resistance, earlier Emily stuck her laptop in the linen closet loaded with a CD which gave a comprehensive but easy to understand explanation of what depression was and how a serotonin deprived brain suffering from depression could benefit from short term use of MAO drugs like Zoloft.

When the CD finished Emily assured her mom that depression was a natural occurring reaction to the earthquake Sarah had just experienced. She was so gentle and persuasive with her mom that Sarah no longer resisted.

"Mom, you can bet, if I find myself needing my own prescription, I will not hesitate to ask Dr. Wells to call in a prescription for me. Will you trust me on this, Mom, please?"

Sarah agreed, took the pill and a sip of water, laid down and went to sleep. Emily sat on the bed and stroked her mother's head as she fell asleep. Then she walked back into the kitchen where Martha had already cleaned up the breakfast dishes and was now getting everything organized for baking pies.

"I'm having a hard time processing Mom's moods and behavior, Martha," confessed Emily. "Yesterday when she left she seemed so distant. This morning before and during breakfast she was her old self; and, then all of a sudden it's like she turned the faucet off and she became distant again. Maybe this is normal. I don't know because I am so far removed from myself when I was six that I don't know what is normal. I'm so used to putting the pain off to the side so I can function like nothing ever happened that it's just difficult to grasp Mom's behavior. Does that make sense?"

Martha felt an overabundance of empathy. "Yes, Emily, it makes perfect sense. I guess we just need to go with the flow right now and let your mom express herself without judging or feeling guilty or responsible. She's trying to process all of this in her mind and I'm sure her mind is playing tricks on her right now. Let's not jump to any conclusions. Just let what happens happen. As long as one or both of us are paying attention, she'll be fine."

"Ok, but let's think about something. Next Wednesday, Mom needs to drive back to Brown to go to my session with me. I won't be here to determine her state of mind; so, unfortunately you'll have to do that. If she begins to behave in the same out-of-it manner as she just did, you're going to have to insist on driving her up there. She could nod out and drive off the road, or even become overwhelmed with guilt or whatever else she's feeling or going to be feeling that she could deliberately cause herself to have an accident. I think we need to watch her for suicidal behavior right now. I'm utterly serious about that. I'm scared Mom will take this all on herself, and blame herself. I'm terrified right now at least until she's had several sessions under her belt."

"I promise you, Emily, I will watch her like a hawk. Why don't you give me Dr. Wells phone number so I can call her to ask for advice if I need to? Let's talk more about this as the weekend progresses."

The two of them cooperated in an effort to maintain a façade of normalcy for Paul and the girls' sake as well as for Sarah.

Around 1 p.m. Emily and Martha had baked two pies and a

third was in the oven. They were cleaning up the kitchen when they both heard a huge rumbling sound outside and ran to the back door to see a beautiful bright yellow 2002 Corvette pull into the driveway.

"Oh, my God. He did it Martha! Paul bought a Corvette!"

They both ran out to greet Paul. He got out of his car and was smiling from ear to ear.

"Paul, this is gorgeous!" screamed Emily as she ran over to her big brother and hugged him tight.

"It is, isn't it? I just picked it up from the dealer in Boston. Now that you know how to drive a stick shift I'll have to take you out and let you drive it." Then he smirked and snickered, "You think Sean's car has power. You ain't seen nothing yet! This will blow your skirt up for sure! This isn't just any ole Corvette. It's the new Z06 which has tons more torque than the run of the mill Corvette or any other car on the market including the Mustang!" Paul laughed at his sister's facial expression.

"Oh my God. I can't wait to drive it! I know how to pop a clutch, but I really want to master the donut. Will you teach me how to do donuts, Paul, Please?"

"I'll teach you how to donuts all day long. By the time we're finished, you'll cause any man to shit his pants at how impressive you are!"

Martha was walking around the car admiring it when Paul, who was now 6' tall, walked over and picked her up off her feet and hugged her.

"I heard you are now a hot mama, Martha. I see the yellow Mustang over there. Mom told me you were racing young guys down Pawtucket Avenue. You naughty girl, you!"

Martha was laughing and squealing like a school girl when Paul finally put her down on the ground.

Paul looked over toward Emily and asked, "Where's Mom?"

"She's lying down. She hasn't been feeling well for the last few days. We think she has a touch of the flu. You know how Mom is. She just refuses to get a flu shot. But Martha and I have been taking good care of her. She's sleeping now, so, we might want to let her sleep."

"Sounds like a plan to me, Emily. I'll just grab my bag and I'll be right in."

Martha couldn't help but marvel at how Emily just does what she needs to do to keep the family operating smoothly.

That evening, she told Sean how much a pro Emily was at faking normalcy. She recalled Emily's comments numerous times to Sean that she could win an academy award for her role as best molested daughter. This insight into how the Callaway family has functioned for years was nothing less than astounding and sad at the same time.

"It makes me completely understand all this poor girl has had to endure for so many years, even after her terrible father died. Now she's charged with trying to protect her brother and sisters from what her mom's going through. I just don't know how she does it, Sean; but she does and it doesn't even seem to faze her, which really concerns me. I don't know if you've picked up on this, but Emily takes everything that happens as her own personal responsibility. I can see how she's acted like a normal part of this family for so long that if I didn't know what has been really going on in the past and the present I would believe the story she's weaving as she makes it up as she goes. It blows my mind to smithereens. My heart just aches for Emily and Sarah. This has been such a disturbingly fucked up environment for so damned long; and you know I never use the word fuck, but there's no other word that describes what I see happening here than fucked up! I'm not only concerned about Sarah falling apart, but I'm also concerned about Emily. I think she's even coned herself into believing she has everything under control."

"I know what you're saying, Grandma. I have noticed Emily's crazy mood swings. She's on cloud nine and confident one minute, then, the next she flies off the handle and behaves irrationally. I just wish I weren't so far away."

"Sean, that's the last thing you need to worry about. I'm taking on that burden. I want you to concentrate on your studies and let me handle the home front. Emily gave me Dr. Wells phone number. I'm going to think hard about calling her and filling her in on Emily's mood swings. Maybe she really does need to take the same medication Sarah is taking."

Sean agreed to leave the burden of caring for Emily to Martha. He knew he had to concentrate on his studies. Besides, being so far away, there wasn't much he could do anyway. Yet

313

he worried. He recalled how Emily was terrified that Sean would find someone else while they were apart. Now he knew in his heart that, if they became distant from each other emotionally, it would probably be Emily that would grow that distance. He fell asleep that evening feeling extremely sad as he thought, *I just hope we don't lose each other. Life without Emily wouldn't be much of a life.*

Chapter Forty-Three

Thanksgiving Day, 2001 was to say the least a very strange day indeed. It started off seemingly normal.

The morning began with Sarah waking up around 8 a.m. and coming out to the kitchen as the two girls ate cereal. Sarah sat down with them and also had a bowl of cereal.

About 8:15 Paul walked down the stairs and greeted his mother.

"Mom, you're up!" He kissed and hugged her.

"Of course I'm up, Paul. What time did you get in yesterday?"

"I think it was sometime between one and two. I wasn't really paying attention. Emily said you had a touch of the flu. Are you feeling better?"

"She said that?" Sarah looked a bit surprised.

"Yea, she said that as in the past you refused to get a flu shot and now you were feeling as if you were coming down with the flu. Don't you think you should be in bed, Ma?"

"Not at all; this is Thanksgiving and there's lots to do. I need to make the dressing and get the turkey in the oven. Where is Emily?"

Lily answered that question. "She's still in bed. I think she and Martha stayed up late last night."

Sarah shook her head approvingly. "Well, that's good. She hasn't been getting a lot of sleep the last few weeks, so we'll just let her sleep. Girls, how about helping me clean things up in here? Paul, what do you want to eat? It's so good to have you home for a holiday. I would have preferred Christmas; but, you're in the Navy now and I'll take whatever I can get."

The two girls began clearing the table and Lily washed and dried the few dishes that were in the sink.

"That's a good girl, Lily. We need to leave the dishwasher empty so we can get all our Thanksgiving dishes in it later."

Sarah turned to Paul. "You didn't tell me what you'd like to eat. How about bacon and eggs?"

"That would be great Ma; but don't go out of your way just for me. A bowl of cereal would be fine."

"No cereal, Paul. Besides, I'd love fixing you bacon and eggs."

As Sarah began cooking she asked, "So how did you get home? You were very mysterious about not wanting me to pick you up at the airport."

"Well, you need to come see in the driveway. I finally bought that Corvette I've been talking about. They came out with a much more powerful version last year called the Z06. I was set to get the 2001 version but the dealer told me the 2002 version was vastly more superior to even the 2001, so I got it. The dealer got four of them just the day before. It's a real beauty, Ma. Do you want to go for a ride?"

"I do," shouted Katie. "Me too," chimed Lily, "Can we go now, Paul?"

"Not now, girls. Maybe later. Let your brother relax a little. But I would like to take a gander. What color is it?" asked Sarah.

Paul got up. Sarah pulled the fry pan off the hot burner then she and the two girls followed Paul out to look at the car. They were all admiring the new car when Martha came back across the street. She had gone home to shower and change clothes.

Lily called to her, "Martha, have you seen Paul's new hot car?"

"I certainly have; and it's a beauty," answered Martha who was now in the driveway.

"We'll all go for a ride later. But it'll have to be one at a time, I'm afraid. There's a back seat, but it doesn't have too much room. Let's go back in now so I can eat something. I'm starving," exclaimed Paul.

Once inside, Sarah continued cooking Paul's breakfast while Martha prepared the dressing, stuffed the turkey and stuck it in the oven.

"Looks like we'll be eating around 3 this afternoon. What do you think, Martha?" asked Sarah.

Martha looked at the clock, did a little calculation in her head and said, "I think you're absolutely right, Sarah. 3 p.m. will be just about right."

Emily finally got up and had a bowl of Capt. Crunch. She didn't want bacon and eggs.

"I want to save my appetite and calories for dinner!" she said.

For Sarah, at least for the moment, everything seemed normal and she was thrilled to have all her sweet children home with her.

Thanksgiving morning went off without a hitch.

****

As everyone except Emily and Martha retired to the TV room to watch the Macy's parade, Emily said to Martha, "This is so strange. I just can't get a handle on where Mom is from minute to minute; but I don't have a really good feeling right now."

"Well, maybe we'll get lucky Emily. Let's just play it by ear," replied Martha.

"Maybe you're right. I'm probably over-thinking this and over-reacting. I'm going to force myself to just not worry," promised Emily which left Martha feeling relieved. Martha secretly remarked to herself that Emily's worrying and over-reacting was wearing thin.

Emily's behavior lately, is getting stranger. She's always on edge; as if she's always anticipating something bad will happen, thought a concerned Martha.

Around three Sarah, Emily and Martha were busy in the kitchen. The turkey was done and ready to carve. Potatoes were boiled and Emily had just whipped them to a fluffy mound.

Emily had already set the dining room table with her mom's good china. It looked beautiful. She was in the kitchen when Lily set one more place at the table and put Joe's picture on the plate facing the middle of the table, *so he can have dinner with us,* thought an innocent Lily.

No one seemed to notice the extra setting or the picture as the food was placed on the table.

Everyone was called to dinner and Paul, Lily and Katie sat down. The three women were the last to come in from the kitchen. They sat down.

As Sarah asked Paul to say Grace, an excited Katie exclaimed, "Oh, Mom, Dad is here with us. See!"

Sarah looked up to see his picture sitting on an empty plate and completely lost it.

She screamed, "What is his fucking picture doing on our Thanksgiving table?"

The two younger girls jumped and started crying as Sarah got up, walked over to the picture, picked it up and smashed it to the floor, then stormed out of the room, went to her bedroom, slammed the door shut and locked it.

Paul was astounded as he sat with absolute confusion on his face. The two girls were crying ferociously as Martha tried to calm them down. Paul finally got up and went to his mother's door only to find it locked.

He came back and demanded, "What's going on, Emily? Why did Mom behave like that?"

Lily cried, "I thought she'd like me setting another place and putting his picture on the plate. What did I do wrong?" Katie was sitting on the floor just crying.

Emily went into auto pilot, stood up and said, "Ok, everybody just calm down for a minute."

"But what's going on?" demanded Paul once more.

Then Emily began making up an elaborate story. "Ok. I'm going to tell you all something, but you need to calm down right now and just listen to me."

Martha was totally freaked out inside and was scared to death of what Emily was about to tell her siblings. She just didn't think it was at all a good idea to tell them the truth right now so she reached over, put her hand on Emily's arm and, using a pleading tone, said Emily's name.

Emily looked at her with unbelievable calmness as she made an exaggerated gesture with her hands for everyone to calm down. In fact, she looked like a maestro who was instructing the orchestra to quiet their instruments.

"Lily, you didn't do anything wrong. That was a wonderful thing you did by putting Dad's picture on his own place setting. Ok, everyone. Mom found some letters last week. This is going to be hard to hear, but everything is going to be ok as soon as Mom gets through this. Dad had an affair with another women about ten years ago and Mom just found out about it,"

Excitedly Paul demanded, "Who was it?"

Emily responded, "It really doesn't matter right now, Paul. I don't even know who it was. Mom evidently knew her but that doesn't matter right now. What does matter is that we all need to cut Mom some slack. She's hurting right now and what she needs is for all of us to just go about our business and let her get over this."

Then she continued, "Dad loved Mom very much and felt terribly ashamed about it. He told me about the affair the day I said good-bye to him at the hospital. Unfortunately I didn't know anything about the letters and therefore, I never had a chance to look for them in order to get rid of them. But now Mom knows and she's having a really tough time with it. When Dad was dying he told her he was sorry for a lot of things including something he had done in the past; but he also told her that he loved her with all his heart and would wait for her in heaven. Mom never asked Dad what he did but just told him it didn't matter because she loved him."

Emily was exhausted from this tale she had just spun; and Martha was so dumbfounded she just remained quiet.

Then Emily began picking up the frame and picture off the floor. "Ok, everyone; let's just have a nice Thanksgiving. I'll take a plate into Mom when we're done."

She stood up, removed the broken glass from the corner and sat it back on the table. She then picked up and wiped up the remaining broken pieces of glass. Lastly she picked up Katie from the floor, wiped her eyes and put her back on her chair.

Lily jumped up from her chair and just hugged her older sister.

Then Paul said, "This kind of thing happens all the time. What we all need to remember is that Dad felt bad about it and told Mom how much he loved her before he died. I agree with you, Emily. We just need to give Mom some slack to get through this. Now, who wants turkey?"

Everyone calmed down and they all ate dinner. When they were finished Martha asked the girls to help her clear the table and do the dishes to which they gladly obliged. Emily made a plate for her Mom and told Paul and Martha she was going to take it to her. Paul agreed as did Martha as her head continued to spin from everything she just watched happen.

Emily went to Sarah's door and tapped on it. She heard Sarah answer.

319

"Mom, it's Emily. I need you to let me in so we can talk."

"I don't want to talk right now."

"Yes you do, Mom. You have three kids out here freaking out; especially the two girls. We need to talk so we can get our story right. Let me in, Mom, please. It's important!"

Martha walked down the hall and Emily gave her the plate back, "Go dump this somewhere while I talk to Mom."

"Ok," was all Martha could muster as she vigorously nodded.

This high pitched chaos was so out of her realm that she did what Emily asked.

Five minutes went by when Sarah finally opened the door. Emily slipped in.

Sarah just started crying. "I didn't mean to lose it Emily. What am I going to do now?"

"Mom, I've fixed it; but you need to know what I told the kids so we can go back to normal. Ok?"

Emily was utterly convinced that she had everything under control that no one including Martha questioned her story or even hinted at bucking her lead. Emily had done what she was so used to doing. She had fixed the situation. She turned an out of control situation into a controlled and orderly one.

Martha knew intuitively how out of control the situation was. Her heart ached watching Emily behave in such a fashion. *Joe created such a hell-hole here while training Emily to turn everything into a false normalcy.* She wanted badly to talk to Dr. Wells but didn't know how appropriate it was. Then, she thought about Sarah and how weak a leader she had been. *I wonder if Sarah did suspect what was going on in her own household but was too scared to do anything about it. Joe sure trapped her as well. He gave her four children and the extra burden of her mother while tricking Sarah into thinking it was out of kindness to not put Bertie in a home. He sure knew how to manipulate Sarah and Emily. God, if he were alive I just might shoot the man myself!* She was so angry at the situation but didn't know what to do about it. She knew she walked a thin line. She wanted desperately to be a positive influence but knew she had to be present to be an influence. So she kept quiet and watched.

She and the girls finished cleaning up the kitchen and dining room. Then they sat down to watch the TV. Katie's favorite

Christmas show, Rudolph the Red Nosed Reindeer, was about to start. Martha was on edge the entire time. She kept looking at her watch and looking for either Emily or Sarah to walk down the hall.

Emily sat down on the side of the bed as Sarah cried.

Sarah repeated herself, "I'm so sorry Emily. I don't know what got into me; but, when I saw his picture I couldn't help myself from exploding."

"It's ok, Mom. I've fixed everything. Everyone is calmed down now."

"What did you tell them?"

Emily told Sarah the entire story she told her siblings.

Sarah listened as her head swam. She couldn't believe how calm Emily was and the story, it blew Sarah's mind that Emily was so inventive. Part of Sarah, the old Sarah who would rather stick her head in the sand wanted desperately to go along with the lie. It was easier to just go along so everything could go back to normal.

However, the other side of Sarah, the side that Emily would catch glimpses of over the years was emerging and that side of Sarah was growing stronger than ever.

In that instant Sarah had an epiphany. She stared at Emily who was oblivious to her mother's changed facial expressions. Emily just talked like an old pro telling her mom that this was how it was going to be so everything could indeed go back to normal. Sarah felt as if she were standing next to herself and Emily as she observed what was taking place and it sickened her. *I recognize this Emily;* and that terrified Sarah because she realized how complicit she had always been.

Sarah was no longer crying. Now, she was the person who was calm and collected as she took Emily's hands in her own and sharply commanded. "Stop it Emily. Stop it right now!"

Emily was stunned, so stunned she slid off the side of the bed and onto the floor. She looked up at Sarah with a face that asked what the hell just happened.

Sarah simply said, "Come back up her, Emily. We need to talk about this whole thing."

Emily got up off the floor and sat back down next to her mom and just looked at her mom with a face full of questions.

"Emily, sweetie, I am not going to let this happen. Not this time or ever again. What you are asking me to tell your brother and sisters is a lie; and, I just won't do that."

"But, Mom, we can't tell them the truth. They didn't know Dad like we knew him. They knew a different dad. Mom, think about how much this shook your world and now think about how shattering it will be for them. I just think we should stick to this story."

But it wasn't at all her other three children Sarah was worried about. Instead it was Emily she was utterly concerned for. Ever since Sarah discovered the diary she struggled in her mind whether or not she always knew the truth yet was too weak to do anything about it. She was terrified of the truth. Right now, however, she was more terrified for her daughter, so she did something very brave and very much out of character.

Emily began to fall apart. "Mom, please Mom." She begged. Then she began crying.

"I'm so sorry. If I had been thinking straight when I went to live at Brown I would have remembered about my diary so you would never have known; because I had no intention of ever telling you. I was learning how to handle it all by myself with the guidance of my counselor. Besides, I had Martha and Sean to help me get through what you never needed to know. I'm so sorry I forgot about my diary and you had to find it."

"Don't you see Emily? That's just the point."

"But, Mom," she pled.

"No, Emily. This all stops today. No one in this family has ever been there for you, including and especially me. I'm ashamed for all these years you've suffered in silence. I'm ashamed that you felt you had to protect us, me in particular, from the truth. This is just wrong, Emily. I should have been there to protect you, and I wasn't.

Your siblings need to know the truth; at least Paul and Lily do. Katie may be too young right now. But in time she too needs to know the truth. Emily, honey, you deserve that they know the truth. The illusion of a happy childhood is false. I have to do this for all of our sakes! You need to let me do this for myself too, because I am equally responsible for that illusion. I was never happy with your father. And, to be honest, I'm not even sure how complicit I was in all of this. That's something I need to talk to Dr. Wells about; and it's something I need to face if the truth is that I was complicit. Emily, I let your father get away with a lot. I let him treat my mother like she was a nuisance and I let him treat me like an idiot. I don't know if deep down I knew something was wrong. I do know I allowed myself to think it was all about me; that he just couldn't stand being in the same bed with me. Your brother and sisters are just fortunate that their father didn't try to destroy their childhood like he tried to destroy yours. I can't allow that lie to remain alive anymore. I am going to tell them the truth, even if I have to pay for counseling for each of them. Emily, this is not about them. This is about you. This has never been a happy family. It's been one big fat lie; and, if this family is ever going become a genuinely happy one, the truth needs to be told. I am responsible for this family now. I am ready to be that in charge mom you always thought you saw!"

Emily was crying. "I'm so sorry, Mom."

Sarah put her arm around Emily and pulled her close. "This is not your fault, Emily. None of it ever was. It's not your fault I found your diary. I did and now we need to deal with all of this as a family. We have a wonderful opportunity to become a real family."

"I love you, Mom."

"And I love you too, Emily. I love you more than you will ever know. It's time to raise the sails and change course. Now, do me a favor and go ask Martha to come in. I want her to know what we're doing. I'm going to ask her to take Katie home with her tonight."

Emily and Sarah hugged. Then Emily left the room.

Sarah was waiting for Martha as she was about to knock on the door. She slipped into Sarah's room and asked, "What's going on? Emily doesn't seem herself."

Sarah smiled and said, "I hope you're right, Martha."

Martha looked stunned.

"Martha, I'm going to tell Paul and Lily the truth about their father. I think Katie's just too young for this information right now; but in a few years, I'll also tell her. I was hoping you could take Katie home with you tonight."

Martha turned white as a sheet. All she could think to say was, "Wow."

"Wow is right. This isn't going to be easy; but I've decided that the lies need to stop here. We all deserve for the lies to stop. I don't want Emily to feel like she has to protect any of us anymore. As hard as this will be, Paul and Lily need to know the truth. I've done nothing else but thought about the night I discovered Emily's diary. Something deep inside me realizes that it was a shock yet not a shock. I can't explain it. It was happening right under my nose and I'm not sure if I was hiding from the truth. I'm not sure if I was telling my own self a bunch of lies all these years. Regardless, of what the truth really is, I have to take charge of this and make it right for Emily. I need to remove that burden from her shoulders once and for all!"

"I'm proud of you, Sarah. I think this is a big step for both you and Emily. I'll be happy to take Katie home with me. I'll pull out that small Christmas tree I bought several years ago and have her help me decorate it."

"Thanks, Martha. Now the healing can truly begin for all of us."

Chapter Forty-Four

Martha asked Katie if she would like to come over to her house and decorate her small Christmas tree with her. Katie got really excited and asked, "Can I stay at your house tonight, Martha?"

"Sure, Katie. It's still early. Maybe we can make a few Christmas cookies too."

Lily watched Martha and Katie walk out the door. She knew something was up because Emily went in her bedroom and shut the door after she came out of her mother's room. She got up from the chair she was sitting in, went down the hall and knocked on Sarah's door. Sarah came to the door and Lily asked what was going on. Sarah told her she would be out in a minute.

"I need to talk to you and your brother."

Next, Sarah stood in front of her mirror and looked at herself. She was scared; but she knew she had to do what she had to do.

Lily walked back out to the TV room where Paul was sitting.

"Where's Mom, Lily?"

"She just told me she was coming out to talk to you and me about something. I don't know what's going on but it's something very strange."

Just as Lily said the word strange, Sarah walked into the TV room, turned off the TV and then knocked on Emily's door. Emily opened her door and looked terrified. She had been crying.

"It's going to be ok, Emily." Sarah extended her hand and Emily took it as Sarah led her to the sofa.

Paul was sitting in the Lazy Boy. He got up and asked his mom if she wanted to sit in the chair.

"No, Paul. I'm going to sit over her on the sofa with Emily. I have something important to talk to you and Lily about."

Paul responded, "Mom, we already know and I just want you to know that I'm here for you, Mom."

"Honey, that's not what I want to talk to you both about. What I need to tell you tonight is going to be the hardest thing

325

I've ever done in my life; but, it's also one of the most important things I will probably do in my life. This is going to be hard for me to talk about and very hard for you two to hear, but it has to be done."

Emily knew there was no turning back now. She bowed her head and began shaking it back and forth as she cried.

Lily went over to the sofa and sat on the other side of Emily. She took Emily's other hand and begged her not to cry.

"What's going on, Mom?" Paul asked.

Sarah didn't know where to begin so she looked at Lily and asked, "Lily, did your dad ever touch you in a way that made you feel uncomfortable?"

Lily shook her head no then said, "But I know what he did to Emily. Two years ago, I found Emily's diary in the attic and read it."

Emily was shocked as she stopped crying and looked at Lily.

"I'm sorry, Emily. I didn't want you to know that I knew what he did to you. I knew he used to come into our bedroom but I never knew what he was doing until I read your diary."

Paul looked completely lost. "What's going on?"

"Paul," Sarah began, "Your father wasn't a very nice man. Your father molested Emily. He began molesting her when she was just six."

Paul just sat there with his mouth gaping open. "That can't be true."

"It is true, Paul. Do you remember the two years your dad coached the little league team?"

"Yes."

"Do you remember a boy named Peter McLain?"

"Yes, I remember him. I hated that kid! Dad loved him. I remember I wanted to pitch but Dad refused to teach me how. Instead he taught Peter. I guess I was really jealous of Peter."

"Well, don't be, Paul, because your dad molested him as well."

Paul was at a loss for words. He just sat there for the longest time. Finally he asked, "So that story Emily told us about the affair and love letters wasn't true?"

"No, Paul, it wasn't true. Emily made up that story in an effort to protect all of us from the truth. Emily has spent her entire life keeping her terrible secret and it was all to protect her family. I haven't had the flu this year. Instead, I've been very distraught because when I was preparing your grandma's room for Emily I accidently found her diary and read it. I've been having a very difficult time dealing with this truth. That's why I flew off the handle earlier today. Emily came into my room after dinner and told me the lie she told you kids. She was trying hard to protect all of us from the truth; but I couldn't live with anymore lies so I decided to end the lies tonight."

Then Sarah turned to Lily and asked, "Lily, now I'm concerned about you. How have you been dealing with this?"

"Mom, I'm more grown up than any of you give me credit for. Besides I have a girlfriend I've been talking to about this. Her step-father did the same thing to her. She's been helping me I guess come to terms with it." Then Lily turned to Emily. "Em, I'm so sorry Dad did all those things to you. I've wanted to talk to you for a long time about it, but didn't know how to."

Then Emily asked Lily which of her girlfriends was molested by her step-father.

"Penny Martin."

"Isn't she the person whose step-dad is in prison?"

"Yes. Penny's been in therapy for two years. He got caught molesting the little girl who lived next door to them and, when Penny's mom found out about Penny she helped prosecute him. He was sent to prison."

Paul was now leaned forward in the chair and had his head in his hands.

"I'm sorry, Paul, that I had to tell you this tonight. Neither Emily nor I planned this to happen but, when I saw your dad's picture, I just lost it. It's my fault that I couldn't control my emotions; but, would you rather I tell you the lie or the truth?"

"The truth I guess. It's just hard to take."

"Would it help to read Emily's diary?"

"Maybe, I don't know."

Sarah turned to Emily. "Do you mind if Paul reads your diary, Emily?"

Emily shook her head no so Sarah got up, went down the hall and retrieved it from her middle dresser drawer.

She handed it to Paul, "This may help put all of this in better perspective."

Paul took the diary and left the room.

Sarah then looked at Lily and asked, "Sweetie, how have you been able to deal with this? Do you think you need to talk to a therapist? I can arrange that."

"No, Mom. I'm really ok with all of it. I hope neither of you will get mad at me, but I still love Dad. He never did any of those things to me and I can't even imagine what it must have been like for you, Emily. I'm just really, really sorry it happened to you because you didn't deserve any of it. I wish Dad had been the same type of father for you."

Emily put her arm around Lily. "Lily, I could never be mad at you for still loving Dad? You knew a totally different father than I did. I wish with all my heart I had known the same father, but I didn't. I just want you to know how much I appreciate that you care about me."

Lily began crying, "Oh, Emily. I do care about you. I know how much Penny's step dad hurt her and he wasn't even her real dad. Your real dad hurt you and it's just not right. Sometimes I'm actually glad he's dead because if he were still alive, I'm not sure how I would feel about all of this. I just don't want you to hurt anymore cuz I really love you, Emily."

The two sisters hugged and cried as Sarah sat on the sofa rubbing both their heads.

****

The next day Paul didn't come out of his room until almost noon. When he did, he asked Emily if he could talk to her. She said yes so they went for a ride in his Corvette.

They drove up to the local Stop and Shop parking lot and talked for several hours. He told her he was really sorry for what their father did to her. He remembered the day they all thought Joe cut himself on the bottle. It was shocking to read the truth, but he also told her she was very brave for having fought back.

"Emily, it's going to take me a long time to come to grips with this. Except for the little league thing I always looked up to Dad. He's the reason I joined the Navy. I am having a hard time in my head putting the father I knew and the one you knew together."

"I know, Paul. I would have a hard time too if the tables were turned. Will you promise me something?"

"What's that?"

"If you need to see a therapist, will you do it? You probably have access to them at the base and it wouldn't cost you a dime. Am I right?"

"Yea, you're right. I don't know if I would see someone on the base, but I promise you if I have a hard time with this I will get help. I'm not so macho that I wouldn't get help. This is pretty heavy stuff. Now, let me ask you something."

"Ok."

"As I read your diary I wondered if Mom ever knew what was going on. Did she?"

"I don't know, Paul. I think Mom is having a hard time with that right now. But after what Mom did last night, I'm trying not to let that become an important issue. Mom took charge last night. I was all ready to continue telling lies to protect everyone. She didn't let that happen. Instead she chose to talk about it because she wanted to protect me. Mom was a victim of Dad in her own way you know. Don't you remember how he used to treat her?"

"Yea, I do. I hated the way he treated her. She didn't deserve to be treated like an idiot so, yea, I remember. I could never treat any woman like that let alone a woman I loved. I guess I learned that lesson from watching them. Dad could be an ass sometimes; now, I know how much of an ass."

Then he put his hand on Emily's which was resting on the console, "Em, I want you to know that I love you. I'm so sorry that happened to you and I'm sorry none of us were paying enough attention to know it was. You're a good person, Emily. Don't ever forget that. I will always be your big brother. I'm proud that I am."

Paul then put his arm around Emily and hugged her.

When Paul and Emily came home Martha and Sarah were sitting in the kitchen while the two girls were watching TV.

Katie ran over to Emily with a plate full of Christmas cookies. "Emily, I made these."

"Awe, Katie, they look wonderful." She took a bite. "Umm. They're yummy too. I love you, Katie."

"I love you too, Emily."

Emily went out into the kitchen and sat down with her mom and Martha.

Martha put her hand on Emily's. "I'm so proud of you and your Mom, Emily, but especially of your mom."

"Oh, Martha. I'm still is a state of shock. I have the mother I always knew was hiding in there. She rescued me last night from my own self. Mom, I'll love you forever for that."

"Oh, honey, it was the least I could do. I just thank God that you always had faith in me because now I'm afraid I'm going to have to face some hard truths about the past; but I'm not going to let it scare me because I have you by my side."

"I'm right here with you, Mom, just like you were right there with me last night and I now know you'll be there with me forever. I love you, Mom. I love you so much."

Soon the house was bustling with noise and activity. There were pies to eat and Christmas specials to watch. They all retired to the TV room, ate pie and watched The Grinch Who Stole Christmas.

Martha sat in the TV room with this family drinking them all in and feeling the blessed joy of having been granted the gift of being an intricate part of this miracle, this family, this *real* family. She was overwhelmed with joy and her heart was filled with the wisdom that everyone and everything would be ok.

Chapter Forty-Five

The Thanksgiving incident left a mark on Sarah, Emily and Paul especially.

It was the Sunday evening after Thanksgiving. Paul was headed back to Norfolk the following morning. Lily and Katy had already gone to bed. They had school the next morning. Paul was sitting in his late father's Lazy Boy watching TV, but he wasn't paying a bit of attention to what was on TV. He was still in a state of shock at what he learned of his father that Thanksgiving.

Emily walked into the TV room and noticed that Paul was watching a show she knew he would never watch by himself.

"Paul, are you ok?" Emily asked.

"Yea, Em, why?"

"Because you're watching a women's movie."

"Oh, yea, I guess I am. I wasn't paying attention."

"Paul, do you want to talk. I mean, you're headed back to the base tomorrow and, well, I just want to make sure you're ok. I'm worried."

Paul didn't say a word. From the look on his face, it was evident to Emily that he was distraught, but she didn't want to press too hard. Finally Paul picked up the remote control and turned the TV off. Just as he did Sarah walked in from the kitchen.

"What's going on you two?"

Emily was the first to talk. "Mom, I think we need to talk about everything before Paul leaves in the morning."

"Ok." Sarah pulled the ottoman so she could sit next to the Lazy Boy.

Just as she sat down, Paul put his hand on his forehead and began to cry. Then, he sat up, rubbed his eyes with his shirt and apologized.

"Paul, it's alright if you cry." Sarah put her hand on her son's arm. "It's ok. If you need to cry, let it happen. God knows I've shed a river of tears over this since I found Emily's diary; and, I know full well that's nothing compared to the tears Emily has

331

shed over the years. Come here, Emily." Sarah patted the ottoman for Emily to come sit with them.

When Emily sat down she too began to cry. "Oh, Paul, I'm so sorry you had to find out about this and especially now."

Paul was sobbing when he lifted his head and looked at Emily. "Em, there would never have been a good time to find out about Dad. I just feel so broken hearted over everything. One thing I don't want to happen though," he said through his tears. "I don't want you to blame yourself. God knows you've suffered long enough and the saddest part of that is that you suffered all by yourself for way too long. I just can't believe Dad would do such a horrible thing to anyone, let alone his own daughter. He sure was a great fake." He almost screamed his last sentence.

"Shh, honey," consoled Sarah. "We don't want to wake the girls."

"Sorry, Mom. But, how come none of us knew what he was doing? Emily why didn't you ever tell anyone?"

Emily was sobbing fiercely, "Because I couldn't. No one would have believed me. And, even if any of you did, I was scared to death I would be blamed."

Paul wasn't crying anymore. "Why do you think none of us would believe you? And, God, Em, why would you think we would have blamed you? You were just a kid."

"I don't know, Paul. I don't know. There's so much about Dad that none of you know and that includes me."

"What do you mean?"

"Over the years I've blocked out so many things that I can't even remember what Dad would say to me to keep me quiet. I've tried so hard to remember thinking it may help me; but I just don't remember a lot. What I do remember is how he made me feel. He made me feel responsible for what was happening and for not telling anyone by keeping the secret a secret. Yet, I can't recall how he made me feel responsible for everything. I'm still trying to figure this out myself; and, it's just hard. I'm so scared that I may have been to blame in some way."

Sarah looked at Emily. "What do you mean that you're scared that you may bear the blame, Emily? Like Paul just said, you were just a child. You had absolutely no control."

"Mom, do you remember the time I broke my mirror and cut my foot on a piece of glass?"

Sarah took a few seconds to pull this memory into view. "I think I do. You stayed up to curl your hair, right?"

Emily continued to cry. It was evident to both Sarah and Paul how painful all of this was for Emily.

"Yes. I remember begging Paul and Lily to stay up with me a little bit longer. I wanted to finish my hair, but (looking at Paul) you and Lily were tired and didn't want to stay up. Dad was asleep in his chair so I hurried as fast as I could. When I was finished I grabbed my stuff and was about to go upstairs but he grabbed my arm and pulled me to his lap. He began doing things to me."

She was crying such a painful cry both Paul and Sarah were hurting inside for her.

"He told me that night that he wished he were 20 years younger so I could be his girlfriend." She looked at Sarah and said, "I'm sorry, Mom. I hated when he would tell me that because it made me feel as if I was taking him away from you. Then, Paul you came back down the stairs to get something from the garage for school and he pushed me off his lap. That's when I broke my mirror and cut my foot. He just pushed me off his lap not caring where or how hard I landed. He didn't want anyone to catch him molesting me."

Now Sarah looked terribly distraught. "I do remember that night!" She spoke emphatically and grabbed Emily. "Damn him! God, Emily! I had no idea that's how you broke your mirror and cut your foot. Damn him to hell!"

"When you picked me up to take me into the bathroom to fix my foot he whispered to me to keep our secret. He asked again when I came back and began picking up my brush. He didn't even help me pick up any of the glass. He just sat there while I picked it all up. He only cared about getting caught and about making me promise to keep what he called *our* secret! All these years I've worried and asked myself why the hell I didn't get up and finish my hair upstairs. And, that wasn't the only time that happened. It happened many times."

All three were crying now when Sarah asked, "Honey, have you talked to Dr. Wells about that and how it made you feel guilty for not going upstairs?"

"Yes. She's told me that I was trying my best to feel safe in my own home. I had a right to feel safe in my own home. But,

Mom, the truth is I was never safe as long as he was around; and, I knew I wasn't safe! So now I'm trying not to feel guilty about staying up alone in the same room with him."

"Oh, Emily, honey. I feel so responsible for all of this. Maybe if I had just been a better wife and mother, none of this would ever have happened."

"Mom, we need to talk to Dr. Wells about this. We've got our second session with her on Wednesday. We need to talk to her about all of this. I don't want you blaming yourself; and, I don't want to blame myself anymore either. Dad snuck up on both of us and made us both feel helpless. I'm just so glad he died before you because I've thought a lot about how things could have turned out if you had died first and left him behind."

Paul was watching his mother and Emily and taking in everything they were saying when he asked.

"Emily, if Mom had died first what do you think would have happened? I really want to know."

"Paul, I've been reading a book called THE COURAGE TO HEAL. It's written by two women and it's all about sexual abuse. I have the book in my room and would love to give it to you to read. I can order another one from the campus book store. The book may help you understand this whole thing and how it effects *everyone* in the family."

"Ok, I'd like to read it and will, but you didn't answer my question, what do you think would have happened if Dad were the one that survived?"

"Well, I'm not 100% sure what would have happened, but I am sure I would have needed to seek help just like I've been doing only Dad would still be in charge of the family. That thought really scares me."

"Why?"

"Because, Paul, think about it? I'm pretty certain that I would have totally turned my back on Dad. With Mom gone there wouldn't be any reason for me to come home or stay in touch with the person who did nothing but hurt me my entire life. I know I would have never wanted to see him again and all of you would have been asking why. Paul, what do you think Dad would have done?"

"I don't know. I'm guessing he would have been pretty angry."

"I'm sure he would be too. In THE COURAGE TO HEAL it talks about how the perpetrator turns siblings against the victim to protect himself. If that would have happened, I'm pretty sure I'd have a lot more emotional stuff to deal with if he were still alive and Mom were gone. I would have been dealing with you, Lily and Katie hating me for turning on the perfect father you all knew. He would have blamed me for breaking up the family. He would desperately need to maintain the lie about his fatherhood so that all of you still honored and loved him. But most of all, he would have needed for the three of you to continue to protect and defend him. God knows what he would tell the three of you was the reason I wouldn't deal with him anymore. But, Paul that's not what happened. Even with Mom alive I was trying my damndest to hide all of this from everyone. I didn't want any of you to find out; but you did. Mom found out by accident and, I even felt guilty about that because I felt careless that I forgot to get my diary. Then you found out because Mom couldn't keep quiet anymore." Then Emily turned to Sarah. "That's exactly why, Mom, you don't need to blame yourself. When the chips were down on Thanksgiving and you lost it over seeing Dad's picture on our Thanksgiving table you could have let me continue to tell the lie about Dad cheating on you and your finding the letters to his supposed girlfriend. If you had, Paul wouldn't feel like he does now. But, Mom, thank God you didn't do that. You rescued all of us that night, me especially. Mom, that took a lot of guts to do. I know you don't think it did, but it did. This is on Dad, Paul and Mom. This is not on any one of us except him. He's the one who chose to deal with what happened to him as a child by hurting other children including me. It was a cruel and narcissistic thing that he did and all I want to happen is for all of us to heal from this. For the first time I can even remember I have a real family. Do you even know how that feels for me?"

All three were crying.

"It feels like hope. It feels like love and it's all I've ever wanted my entire life from my family. It's too late for Dad. He's dead. And, wherever he is right now, he's going to have to deal with what he did; but, that's his problem. It is not ours. Our challenge is to get through this as a loving family who supports each other 100%." As she finished she cried painfully.

Sarah and Paul both reached for Emily and began hugging her and each other.

Five minutes later Emily wiped her eyes and looked at Paul. "Paul, do you remember what I asked of you the other day in your car?"

"Yes. You asked me to talk to someone when I get back to the base."

"Do you promise me you will do that?"

Sarah looked at Paul. "Honey, when does your ship leave port?"

"In forty days."

"Please promise us you will talk to someone. Even if it's an off base person, Paul, I can pay for it. One thing your Dad did right was leave me and the girls in a good financial place. I can afford to pay for you to see someone. Can you do that for all of us?"

"Yes, Mom and Emily. I promise I will do that. I think it would help me out. I also really want to take that book back with me. I need to understand this whole thing because it's totally fucked up."

The three of them sat and talked a little longer when Paul said he needed to turn in.

The next morning he got up at 6 a.m. and prepared to leave by 7:30. Sarah got up and fixed him a hot breakfast. Emily was up at 6 as well so she could help Sarah get the girls off to school. She wanted to be there when Paul left. She didn't need to be back to campus until the next day.

As Paul was about to back his car out of the driveway he lowered his window. "Thanks, Mom. Thanks, Em. I'm really glad we talked last night." Then he kissed Sarah's hand, "Mom, Emily is right. This is on Dad. This is not on you or any of us. He's the one who created the lie. It's time for us to deal with this and to become the family he fooled us into thinking we already were. I love you both."

Sarah and Emily stood in the driveway holding hands, sobbing and waving goodbye to Paul.

Chapter Forty-Six

Emily got up the next morning and packed her bag. She needed to leave by 9. Her first class was at 2 p.m.

On their way out the door, both Lily and Katie stopped by her room to say good-bye.

Katie hugged her big sister. "When are you coming home again? I miss you already."

"Awe, Katie, I miss you already too. I'll be home at the end of the week for the weekend."

They kissed and Katie left the room and ran out to join her friend as they both walked up the hill to the bus stop.

As soon as Katie left Emily's room, Lily walked in.

"Hey, sis, are you ok?"

"Yes, Lily. I'm good. This is a lot to deal with for all of us. Are you ok? I'm still in shock that you've known all this time."

"I really am ok, Em. It was hard in the beginning but like I said the other night, Penny is helping me cope. I don't know what I would have done if Dad had done those things to me. I just feel bad you've had to suffer all this time all by yourself. I also wish I had told you about finding your diary; but, I was scared. I was afraid you'd be mad at me."

"You know, Lily, that's one of the really screwed up things about all of this. Dad developed an atmosphere in our house which caused us all to not trust each other. He manipulated all of us and the environment so well that we all lived in our own world apart from one another. Look how long it took for you and me to trust each other. If you would have told me, I would have been upset, but not at you. I would have been upset at myself for not hiding the diary better. I would have blamed myself while you would have blamed yourself. How screwed up is that? Now that Mom is in charge though, I think everything will be different. I'm also kind of glad you already knew and had at least a little time to deal with it."

Emily paused for a minute as she stared out the window. Then she looked at Lily with tears rolling down her cheeks.

"Most of all, Lily, I have to tell you it is wonderful to finally have my family caring about me. At least now I have proof you all care about me. That helps more than you know! I've felt so alone for so, so long. I've been in silent pain for so long and now I'm not alone anymore."

Lily dropped her backpack on the floor, walked over to Emily and threw her arms around her. She was crying as well. "Oh, Emily, we all love you. We always have. I'm so horribly sorry about all of this. Dad was so cruel to have done this to you and then left you with the responsibility of keeping *his* secret. I love you, Emily and I don't want you to hurt anymore. I honestly don't."

Emily was rubbing Lily's back. "I know, Lily. Thanks for loving me so much. I love you so, so much. We're going to get through this. All of us will. Now I know I'm not alone in this and that, in and of itself lifts the heaviest burden from my shoulders. I think that's actually been the biggest fear in my life."

"What?" Asked Lily.

"That I would never feel complete love and compassion from my family. I think I kept the lie alive to protect myself from what I believed was the truth, that I was an outsider in my own family."

"God, Emily. I hate that you felt like that. It makes me glad all of this happened. I just with it could have happened sooner."

"I know, I know. I do too now. Listen, you better get going so you don't miss your bus."

Lily looked at her watch, "Damn, you're right I better hurry up."

"Do you need me to drive you up the street? I can do that."

"Yea, maybe you better. I don't know if I can make it all the way up to the bus stop in time."

Emily grabbed her keys as the two girls walked out into the TV room telling Sarah what they were doing.

On the way up the street, Emily said, "I know it's going to take a long time for me to work through all of this; but, I'm determined to do it. I refuse to let this control any aspect of my life...ever! I also want you to promise me that you'll talk to me when you have questions or are feeling sad about everything. This may have physically happened to me, but, believe me his

338

abuse didn't stop there. Just the fact that you knew he was coming into our room left you with trauma. Lily, you're a very bright person. I know you thought something wasn't right when he would come into the room in the middle of the night"

"I know what you're saying, Emily. Penny gave me a brochure about sexual abuse within the family and it talks about all the members of the family including the non-abused siblings. It was hard for me at first because Dad behaved so differently toward me. I felt love from him. I'm just glad I know about Penny's situation because it's helped me to realize that the family life I thought we all had wasn't real. I just wish this had never happened to you, Emily. I also want you to know I think you're really brave. I promise to talk to you when it bothers me. You too. I want you to know that I'll always be here for you."

As they reached the bus stop, the bus was already there. Lily squeezed Emily's hand and said, "I better get going. I don't want to miss the bus. I heard you tell Katie you'll be home this weekend. I love you, Emily. I'll see you later this week. Ok? Maybe we can talk more. I'd like that"

"I'd like that too, Lily. Also, honestly, thanks again for my door plaque and I just want to say I'm glad we're getting closer. It feels, well, special."

They hugged.

As Lily got out of the car, she looked back and said, "I love you, Em."

Emily sat in her car and watched Lily get on the bus. When the bus shut the door, she saw Lily wave. She waved back, turned the car around and drove back down the street. As she got out of her car she heard Martha calling. Martha was walking across the street.

She put her arm around Emily and said, "Hi sweetie. How are you doing today?"

They hugged. "Hi, Martha. I'm doing ok. I must admit I'm apprehensive about everything that's happened the last few days, but I know everything will be alright in the end. Now, at least, I have a real family who I know cares about me. Mom, Paul and I had a really good talk Sunday night. He's going to talk to someone before he ships out in a month. I also just had a nice talk with Lily."

"A little while ago your mom told me about your talk with Paul. I can't tell you how proud I am of your mom for taking control like she did. I think your mom is going to become a very different person than she has been in the past."

"I know you're right. I'm looking forward to that. Have you talked to Sean? God, I haven't talked to him since early Thanksgiving. With everything going on…I just…I'm going to call him this morning on my way back to campus."

"Honey, don't worry about Sean. I've been keeping him up to speed. He's just very happy and relieved everything is happening the way it is. He loves you very much, Emily."

"Oh, Martha. I love him with all my heart. I just hope I can keep my shit together over the next several years. I don't know what I'd do if we split up."

Martha patted Emily's hand, "Honey, you've got a lot on your plate. You always have; but now, the full plate is different. It's still full though so just remember, if you do drift apart, it will have been meant to happen. I have a really strong gut feeling though that if that does happen, it will be temporary. Yours and Sean's bond is too strong for it to be permanent. I don't know why, but my gut tells me that's true. Is your mom in the kitchen?"

"She was a little while ago. I love you, Martha. I don't know what we would do without you."

"I love you too, Em."

Emily finished packing then brought her belongings out to her Beetle and came back in to say a final good-bye to her mom and Martha who were sitting in the kitchen drinking coffee.

"You all ready, Emily?"

"Yes, Mom. Don't forget we have our second meeting with Dr. Wells tomorrow. Do you feel ok about that?"

"I'm nervous, especially after everything that's happened; but, I also feel sure things are on the right track. We're going to get through this, Emily. I know we will."

"I know we will too, Mom. Ok…I'm going to get going. I want to get back early so I don't have to rush to my class. See you this weekend, Mom. Love you. I love you too, Martha!"

She hugged both her mom and Martha then left.

It was 9:30 when she turned right off her street onto Pawtucket Avenue. It was only 6:30 in California so she waited to call Sean until she was nearly to the campus. He picked up immediately.

"Hi sweetie. I was hoping you'd call this morning."

"Hi Seanie. I was trying not to call too early, but I was also dying to hear your voice."

"What time's your class today?" He asked.

"At two. I'm almost to my dorm now. I wanted to get here early so I could catch my breath before going to class. Lots happened the last several days since Thanksgiving."

"Phew. I know. Grandma's been keeping me up to date. You ok?"

"Yes, I think so. Paul's gone back to Norfolk. He really took everything hard but promised he would talk to someone before he heads out to sea in a month. I'm a little worried about him; but, I think he'll be ok, at least over time. Did Martha tell you about Lily?"

"Yea, she did. I'm not at all surprised. She's always been a little snoopy; but, maybe it's good she knows and has had a little time to process everything. How's your mom?"

"She's ok. I know it's going to be rough for her for a while and maybe even rough for the two of us together for a while; but I feel like she's made a huge shift in her life and won't back track. You know Paul asked me if she knew what was going on. She's really struggling with that one."

"What do you think, Em?"

"To be honest, Sean, I'm pretty sure she knew something was going on. Maybe she didn't know what it was; but then, she was so beaten down by Dad and so under his control I think it was just easier for her to stick her head in the sand by convincing herself it had everything to do with her. By doing that she didn't have to ask questions or do any investigation."

"From what Grandma tells me, I think you're right, Em. Are you going to be ok with that?"

"I think so. I guess I'll have to see what happens. I do know that when the chips were down and she realized she could begin to turn everything around for me, she stepped up. That's huge. I'm going to do my best to make it enough. It's so much easier to forgive and forget with my mom just because of everything she went through. But…we'll see."

"You getting excited about coming out here for Christmas?"

"Oh my God, Sean. Yes. I haven't had a lot of time to think about it the last several days but when I have and then realize how close it is I get butterflies in my stomach. I just can't wait to be in your arms again. I miss you, Sean."

"I miss you too, sweetie. We'll have a good time even though it will be short. Sounds like you just pulled into the dorm parking lot. Did you?"

"Yea. I'm here."

"Well, listen, why don't you go on up to your room, get ready for class and I'll talk to you tonight. I'll call you, ok?"

"I'd like that. I love you a lot, Sean."

"I love you too, baby; and, don't worry about the future. It's going to work its way out."

"Ok, bye."

As Emily collected her belongings and trudged up to her dorm, she thought about seeing Sean. It was Tuesday, December 3rd which meant that in only 18 short days she and Sean would be together again. She felt ecstatic!

www.ingramcontent.com/pod-product-compliance
Lightning Source LLC
Chambersburg PA
CBHW072120250626
47159CB00007B/2511